Ties That Bind

James H. Lehman

Brotherstone Publishers
9 North Union Street
Elgin, IL 60123
www.brotherstonepublishers.com

ISBN: 978-1-878925-05-3

Cover design: Paul Stocksdale

To Hal

Who for nine years reminded me every week,
without fail, to show up and keep writing

and

To Peg

Whose support and love astonish me
and fill me with gratitude

Acknowledgments

My wife Peg read the manuscript three times with many words of encouragement. She liked it far more than I expected. She offered innumerable editorial suggestions and proofing corrections. Most importantly, she showed me the book through her eyes. Bill Jolliff read the manuscript twice with deep attention to its strengths and flaws, and his sometimes astringent and always right-on suggestions improved the work immeasurably. His conviction that the book deserved publication gave me reason to think it had a future. Don Skelton understood the spirit of the book and was moved by it in ways that went far beyond anything I could have hoped for from such an old and dear friend and helped me see why writing it was a good thing. I also want to thank Kevin Kessler, Shawn Kirchner, Wendy McFadden, Dan McFadden, and Hal Sheller for their careful reading and helpful responses.

Editorial note:

The speech by Mona Mackie in chapter 31 is based on and inspired by the words of Helen Sartin Sample. She is the mother of Tex Sample, sociologist of religion, author, lecturer, emeritus Professor of Church and Society at the St. Paul School of Theology in Kansas City, Missouri, and storyteller. His mother's words appear in a video version of his story "That Hussy!" which is part of the DVD collection: *Tex Mix: Stories of Earthy Mysticism*, Tex Sample, © 2008 livingthequestions.com, LLC.

Table of Contents

BOOK ONE

Prologue

Two old men sat on a bench inside the mall across from the designer Christmas tree at the entrance to an upscale department store. The scent of expensive perfume drifted out from the cosmetic counters done up in cool silver and dark red.

"Rich and delicious aromas," one said cheerfully. "How fitting for a holiday that honors an expensive perfume."

"Perfume. There's no perfume in Christmas," said the other, then adding, "Oh, I suppose you mean Frankincense."

"Indeed. The Magi might have been at home in that store." The speaker wore a tweed jacket, dark green turtleneck, red scarf, and a brown leather cap. He crossed his legs and leaned back. "The Wise Men add a note of interest to the story, you know. A counterweight to the poverty of the holy infant."

"That's not their purpose," said the second old gentleman, dressed more soberly in a suit, dark tie, and black cashmere overcoat.

"Oh. What is their purpose?"

"To show that all faiths recognized the savior."

"Ah, and just what was their faith? What Gods did they worship when they went home?"

"We don't know. Historians can only guess."

"Here's a thought. Were they 'saved' by this Savior?"

The second gentleman nodded indulgently. "Good question."

"I just wonder how a fundamentalist would answer."

"I'm glad I'm not a fundamentalist."

"So am I, Preston. I have a great appreciation for the vagaries of your faith, but I draw the line at certainty."

Just then the mall Santa Claus came by. Kids were following him and calling out to him, and he was waving and gesturing with open arms like the pope in procession. Suddenly he ducked down the corridor to the men's room, turning to make one last grandiloquent gesture.

"The wonderful silliness of Christmas," said the cheerful old man.

"I like it, I confess," said Preston, with a touch of embarrassment.

"Oh, indeed?"

Preston shrugged. "It's a holiday for children. Happy, innocent. A time of joy."

"Not for the homeless under the bridge. Not for the bereaved."

"There is always pain and trouble," said Preston intently. "We have to make the best of things. Find the joy in the struggle. Christmas helps us do that."

"Strength through suffering," the other said with a smile. "I like your philosophy. I'm in favor of misery. I salute it."

"Oliver, stop your nonsense and be serious."

"Preston, I am serious. This is a sad and sober world, and I very much wish to avoid straying into idle enthusiasm or dizzy optimism."

The earnest and well-dressed man, whose name was Preston Krunsch, just shook his head, while his eccentric friend, Oliver Larkspur, clapped him on the shoulder and said, "Come on, Preston, let's move over to the coffee bar where we can continue this uplifting conversation."

"So, Preston," he went on as they settled at a table with their cappuccinos, "I understand your church is considering a building project. I'm glad to hear it. It's admirable—the care people show for their churches. It's a sign of Christian civilization. Lovely cathedrals rise up to shed their light on the poor who live in their shadow."

"We're not in that category, Oliver. You know our reputation for community service."

"Yes, it's well-deserved. Still you are not going to tell me there is no one in your congregation who says you need a fine facility before you can be of service. That's what people always say, Preston."

"Why shouldn't they? You tell me how in this day and age you can have an active church program without a good building."

"Ah, that's true. It certainly is true! People aren't sufficient instruments. The almighty has got to have bricks and mortar. The whole history of Christianity attests to it."

"Oliver, you are wealthy; you have a beautiful house. You take good care of it."

"Indeed, I stand in blissful solidarity with the finest Christians."

"Oliver, are you angry about something?"

"Not at all, Preston. When I think of the wonderful state of the world, I am filled with admiration for the Christian church."

Krunsch sighed and peered at the frosted angels that flitted across the glass next to them.

Oliver guessed his thoughts. "They could be worse," he commented. "Have you noticed the baby's been missing from Christmas? Wise Men, shepherds, and especially angels—they're all rendered in exquisite and nauseating detail. Robes, gowns, crowns. The church-lawn Marys and Josephs with their ruddy faces and plastic personalities. But the baby Jesus is buried in the hay. Why aren't the store windows full of bouncing infants, with rosy cheeks and cherubic smiles, flashing divine light from their eyes? You know the kind I'm talking about. The ones they have in baby food commercials. People used to know how to show the holy infant. Think of those Renaissance Madonnas. True babyness today has shifted to the cherubs. Sweet, chubby cherubs! I put it to you, Preston—What has happened to the baby Jesus?"

"Maybe Mary put him in daycare."

Oliver grinned. "Preston! A joke. And about Jesus yet."

"Sometimes it's just better to humor you."

"And just when I think I've lost you in thickets of probity!"

"Oliver, I like Christmas. I don't ask all these questions. I suppose I should be offended by the commercialization. A lot of Christians are."

"But I am proud of Christians," Larkspur said. "Despite what they say, they know their job. They run up their credit cards, buy too many presents. I really don't know what we'd do without Christians at Christmastime."

"What do you think Christmas should look like?"

"You tell me."

"I like the colors and sounds and images. Maybe it's crass, but there's something lighthearted about it all. Business people, politicians, store clerks, teachers, stressed-out parents, bank tellers—don't you think there's a little lift of the spirit when they're stringing up the decorations? Think of the guy who covers his house with such a wretched excess of Christmas lights and do-dad lighted lawn ornaments that every kid in town makes his parents drive past. The kids know. They don't see the bad taste. They see the magic of color and light."

"So, Preston, Christmas is the holiday of excess. Star in the sky. Angels on wing. Cosmos filled with song. The Magi in rich retinue bearing ridiculously expensive gifts. God overdoes it and we're following suit."

"Why not? Why can't God be lavish?"

'Of course! But this brings us back to the baby. He was poor. Working class. No room in the inn. No money. No rich relatives to stay with. Born in a barn after his mother walked 100 miles. There's no donkey in the Christmas story. You read the accounts. I don't know how the donkey got in there. It's a fine prop, though. Mary looks good on it, especially in silhouette with the Star overhead. The baby grows up to be a carpenter. So where's the lavishness in that story?"

"You know, with God, sometimes you just have to take what you get."

"Now, that remark I can appreciate!"

Chapter 1 – Arriving

John Engelsinger stood in the doorway and looked down the meadow, across Cassell Creek, and up the other slope toward the farm where he was born. A large tent, blue and white with open sides, stood in the yard between the house and barn. Under the canopy a man and two women were examining papers in front of a platform where another man was setting up a microphone. One of the women crossed to the barn and entered a door under the forebay. There in the old stable, now swept clean, the goods of six decades of family life were spread out on tables and makeshift shelves.

To the left a bit back from the tent, Davy Snider was putting up the awning in front of the refreshment booth he'd pulled in behind his four-by-four, getting ready to sell hot dogs, snow cones, and chicken corn soup. Already cars were coming down the lane and pulling into the barnyard or onto the grassy verge along the lane. People who wanted to get a good spot were walking toward the tent carrying folding lawn chairs.

John was remembering another scene more than forty years earlier. It had rained hard, the creek had risen. Cars had flooded out, splashing through the creek water flowing across the lane, or they had sunk to their axles in the soggy ground when they pulled off to park. Marvin Hess's tow truck had been kept busy all day winching people out of the water and mud. Angry and helpless as he had been then, he really hadn't known what losing the farm would mean. At sixteen he hadn't had enough experience to imagine loss, even though he had recently lost his dad. And then, of course, the strange old man had appeared and bought the farm—with the stolid advice of Wilbur Rutt, buying the implements and machinery piece by piece and then outbidding Amos Hacker for the farm itself. People had talked about it for weeks.

Well, there was no old man to bail him out now. He had borrowed against the farm to buy his mother a cottage in the retirement village, and then to pay for her in the nursing center. She had died five years before at 87. As long as Mary was healthy, they'd had two incomes and had been able to keep up with payments. He had hung on for two years after Mary died. Now with the downturn in the economy he had to sell the farm to pay the mortgage and cover his other debts. The beautiful stone house where he stood, where he and Mary had lived, built by the old man on the edge of the farm, was already sold, along with an acre of land, broken out of the farm property. The new owners would take possession tomorrow. The money from this sale, after the last of the debts were paid, would leave him a very modest sum, almost nothing for someone his age.

Now in his sixties he thought he knew something about loss. He suspected sadly that he would never own land again. He thought of his father, who had received the farm from his father and who had worked too hard and died young, only to have the farm sold out from under his widow and 16-year-old son to the improbable old man who then gave it back in his will. He would never live in East Henrysburg again. Strands went back through three of his grandparents eight generations each, sometimes connected by intermarriage so that he was his own fifth cousin once removed. They had all lived within 20 miles of this farm. He would not come back to the East Henrysburg church, where his grandfather and his great grandfather had been elders. These roots were almost beyond reckoning. He loved these people. But his time here was over. He would come back to visit. He would remember. He knew as surely as he felt the power of this lineage that he must go.

He watched the stuff of his family's life bid on and passed to the buyers sitting in their lawn chairs. Neighbors, cousins, people from the surrounding towns, Amish from further down in the county and now recently from nearby farms. When his wooden toy train set went for $90, he wished he had kept it. It was a link with the past. But he had no need for it. Let a child enjoy it. Then he saw it was a collector who bought it as an antique. Its child-pleasing days were over.

The auctioneer moved from the house to the barn. The day passed quickly. By 4:00 in the afternoon, the auctioneer's clerk was tallying up the sales. The men from the rental company were striking the tent. The farm house was empty, cleaned from top to bottom. The auctioneer and the tent people pulled out. The Penny Man loaded everything that hadn't sold onto his old flatbed truck. John went into the farmhouse and walked through the rooms from attic to basement, remembering. Last he stood in the kitchen. He could picture his father sitting on a chair leaning down to lace up his work shoes. He could see his mother at the sink. He locked the door.

The stone house was empty too. He sat in the turret room and thought about the old man and about Mary. He saw her sitting on the loveseat with her legs tucked under, poring over a book. She had her glasses on. She looked cute, perky, and intelligent at once, something he never understood, how glasses could produce that combination of appearance. A high, empty, piercing grief passed through his chest and into his eyes. Tears came. He let the sorrow have its way. It was almost too much to bear. It passed. He shook his head and went out and locked the door.

The last thing he did was to drive to the older part of the retirement village to a small, brick, bungalow-like duplex. When he knocked, the door was opened by a thick, squat, powerfully built old man in bib overalls. He said nothing, but he smiled slowly, and his eyes lit with pleasure.

"Hello, Wilbur," John said.

"Vell, I guess it's good-bye," said the old man. He stood back so John could come in. He indicated the sofa next to the recliner in the small room. There were no knick-knacks in the room, no pictures except some photos of grandchildren, but someone had gone to the trouble to put simple, dark red curtains at the windows that picked up the red hues in the braided rug. With the brown upholstered furniture, the room was cozy and pleasant, not dark as one would expect of the room of an old man living without the wife who had always taken care of him. The luxuriant house plants at the front window were out of character for a retired farmer. It amused the women of the church that stolid old Wilbur Rutt, who had never paid a bit of attention to anything indoors, had domesticated his gift for making things grow and brought it inside after his wife died. They also knew he had chosen the curtains and the braided rug and were heard to comment that Wilbur had depths no one had guessed. Of course, John had always known this. In all his friendships and the many connections he took for granted as a man living in a place where his family had been for generations, Wilbur was the person with whom he felt most comfortable.

They sat in companionable silence for a bit.

"I'll miss you, Wilbur," John said.

"Yup," Wilbur replied.

"I have to do it, you know. Have to get away. Don't know why, exactly. Well, I do know why, but the reason doesn't matter as much as the necessity.

Wilbur nodded, "Vell, you miss Mary."

"That's part of it."

There was more John could say but knew he didn't need to and was glad. He nodded and stood up. He almost embraced Wilbur. He thought it would have been okay, thought he caught a whisper of a smile as though the old man were reading his mind, but he reached out for Wilbur's thick, work-hardened hand.

"Vell, I'll see you sometime," the old man said.

"When you come out to visit Nancy and Kirby? Yes, I'll enjoy that."

****

He took the Skyway and drove up Lake Shore Drive just for the pleasure of seeing the skyline at dusk. It was a moment lifted from a popular print, where the lights are preternaturally glowing and the edges between objects are too sharp and the relief is too high and the whole scene is suffused with a glow that cannot possibly be real and colors that cannot possibly be true. The tall buildings stood silhouetted against the sunset colors, and the lighted windows glowed unnaturally bright against the dark shapes they populated. The blue black night rolled slowly in overhead pushing the sunset down but only making it brighter by contrast. And in that unreal mix of dark and light, the lake on the right had turned deep turquoise, shading to darkest blue out beyond the breakwater. How different from the first time he had come this way, one sunny morning when the Prudential Building was the tallest in Chicago.

He left the Drive in the Loop and went north on the Magnificent Mile. The tiny lights in the trees had just come on—odd to be in a Christmas-like scene with a mild autumn breeze blowing in the car window. At the Water Tower he turned and went over to Rush Street. At Rush and Walton he stopped. The parking lot was no longer there. No gas pumps. No mechanic's bays. A high rise was going up on the spot. It was hard even to imagine the large oil-stained blacktop tightly ringed by a chain-link fence, to think of packing the cars all the way into the back, then having to move three or four cars if someone came back early for a vehicle they had put in the rear by the fence. He remembered the day they had been short-handed and he had to run the lot himself, pulling lines of cars out past the pumps, backing cars in tight arcs to put them precisely in spaces with only a foot on each side, sprinting into the back of the lot to move yet another vehicle. Bringing out the one that had been called for, then putting all the cars back in place so customers could get to the pumps to buy gas. Then doing the whole thing again. A guy, watching as he waited for Calvin, the mechanic, to finish the lube job on his car, had laughed and called it vehicular ballet. After all these years, that compliment still gave John pleasure.

Not much else was the same. Mammy's was gone. So were Burger-on-a-Bun and Punchinello's farther up the street. The recording studios on the second floor across the intersections—once the source for thousands of commercials—were closed.. Remembering made him uneasy. Why he should he miss a world he had lived in more than 40 years ago? What had he done with those years? He thought of a girl he'd admired. He could see her walking down from Oak Street where she worked. He thought of Mary. He sighed. Everything was sad. He smiled and shrugged in silent conversation with himself, disgusted with this self-indulgent sentimentality.

He looked at his watch. There was still time to hunt his way back to Hyde Park and find the restaurant where he was to meet Viona. It was a pancake house in a small mall on 55th Street. The hostess seated him. He was the only white person in the room, until Vi came through the door. She walked briskly to the table and sat down as though she were in her natural habitat. She'd been working for three years in a center for homeless and abused women on the South Side. Before that she had spent many years in Guatemala. She had once swum a river with women and children fleeing government troops who had burned their village during the civil war. She wore jeans, white shirt, and sandals. Her one concession to style was a wine-colored scarf tied and laid to the side over one shoulder. He noticed she still had her figure. He'd known her for many years, ever since she'd done a speaking tour in Pennsylvania and stayed with him and Mary; the two women had kept up a correspondence. When she was exhausted by her work and needed sabbaticals, she would come to the farm, sometimes staying for a month or two. She'd never married, was in her mid-fifties. He had not seen her since Mary's memorial service.

He was surprised at how much his heart lifted just to see her smile and feel her vitality. Suddenly desire washed through him—the first time in two years. He had forgotten how good it felt. He had always found Vi attractive. He and Mary had joked about it. A wave of longing swept over him—for Mary and the good company she had been. This passed rapidly in the time it took for Vi to slide into her chair. He hid behind a rueful smile. But Vi raised an eyebrow as she picked up her napkin.

"You sold the farm?" she said, pausing.

"I did."

"I can't imagine you without the farm."

"I can't either."

"What will you do?"

"What do you advise?

"You want my advice?"

"I have no marketable skills or experience."

"You ran a farm and a small business for many years."

"Not particularly well."

"Why ask me? Most people would say I've lived a vagabond life. I've had no career path. If I quit what I'm doing, I'd be in the same fix you are."

"At least you understand the consequences of unorthodox choices. And you know how to live without much money. Money never mattered to you. I expect I'm going to have to live without much money."

"Can you do that?"

"Don't know. I had it pretty easy with the farm and the old man's inheritance."

Vi leaned forward and looked closely at him, "You're still grieving?"

John pulled back from her sharp gaze. "Of course I am."

She reached across and took his hand. "I wasn't accusing you. I'd forgotten for a moment." She paused, "It's hard to make decisions when you're sad."

John shrugged, "They still have to be made."

"Do you prefer not to talk about Mary?"

"No, I like to talk about her."

Vi was quiet, looked at him expectantly.

"So, are you wanting me to say something?" he said.

"Only if you want to."

John sat quietly. "It's little things." He shook his head. "She used to write Post-It love notes and stick them on my monitor. I left them there for months. I used to wonder what my computer guy thought." John laughed. "She was always putting my coffee mug in the dishwasher before I was done with it. Irritated me! She was hard on equipment. I hated to lend her my camera. She wore stuff out. In recent years she started taking pictures. She was good. Had a natural eye. She was a natural hugger. I miss her hugs. She was good company. We were busy most of the time. She had her practice. But when she finally quit working, she was good at doing nothing. That was the best time, doing nothing together in those months before she died."

"Do you believe people are destined for each other?

"I don't know. Do you?"

"Maybe."

"Are you saying Mary and I were soul mates?"

"I thought you were."

John took a deep breath and sighed. "Well, she's gone. Here I am in Chicago. No job. Enough money for a few months. So give me some advice."

"Are you interested in service work?"

"I might be."

"Doesn't pay well."

"I'm going to see if I can live on less."

"You might consider a volunteer program. Give your time for a year, maybe two. Your living expenses are paid. You get a small stipend for incidentals."

"Those programs are for young people."

"Not any more. There's one for the post-30 set."

"I'm post-60."

Vi shrugged. "People your age do volunteer, you know. Where do you go from here? I mean tonight. Where are you staying till you get settled?"

"Kirby and Nancy are putting me up."

****

He made his way through the tangle of expressways west of the Loop and took the Kennedy and then the tollway northwest to Selby. He found the house not far from I-90 in the Birch Tree subdivision. It was not much to look at in the dark—aluminum siding, two-stories, brick façade at the entryway, two-car garage. Some pines and bushes grew on the corner, and a pin oak stood between the streetlight and the house and threw shadows on the front. That was all he could make out. Not what he expected of Nancy. He rang the bell. The door opened and a handsome woman in late middle-age peered out.

Just for a moment she paused, and John saw the shy girl she had once been. Then she exclaimed, "John! At Last!" She hugged him and kissed him warmly on his cheek.

"Kirby's beside himself, waiting for you. You know how he gets."

John could not remember when he did not know Nancy Beahm. They grew up together in the same church in East Henrysburg. Their parents grew up together in that church. Nancy's father was Wilbur Rutt. When John's father died, and then the old man who bought the farm died, and later John's grandfather too, Wilbur had always been there, sometimes substitute father, always friend.

Kirby had been the second friend John brought home from college. The first was Jack Frisk, an insouciant and irresistible charmer who was smitten by Nancy's sweetness and inexperience and took advantage of it. When she became pregnant, he ran away from college and from his friends. It pushed Nancy's mother Miriam further into her chronic depression. Wilbur grieved deeply and silently. People in the church watched helplessly. They thought Nancy would turn out like her mother, never hold up her head or amount to anything. But she gave birth to Jacqueline, finished college, started teaching second grade, and earned her master's degree.

Kirby had made a threesome with John and Jack. He came home with John too, but it was not until he was in his PhD program that he met Nancy. Little Jacki was four by that time. After they married, their ambition, which still surprised John because it was not obvious, led to advanced degrees for both. Then Kirby changed course, gave up his scholarly interests, and went to theological seminary. Nancy became an elementary school principal and Kirby became a pastor. They had two more children, Joel and Janelle. Little Jacki grew up, went to business school, and started her own company. Several years earlier they had moved to Illinois where Kirby became pastor of the Westbrook Church in Selby and Nancy principal of Jefferson Elementary School.

The entry hall was narrow. Nancy showed John past the stairs and through a door. Suddenly the kitchen opened into a great room with a peaked cedar ceiling, large windows, high stone fireplace, and an oriental rug on the hardwood floors. John stopped to gape. He knew now why the Beahms had bought this house. The great room was hidden from the street. Through sliding glass doors to the right, John saw a large, enclosed, multi-level lighted patio, with flower boxes on the cedar fencing and pots of mums.

"Is that a pool?" John asked in surprise, after greeting a small border collie named Tillich.

"Yes, yes, it is," said Kirby, "I know, I know. A pastor has no business with a pool, even though it is very small and above ground. Of course, it was here when we bought the house. I don't think of myself as a man with a pool. I'd never put one in. But here it is, and here we are, so we're doing our best to enjoy it and not feel guilty."

"The house is huge!"

"Yes. Six bedrooms if you count the room in the basement. But we have people living here. Last summer the Millers—you know Ralph and Sandy—back from Africa, stayed with us for three months. Their sons were here too, and Joel and Janelle were home. Eight of us in the house. Never felt crowded. Never got in each other's way. It's a little experiment in community living."

"So that's how you justify it," John said.

"An exquisite combination of pleasure and chagrin."

****

The guest room was just off the hall at the front of the house on the main floor. John awoke to the sun filtering through the copper-toned leaves on the pin oak. It was early. He heard Nancy stirring in the kitchen. He threw on sweatshirt and pants and went outside. Tall pines, whose cone shape came all the way to the ground, framed the large side yard. Typical, mostly one-story, ranch-style houses on large lots ran down both streets that formed the T where the Beahms' house sat. After a brisk walk John joined Nancy for breakfast.

"Was it hard when you moved here?" he asked.

"At first."

"After fifteen years in the same place—at the church in Maryland?"

"I missed the school the most. I was principal there for 10 years."

"You give up a lot by being a pastor's wife."

"Some pastors move every six or seven years. I count myself lucky that Kirby stayed 15 years. I found a principal's position here quickly—not easy in a different state and at my age. Kirby thinks we should have moved five years earlier. He thinks anything over 10 years in one church is too long. He stayed because I loved my job."

John looked surprised. "He thinks he overstayed his usefulness? I thought everyone loved him."

"Oh, they did." Nancy smiled. "It's Kirby. Never quite satisfied with himself. He thinks he needs to grow."

John looked at Nancy across the table—slender, fit, carefully dressed in a suit with the right combination of style, properness, and femininity; her dark hair short, neatly-styled, sprinkled with gray; her manner competent. He recalled the timid, innocent girl he grew up with.

Nancy pulled back her head slightly and squinted.

John saw this and smiled. "I was remembering. How much has happened since I was that angry, confused college kid bringing home friends to meet you!"

"You were never confused, John. You were tough. I admired you. You weren't afraid to ask questions. I was the confused one. I was sheltered. If I were to fault Dad for anything, it was that he treated me like a little princess."

John smiled.

"You smile. It was true."

"Yes, it's just hard to put the word princess and Wilbur Rutt in the same sentence, the stolid old Pennsylvania Dutchman. Even people who've known your dad all his life don't realize how tender and senti-mental he is."

"He was, and is, a wonderful father. I am startled sometimes at how fierce my affection is. I miss him; here in Illinois I'm so much farther away. I could see him twice a month when we were in Maryland."

"And Jacki—you left her behind too. How's she doing?"

"Well, you know Jacki. I worry about her. So ambitious. She eats and sleeps her company. Not much social life. She's not even dating anyone."

"Typical mom, wanting to marry off your daughter."

"Maybe, but you ask Kirby. He thinks she's running away from some-thing, throwing herself into her work."

John paused, then asked, "Does she see her dad?"

"She considers Kirby her dad."

"Of course, she does, Nancy. I mean Jack. Does she see Jack?"

Nancy sighed, "Yes, she does. And I'm glad she does. She needs him in her life. It's just..." she paused. "He's a troubling reality. You know Jack. She loves being around him. Charming, engaging, so much fun..." She stopped, remembering. "He'll show up for a few days, wine and dine her. They have a wonderful time. Then he disappears for months."

"Are you and Kirby happy?"

"That's rather abrupt...and personal, isn't it?"

"We're old friends, Nancy. I don't see Kirby for months. Then we get together, and we pick up right where we left off. You're the sister I never had. So, yeah, it is personal. This is a big change—uproot yourselves after all those years. Joel and Janelle off to college. What's it like to have the nest empty? Are you enjoying one another?"

"Well, of course."

"You say that so quickly."

"John! Are you asking if we're having problems?"

"No, I'm envying you," John said quietly.

Nancy suddenly smiled, the bright shy, slightly sad smile John remem-bered from their childhood, and tears came to his eyes. "It's good to see you," he said. "I wish Mary were here."

****

John stood in Kirby's office at the church reading the titles on the bookshelves. Kirby was sitting at the desk fiddling with a small cinnabar box he kept as a plaything. "We want you to stay with us—as long as you like. John, there's plenty of room. Amazing really, the way that house multiplies space."

John sat down and Kirby poured him some coffee. "So..." Kirby said, "Seeing you here, knowing you're not going back, realizing that you sold the farm! It's not like you. We thought you would die on that farm. Remember when you went back—and why. What happened to that fierce feeling for roots?"

John shrugged, stared into his mug, swished the coffee around. "Maybe the roots left me."

"Oh, well, now, that's an interesting idea," Kirby said.

"The church has changed. It doesn't feel like the old community. When we were plain, sectarian, and mostly farmers, there was a certain theological openness—at least in my congregation. The question was not first of all 'Do you have the right ideas? Do you think right?' But, 'Are you right with each other? Are you doing right?' Now we look like any other American protestant church—have the same education, live in the same houses, have the same jobs, have the same cultural and political values. But we've lost some essential quality."

"What is it?"

"You're the historian, Kirby. You can answer that better than I can."

"But you've been living in the middle of it."

"I guess I would say it's a kind of naïve, innocent trust."

"Really," Kirby sat up and leaned across his desk.

"You remember when I was a kid and I came back from college asking all those questions and just generally being an arrogant sophomore agnostic. My grandfather, the elder, wasn't troubled. Old Henner Musser wasn't worried. George Bricker thought I ought to be asking the questions. It was Amos Knacker who made me an issue in the congregation. Amos was the fundamentalist. Many others were Biblical literalists. But no one knew anything about historical criticism. Their literalism was innocent and full of trust. Amos's was aggressive, defensive, and full of judgment. In those days the Bible was important but it was read in the context of the community. It gave shape to the church, and it was read and interpreted in the church. Amos was different. Getting the Bible right was more important than the community. He would have put me out for my questions."

"But at one time the church did put people out. You know that."

"Yes, and thank God, that ended in my congregation when I was a kid. But even when the church did that, it was for behavior and action, not belief." John paused, "I just don't feel at home there anymore. It just doesn't feel like the church I knew and loved. More rigid in some things and more lax in others. It's just not my mix anymore. And for God's sake, we have a 'Praise Band'!"

Kirby laughed, "Come on, John, what's wrong with drums and guitars in church?"

"Not a thing. It's the style I dislike. Fluffy, happy melodies. It's all about victory and being with Jesus. There's nothing about peace or the poor. That Jesus walks a heavenly road. My Jesus walks with the homeless."

Kirby was nodding his head.

"I'm not saying anything you don't know," John said, "but…"

"But I haven't had to deal with it, that's what you were going to say."

"You always pastor a liberal church. You never had to live with this other stuff. It's funny, isn't it, that this same small denomination could produce a church like this one in Selby and one like mine at home."

"When the old identity broke apart," Kirby said thoughtfully, "the liberal congregations took the concern for nonviolence and people and translated it into peace activism and social justice. The conservative churches translated the centrality of the Bible into Biblical clarity and right doctrine. The liberal churches kept the belief that new light can come and translated it into a faith where searching and seeking are more important than finding and arriving. The conservative churches translated the conviction that Christ gives new life into contemporary-style evangelism. Both believe in the value of the community, but the liberals want to create a broad and inclusive place where people of many ideas and needs can find a home. The conservatives want to create a dynamic place where assurance fuels church growth. Do you ever wonder if we are both wrong—or right?"

John laughed, "Not right at the moment. I'm just glad to be out here in this nice liberal church with you as my pastor."

"Well, no church is just one thing. You'll have to see what this one is like. But John, how are you really doing?"

"Meaning I suppose that I didn't move out here just because the home church has turned into a bunch of Baptists. You want to know. So do I."

"People do take an interest in you. Everyone wants to know what you're up to. But I don't believe you don't know. You always know."

"It's not just one thing. It is really the church. And I am still missing Mary.

"It's not in your nature to run from conflict, John. You have not really fit in at that church for a long time. Why leave now? You don't run from grief. You didn't leave when your dad died, when you lost your grandfather, when the old man died, or when your mom died."

"I saw Vi yesterday in Chicago—she said Mary and I were soul mates."

"What is it really, John?"

John closed his eyes, then looked out the window, then stared into his coffee as though it were a divining fluid. "I failed, Kirby. I *had* to sell the farm. My little business never got off the ground. And without Mary's income, I couldn't meet my obligations. I had to start borrowing, just for upkeep. And then to set Mom up at the retirement village and to keep her in nursing care. I wasn't making anything off the farm. I borrowed as long as I could and then sold out. The farm was in the family for four generations. And I'm the one who lost it. The old man rescued it once. Then it looked like it was lost again when he died and we couldn't find the will. Well, you figured out where it was, and more than that why he cared so much about me in the first place. Saved again. He willed it to me. So I had a farm that was in the clear and that beautiful stone house. And a wife who was an attorney making good money. I'm 62, Kirby. I should be well-off. Instead, I'm almost back to zero. Just a bit toward retirement. No farm, no stone house. I am too proud to move to an apartment and face people's pity or judgment. Maybe if Mary had lived, I could have brazened it out. But, of course, if Mary had lived, her income would have kept us going. I am the beneficiary of such richness and I have frittered it away. I am deeply chagrined."

Kirby stood up and reached for his coat. "Do you have time to go for a drive?"

"Do I have time! It's all I have!"

The church was called the Westbrook Church and was on Westbrook Avenue. They climbed into Kirby's car and drove four miles due west on Westbrook. He pulled off the road, bounced across a right-of-way, turned into a field of corn-stalk stubble, and stopped. "All that," he said with a grand sweep of his arm as he stood in front of the car, "belongs to our congregation."

A nice piece of land, John thought. About 25 acres, he guessed. Rimmed by hedgerow on the west, a housing development on the east, and what looked like a stand of trees off in the distance on the north. Flat except for a little swell that no one but an Illinois native would call a hill. Nothing like the rolling farmland and tree-lined ridges back home where land had definition.

"Why are you showing me this?"

"This..." said Kirby, "might be a problem. This might tie up a great deal of our energy. Land always ties up energy. Except when it frees up imagination. You just never know with land."

"What are we saying here, Kirby?"

"He who has ears…"

"You're giving me an object lesson! I come all the way to Chicago to get a sermon from my old friend!"

Kirby lifted his hands in mock disclaimer.

"Okay, which was it for me? My land?"

"Different things at different times."

"You think it was good for me to lose it?"

"Don't know, John, but isn't it worth thinking about?"

"What do you mean—this is going to be a problem for your congregation?"

"It might not be a problem. It might be a blessing."

"But you don't think so!"

"I don't know, John."

Chapter 2 – Faith

Was God testing him? This was not a question that came to Sam Ellerby with great force, but as a nagging doubt he would have preferred to put out of mind. Would God cause or allow misfortune to see how tough he was—or to make him grow?

He was sorting bills. He had a system that showed him what he owed and when it was due. He updated this list on his computer—except when he had no money. Then he let the bills pile up because he couldn't face them. This denial wasn't really very effective because he knew anyway they were big and growing.

Sam put the stack of bills and loan payments aside and stood up. He thought he ought to pray, but it seemed odd to pray about debts. He thought of his parents, now in their high eighties. They'd never had bills they couldn't pay. His grandfather had been a farmer and preacher—his word was good—when he said he'd pay, he did. There was nothing in this family history that helped him.

He walked down the hall to find his jacket. Hardly any of his friends knew. When people asked how he was, he would say he was okay, which was true. He wasn't in despair. He'd been through this too often. He wasn't riddled by anxiety. Occasionally he would say something like, "Things have been tight financially." But he never let anyone know how desperate his situation was.

He left the house, carrying a paperback mystery, and began to walk. At the Starbucks he took a table, drank coffee, ate pound cake, and followed the contrivances of the crime writer. This gave him escape for maybe an hour. Then he was back outside walking.

No solution suggested itself. He smiled bitterly—he who could always see options where others saw only obstacles. Back at the house later he decided praying was the only thing he could do. But he was embarrassed. He never thought of praying when things were going well—except maybe a muttered "thank you." What right did he have to pray when things were going badly? He had been told—had believed—that God was patient. God forgave and started over with you. That troubled him a little. Shouldn't God be more tough-minded—not just settle for whatever he could get? Expect you to stand up like a man and take responsibility for your screwups and suffer their consequences? Expect some courage and maturity? Expect you to launch your prayers from high moral ground?

What kind of God responded to weakness! Sam felt like a failed child. He wanted God to put things right. Nevertheless he sat in the chair in the living room. He could hear his wife cooking in the kitchen. And he prayed.

Nothing happened. His heart did not lift. He tried to settle himself, to find his center. He couldn't find it. He was empty, numb. He sighed, slumped forward, his elbows on his knees. He was too old to panic. There was a place of light and freedom somewhere, but a veil was drawn across it.

Sam knew that most people don't really believe God is involved in ordinary financial affairs. Sam didn't quite believe it either. But the possibility persisted in his thoughts. He tried to act on it. He never admitted this to anyone, but his wife. It embarrassed him.

He kept up the appearance of being conventionally religious, which meant he stayed active in his congregation and promised to pray when people got sick or lost loved ones or went through job changes—the sort of thing put forward in the sharing time during worship. He noticed people almost never stood up and asked for prayers to help them through really unpleasant things like divorce. Too much shame. They sometimes dropped out until they had gotten through the worst. People never stood up and said they were out of money and couldn't pay their bills. That was nearly the worst. Marital misadventure was easier to admit to than financial failure.

Still he could not imagine himself not connected to a congregation. Most people thought you had to belong to a church to be a Christian. That's where you found Christ. Christ! That was another matter! His mind veered away from thinking about Christ. He thought he needed a congregation. He needed the ordinariness of the people. It did him good to have to tolerate and even appreciate people he would probably not choose as friends. The congregation was "progressive," a word in vogue now that "liberal" was an epithet. That was good. He was glad to be progressive. God! He wondered where God was.

He went to the kitchen. His wife, Eve, was in good spirits. They ate a quick meal. They dressed, and they got into their car. He watched her from the corner of his eye as he drove. She was as full of worry as he was, but tonight she seemed to have put it aside. They waited in the traffic jam where the tollway emptied into the expressway. If traffic didn't open up soon, they would miss the opening concerto.

He was grateful he could talk about anything with Eve. For some time they had been trying to pray together every day. They laughed about it. Two people could not have been more poorly equipped to be people of faith. He was skeptical, intellectual, self-reliant, self-preoccupied; his instinct was to figure it out and do it on his own. She was passionate, turbulent, willful, guilt-ridden, charming; her instinct was to plead and badger and cajole and apologize and be outraged.

What did God think of them? He really didn't want to know. Well, actually he did. He even imagined God's reaction sometimes—a wry combination of affection and disappointment. Then he remembered that God had made billions of galaxies, and he wondered how a being that large could be interested in him at all.

For years season tickets to the symphony had been a lavish gift from his mother-in-law. She had died last year, but Eve had continued the subscription, though this would be the last year. Tenth row, main floor, center—they could see the rosin dust on the concert master's violin. It seemed ironic to him, not for the first time, to be surrounded by lawyers, doctors, professors, business people—the elite of the city. He had no credentials in their world. He was beyond or beneath any competition or professional jealousies.

He looked his seat mates over coolly. A huge, florid, slightly seedy man with flushed cheeks and a baggy, ill-fitting suit spilled out of the seat in front of him. This man and his wife, who wore a sort of turban and looked like she chose her rumpled clothes at the thrift store until you looked at them more closely, always came with an elegantly turned-out couple who dressed in black. He liked watching these four because they enjoyed the music and what must have been an old friendship. Two rows down sat an attractive woman he'd been watching for 20 years. He had always tried to guess what she was—law intern or grad student with book bag at first, then young professional wearing muted colors—clothes stylish, expensive, but conservative—now settled professional, assured, streaks of gray in her hair, superbly made-up, tired eyes. Two rows forward on the left sat a man—maybe fifty-five, handsome, hard, wearing an expensive suit, beautifully-fitted—with a twenty-something wife or girlfriend leaning into him, laughing when he spoke—politely attentive to the music, looking around surreptitiously. Did any of these people have troubles like his? Maybe in this economy. Still it was hard to imagine.

At the intermission he leaned against a post in the lobby and sucked on a mentholated lozenge offered free by the management so coughing wouldn't disturb the sacred sound space in the hall. He watched his wife come up from the ladies room and cross toward him. He wished he weren't putting her through all this. They were both professionals, but he was the man. He felt responsible for their finances. He saw her for a moment as though she were not his wife. Petite, quick, in a dark, elegant dress that showed her youthful figure, narrow hips, brisk walk, nice legs—a touch thin—good ankles, looked twenty years younger than her early sixties. Her face lit up when she spied him across the lobby, as though she hadn't seen him for a long time. She was always like that—her enthusiasms on her face. His heart turned over. She loved him. This still surprised him.

Two people, a couple, came into focus from the surge of faces and dark clothing as people began to move back into the hall. The man was tall and lean with thick white hair and a delighted, almost childlike smile. The woman was large-boned and carried her weight confidently, under a loose, flowing dress, with the impishness of a girl and the confidence of a matron. Sam knew he knew the man—knew him well—but from some other part of his life. This was someone he had liked—very much—someone who obviously knew him. They were heading this way.

Of course! This was Will. From graduate school—when they were both single, sharing an apartment. How long had it been since he'd seen him? He lived on the West Coast. What was he doing in Chicago? This must be his wife Rae—the one he'd heard so much about, whom he'd never met.

There was just enough time for introductions. Sam was surprised at the warmth of Will's hug. As they moved into the hall, Will put his hand on Sam's shoulder and gave him a careful, searching look. A small rush of remembrance and feeling went through him. He looked away, afraid to meet that frank gaze. A sudden need to unburden himself unnerved him. He took his seat and tried to compose himself. When the concert was over, Eve suggested they find Will and Rae and go out for coffee, but Sam said he was tired and wanted to go home. They waved at the couple across the crowded lobby as they headed for the underground parking.

Sitting in his office thinking about it the next day, Sam wished they had talked to Will and Rae after the concert. Simple politeness should have dictated at least that. They were here all the way from Seattle. How long were they in town? Why had they come? Where were they staying? These were questions he should have asked.

He remembered how Will used to walk in the swamp on the edge of campus early in the morning and come back to tell him about the birds and frogs. Will would talk about his father, an aggressive businessman and church leader with high standards, whom he resisted and tried to live up to. When no one was around, Will would sit for hours at the piano in the student lounge playing with a virtuosity that deserted him when he had an audience. He had a habit of letting out a shout and a quick, cascading laugh when something caught his imagination. One day for no apparent reason but a burst of friendship that embarrassed Sam, Will gave him a copy of *Testament of Devotion* by Thomas Kelly, a Quaker mystic, which Sam read and reread and thought was one of the best pieces of devotional writing he owned. That next fall Will came back in the buoyant afterglow of a summer relationship with a girl named Rae. She was seven years younger, only 19, but, oh my, how he talked of her. What a spirit! He finished his degree that year, moved back to the West Coast, and married Rae. Sam had never met Rae, and he hadn't seen Will for almost 40 years.

How could someone be in your life for a short time, make an impact, pass out of it for 40 years, and then show up suddenly, brush past the small talk, look you in the eye, and seem to see into your heart. Will was intense. Other students had felt awkward around him because he didn't know how to chat, wasn't much interested in sports, didn't like breezy intellectual chatter. But when somebody was in trouble, Will listened.

The phone rang. Sam knew it would be Will; he picked it up, but it wasn't Will. It was a woman—a voice he didn't recognize. She identified herself as Rae. She was calling with an invitation, she said. They were staying at a hotel at O'Hare. It had a good dining room, she said, well not great, but the food was edible. The point was to get together. Would he and Eve drive down and meet them for dinner? He said yes. His heart was beating, like he'd just been accepted for a date. Why all this feeling? He'd have to check with Eve, but he was sure she was free. Eve had wanted to meet for coffee last night anyway, he said. She only knew what he'd told her about Will. She wanted to observe him first hand.

"Yes, he is a rare creature," Rae laughed.

"Forty years ago Will thought you were."

"Well, I guess now you'll find out."

"I'm looking forward to it."

Driving down the tollway Sam was having an anxious inner debate. Why had Will and Rae shown up at this moment? Was he going to tell them what was going on? Were they here so he could? It was so hard to talk, even to their closest friends. The advantage in talking to Will and Rae was that he wouldn't have to see them for another 40 years.

Eve was leaning back against the headrest with her eyes closed. He knew she wasn't asleep. Her brow was puckered, as though she was trying to convince herself that she would fall asleep.

"Well, are we just going to chit chat with Will and Rae tonight?" he asked.

"Do you think we can? I'm not good at faking it."

"The Will I knew would understand. But who knows what he's like now."

"So what do we do? Can we get through a whole evening of polite nothings?"

The four of them were seated at a round table that looked out over a small artificial lake. Some ground lights were shining up through the trees around the lake. The dining room was decorated in dark wood and mauve and light green with hardwood floors.

The exquisite agony of table talk, Sam was thinking. You comment on the weather or the Chicago Bulls or maybe even politics. You may even make some profound observations about the election coming up or the gentrification of neighborhoods on the near north side. Your heart isn't in any of it, and you wonder what you really want to say or if you want to be there at all. You begin to eat the hot bread, spreading it with butter embossed with the restaurant's seal, after expending an unreasonable effort to slice it on the cutting board on which it's served, scattering crumbs all over the tablecloth. The salad arrives, and you are already feeling full, wishing you hadn't eaten that bread and wondering how you're going to get through the entrée you thought you wanted. You've lost all track of what you are feeling and what you really want to say. If you have had the misfortune of having had a before-dinner drink or some wine, you're already feeling fuzzy-headed and even sleepy. If you are actually burdened with the gift of small talk, you've been babbling right along, maybe even being witty.

Tonight Sam had resolved to say nothing unless it was meaningful. But Will and Rae said nothing too. Eve said something that dropped like a stone into a deep well. Will laughed, "Maybe long awkward silences are good. Speech is overrated. Let see if we can go through the whole meal in silence. A Quaker Meeting meal. I'll bet we can't do it."

"Why should we want to?" said Rae.

"I like Will's idea," Sam said. "Are we scared of silence? At least it takes less energy than words. Well, maybe not. I know people who explode without the safety value of talk. Suppose we sit around this table and refuse to speak until something scintillating or sincere or profound bursts out. Think of it!"

"You've expended a lot of speech to talk about the values of not speaking," said Eve drily.

"Authentic speech is hard to come by," said Will, ignoring her. "What does it sound like?"

"It comes from the deepest place and it makes no effort to please or persuade or impress," Sam said.

"Is it feeling or thought?"

"Both, but there's no sentimentality, or intellectualism. Maybe it's what we mean when we say something is heartfelt or has been thoughtfully put."

"Are you practicing authentic speech now?" Rae asked, laughing.

"Of course we are," Will replied with a knowing smile. "But if you have to ask the question, it means we probably aren't."

Sam said nothing more, and Will fell silent, as though he'd been talking to no purpose. Sam pushed his food about on his plate and seemed to forget everything around him. The two women looked at each other awkwardly.

"There is something Eve and I have on our minds," Sam said. "Something heavy. If we don't talk about it, our talk will be pretty empty." He hesitated.

Will and Rae became attentive.

"Some time ago, Eve and I made a decision. We don't say much about it because it seems crazy. We decided to conduct our finances by faith. This means when we take on a project, we don't ask, 'Will we be paid enough?' We ask, 'Is this the right thing? Is this what we are being called to do?' If we sense that the answer is yes, we do it whether there's money in it or not."

Will smiled and his face lit up. He leaned forward with great interest. "So how do you pay your bills?"

"Sometimes we can't, and this is one of those times. But I haven't told you everything. We are trying to meet our daily needs by praying about them."

"You pray every day about your bills!"

"Well, no, not every day. That's the rub. We aren't very good at this. We pray a lot better and more often when debts are staring us in the face." Sam paused and then added, almost compulsively, "I know it sounds nuts."

"What do you ask for?"

"Money sometimes. Guidance. Help to find work. Sometimes patience."

"So does money come?"

"Yes. Sometimes in ways that startle and amaze us, that fill us with gratitude and discomfort. Through connections that have no logic. Through a series of events that can only be called providential. And sometimes no—no money, no help. Just anxiety and emptiness.

"I always feel I have to put in a disclaimer. Even the most religious, the most evangelical, don't really put their finances in God's hands and certainly not self-assured liberals like me. In our culture many, probably most, don't have an everyday sense of the holy—in the land, in the weather, in the animals and birds that survive in our urbanized spaces, in the ebb and flow of economics, especially in the realities of contracts, salaries, pensions, insurances, taxes. Where's God? Who believes their income comes from God? I mean who feels God when they walk into a bank the way desert people feel God when they ride in the wind? I don't feel God's presence most of the time. I practice a presence that's sometimes more an idea that than a living reality. I am at the disadvantage of trying to follow this way of living without the benefit of a lively faith."

"Why do it then?"

"Well, because we—Eve and I—feel this is part of the central purpose of our life."

"Do you really feel that God has a purpose for you?" Rae asked.

"I'm afraid so."

Will broke in, "You said there are times when money doesn't come, when you can't pay your bills?"

"There are. Often. We don't panic as we used to. Still, not having money is a tremendous drain. It's the measure of value. When you tell someone you can't pay your bills, there are about three standard reactions. You're a failure and a bad manager, and people feel superior to you. Or you're a victim and they pity you. Or you need rescuing and they feel they should help you, but they don't want to do it, so they feel guilty. It never occurs, even to people of faith, that what you're going through may be necessary to your spiritual growth and not something to judge or remove or rectify—something to be lived with, to be suffered or surmounted."

Eve watched Will and Rae closely while Sam talked. They were listening with interest. She relaxed a bit. They asked questions and they talked about their own lean times.

"So," said Will, "what are your circumstances now?"

"Meaning...?" said Sam.

"Do you need money now?"

Sam sighed, "Yes, of course we do. That's why it's on our mind. If we were in one of our flush times, we probably wouldn't be telling you this. But the money we need is not the point. We're not hoping for sympathy."

Rae put in, "But suppose God heard your prayers, and we're expected to be God's instruments."

Eve suddenly spoke, "Then we would say 'Thank you.'" She laughed, "Are you?"

Will shrugged, "I don't know. How do *you* know it's God's hand when something you need comes to you?"

Sam shrugged, "We don't. Not with any certainty. If we were fundamentalists we'd know when God speaks and acts. It'd be a lot easier. Instead we sometimes wonder if the good things that happen after we've prayed are coincidences."

"I don't!" Eve exclaimed.

Sam turned to her and laughed, "You have this sophisticated university education, and yet you have this simple faith." He looked at Rae, "Eve drives up and down a crowded street and prays for a parking space. And she finds one. Here's a theological question. Is God interested in parking spaces? Or does God delegate the parking duties to minor angels— cherubic valets?"

"So, Eve," Will said, laughing, "How do you know God helped you to the parking spot?"

"I don't need to know. I'm just glad I found it."

Rae was nodding her head, grinning and agreeing with Eve.

"So is this a male/female thing!" Will exclaimed. "Women are down to earth and see God's hand in ordinary stuff?"

"I would say so," Rae replied and Eve nodded.

"Okay, my question still stands. How do you know it's God?"

"You know the answer, Will," said Rae with some impatience. "Why are you pressing this question? Answer it yourself."

"It's a deep feeling, hard to put into words, that God is real," Will replied.

"Is that all? Is there more to the feeling?"

"Yeah, the sense that God cares," Will said.

"And that God has something in mind. God knows where it's all going," said Sam.

There was a silence, and Sam was getting ready to launch into his ideas about the difference between plan and purpose. He wanted to explain that the fundamentalists get it all wrong. But he felt an inner check that told him he'd said enough. Eve remarked that it was time to go home.

****

A few weeks later Sam got a call from Will who had flown into Chicago O'Hare to visit his sister in northern Indiana. He said he had an extra day before his return flight to Seattle and wanted to know if Sam was free. He had a rental car and could be at Sam's office in an hour. Sam knew they would spend rest of the day together, wondered if he could spare the time, knew he probably could, wondered if he should, knew he would anyway, so he cleared his calendar.

"I want to know more about this thing you're doing," Will said

"I'm embarrassed," Sam hesitated.

Will shrugged, "Why?"

"It's corny, like something a televangelist would say."

"So—I won't report you to the *New Yorker*."

"I suppose everyone lives by faith, but when you have money you don't think you do. You think you control your life. We have a name for it—financial security. So I have trouble talking about it. It's nuts really. It'd be a lot easier if I had the gift of a single mind. A professor once told me that I have the ability to see seven sides to every issue. I'm at a disadvantage, trying to follow a radical faith with an open mind."

"So what does this mean in practice?"

"I pray about the money I need. I try to follow the promptings I get during prayer."

"Give me an example."

"The house we bought years ago wasn't on the market yet. Our friend, who lives in the neighborhood, happens to find out that the owners are getting ready to sell. He doesn't know them, but he overhears a conversation at parents' night at the elementary school. Ordinarily, he wouldn't pay attention—he's there to talk to his son's kindergarten teacher—but he admires that house. A Sunday or two later, during the coffee hour at church, Joe—that's the friend—rhapsodizes about the house and tells me how he almost buys it, but he can't find a buyer for his present house. This piques my interest. I ask him if I could look at the house—we're thinking about buying. We need more space. We're running our businesses out of our house. We've been renting, but we'd like to buy. Joe's eyes light up. 'Yeah,' he said, 'if I can't have it, I'd like to see you get it.' So we look at it. Charming. Corner lot, trees. Extra bedroom for Eve's office. Large room in the basement—at garden level with windows—for my office—

and a fireplace in this room, as well as one in the large living room upstairs. And a deck! The minute I see this place, I know it's going to be ours. It's the right place!"

"Wait! What do you mean 'right place'? Are you saying God was leading you to this place?"

"Well, it felt that way. But, see, we didn't really have the money to buy it. But the owners liked us. I don't know why, but they really wanted us to have the house. They offered to sell it to us on a one-year contract. That gave us a year to find financing. Seemed like God's hand was in it. So we bought it and moved in.

"A year later we're having trouble finding financing. It's coming down to the wire. The contract's due. We're desperate. We pray. I'm writing in my prayer journal. It comes to us—I'm writing this down—to drive to a bank in a nearby town. It's a Saturday morning. We talk to the loan officer. No interest. We don't have enough income. What now? We're scared. We stop at a pay phone—this was before we had our cell phones. We look in the Yellow Pages. We're standing there in the open, the breeze blowing the pages. We look under "Lending." We don't even look at the finance companies; even then they were predators. We stay away from the banks; we already know they won't help us. There's this one entry for a loan consultant. We don't know what that means, but it's different. We call. A man answers. No, he can't help us, but he knows someone—the loan officer at a nearby bank. It's a branch of a big bank that's already turned us down. Doesn't give us much hope. But we call. He says come in."

Sam paused, wondering what Will was thinking of all this, but saw he was leaning forward intently, so he went on.

"It's almost noon. The banks close at noon. Still, he's willing to see us. We pour out our story. He looks at us thoughtfully. Maybe he thinks we're crazy. But he's intrigued. Maybe he has a fondness for struggling self-employed small business people. He says his bank can't help us. I interrupt to say that we already know that. But he goes on that he knows the president of a small independent bank in a town north of us. He calls this guy, tells him our situation, makes an appointment for us to see him on Monday morning. The guy sees all the same things everyone else sees, but he gives us the loan—based not on our income, but on some money, a rather small amount, that came from Eve's family, that's still invested. I had the strangest feeling that he wasn't seeing with his banker's eyes. He made a loan he shouldn't have made."

"You think God closed his eyes?"

"No…well, I don't know what happened. But we got a loan we shouldn't have gotten."

Sam couldn't tell what Will was thinking. "Does this happen often?" he asked

"Yes. Not this dramatic. But yes, there are times when something we need comes to us in inexplicable ways. The trouble is, instead of praying thoughtfully each day, I drift along and then hope for rescue, for a bail-out. I read about people who have prayed with discipline. They knew to the penny what they needed and when. Their minds were alive to the possibilities of the moment. They knew how to seize them. But they knew how to wait too. They were sure God would come through, even when it looked as though he wouldn't."

"So they looked for bail-outs too?"

"No, for plans to be fulfilled." Sam sighed and shrugged. "God could work with these people. Me? I'm a washout as a person of faith!"

"Quit and get a job with salary and benefits."

"No. I have to see this through."

"Lose all you have? Go bankrupt?"

"If that's what it takes."

"Why would it take that?"

"Maybe there's a lesson here. Maybe the lesson of my life."

"Are you saying that God would lead you into bankruptcy to teach you a lesson?"

"Not *lead* but *allow*…well, maybe even *lead*. I don't know how God works. My friend Joe and his wife Anne—two weeks ago their son Michael died suddenly. He just fell over. The autopsy showed nothing. He was playing table hockey with his friends in the basement family room, and he passed out and died. Joe and Anne are wonderful people. Michael was smart. He was gifted. Everyone liked him. He grew up in our congregation. A child of the church. Everyone had known him since the day his dad stood and announced his birth. So why did Michael die? One of the guys in our breakfast group said maybe God had a larger purpose for Michael. He said he pictured him moving about the universe full of energy and large vision. But others said God had nothing to do with Michael's death. God would never do something that causes pain, especially to teach a lesson. Especially to a kid! Bad things happen because God allows for freedom.

"Here's the thing. Neither works for me. Maybe God does make things happen, even painful things. And maybe sometimes God lies back and does nothing. And maybe other times God just lets things happen. Does God have a plan? Well, I hope so. If there is a creator, how can this creator not have some kind of plan, or at least some intentions?

"So, are my financial struggles of my own choosing? Of course. Is God's hand in it all? Did God lead me or allow me or nudge me? Does something have to work itself out in me that has to do with money? Why not?"

Will said nothing in reply, just gave Sam a thoughtful look.

Sam met his gaze, then looked down, aware that he didn't really know Will, could not assume he was interested in labored theological analysis. "I'm sorry. Probably more than you needed to know."

Will reached into the inner pocket of his jacket and took out a check-book. Deliberately he wrote out a check and handed it to Sam. "Part of God's plan," he said.

"Oh, come on, Will. You're not going to tell me that God told you to write me a check."

"Maybe he did. Or maybe he just allowed me to do it."

"My God, this check's for $2,000! I can't accept this."

"Sure you can. If it makes it easier, consider it a loan and pay it back at some indeterminate time in the future."

"Why, Will? Why are you giving me this?"

"Your experiment intrigues me and moves me, Sam."

Chapter 3 – Knowledge

Sam took the usual table in the Athens House, arriving just before Kurt Wampler. Kurt usually got there first and sat quietly by himself, with his coffee, reading a book. Most people didn't see this subdued side of Kurt. They heard his booming voice and felt his knock-you-down friendliness. They laughed at his store of pithy sayings. Sometimes, like this morning, Sam went out of his way to get there early so he could share these muted moments with Kurt before the others arrived.

Vern Keller dragged himself in next. Vern taught history at the community college. He looked tired. Vern always looked tired. He had bags under his eyes. He was carrying 70 pounds more than he should. Once the conversation got going, Vern came to life, but usually he plopped down and had little to say until his first cup of coffee.

Joe Kurtz came in and sat down, sadness etched on his face. Then came the pastor, Kirby Beahm. When Beahm had come to town some years before and Sam and Kurt had invited him to join the group, they wondered if he would be comfortable just being one of the guys. Some pastors weren't. But Beahm fit right in. No false piety. They all liked him. At these Thursday morning breakfasts they forgot he was their pastor. He brought a new guy with him this morning, introduced him as John Engelsinger.

Jack Foster was the last one. "Did you ever stop to think how ignorant we all are!" Jack said, as he pulled out a chair, sat down, leaned forward, and put his elbows on the table.

"Please!" exclaimed Kurt. "It's early! Drink some coffee."

Joe leaned back as though he wanted to leave. Sam gave Jack a tired smile. Kirby pricked up his ears and cocked his head as though expecting to hear something interesting. John, the new guy, looked surprised and intrigued.

Sam watched with interest as Vern hauled his eyes away from his coffee cup and glanced at Jack. "Let's see," Vern said, "you were listening to the radio as you drove over here. You heard something that shocked you into this admission on behalf of us all."

"Well, you got the radio part right. I was listening to NPR. And it suddenly struck me: the commentator didn't know a damn thing! Didn't know what she was talking about."

"Why is this a revelation?" Kurt asked.

"This wasn't some 30-second news blip. This was in-depth reporting from a correspondent on the ground. She'd done her research. She was reporting on Afghanistan, but it wouldn't have mattered. It could have been rural Wyoming. She was full of information, but she didn't know a damn thing."

"So why is this a new idea," said Kurt, "that the news media gets it wrong?"

"NPR usually gets it right."

Vern smiled condescendingly. "Seriously, Jack, is this your epiphany? That knowledge is limited?"

Jack hesitated. "Just less than it claims to be."

John Engelsinger spoke, "Can the new guy say something?"

"Only if it's profound," said Kurt.

John smiled and shrugged, "Isn't this what we learn in any beginning philosophy class. Knowledge is never complete. It's a mix of what we see and our own preconceptions."

"Yeah! With an emphasis on the preconceptions. Only, I'm not talking a theory of knowledge," said Jack. "I'm talking practical here. We know far less about the other guy than we think we know."

"You mean people can't really know what someone else's life is like?" said Joe Kurtz quietly. "This is true. Believe me, I know it!"

No one spoke. Everyone, even John, the new one, knew that Joe was talking about his almost unbearable grief over the loss of his fifteen-year-old son, Michael, who had died suddenly and inexplicably just a few weeks earlier.

Jack softened his tone, "You do understand what I'm talking about, Joe. We don't know what it's like for you."

Sam had been listening, thinking. He knew what Jack was getting at. He felt it all the time, the sense that even your closest friends don't understand you, though they have known you for years. He wondered why Jack was bringing it up. Jack was always so sure of himself. He drove himself hard and had already had a heart attack. Sam did know what he didn't know—the limits of his own understanding. It put him at a disadvantage. He wasn't much good at arguing; he always saw the other side.

"So why all of a sudden, Jack, does this matter to you?" Vern asked.

"I don't know. Why do people get sudden inspirations? Why do people change jobs? Or get married? Or quit smoking? Why does anybody ever change at all?"

Jack seemed to be searching his deepest thoughts. "I think I am embarrassed at our arrogance as a nation—and at my stupid assumptions as a person and a citizen."

He said this with such intensity that the rest around the table fell into silence, uneasy with his naked feeling.

Jack went on as though the silence were a pause in his own thoughts, "I think I have to do something!"

Vern laughed, "That's the first thing people say. I have to *do* something. As though another well-intentioned person trying his hand on the political levers will finally make the big difference."

"Politics!" Jack exclaimed. "God, that's the last thing on my mind!"

"So where are you going with this?"

"You know, I honestly don't know."

"Come on, Jack. You always know what you're going to do."

"Not now. This has been coming on slowly. This is new. You know me. I'm the guy who accepts things the way they are. I go along. I'm a realist. I *benefit* from the status quo. You're the ones with the social conscience. I'm just glad when the economy's humming along. Business is booming. Money's rolling in. But I am ill at ease just now—I have this feeling that in some way we've gone too far."

Vern leaned forward, really interested. "What do you mean? Who's 'we' and what has gone too far and how far is 'too far'?"

"You tell me! Have you ever had a gut feeling that something's not right, but you don't know what it is?"

Before Vern could begin to pontificate, Sam, who had been watching Jack closely and with curiosity, asked, "Does it have anything to do with being isolated?"

Jack looked up quickly. "Odd question. Why do you ask that?"

"You're a tough guy. You get things done. Always on the move. Often helping people. Lots of friends. But do you ever stop and do nothing?"

"What do you mean 'nothing'?"

"There's a folk song with the lyrics, 'It's the time you waste for them that makes a friend a friend.' Do you ever waste time with your friends?"

"I eat breakfast with you." Jack shot back. There was some uneasy laughter.

Jack paused, lifted his shoulders, and cocked his head as though he wanted to shrug off the question, but found it troubling and arresting..

"Well, I guess none of us wanted to hear that question!" remarked Kurt.

"We're always working at something. We're doers," said Vern, "diligent, dutiful. It's the curse of the middle class. We have the possibilities of leisure without the capacity to enjoy it. One of the great anomalies of the modern world. The rich and the middle class have leisure. The poor know how to use it. They often do nothing because there's nothing they can do."

"I think we ought to feel guilty," said Kurt.

"Sorry! I'm usually not the guy raising the uncomfortable questions. Or trying to find answers. New role for me," Jack said with a crooked smile. Then he looked at Sam, "Are you saying I'm isolated?"

There was bite in this abrupt question. Sam felt everyone tense up. Their unspoken rule was that they would never cross the line to argument or attack. But Sam was calm. He knew what Jack was really asking. He waited before answering. "It was just an observation and not only about you. Here it is. We live in the appearance of community, not the reality."

John Engelsinger leaned forward with sudden attention, "Do you know why?"

"I think I do," said Sam. "Do you?"

"Cable TV, newspapers, magazines, the radio, the web," John said. "Especially the web! Facebook and Twitter. Talk about the illusion of connection! We have Wal-Marts, the shopping mall, the fitness center, the supermarket. Everywhere we go we're surrounded by people! We live in a huge village. But how many people do we *know*!"

"This is not a new idea," Vern said. "It's been around at least since Martin Buber's *I, Thou*, David Riesman's *The Lonely Crowd*. Harvey Cox's *The Secular City*."

"We don't need a history lesson," Kurt snapped. "But you are right. We do know this about ourselves. But we forget. We're too damn busy."

"Do you know why?" asked Vern sharply.

"I know you want to tell me!" Kurt shot back

"It's money," said Sam quietly.

"The tired old 'materialistic culture' argument!" exclaimed Kurt. "Come on, Sam. Jack's the only businessman around this table." He paused, still looking at Sam, "Well, you are in a small way, but you're not in Jack's league. We're teachers, social workers, church workers. If we wanted money, we'd be doing something else."

Sam did not reply. He had no moral ground from which to speak. No one around the table knew how embarrassingly far in debt he was or about his experiment.

"Is it only those who crave money or who have a lot of it who are bound by it?" asked John Engelsinger.

Sam looked at the visitor with surprised interest, "I don't think so."

Joe shrugged, "It doesn't matter much to me at the moment."

No one knew what to say to that until Kirby, the pastor spoke, "Of course it doesn't, Joe. Grief changes things."

"It does!" Joe said. "We were going to add a family room—with a vaulted ceiling and a stone fireplace. We've been planning it for years. Since Michael died—I don't care. It seems so...unimportant! I used to love upgrading my computer. Tried to get as close to the bleeding edge as I could. Shopped for the best deal. I relished it. I used to enjoy planning for retirement. I felt so secure! What's all that now!"

"Damn it!" said Kurt. "I can't even imagine what it's like to lose your son. But don't you think those interests will come back to you?"

Joe shrugged, "Should they?"

"That's my question," said John.

"I thought we needed a new car," Joe went on. "I like buying new stuff. Well-built stuff. Precision-made. I was looking forward to it, thinking about a Prius. What the hell difference does that make in the great movement of the universe whether I have a Prius or drive a beat-up old Ford Escort?" Joe paused. "Well, you could ask the same thing about Michael. What difference does it make in the universe, if Michael lives or dies? But it does! And not just because he was my son!"

No one spoke.

"Damn it. Don't we all know that a child is more valuable than a Prius. The hell of it is we don't! We worry as much about the car as the kid. You know we do. We all do it. We get wrapped up in all this stuff!"

"You can't serve God and mammon," said Vern with mock sententiousness.

"It's about time we brought God up," said Jack.

"What the hell is 'mammon' anyway?" Kurt exploded.

"A word that's safe because it's lost its meaning," said Vern.

"Come on. No one uses 'mammon' any more. That's the King James version," exclaimed Sam.

"You tell us, Kirby, what do later translations say?"

"They are more direct. They translate the Greek as "wealth" or "the power of money" or simply "money.""

"I'm glad you know your scripture!" exclaimed Vern.

"That's what we pay him the big bucks for," said Kurt, as others smiled, knowing that pastors' salaries were notoriously low by secular standards, though the church Kirby pastored, and they all attended, paid better than most.

"Let's get back to Joe," said Sam. "He just poured his guts out. It's not just an intellectual question for him, or something that makes him vaguely uneasy. He just said that it took the death of his son to make him see that he was mired in an unthinking materialism that had sort of slipped up on him. 'Stuff' seeps into our soul and we don't know it."

"So we have to lose someone to know it?" said John Engelsinger.

"Jack didn't have to lose something to start asking questions."

"I'm not asking the wealth question," Jack said. "You're asking that. I'm asking the knowledge question."

"We're going in circles."

"We're as clueless as the radio reporter," said Jack.

"There's at least one thing we know," Sam said softly.

"What's that?" snapped Vern, who thought he should be making the wise, conversation-stopping comments.

"Joe's son is dead and he's grieving," Sam answered.

No one spoke. The comment seemed harsh. It was hard to tell if the words pained Joe or relieved him or both.

"Yes, we can be sure that people will suffer and die," said Kirby.

"And that they will take joy and live," said Sam, trying to atone for his bluntness.

"Dying and living—is that all we can really know? And how much do we know about that?" Kurt said.

"*That's* what was missing from the radio segment!" exclaimed Jack. "The reporter couldn't tell us what it was like to live in that place. She reported accurately. She rolled tape with crowd sounds. She interviewed people. She talked about people dying, but it wasn't real."

"The disconnect is not just between us and them. How about right here? How long have we been eating breakfast together?" asked Sam.

"Some of us twenty years," said Joe.

"How much do we know about each other?" Sam said. "Jack, I've known you for 25 years. But I've never seen you on a construction site. I mean you're a nice guy here around the table, but for all I know you may be an S.O.B. with your workers. You have to be around someone to know what they're like. You have to see how they treat their kids. You have to see what they do when they're pissed at their spouse."

Kurt cocked his head toward Kirby, "What about the pastor? He's supposed to know his parishioners."

Kirby smiled and shook his head. "People are on their best behavior when I come around. Unless they're in crisis. Then they don't have energy to keep up a front. It takes years till you really know your people and they know they can trust you."

"Well, that's proof for our argument," Sam said. "There's no substitute for being with people over time in all sorts of circumstances. Without this we don't know each other."

"That's true," said Kirby. "But it's much harder than it used to be. My uncle was a pastor fifty years ago. He could visit all his parishioners at work, during the day. The women were at home. The men were in the fields or the barn or the workshop. He spent hours visiting. He did know what they were like in their ordinary lives. He loved engines, so sometimes on his day off he worked for the local mechanic, just to get his hands dirty and let his mind rest. People liked him. They felt he was connected to them."

"So why can't you do that too?"

"I do try."

Jack laughed ironically, "You can't ever find me. My construction sites are spread over three counties."

"Yeah, think about it. How many of you have a schedule or a workplace that invites someone to drop in!"

"Instead, we meet for lunch," said Vern.

"That's true," said Kurt. "That's how I stay in touch."

"Or have breakfast together." Vern lifted his hand in a broad sweep indicating their whole circle as though introducing the table itself to the conversation. "That would make an interesting study. The role of food in sustaining community."

"Food has always brought people together," growled Kurt.

"That's right," said Vern. "Stories around the campfire. Revelry in the castle hall. Pilgrims feasting with Indians. Farm families around the groaning board. Fourth of July picnics. Church potlucks. Fried chicken on the political hustings. $50,000 a plate fund-raising dinners. Soup kettles for the homeless. Even Jesus loved food. His critics accused him of gluttony and wine-bibbing. There's the little matter of turning the wine into water. How's that for a first miracle! Then at the end of it all the great messianic banquet!" With a beatific glance and a mock smile, Vern sighed. "I like to imagine that. Eating in heaven! Food's at the heart of history! And—we can hope—eternity!"

"By God, Vern!" said Kurt, as smiles ran around the table.

"I offer physical evidence," he said clasping his hands across his paunch.

"No one's better qualified to think about food."

"Or a better observer."

"That's true. I watch what I eat."

"We can see that!"

"Actually, I do. I'm going on a diet."

Surprised glances around the table.

"So is this why you're waxing eloquent on food? People on diets always think about food."

"Maybe. I don't mind telling you I'm worried about the whole thing."

"Worried! Why worried! Hungry or restless or weak from deprivation—these I could understand. But why worried?" Kurt said.

"I'm going to have to eat all sorts of nutritious and dreadful food—probably forever. I know I'm a candidate for a heart attack or high blood pressure or one of those other diseases you read about. I know I'll live longer if I keep my weight down, though I have to admit I'm sometimes tempted to go out in blaze of steak, fried eggs, chocolate cake, and bagels dripping with butter. But I'm opting for the miseries of healthful living.

"What bothers me is that I like being fat. I've always been fat, except for one year long ago when I lost 50 pounds and positively glowed with emaciated good looks. I think of myself as someone who carries weight. These extra pounds give me authority.

"Weight to throw around?" asked Kurt.

"Do I do that?"

"Does he do that?" Kurt asked, looking around the table at the affectionate smiles.

Vern shrugged. "Frankly, I think slenderness is overrated. I like to see fat jovial, comfortable people, not your hatchet-faced, hard-bodied junior execs in designer jogging suits who can crack your sternum if you hug them too hard.

"And I like being warm when everyone else is cold. I like these layers of organic insulation. My wife weighs 110 and she's always cold. I like the friendly, roly-poly look. I can't imagine being lean and fit. I like to feel my belly bounce up and down when I walk or, heaven forbid, when I jog. I like wearing tweed jackets that I never have to button because I can't."

Vern was saying all this while he was putting away a plate of eggs, sausage, and hash browns.

"So when do you start this diet," Jack asked.

"Today. This is my last meal," he said mournfully.

"This is sort of dieter death-row then," laughed Kurt.

"I do feel like something is going to die. It's biblical, you know. You have to lose yourself to save yourself. Hah, Jesus didn't know he was talking about dieting. Well, I'm going to lose all this lovely weight. I'm going down to a wonderfully healthy 165. Everything will be splendid. I'll feel great. I'll have lots of energy. My teaching will take on new vitality. Students will flock to my classes. I'll be famous. I'll be attractive. People will turn and look when I walk by in my three-piece suit with the vest buttoned. I'll have sex appeal. Ah, it'll be wonderful."

Laughter around the table. Vern was enjoying himself.

"Well, I'm going to watch these lovely pounds melt away. I'll mourn their loss and do my best to live with my new svelteness. But all the same, I think I'm going to miss myself."

After Vern's soliloquy the conversation lagged until Vern looked up from his food and said, "Do you know how unusual this is?"

"The silence or thinking of you eating dry toast and oatmeal?"

"This gathering around this table."

"Why is this unusual, Vern?"

"We are a bunch of middle-class people, well-fed, a bit overweight (I'm not the only one), well-educated, with enough free time and money to take an hour and a half out of the beginning of the day to eat together, and pay for it, for no purpose except friendship. Until the last century or so, only the rich could afford this. In most of the world still, only the rich can afford this. Even in the farm community where I grew up, people didn't do this. In the great sweep of history, not to mention, the evolution of creation itself, we are a little blip. An intelligent, free, thoughtful middle-class is a new phenomenon."

"The way our economy is going, maybe a passing phenomenon."

"Exactly.

"The middle class is shrinking. The rich are getting richer, some obscenely so. It's harder for working class families to make it—even with two wage earners. Young people think their life won't be as good as their parents'. Kids finish college with huge loans."

Sam was watching faces around the table, looking for an opportunity to nudge the conversation in a different direction. "We're all working against each other," he said. "Would you give up a large pay raise if you knew that someone in another department was being laid off to tighten the budget?"

"That's too simple."

"Depends on the situation."

"I don't know enough to answer."

"Maybe I'm worth more to the company than that other guy,"

"Okay," Sam went on. "Let's say you're in top management and you know a lot about the company. And you believe there is another guy who is valuable to the company in a way that the president doesn't see. Would you argue to the president that money being offered to you be used to keep that other guy?"

"I might," said Joe.

"I'd like to think I would consider it," said Kurt.

"But here's the real question," Sam said. "How many people in this country would do it or even think about it?"

"Get as much as you can and if you can get more, get it," said Vern, "and don't think about the consequences for anyone else. That's the American way. And if you get a lot, give some of it away to help the people who aren't as good as you are at the getting. Is there anything wrong with that picture?"

"People don't make money just to have it," Jack said. "People do things with money. You have to concentrate wealth to get things done. You have to have capital."

"How much? What is enough? Is there an 'enough'?" Sam asked. "We think it's a good thing to have more. Even us around this table. We say we don't. None of us around this table have gone after big bucks. Well, maybe you, Jack. But not even you. You're not trying to create an international construction firm. But we still identify ourselves with the upwardly mobile. Look at where we live. We began in "starter" homes. We moved to bigger houses, bigger yards, farther away from the poor people downtown. We don't have the money lust of the Trumps of the world, but we're closer to them than to St. Francis."

"Why do you suppose people automatically want more space, want to move farther away from problems?" asked Kirby Beahm. "That's what money buys, you know. It buys distance."

"Isn't it obvious?" Kurt said. "Who wants to live in a cramped apartment on a street with drug dealers!"

"Of course," Kirby went on, "but there are a few people here and there who make another choice."

"You mean people like Mother Teresa or Dorothy Day?"

"Yes, why weren't they moved by the same desires? Or were they, and they resisted them? And if they resisted them, why?"

"And what I would like to know," said Sam, "is what the world would look like if more people made their choice."

"But they didn't have a family and kids who needed safe streets, yards to play in, and good schools."

"There are families and kids all over the world who don't have those things," Kirby said. "These are the people Mother Teresa and Dorothy Day lived with. Actually, Dorothy Day did have a daughter."

"I guess my question is why is it more natural—or maybe the word is instinctual,' Kurt said, "for human beings to move away from each other's suffering than to move toward it?"

"Is it more natural?" asked Sam. "Or are there two competing instincts in each of us—one toward compassion and connection, the other toward self-interest and separation?"

"Well, folks," said Jack, "I don't find much interest inside myself to move down on River Street. Maybe I shouldn't, but I like it a lot better out on Cotswold Court. And I wonder how many of us would choose River Street over Cotswold."

"We're all going to have to make that choice soon," said Kirby quietly. Everyone suddenly knew that he meant the possibility of moving the church from its downtown location to the land out west in the new upscale subdivision.

"There are other questions to be answered. It's not quite that simple," said Jack. "It's too expensive to fix up the old building. And for God's sake, the people on Cotswold Court need ministering to, too. Just look at me."

"You really think it's not the prospect of a large new, highly equipped, sprawling building with grass and trees and plenty of parking and a ball field and a picnic pavilion that's really on people's mind?" Sam said. "Jack, how would we know how to minister to the folks on Cotswold Court? They wouldn't even come to our church. Their income bracket is Episcopalian. Or they belong in one of those upscale independent churches with the BMW's in the parking lots."

"We don't know that! That's like saying all the blacks on Ann Street are gang members."

"Isn't there something in between?" asked Kurt.

"That's a good middle-class question," said Vern, who had been uncharacteristically quiet. "Find some happy medium. In a way, that's what most of our subdivisions are—a medium between River Street and Cotswold Court. Whether happy or not is another question. And really that's what our church is now. We're in close to downtown, but it's still a safe neighborhood, old, but still middle-class. Isn't there a place for people who protect themselves from poverty but aren't out for riches—an enlightened people who don't forget to serve the community? Like you, for instance, Jack. Maybe you live in Cotswold Court, but you could buy some of those buildings on River Street and rehab them for low and moderate-income housing."

"Can you do that really without living there?" Sam asked. "Would Jack be like the reporter who ticked him off this morning?"

"Well, hell, probably not," Kurt said. "I mean maybe he could do it better if he lived there, but doing it at all would be better than not doing it."

"So what are we saying here!" exclaimed Jack. "That I'm isolated, my friendships are superficial, I work too goddamned much, I'm obsessed by money, and I don't know jack about life and death! That the only way I can really get connected is to live in the slums and do rehabbing. And that's why I got pissed off at a radio broadcast."

"You have a gift for understatement," said Kurt.

"But we still love you, Jack."

"It's time to go," said Kurt, peering at this watch. "Does anyone have a last word?" He looked at John Engelsinger. "The new guy. Don't you think he ought to give it?"

John's face lit up, "If I speak in the tongues of men or of angels and have not love, I am a noisy gong or a clanging cymbal."

"Ho, he quotes scripture!"

"What I want to know," said Vern, "is: who's the angel and who's the gong?"

San wondered, as he stood behind Joe and Kurt, waiting to pay his check, if he should have said more about his own situation. Was he being false, or just smart? And what right did he have to raise these questions about money?

Chapter 4 – Two Women

John liked being left to his own devices. This is what Nancy Beahm did each morning, when she had to leave the house at 6:45 a.m. to be at her school before the teachers and students began to arrive. John had known her longer than he could remember. She was the sister he never had. They were born only a year apart, in the same hospital, to mothers who had known each other since their own infancy. They went to Sunday School together. They went to elementary, junior high, and high school together. She was a quiet, pretty girl; John never thought of her as a possible girl-friend. She was the confidant he turned to when he came home from college lacerated and dumbfounded by his efforts to be loved by Mary, who years later would become his wife. Nancy was one of the close friends who consoled him when Mary died. When they were kids, he had not even no-ticed Nancy's desirability or innocent sexuality until his friend Jack Frisk took advantage of it.

John still could not think of that without pain, and he often wondered about Jack and was tempted to look him up. Nancy knew where he was and had kept in touch with him all these years for Jacqueline's sake. He knew that Jacki saw her father from time to time, though she had taken to Kirby as her real dad long ago. John counted it one of the finest of Kirby's many thoughtful and praiseworthy actions that he had carefully and pa-tiently courted the four-year-old Jacki, paying as much attention to her as to her mother and he knew it was one of the things Nancy valued above all else. He never doubted her love for Kirby, but he wondered about it. Nancy was the kind of girl who had only one place in her heart for ro-mance. She had given that so completely to Jack, that what she gave Kirby, John thought, was a wiser, steadfast love and appreciation, the kind actual-ly that a marriage is based on. But he wished sometimes Kirby could have been the recipient of that earlier pure, whole-hearted fascination Jack had inspired.

After Jack got her pregnant, abandoned her, and left school and his friends behind, John could hardly bear to look at the pain in Nancy's fami-ly. Her father, Wilbur, had been taken in by Jack too. John loved Wilbur's mix of country canniness and simplicity. Of the men John had turned to after his father died and over the many years since, Wilbur was the best company. Wilbur made no demands. He offered no advice. He was elemental, simply there like the fields and fence posts. Yet when something roused him, he displayed quickness and insight and humor that were as effective as they were unexpected. John loved watching him to see when these hidden depths would suddenly surface. He knew how much Wilbur loved his oldest child, this precious daughter who in ways John only later discovered mirrored her father's nature.

Miriam, called Mim, Nancy's mother was a frightened, overwhelmed woman. John often wondered why Wilbur had married her. He showed her tenderness and patience, but he never turned to her for advice, and she abdicated most of the decision-making to him. He had a small room in the barn that he had outfitted with a potbellied stove and later with an electric heater, and he spent much of his spare time out there. The kids loved to be out there with their dad, but Mim rarely came out to sit with Wilbur. She was not a woman who could sit, though despite her nervous activity she always seemed to be behind in her housework. When Nancy became pregnant, Mim went to pieces. The women of the church brought in food and helped with the housework, but their attention was not needed for long. Nancy took over. The work seemed to give her purpose: she had been doing a lot of it anyway since she was a young teenager and even through her college years which were spent going to the local state teacher's college and living at home. Between the two of them, Nancy and Wilbur, they managed the household and the younger children.

Nancy gradually grew from that quiet, easily seduced young girl, who John had sometimes thought would turn out to be more like Mim than Wilbur, into a forceful, highly competent, thoroughly well-organized woman who was not like either parent except that she sometimes, like her dad, hid her savvy behind a seeming uncomplicated nature. She was amused as each new teacher on her staff misjudged her and was suddenly brought up against her toughness and perception.

After that huge effort in early adulthood to go on and finish her degree as an unwed mother suffering under people's disapproval and judgment, then to get advanced degrees while managing a household and more children with a husband who was himself in graduate school, to deal with the heightened expectations placed on a pastor's wife, while becoming an elementary school principal when she was one of the first women to do so—after all this, there was not much Nancy could not do. Her confidence was as elemental as her father's stolid immutability. John enjoyed being around her because she made the world seem like a place that could be managed.

But now she was bringing her powers to bear on him. Nancy had decided John needed a relationship. She never said he needed to marry again. She understood what Mary had been to him, and Mary had been her friend. But she was convinced he needed female company and had talked him into meeting a friend she had in the local service club—a woman who taught history at the community college.

The plan was for John to be Nancy's guest. He knew Kirby had joined a morning club because it had been a good entrée into the community when he was new at the church; this was the one that teachers, ministers, retirees, and a few small contractors who did not take long lunch breaks belonged to. Nancy went to the noon club where the business leaders, bankers, and lawyers belonged. She intended to keep her school connected to the business community, and she made those connections work. Jefferson Elementary had a fully outfitted video studio that Ron Eggert, who owned the local AM and FM stations, had underwritten. She had persuaded Robert Stokes, who ran a chain of lumberyards, to build playground equipment to her design.

John smiled as he dressed. He did not see himself as a service-club-type guy. He wondered what they wore. He supposed sport coats and ties. He put on some clean Levis and a cotton shirt, open at the neck, and shrugged into a blue blazer. He looked pretty good, he thought, glancing in the mirror, maybe ten years younger than he was. He wondered if that was important to him.

He found a parking spot outside the sprawling one-story brick building with some bushes nicely positioned beside a short course of steps up to the double doors, wood with etched glass. Nancy was waiting for him in the lobby. She hurried him into the room where there were a dozen large round tables fully set. The tables were about half full, mostly with men, maybe a quarter women. People were filtering in. Nancy maneuvered him to a table and introduced him to the woman and several men who sat there. John knew this was the person he was supposed to take an interest in. Her name was Barbara Nichols.

She was about his age, maybe a few years younger. Her black slacks, silver-gray blouse, and wine colored jacket showed her slender figure and set off her short, dark, nicely trimmed hair. Suddenly Mary flashed to his mind, and her unerring instinct for knowing when another woman was helping her hair color along. She would have known this woman's hair couldn't be as black as it was. He smiled, which the woman thought was meant for her, and she smiled back. He was jarred by her voice, which was high and childlike, but he listened to her talk and soon forgot the baby voice for the sharp mind behind it.

What really drew his attention was the guy across the table, whose name was Ben Norton, an acerbic wit who couldn't keep from making sarcastic remarks. John figured out that this guy was a lawyer and that he was the program chairman. His job was to line up the speaker for each meeting. It came out that he'd been doing this job for 30 years. John's interest picked up. He liked this guy. Maybe lunch was going to be more interesting than he'd expected.

They slogged through Salisbury steak and mashed potatoes and steamed vegetables and dinner rolls that left John with the feeling that food sometimes really does stick to your ribs. He was impressed that Barbara acted as though he was just another person at the table. Apparently Nancy had not told her why he was there, or if she had, this Barbara was not on the prowl.

After the meal a retired high school bandleader and 40-year member rose and led the members in song, from a book with mostly show tunes from before World War II and written from the male perspective. John wondered how these professional women felt about that. He noticed that Barbara was not singing. Then the chapter president got up and made a few announcements and called on Claude Framington, another attorney, who stood up and told some tasteless jokes. John was amazed and embarrassed as he watched this guy in his mid-seventies smirk and show an astonishing capacity for sexism and misogyny. He heard Barbara lean over to Nancy and whisper, "Where is Jane Nevers when we need her." Nancy told him later that Jane Nevers had lobbied the board to take the job away from Claude and had finally resigned in protest. John asked Nancy why she didn't resign. She shrugged and said she thought she could out-wait the Claudes of the world.

The president turned the meeting over to the program chair who reminded everyone that next time Moose Skowron, former New York Yankee great, now retired Chicago businessman and greeter for the Chicago White Sox, was the speaker. The week after that the Republican candidate for States Attorney would speak, and the week after that Mrs. Jerymin Jessup would talk about Nature's Gift Nudist Colony. She was bringing videos, he said, evoking laugher and some raised eyebrows. John was beginning to understand why the chapter kept Ben Norton as program chair. Today, he wanted to introduce the Reverend James Merrill, pastor of the Walters Park Church in Chicago. "You may remember that Rev. Merrill was in the news for performing gay unions and being suspended by his denomination." As Merrill rose to speak there was dead silence. John was astonished. This town and this county were overwhelmingly Republican and conservative. Norton, apparently was willing to book anyone to get an interesting program. But Merrill must be a masochist to come to Selby to talk about gay parishioners.

John was surprised at how simply and skillfully Merrill disarmed his audience. He talked about the gay young men in his parish—a lonely, young divinity student with no interest in cruising the bars, a man whose family disowned him, another whose partner died of AIDS. No stridency, just human stories, unusual only because they put an ordinary human face on something most people in the audience were uncomfortable with. He spoke with a mix of frustration and patience of the church hierarchy who had imposed his suspension. When he finished, there were no questions. The room was quiet as people got up to leave.

John turned to Barbara, "Is that typical?"

She smiled, "You mean presentations on homosexuality?"

"Programs that run counter to the received wisdom."

"Ben will book anyone. About half the time the speakers are local politicians or leaders of civic organizations. The rest of the time is evenly divided between business people, elderly members of the Selby Symphony, sports personalities, and a stripper or two. It doesn't matter. I think he's really a closet liberal and likes to shake up the members. But he'll cheerfully book a racist if he thinks it'll be good theater."

Another woman had come up to Nancy while Barbara was talking. John caught her out of the corner of his eye. He could smell her perfume, something subtle and disturbing. She was saying something about coming to Nancy's school to do a workshop on writing. He turned and took her in in one long glance that he could not have ended had he wanted to. Her skirt was short. Her legs were good. Her breasts were high and full. She wore a sweater that was tight enough to show them and loose enough and tailored enough to say that you were supposed to see its style and value as well as what was inside it. Her face was not young. She must have been in her early fifties. Her make-up gave her color and set off her green eyes, but she had not tried to cover up the small wrinkles around her eyes or at the edge of her mouth. Her skin had a patina, aged but cared-for, and it still had some freckles. The face had character and determination. The lips were full. The red hair, streaked with gray, looked real. It was drawn back and pinned up with a silver barrette to accentuate her cheekbones and forehead. John had an instinctive desire to pull the pin and watch the hair cascade over her shoulders. He quickly looked away wondering if anyone saw him staring.

The conversation with Nancy was short. The woman moved off. John watched her go. Her waist was narrow, her derriere compact. She walked with purpose and some grace and with a pleasing sway. Her black pumps had medium heels and were of the latest style. He dragged his eyes back to the table. Barbara was smiling at him. He was caught in the act. He smiled and raised his eyebrows.

"She has that effect on every male," Barbara said.

"You're remarkably sanguine about it."

"I'm used to it. I've known Angela for thirty years. She was my student when I just started out. She's a first-rate teacher. Well, I've got to get back. It was nice to meet you, John." Barbara held out her hand. John suddenly had the feeling that Barbara did know why he was here and seated next to her and that what had just happened was like most blind dates, only it had been carried off with more aplomb and less embarrassment. With the slightest touch of irony she said, "Enjoy your stay here in Selby. You're in good hands with Nancy."

Later as he walked with Nancy to the parking lot, he asked, "Who was the woman who came up to talk to you there at the end?"

"John Engelsinger, I expected better of you."

"Come again."

"Barbara Nichols is one of the nicest and sharpest women I know. Intelligent, good-looking, sensitive, excellent teacher, widowed after a good marriage, mother of two grown children who are a credit to her, community activist, active church member, and by the way a pretty decent jazz pianist, who values herself enough that she would never throw herself at anyone. And the only person you notice is Angela Feladucci!"

"Nancy, I made no promises. I liked Barbara. What's wrong with Angela Feladucci? Even the wonderful Barbara told me with a certain dryness in her tone that she was a first-rate teacher, as though there was something else that trumped her classroom powers."

Nancy sighed. "Angela is a good teacher. She's a good friend too. She has never married. She has had a string of affairs and boyfriends, some alleged some actual. She has a reputation. She doesn't care, seems even to enjoy it. But if you ask me, I think underneath it, she feels bad. She attracts men who want only one thing."

"I'm surprised you trust your elementary school kids with her."

"She's wonderful with kids. She makes writing exciting. Kids come out of her workshops fired up to write, even and especially the ones who hate writing and believe they can't do it."

****

John found her in the online White Pages. There was only one Angela Feladucci. The listing gave her age and address as well as her number. This had to be the person he was looking for. He printed out the information and, holding the paper in his hand, paced the length of the Beahms' kitchen and dining room—as disturbed as he'd been as a college student calling a girl. Women still produced this suffering, even after more than thirty years of a marriage that should have convinced him once and forever that he was a worthy companion. How could someone like him be wanted by someone like her! His anxiety rose by so many decibels that he could almost hear it—like the hum in high-tension wires. He laughed and told himself he was old and wise—he was sixty-two years old—which reminded him that this woman was much younger. He broke into a nervous sweat. This was ridiculous. He dialed the number. An answering machine picked up. Relief and disappointment washed through him. He steadied his voice and left a message.

Later in the day when he finally found Angela Feladucci at her work number at the community college and made the date, he was off-handed. He hardly cared; he was so wrung out and so relieved to have it done with. This jaded feeling carried over to the next day. He arrived early for lunch at Emma's and sat waiting for her. But when she walked through the door the rush of anxiety and desire startled him and left him weak. He cast about in his flushed thoughts for something to say as he quickly got to his feet to help with her chair, trying to show the poise he thought he would normally exhibit but could now only dimly recall. He wondered if this woman knew. Of course she did. She was quick and intelligent, and she was used to the effect she had on men. He wondered what he was doing having lunch with this kind of woman.

She lifted the menu smiling to herself and glancing past it into John's eyes, she said, "Have you read Meister Eckhardt?"

"Excuse me."

"The thirteenth-century mystic."

"Yes, I know who he is. I've never had a…" he paused "…woman ask me that."

"Women don't read mystics?"

"No, I mean, yes…"

"Careful, you're getting yourself into trouble…"

John laughed, "You don't look like someone with a taste in mystics."

"What do I look like?"

"Someone with a different kind of taste."

"So, my reputation has preceded me."

"I didn't need to know your reputation to answer the question."

"So I have that effect on you?"

"Are you always this frank with your conquests?" John asked.

"Are you a conquest?"

"I'm afraid I might be," John said. "Why the question about Meister Eckhardt?"

"You belong to Nancy's church. I thought I'd start the conversation with something religious."

"Surely you know enough about us to know we have no mystical tradition."

Angela laughed. "You're a little different."

"You think I'm mystical!"

"No, just not so earnest."

"Earnest?"

"The people in your church are some of my dearest friends. People I've known for years. People I'd trust my life with. Good people. Wonderful people. But they are earnest. They are seriously good people."

"You mean self-righteous?"

"No, that would make them insufferable."

"*Do* you read Meister Eckhardt?"

"More than that. I teach him."

"I thought you taught English lit."

"I do. I head the department."

"Eckhardt was German."

"The dean trusts me. I have leeway to add some courses just because they interest me or my department faculty."

"So Eckhardt is part of a course you teach? What do you call it?"

"*Mainly Mystics: Meister Eckhardt to Thomas Merton.*"

"Are you Catholic?"

"Lapsed."

"Are all your mystics Catholic?"

"No, I have George Fox and Thomas Kelly and Kathleen Norris in there."

"Norris came after Merton and isn't really a mystic."

"Doesn't matter. I put what I want into the course. I liked the alliteration in the title."

John stopped. The day, his life—everything seemed to have narrowed to this table in Ella's Café and Creamery. There was only Angela's red hair. Her breasts filling out her white blouse. The open, embroidered vest that framed them. The full red lips. The pert nose. The schoolgirl freckles. All this in spite of or mingled with the delicate lines on her face and slightly world-weary manner. The memory of her legs tucked under the table. Her subtle and provocative perfume. Her brisk, witty, teasing voice.

"Are you still with me?" she asked, waving her hand in front of his face.

He shook his head. "More than you can know."

He carried thoughts of that lunch with him like warm fire and blushed with the memory of his candor and was pleased and proud of himself. Two days later he drove down to Chicago for the day. He watched the five-story video faces in Millennium Park. He enjoyed the stretched out, funhouse images of the skyline reflected in the giant stainless steel bean. He contemplated the rolled-steel roof of the band shell that looked like scraps from an air-conditioning duct installation.

He met Vi at Miller's Pub in the Loop, which she had suggested. "I need to get out of the neighborhood sometimes," she said. "They have a nice fish for lunch here at a good price for a low budget."

"So you're free for the afternoon? You'll spend the day with me, have dinner later?"

She nodded. She looked tired. She was wearing pressed jeans, an open-necked blue shirt, her trademark scarf, and sensible walking shoes. "What do you have in mind?"

"Talking, walking, maybe down along the lake. Talk, mostly. I need to talk." He paused, "I'm in new territory. I have no ties. There's no 'next thing.' Everything is out there for the choosing or creating. This might be all right if I were 25 or even 45. But I'm past 60. I'm not supposed to be in this place at this age."

"Why do I have the feeling that you like this?"

"Why do you say that!"

"You look good, ten years younger than you are, actually. Color in your cheeks, glint in your eye. You look a lot better than I feel, and I'm the one with purpose and direction."

John smiled, "I do feel good. The best I've felt since Mary died. I even feel guilty; I don't deserve to feel this good. It's too soon."

"You know that's nonsense."

"Yes, of course. The feelings are real, all the same."

Vi reached across and put her hand on John's. Her fingers were long and delicate, the nails beautifully kept, her touch soft and cool, and reassuring. It surprised him how good it felt to be touched by a woman. And how odd. He thought of Vi as a crusader, a tireless worker for justice, a person of extraordinary courage. He rarely thought of her as a woman, much less a desirable one. It confused him.

She looked at him with a smile and withdrew her hand. "You were saying?"

He gathered his thoughts. "I have enough money to live for two or three months. Then I need to get some kind of work. I really don't care what I do. I suppose I should care. I've always thought I should care. There's always been something that needed to be done. Work is good; idleness is bad. Do we ever stop listening to those voices from childhood? Expectations and assumptions are in the air I breathe. My value is measured by what I do. Do you ever question that?"

"Not much. No."

"No, you wouldn't. You have a certain purity of intention. I once thought you were self-deluded. I thought you needed people to be poor and oppressed and in trouble so you could do your noble work. I thought you would be secretly disappointed if the world suddenly became good."

"What changed your mind about my self-delusion?"

"I watched you when you came to visit us on the farm. You luxuriated in your leisure. You enjoyed the good things in the US even though many are only possible because we exploit our position in the world."

"That troubled me—and still does—but I needed rest."

"Some people coming back from international postings are sickened, for instance, by all the stuff at the local supermarket. Instead you were amused that you had once taken this for granted and would again if you stayed long enough. Sometimes you didn't want to go back to your work, yet you did. I realized your reasons were more complex. I began to think you needed to suffer."

"Do you still think that?"

"Well, maybe. But it's the suffering that comes from a valuable and positive discipline—like the pain a runner feels, who gets a health benefit and a "runner's high," You got more satisfaction from your life with the poor than from a comfortable life here at home. You knew your own life flowered in more demanding, and therefore more authentic, circumstances."

"That doesn't seem much different to me. In this view I still need the poor so I can live in authentic circumstances."

"I thought you got pleasure out of providing opportunities for the poor to make the same mistakes we all make when we acquire wealth."

When they finished lunch, Vi took John firmly by the arm and guided him to the El. They got off on the South Side and she walked him through the neighborhood of older brick buildings, once the homes of the comfortable middle class, now divided into apartments, with sagging porches, scuffed doors, dark windows, and bare yards, some enclosed by broken picket fencing. The streets were crowded with battered cars.

They stopped in front of a square building, with a flat roof and stairs running up to the front door. She explained that this had once been the parish center for the church next door. Inside, they were accosted by stale kitchen odors from countless meals of cheap food and the smells of institutional cleanser and unwashed clothing, overlaid with the aroma of chili bubbling in a huge kettle. They were in a long room with two rows of tables already set for the evening meal. The sounds of banging pots and laughter and rapid-fire speech came from the kitchen in the back where two large and raucous black women were cooking while teasing and bossing two young white women in jeans and t-shirts and Birkenstocks.

Two gnarled and wizened old men sat in battered recliners in the lounge, leaning forward over a game of checkers on the scuffed and scratched coffee table marked with the moisture rings of innumerable glasses and coffee mugs. In the corner another, younger man, wearing a hooded red sweatshirt, sat rigidly staring into space.

In all the hugeness of the universe, John wondered, was anyone paying attention to these people? They were making no impact on the city or the world. They were surviving. The man in the corner began talking loudly to himself. The two old men playing checkers looked like junkies. The shouting, laughing women in the kitchen were embarrassing the white girls by talking about sexual escapades in crude and explicit detail. There was nothing beautiful or refined here, or even admirable. But, as though a curtain in his mind were drawn aside, John saw that the human spirit was precious even if it came in a damaged and disfigured package. He remembered once hearing a priest lecture on the "preferential treatment of the poor."

Vi had been talking quietly, telling John about the shelter. Now she introduced him to the checker players who gave him the smile they kept for white do-gooders who invaded their haven. This veiled distrust jarred John out of his epiphany. Vi noticed his silence, but she said nothing as she showed him where the people who came to the shelter slept. She called them "guests."

Later when they were outside, Vi asked him about his distracted manner. "I felt at home for a moment," he answered. "It was very strange—but comforting too."

"Comforting?"

"When you are as poor as those people are, you don't have to play a role. I think I'd like to live like that—not poor, but free. I've lived where everyone knew me and my family going back generations. I resisted living up to expectations, but they were always there in the background, annoyingly present like a sore lower back."

Vi smiled.

"You think I'm romanticizing the poor?" John said.

"I think you are thinking about yourself and not the people you just saw."

John stopped and looked right at Vi, and then he laughed. "Is that an occupational hazard of your line of work—to think you've understood someone when you've really only projected yourself into their world?"

"That question may be the beginning of wisdom."

Chapter 5 – Getting to the Bottom

The money from Will and Rae went quickly. Sam thought people who had a regular paycheck could never know how quickly $2,000 can go when there is no assurance where the next $2,000 will come from.

He liked the Old Testament story about the jar of oil and the canister of flour that never went empty. He wondered if the woman looked in the vessels each day and worried if this would be the last day. Or was she just happy that the oil and flour were there once again. Did she believe they would be there tomorrow and the next day too?

He himself was of two minds. Some days he looked at the bills and expenses coming up and knew there was no way to meet them. Other days he was buoyed by a deep certainty. The creation was rich; its bounty could never be exhausted. The anxiety that drove human economic life had it wrong. There was enough for all, if people trusted and helped one another. If they were reassured that they did not have to acquire and protect but could hold their labor and needs lightly, God would indeed provide.

Then he thought of the natural world where creatures killed and ate each other to survive. The air went out of his faith. The world was a place where you had to get what you could, protect what you had, and put as much aside for the future as possible.

He heard the sound of the lid on the mailbox, then the ringing doorbell. The mail carrier stood at the door with two certified letters. Sam signed for them. They were from the Internal Revenue Service. He sighed as he closed the door. One was for him, one for Eve. But they said the same thing. He knew this from past notices. When you filed a joint return, the IRS sent notices to both of you to be sure you both knew of their action—presumably in case you were living together in separate hostile encampments.

He wondered how many other people were getting notices. Once he had thought he was alone. When you have been careful and proper all your life, and you falter for the first time, you have this awful sense you're the only one. Everyone else is paying bills on time. No one else is in tax arrears. The rest of the world—everyone—is righteous and compliant and good. They disapprove of those who are not. They react in horror and shake an accusing finger at you like your third-grade teacher when you forgot your homework.

When he began to look into companies that did debt consolidation and debt settlement and tax settlement, he was amazed at how many there were. He realized there must be thousands, possibly millions of people in his situation. That was comforting in a tawdry way. Did this make him part of the unwashed lower orders, who kept junk cars in their yards and lived in slums and made no effort to keep orderly lives—the world of poverty, of people who gave up, of the mentally ill who had no idea how to carry out their financial affairs much less put them in order. He should feel compassion and understanding, now that he was one of these people, but he felt distaste and then guilt. How could he see them as fellow human beings! He wondered how many people thought they were the only ones too. Were millions in deep financial trouble, suffering in terrible isolation, known only to the IRS and the collection agencies?

Still, he hung onto his faith. Was the check from Will a lucky accident? Yes, of course. He knew it was. Yet he had a persistent sense that behind what he saw and experienced were connections and movements that made such things not coincidences but the powerful and purposive movement of providence itself. He smiled. He liked the sound of that—"powerful and purposive movement of providence."

If he had a full and deep and simple faith, he thought, he would be led to ways of earning money or finding money or receiving money. But his faith faltered. When he was without it, he did what a person does who knows anything about money. He borrowed or postponed or renegotiated. So now he was in debt and living just a few steps ahead of creditors. Still, somehow he managed to stay afloat and meet the bills that came to him each day.

A person of real faith would not go into debt. When the money ran out, he would let the chips fall. He would go financially naked on that empty day, not try to cover his nakedness with borrowed clothes. That's the way all the people he ever knew or read about did it.

At the edges of Christianity there were people who had made such a radical experiment—trusting their needs for food, clothing, shelter, and money to God. They prayed for what they needed. If it did not come, they went without. These people had an intense, day-by-day, hour-by-hour sense that God was present and involved. God guided and provided. This idea affected him deeply. This was the pattern by which he was trying to live.

He wondered sometimes about those who made lots of money by the usual means. Were their opportunities less of their own making than they realized? Were they the unwitting beneficiaries of providence?

He could not imagine providence urging anyone to go into debt. Still there was something about his situation that seemed right even in its awfulness. Being poor, being among the dregs of the financial system—this was stripping away his sense of his own goodness, his self-satisfaction, showing him how the majority of people in the world lived—from day to day and hand to mouth. It was keenly painful to do it in hiding behind a middle-class façade. He often wondered what might have happened when they began to run out of money if he had just begun to sell everything, until they were down to nothing.

He knew why he didn't do this or even tell his friends. People had hidden fear, lost to consciousness because salaries and benefits protected so well. It surfaced fast when they were laid off or lost a job. They panicked. They went from financial security to the appalling fear that they could lose everything. He knew now that most middle-class families were so heedlessly well-off that they had resources they didn't even think of—equity in insurance policies, 401(k)s, premiums that could be reduced, payments that could be deferred, extra cars, accumulated stuff in the house and garage they could sell. Add to this their savings and credit cards, and most families could survive for months on little income and not significantly alter their lifestyle. But viscerally people felt the disordered ranks of the lower classes were only a few missed paychecks away.

When his friends did know of his struggles, it made them uncomfortable. They pitied him and felt they should help. Most of his friends could find $5,000 if they had to. They always seemed to come up with a down payment for a car. But a sum like that feels big. One time a friend had said, "Look if I can help, let me know." He could not tell him how unhelpful that statement was. He'd just swallowed enough pride to admit he was struggling. How in God's name was he ever going to be able to say, "Uh, would you be willing to lend me $2,000?" What an awkward moment that would produce. He figured the "let-me-know-if-I-can-help" comment had about a $100 ceiling. The best kind of help was the kind Will had given. Say nothing and write a check. It's not just the money, it's the spirit. A simple act unasked for does more than pay the bills. It lifts you up. It says, "I know! I am willing to know what it's like. I'm with you." It lifts the awful burden of financial isolation.

The part Sam knew his friends really couldn't understand was that he was not hoping for a bail-out. This was the crazy part. He believed he had to go through this. There was something he had to learn. And it could only be learned through suffering. He did not like the sound of that, but he thought it was true. Whether God produced the suffering or he himself caused it by playing out some deep ambivalence at the roots of his personality—he didn't know. Didn't need to know. This was part of his deeper purpose—to understand money and how it affected spirit.

Money was a measure, Sam thought. One would never willingly choose debt or deprivation. Some religious people said that money and riches were a gift from God and confirmed one's goodness; they were one's just desserts. Debt and deprivation were signs of spiritual failings. Even voluntary poverty was suspect.

So to hear of his struggles and hold him in concern and support as if he were struggling with a demanding job or a serious illness—this was simply not something that occurred to people. Sam smiled. The only one of his men's group who might understand would be Jack. He was hard-nosed. He figured you made your own bed, you lie in it. If he gave you something, it was from generosity, not guilt or a sense of responsibility. He had made it the hard way; you should too.

People who worked for themselves knew what it was to have bills and not know how to pay them. They knew they could survive. The fear that the jar will go empty doesn't go away, but you live with an empty jar often enough to know you can survive; the world doesn't end. He wondered if that's why poor people sometimes have a strong faith. They've seen the worst and survived.

When everything else is gone, there is God. Choices narrow. You can be cynical or angry or sad—it doesn't matter. There's no place to turn. God is all you have left. Was that why Jesus told the rich young ruler to sell everything? Was that why St. Francis actually did it?

He had a disturbing thought. Was that what he'd been trying to do? Unconsciously sell it all? Without the courage either to keep it and enjoy it or to walk away from it, he'd been doing it by default?

He heard the garage door opener, and Eve came through the door into the kitchen. She walked down the steps to his office.

"I tried to use our debit card to buy groceries. The card was rejected. I don't know why. There should be enough in the checking account to cover the stuff I was buying. Why wouldn't it accept the card?"

Sam shrugged. "I have no idea. I'll call the bank and check it out."

Eve sat down, "Did you write a check we forgot to record. Or did I?" She sighed, shook her head, "I don't think I did."

"Maybe it was just a computer malfunction."

"I hope so. I am so paranoid. Whenever something like this happens, I'm sure I've done something wrong and someone's going to accuse me."

Sam checked their account online; there was still a balance. He dialed the bank's number and patiently waded through the quagmire of electronic options until he finally got a live human voice. The customer service rep put him on hold. Sam and Eve looked at each other. They'd been through this before. But it never got easier. They'd developed a kind of dumb patience.

The bank representative came back on the line and explained that a hold had been put on their checking accounts. The Department of Revenue was levying their joint account to claim the state income tax they had not been able to pay. Sam hung up, stunned. He hated to tell Eve. Her anxiety would shoot up. He could control his own, but he was not sure he could handle hers. But, of course, he told her. They sat in silence.

"Is it just our joint account?" she asked. "If it is, we can use our business accounts."

Sam called the bank back and found that both small business accounts were levied too. "They put the hold on any account with your name or my name on it."

Eve looked up suddenly, "Does that mean they've claimed the money Will and Rae gave us."

Sam smiled ruefully, "No, that's already gone—to pay the mortgage and health insurance and a lot of other bills."

"So what are we going to do! We can't even use the little bit of money we have."

Sam was numb, sitting there in his chair. Eve had gone back upstairs. Gradually he stirred. He gathered together the papers on his desk and put them in a neat pile. He took out the file with the tax returns. He had carefully filed the returns. A principle had slowly evolved out of this struggle to survive. When he could not pay something, he could at least stay in regular touch with the creditor, indicate when and how much he could pay or why he couldn't and how he hoped eventually to do it. So he knew what he owed in state tax. He had carefully filed the return with a letter saying that he could not pay it, but would be working toward paying it. He looked at the tax forms. He owed $1,487. That was the figure from two months ago. The amount would be higher now—penalties and interest. It was one of the great injustices that the less you had and the less able you were to pay down your debts, the greater the interest and penalties grew. He understood why the system worked that way—it cost money to service debt and to collect it. The risk was greater. The creditor could lose the principal completely. But think of it! The more you didn't have money to pay, the more rapidly the amount you had to pay rose. It was a craziness you couldn't really appreciate until you were in the situation.

It took Sam several hours of phone calls to find out how the levee on his accounts worked, what he would have to do, what would happen if he couldn't do it. The state Department of Revenue would take any amount in the accounts until the tax burden was paid. There was nothing the bank could do. They were obligated to keep the hold until the state released it.

As Sam made the calls, talked to people, his spirits began to revive. His faith stiffened and grew stronger. He would find a way. Doors would open. This upsurge of will had happened before, and Sam was always grateful for it. He seemed to have some deep resilient life that simply would not give up. It wasn't something he produced. It was something he found and was faithful to. It was dormant when he was immobilized, but as soon as he began to move forward—one foot in front of another, one phone call and then another—slowly hope returned. A disaster became a challenge.

But it was Friday morning. There was no way he could find the money and have the hold removed still today. It would have to wait until Monday. He thought about money for the weekend. Fortunately they were not going anywhere. But they needed groceries. He called his life insurance company to check the cash value in his policy. It had increased only a few dollars since the last time he taken money out—not yet enough to do it again.

He had a check on his desk for a bit over $200 for a project he'd done in his graphic design business, for a local gourmet coffee shop. He could probably cash that at the currency exchange. He had to use most of it for a new toner cartridge for his laser printer. It was an expensive cartridge. There were brochures he had to print over the weekend. He needed them Monday morning. He could not put them off. After the cartridge he would have about $45. Would that get them through the weekend?

He drove to the huge discount computer and electronics store, where prices on cartridges were better than at the big-box office supply store. It was good to be able to buy something, even something as basic as a printer cartridge. It meant a small movement forward. He smiled to himself. It wasn't a movement forward. It was floundering in place. Still he had a small burst of energy as he walked into the store. He walked past the high-definition televisions. He watched a swashbuckling movie, reveling in the surround sound. He could picture one of those in his home. He sat in the simulated living room and watched a few minutes of a popular animated feature, immersed in the sound and vivid pictures. A palpable yearning rose in him. He could feel it in the pit of his stomach and behind his eyes, a desire to have these pretty and wonderful things. The racks of DVDs, a digital camera, a new smart phone. He looked longingly at the iPads. He didn't need one, but he wanted one.

He imagined a large, well-appointed home wired with the latest technology. What a luxury it would be to buy whatever he wanted, whenever he wanted it. For a few moments he gave himself over to a paroxysm of imagination and longing. Anything could be made. Anything could be bought. The world was limitless in its possibilities and richness. It was good to revel in its richness, to enjoy it, to savor it, to have it. God was a God of beauty and creativity, of joy and enjoyment, lavish in his decoration of earth and heaven, wanting his creatures to take pleasure in creation, not deny themselves. Having things wasn't bad.

He picked out the cartridge and stood in the checkout line. The mood began to collapse. He felt tired, his eyes heavy and sad. He felt as though he had eaten too much candy. He thought of thousands of homes filled with all the stuff people bought at this store, men sitting in front of large screen TVs, eating chips and dip and drinking beer or kids spending hours playing video games. People over-eating in the fast food restaurants that ran in a long row outside the store. He wondered if they were happy—all these people. Sadness filled him. Where were the sweatshops that produced the computer chips and circuit boards?

By the time he left the checkout counter the whole scene seemed alien. The guy who watched people leaving the store to make sure they weren't sneaking out stolen stuff seemed to give him a second look. He felt vaguely guilty, paranoid. Somehow people would find out how little money he had. They would tell him he couldn't buy the thing he had in his hand. He was separated, cut off. All those people in there could buy all that stuff. He could buy none of it.

Crossing the parking lot, he heard someone call his name. He glanced around, slightly disoriented, trying to figure out which direction the voice came from. His eye spied a head wearing a Greek fisherman's cap poking above the car roofs and eyes peering across the long line of vehicles. He recognized Oliver Larkspur, a wealthy local eccentric he'd done a project for the previous year, who'd engaged him in some lively conversation. He walked down the row as the old man closed the door of his car and began to open the back. Not for the first time Sam thought how incongruous his car was. It was one of those retro vehicles that looked like something from the 1930s souped up by a kid in the 50s and then just slightly smoothed out by a 21st-century designer—a car that didn't know its decade. It was popular with young people; he'd never seen one driven by anyone over 70. He wondered what part of the old man's personality the car fit—his throwback politeness and formality or his unexpected, sharp contemporaneousness. Not to mention the fact that he could afford a car six times its value.

The old guy had lifted the car's hatchback and was beginning to wrestle a large box out of the rear luggage area. Sam quickly corralled a shopping cart and began to help him. "I believe in the wonders of modern technology," the old man said. "I just don't have much faith in the manufacturers. I paid $3,000 for this. It took two of my neighbors to help me maneuver it into my house. Plugged it in. Hooked it up to all the ancillary image-producing gadgets that go with such a miraculous machine, tangled in cables up to my neck. Turned it on. Nothing! Went over the whole manual again. It was like reading Sanskrit! Still nothing."

Sam saw it was a 60-inch, flat screen, high-definition TV. They wrestled it onto the top of the shopping cart—it wouldn't fit inside.

The old man kept talking, "I even asked my neighbor's eleven-year-old son to take a look. You know, of course, that no one over the age of twelve really understands DVDs and DVRs and AT&T broadband and all those other acronymic components and connections that define and ennoble our civilization. Think about it. The first time in the history of human culture that the ones who know best about the construction and use of the tools that keep the culture going are just barely out of puberty and have no understanding or experience of the culture they are enabling. "

He was shaking his head as the cart wobbled across the tarmac with the TV balanced precariously on its frame. "I don't know what all this is going to lead to. Certainly, bomber pilots with video-game precision wiping out homes and people on the ground they cannot even imagine, much less feel for, or worse, drone operators sitting in bunkers thousands of miles from the people they are killing. Ah, for the old battles where you had to look your enemy in the face before you dispatched him. Well, even the gigabyte genius next door couldn't get this malignant monstrosity to work."

The old man gave the exit police a friendly glare, and they waved them on through. It took only a few minutes to go through customer service, to have an identical replacement unit tottering on another cart, and to be heading out the door. It seemed the old man was not the only shopper to bring back defective merchandise. Sam wondered what the percentages were. Management certainly had the replacement wheels well oiled.

With the box stashed in the back of his improbable vehicle, the old man thanked Sam and invited him to lunch. Sam smiled to himself. He had two dollars in his pocket and would have had to head home and make a sandwich instead of picking something up, so he accepted. The old man took him to Emma's Café and Creamery, which catered to the health-and-nutrition-conscious crowd. Quilted pieces by a local artist hung on the walls.

"Of course it's wholly impossible to find anything edible in this town," he said cheerfully, "but Emma seems to understand that flavor can be coaxed out of food. Though I will never understand why she puts sprouts in salads—and on sandwiches, God help us. I suppose it shows my age, but they look like something that poked out of the potatoes my mother left too long in the root cellar—which is probably not too far from what they are. I have to make an effort to care about nutrition, but I admit to having an interest in taste. So, Sam, do I sense a despondent air?"

"Is it obvious?" Sam asked.

"There are four kinds of people," said the old man.

Sam smiled and raised his eyebrows.

"Those who have feelings, know they have them, and express them. Those who have feelings, know they have them, and choose not to express them. Those who have feelings, don't know they have them, and express them indirectly. And those who have feelings, don't know they have them, and don't express them."

"So which am I?" Sam asked.

"I hope the first or the second."

"The other two are not good, I take it."

"Neurotic. There are two things you can be sure of."

"You're full of bromides today."

"Not bromides, I hope. I shouldn't want to dull your pain."

"So I seem to be in pain?"

"Sam, it is acceptable, even desirable, to meet life with anguished stoicism. We all know what a blessing it is to be able to stand alone on the windy heights of one's soul, facing into the gales of eternity, and peering over into the abyss of existence."

"You're poking fun at me."

"Simply acknowledging what a wonderful thing solitary suffering is."

Sam looked away, over at the quilt hanging on the wall, "I'm broke. Out of money and falling deeper in debt."

"Is this good or bad?"

"I'm surprised you asked that question."

"Why?"

"No one believes being broke is good."

"Do you believe it's good?"

Sam hesitated, "Yes…sometimes…but not today."

"So it's not that you're broke. It's that you've lost heart."

"Lost faith is more like it."

"Do you like money?" the old man asked.

The questions surprised Sam. "Why do you ask that!"

The old man raised an eyebrow. His face grew serious but his eyes gave him away. He seemed to be laughing inside. "You're a good Christian—a liberal one at that. I like to talk about Christianity with my good friend, Preston Krunsch, who is a member of your congregation. It's my observation that people who follow Jesus almost always feel guilty about money. And it's a fine thing too. I recommend guilt. Very bracing. Keeps one on one's toes. No rest for the guilty. Keep doing good. Keep working. Keep wrestling. Like Jacob. He always reached out and took what he wanted. Never felt good about it. Wrestled with the angel, till it lamed him. Still I wonder even then if he got relief. A guilty conscience is a fine thing. Are you wrestling with your angel?"

"That's a perceptive question!" Sam exclaimed.

"Are you insulting me?" the old man laughed. "Am I not permitted to be perceptive?"

"No…yes. Of course." Sam fell silent. The old man said nothing. Sam became aware of the clinking of silverware, a waitress calling to the cook in the kitchen, the front door opening heavily, the, rapid rat-a-tat of the cash register printing out a receipt, an occasional word rising above the quiet buzz of conversation. Still the old man did not speak. "Are you waiting for me to answer your question?" Sam said, feeling uncomfortable with the silence.

"Do you want to answer the question?"

"I don't think I'm like Jacob. I don't reach out and seize things."

"But do you want to?"

"No, I am not a grasping person. Money doesn't satisfy. I know I have no right to say that. People always say that when they don't have money, probably to make themselves feel morally superior to those who do have money. You have to find some way to feel good about yourself." Energy came back into Sam's voice and face. "You have money. People say you have a lot of money. Are you a grasping person? Does your money satisfy you? I'm not being nosy and argumentative. I really want to know. I've always wanted to ask." Sam said this with an almost exultant curiosity—as if to say—What the hell? I've nothing to lose. I'm just going to ask this old guy what everyone has always wanted to know. "Do you know what people think of you?"

The old man smiled. "Should I know?" he asked.

"You really mean, 'Should I care?' But I expect you do know. Not much escapes you, I think. You must know that people find you eccentric. The word is that you have piles of money, that you could buy most people in this town. There's a disagreement between those who think it's admirable that you live rather simply—except for high-end electronic gadgetry—and those who can't imagine why you wouldn't lavish your money on yourself. Mostly people envy you."

"Do you envy me?"

Sam paused. "Yes, I think I do. I wish I didn't. I think I'd like to have enough money to be able to choose not to use it."

"Is that what you think I'm doing?"

Sam sighed deeply and shrugged. "I don't know what you're doing. I don't even know what I'm doing."

"Do you want my help?"

Sam's heart lifted. He resisted this eager hope. Pictures of paying off his debts passed through his mind. Images of all the things he and Eve needed that they had postponed buying, of all the things he wanted, flooded him. He felt sick with desire and hope. This old man was in a position to make all his financial struggles go away and he would not even miss the money.

"There—right there—what went through you?"

"I'm embarrassed to tell you. But you probably know."

"Did you think I was asking if you wanted financial help?"

"How could that not be what I thought! I'm desperate. Suddenly I saw myself begin saved, rescued…And mixed with it was this awful craving for money."

The old man waited, saying nothing, peering at Sam with a penetrating, questioning gaze.

"I don't believe I could accept your help, even if you offered it," Sam said.

"Do you mean if I offered you money?"

"Yes."

The old man smiled and his interest quickened. "Why?" he asked.

"Being rescued saves me from what I need to learn. I don't deserve to be helped. I need to suffer a bit more."

"An honest answer!"

"That's what this is about. Getting to the bottom of money. Being honest about it. About the desire and the guilt. Maybe money is an illness for me. Maybe for a lot of us. But forget that. All I know is myself. Maybe for me."

"What would a cure look like?"

"You tell me. If I knew, wouldn't I be getting better?"

"Not necessarily. Knowing the cure is not so difficult. It's allowing it to work. That's the hard thing."

"Well, if you see what it is, tell me."

"I will, but I think you know."

"Oh, well, another cryptic comment!"

The old man chuckled as the waitress put bowls of soup before them.

"Why do you say things that are intentionally obscure?"

"Not, obscure, surely. Obscure means cloudy or unconnected. I prefer to think of them as elliptical—short, leaving something out, but implying it."

"What are the two things?"

"I beg your pardon."

"You said earlier there are two things you can be sure of?"

"Ah, you want me to be obvious."

Sam shrugged.

"Nose hairs and lower back pain."

"You're laughing at me now."

"Certainty is always in context."

"You mean the things you can be sure of change depending on what's happening?"

"If you wish," the old man said and smiled.

Chapter 6 – Poetry

Sam came to the Athens House early as usual and was surprised to find Jack Foster already sitting at the table and joking with Guillermo, the busboy, who was a well-mannered, intelligent man. Sam always wondered why he was only a busboy and whether it was because he spoke so little English. He was briskly setting out the glasses of ice water and beginning to fill the coffee cups.

Sam saw that Jack's cup was already half empty, and he noticed a book Jack had been reading, which he had turned facedown on the table. Jack always managed to look relaxed and well-dressed. If Sam hadn't known how hard Jack drove himself, he would not have been able, looking at him, to imagine he'd had a heart attack two years before. Jack always had a tan, but it was hard to picture him in a tanning parlor. Sam never saw him in a coat and tie, yet his well-pressed slacks, monogrammed shirts, and tasseled loafers put him easily in the country-club crowd and among his well-heeled clients. Given the circles where Jack moved, Sam wondered why he ate breakfast with teachers and social workers and a minister—who were all liberals. Sam did know that when Jack ate lunch with a friend, as opposed to a business associate, he came to the Athens House, not the country club. Jack could make anyone he was talking to feel important. He had energy and he liked people. There was always something stirring in his brain. He had a certain glint in his eye. He was good company. Jack smiled at Sam. Sam felt good.

"So what are you reading?" Sam asked. "May I see it?"

Jack handed it over, with some embarrassment. It was a book of poetry by Rainer Maria Rilke. Sam handed it back with a grin and without comment.

"So I can't read poetry?" Jack said.

"I'm not saying anything," Sam replied.

"I read every morning before I leave for my office."

"I'm impressed."

"Incredulous is more like it," Jack retorted.

"At least you're not *writing* poetry. That would really worry me."

Jack paused.

"It isn't possible!" Sam laughed. "You! Now, I know there's a God!"

"What! I can't be creative?"

"Oh, there's no question of your creativity. I see it all the time in your building designs. Even in the way you run your business. But poetry!"

Sam could see that Jack was dismayed, vulnerable, like a child who needed approval—this tough, good-natured, take-it-as-it-comes guy. Sam tried to cover his astonishment and say something nice.

"Jack, it's wonderful that you're writing poetry."

"Bullshit! You can't believe it!"

Sam laughed. "No, I can't."

"This is a great beginning!!" Jack groaned. "You're the artist in this bunch and you can't see it. What about these other guys!"

"Maybe we'd better not tell them." Sam was still laughing.

"You find this funny!" Jack said indignantly.

"I find it amazing. It just tickles the hell out of me. I suppose you're going to tell me next that you meditate."

"Well," Jack said.

Sam hooted. He pushed back his chair. "By God, Jack. This makes my day!"

"You son of a bitch!" Jack exclaimed. "You think you're the only one around here with imagination and a spiritual life."

"No, it's not that," said Sam, still struggling for control.

"So you think I'm the only one without it?"

Sam shook his head.

"Well, what the hell is so funny?"

"This is not ridicule, Jack. This is delight," Sam gasped.

"Delight! What the hell does that mean? Like you found a kindred spirit all of a sudden? Where before there was only this—what—this business guy with no feelings? This money guy! Like now I've come over from the dark side?"

"Yeah," said Sam, wiping his eyes, "something like that."

"I suppose you're going to ask me how long this has been going on. When did I see the light?"

"No. No, I'm not going to ask that."

"Good, because that would be goddamn insulting!"

"I wouldn't want to insult you, Jack. We'd better compose ourselves before the other guys arrive."

"Why?"

"Well, are you going to tell them?"

"You tell them if you want to. Frankly, I don't give a damn. I have other things I want to talk about."

"My lips are sealed."

"What! This is not a secret."

"Good. Then I think you should tell them. I see Kurt coming through the door."

"They'll react worse than you."

"Then I think you shouldn't tell them."

"You're not taking me seriously."

"Yes, I am," Sam protested trying to keep his face straight.

"Bah!"

"What's so funny?" said Kurt, hanging his coat on the back of his chair and looking around for Guillermo to get his coffee started.

Sam said nothing and Jack looked vaguely disgusted, and both of them were saved from answering because Vern seemed to come from nowhere and drop into his chair with a sigh. Kirby and the new guy John were making their way across the room, and Joe was pulling a chair from another table so there would be enough places for everyone to sit.

"So, Vern, you look tired," said Sam.

"I always look tired. I looked at myself in the mirror this morning. Do you see these bags under my eyes? These are tired eyes. It makes me tired just to look at myself."

"How's the diet coming?"

"Don't talk to me about the diet."

"Okay…"

"The diet is hell!"

"Do you want to tell us about it…"

"I'm hungry all the time! Every bloody minute of every bloody day. I am ravenous! And after I eat the miniscule amount I'm allotted, I am even hungrier. These minute bits of food—these mere morsels—arouse and enrage and insult my hunger. I am in agony!"

"Maybe you're not eating enough. Maybe you've cut back too far."

"I'm still eating 2000 calories a day!"

"Morsels!" exclaimed Kurt. "That's not much less than a normal person would eat—your wife for instance."

"Tell me about it!"

"So what's called for here, Vern?" Kurt asked. "Do we give you a stiff pep talk or lay on the sympathy?"

"Sympathy. Pity. I want you to feel my pain."

"We do, Vern!"

"We are so sorry!"

"You look wasted, Vern."

"Like something out of a third-world famine report."

"Yeah, right! That's what's so sad," Vern said. "I'm still eating more that most of the people in the world, and I am miserable. Now, what's wrong with that picture?"

"Aw, you're being too hard on yourself," said Jack. "Everyone has his private battles. Food is yours."

"What's yours, Jack?" Kurt said.

"I'll tell you later. What's yours, Kurt?"

"Computers. The latest gadgets."

"Kirby?"

"We all know that. Books, of course!"

"Sam?"

"I can't tell you. Too personal."

"Ho, he hides himself. Sam's secret mania." They laughed, and Sam thought to himself how true it was.

"The new guy, John. What's your deep inner conflict?"

John Englesinger paused, and in that pause the mood seemed to change. "Commitment," he said.

"That did it! You downshifted us into seriousness."

"What do you mean? You've never had trouble with commitment," exclaimed Kirby, who as John's oldest friend was surprised.

"The roots and relationships that defined me and my family for generations are behind me. I'm starting over. I haven't settled on what I'm going to do."

"You don't look too upset about it."

John shrugged. "It's a new experience. I haven't felt this way since I came to Chicago when I was a kid. But I went back home that time. Now, I'm here to stay. So what do I do? No, I'm not unhappy. Actually kind of curious. But I am wondering if I'll commit to something or someone. I'm in my early sixties. I don't have to. I mean I have to make a living for a few more years, but I can really sort of play around with the rest of my life."

"Do you want to do that?"

John smiled. "I don't think so. Someone with my history? I'm not sure I could even if I wanted to."

The waitress came to take their orders and Vern groaned and asked for oatmeal with skim milk. Joe gave Vern an appraising look, "We do applaud you, you know! You are an inspiration! Your diet is truly a Sisyphean effort!"

There were smiles. Sam laughed and pictured Vern eternally rolling a rock uphill.

Kurt peered across the table at Joe, who seemed suddenly self-conscious. "That's the first time you've said something funny."

Joe shrugged, "One of my better days, I guess."

"We walk a fine line," Kirby commented.

"Yeah," said Kurt. "we want to give you room…"

Vern interrupted, "But we want you to feel better."

"Yeah, well, I walk that line too," Joe replied. "When I feel better, I feel guilty. I think: 'My son died! How can I ever feel okay!'"

"How do you handle that?" Jack asked.

"I have some things I do. Sometimes they help. Sometimes not. Why do you ask? Did you have something in mind?"

Jack paused before speaking, "Meditation. Journaling. Things like that."

There were some surprised looks and raised eyebrows.

Jack shrugged and said in hard voice. "The hell with you guys!"

"I don't get it," said John. "I'm the new guy. Is there something here I don't know about."

"We don't usually put Jack and meditation in the same sentence," Kurt laughed.

"I would," said Kirby.

"Well, you're the pastor. It's your job to see things that aren't there."

John turned to Jack, "Help me out here."

"They think the only thing I'm capable of is making money and being a tough guy."

"Jack, what's up?" asked Joe.

"I bought that old 24-flat on River Street," Jack said abruptly.

"The one that's supposed to be full of drug dealers? With the caved-in garage next to it?"

"I've already bulldozed the garage. I don't know about the drug dealers."

"Why, Jack?" Sam asked.

Jack shrugged as though he didn't want to answer. "I'm going to fix it up."

"Probably a good move," Kurt said. "I read somewhere in the paper that the neighborhood is ripe for gentrification."

"I'm not rehabbing it for yuppies or rich retirees."

There was silence. Jack seemed uncomfortable and defiant and oddly pleased. He gave them a lopsided smile and reached for his empty pocket.

"Damn!" he said. "It's been three years and I still want a cigarette!" He paused. No one spoke. "I'm going to fix it up for low and moderate income people. Some of the apartments will be Section 8. Four or five of them will be transitional housing for homeless families."

"This is good," said Joe quietly.

"This is the real thing," Sam said, toying with his spoon.

"What do you mean 'the real thing'?"

Sam rapped the spoon lightly on the table. "Meditation is great. So is writing poetry." Sam smiled around the circle. "Jack admitted to me before the rest of you got here that he's been writing poetry. But those are private things. There is no risk, except that your buddies," here Sam looked around the circle again, "will make fun of you. But buying this building—you're moving into territory that's completely new for you. You know all about the rich and upper middle class people you build homes for—what they need and how they get and spend their money. How much do you know about poor people?"

"Not a damned thing!"

"Don't be a Nick Stoner," said Kurt.

Jack raised his eyebrows. Sam looked down. Joe seemed pained. Vern nodded knowingly. Kirby looked puzzled.

"Excuse me," said John. "Who is Nick Stoner?"

"A community legend, and a sad story," Kurt replied. "Someday you'll hear someone refer longingly to "Stoner's." Before your time, too, Kirby. Local supermarket. Well-run. Won awards for being one of the few successful independents. Everyone loved that store. Nick and his family owned it, ran it. He was there every day. In a middle-class neighborhood. Had everything. Even some of the gourmet stuff you find only in the trendy markets down in the upscale Chicago neighborhoods. So there was a new strip mall going in on the southeast end of the city, down where the old linoleum factory used to be. Stoners decided to expand. Built a beautiful new store, a clone of their flagship store. It failed! In just a few months! All the people in that neighborhood were Hispanic, Asian, and African-American. Weren't interested in the stuff Stoners stocked. Store went under, took the flagship store with it. Sold the new store to a discount chain that knows how to market to the neighborhood. Flagship store was closed, the space divided up, turned into a video store, some insurance offices, a furniture rental place, and a bagel shop."

"So, Jack," said Vern, who had been unusually quiet. "Does the comparison fit?"

"I guess we'll have to see, won't we. Well, gentlemen," he said picking up his check and pushing back his chair, "I have work to do." He paused by the table for a moment, looking down at his friends thoughtfully. "At least I know I'm a damn fool."

"We were pretty hard on him," Vern commented, when Jack was out of earshot.

"Kirby, what's going on with Jack?" Kurt asked.

John watched thoughtfully as Jack walked to the cash register. "I have to be on my way too," he said quickly, taking his check and putting down a tip. He caught up with Jack in the parking lot, opening the door to his Lexus.

"Nice car," John said, immediately wishing he'd said something wiser or nothing at all and wondering why cars were a default subject.

Jack shrugged, "It gets me around."

"Listen," John said earnestly. "I liked what I heard in there."

Jack laughed, "You don't think I'm crazy?"

"They don't either. I think they're just puzzled. You've apparently stepped out of character. Me—I don't know you. I don't have any history with you. All I have is what I see."

John stopped. Jack waited, offered nothing to help him along.

"There was a guy who did what you're planning to do back home, in Harrisburg, a city about the size of Selby. He was a lawyer, in the same firm as my wife. Smart guy. He made it work financially, but I remember what he said. He said the bottom line was not the hard part. It was the people. Eventually he turned the project over to a local church. They employ a full-time person now to run it, not a real estate management type, but a retired social worker."

"Would this guy talk to me if I called him?" Jack asked.

"I'm sure he would. Listen, I don't know what this project means to you. I don't know why you're doing it, except everyone inside there seems to think something's changed in you and this isn't just another business venture. I don't need to know. I'm interested in the idea. I'm looking for something to do. I have about a month's grace here until I need to start earning some income. I don't have any experience as a social worker or with government programs and only a little with real estate." John stopped, then quickly went on. "What the hell! I want to help you with this project, the human side, with the people. I'll give you a month—volunteer. If I'm useful, then you employ me. If not, we shake hands and part ways."

Jack grinned, thought for a moment, "Okay, you're on. But not just with the people side. With the whole process. Remodeling, working with contractors, government programs, local service agencies, rent collection, putting tenants in touch with services they need. The guys in there seem to think it's one or the other—either you're a tough businessman or a humanitarian."

"You think you can be both?"

"Do you?"

John shrugged, "I don't know."

"I guess we'll find out."

Chapter 7 – Congregation

John was thinking about Kirby's academic credentials early one morning when he stopped at the church—the Ivy-league Ph.D Kirby had earned before he went to theological school. Kirby's research skills had actually helped him many years before when there were questions about a will. John was wondering how Kirby kept his intellectual interests alive. John found him on the third floor sitting on a low children's chair in one of the Sunday school rooms.

"I like to get here before, Geraldine, my secretary," Kirby said. "She's a talker. Friendly to a fault. A transplanted Southerner. First-rate organizer. Computer guru, loved by everyone in the congregation. Smart enough to be pastor herself. She's everything I could possibly want in an administrative assistant. But when she arrives, the church building fills with energy and speech. Sometimes I just need some early morning peace, a little time before the mystery flees into that part of the universe where it stays while we carry on what we call daily life."

John turned another small chair around and sat with his arms resting on the chair back. He smiled and felt sudden affection for this old, old friend.

"I was walking through the sanctuary before you got here," Kirby went on, "and I stopped to sit for a moment. I looked up at the peaked wooden ceiling and curved laminate beams and they seemed ordinary—solid, even pleasing, but commonplace. And I thought of the smoky heights of Notre Dame in Paris that seem to open out into the very depths of God—and of the gorgeous celestial light pouring through the windows. And then I looked at our pastel panes with the one interesting detail in each center." He sighed. "It's a nice enough sanctuary, comfortable.

"Then I came up here. I like to walk through the empty Sunday school rooms sometimes, thinking of the generations of kids who'd inhabited these spaces. I remember a photo from the 1940s, and for a moment I could see those children sitting around this table, the little girls in neatly patterned pinafores with large bows tied in back and shiny black patent leather shoes and the boys in dark slacks, white shirts and small ties.

"There's another earlier picture—taken in the first years of the century at the beginnings of the congregation. It's a class of young adults, dressed severely, some of the men still in plain coats with standing collars and no ties, the women in white blouses and long dark skirts. They have an air of innocence and confidence. Where have those people gone? Who remembers them now—their work, their fears and failures, their faith? Did they marry? What sort of joy and pain marked their lives? Does their presence still linger in these walls, their energy and effort still at work in the hidden life of the congregation?"

John saw sadness in Kirby's eyes.

"Will all this be forgotten when there is no longer anyone to remember? Does God keep these things in memory? Are we, the members of this church, entrusted with remembering? Will remembering tell us something we need to know?"

"You must know more than most pastors about the history of your congregation," John observed.

"There are always a few members who like to remind everyone else that the new things are only slightly altered repetitions of things that have been done before. Most pastors tire of these people. I like them. I cultivate them. Members are myopic. They forget the events and experiences that shaped them, and so the tangled reality that is the congregation's history moves into the congregation's unconscious with hidden power. The history of a congregation holds forgotten keys to present behavior. So I welcome the people who remember how it used to be."

The phone rang down on the main floor. They heard Geraldine's voice as she picked it up. Kirby sighed. They put the chairs back in place. John thought Kirby still needed to talk so he followed him down to his office. They sat facing each other at the ends of a sofa across from Kirby's desk. Kirby picked up a new book on urban ministries.

"This church is in an older neighborhood," he said, "on a smaller lot without room for expansion or the extra parking we need. Once, many of our members lived in these pleasant old homes near the church. Now they live further out where the yards are larger and the strip malls are nearer. I find myself wondering why. The neighborhood around the church is still middle-class. These older homes are in good repair. Some are even fixed up as show places for the yearly Historic Homes Walk, with three-color designer paint patterns, and turn-of-the-century wicker porch furniture. But it feels like a city neighborhood, not the suburbs. Why do we want to live in the new subdivisions?

"The land I showed you is exerting its pull. There's a new church building in Indiana. The congregation's downtown building burned. Only a few wanted to rebuild on the spot. Instead they bought 10 acres on the edge of town. I like their handsome, sprawling new building. Plenty of parking. Room to put up a picnic pavilion and lay out ball fields. A narthex as big as the sanctuary," Kirby smiled. "The architect noticed that people spend as much time socializing as worshiping. So he turned the narthex into a fellowship hall. You enter the sanctuary through this large comfortable space where coffee and refreshments are always laid out and where at a moment's notice tables and a podium or stage and sound system can be set up for coffeehouses, receptions, dinners and meetings, and where people can stand around and visit for as long as they wish. There's a gymnasium! Can you imagine that! A gym in a church! And a multi-roomed office suite! Dozens of church school rooms that could double during the week for community meetings. Space! People like space! Inside and outside!

"Our people are going to want this. They are going to be disappointed if someone can demonstrate that staying here is better stewardship. People can already see themselves out there. That's a powerful picture. All that green space and glistening sprawl!"

****

John was still thinking about this conversation on Sunday as he took a seat off to the side and waited for the congregational business meeting to begin. It had seemed out of character for Kirby. John was usually the restless, skeptical one. He knew Kirby held a more sanguine view of congregational business meetings than he did. Often over the years they had talked about this, beginning when John was called before the church council as a college student. Of course, congregations didn't call people to account anymore—or seldom did. He knew of a congregation in Indiana that had called two young women in front of the church council for signing a statement in support of gays and lesbians in the ministry—the only instance in John's recent memory of the old practice.

John was remembering how he would tell Kirby it wasn't the Holy Spirit that moved in church business meetings. It was people's own judgments mingled with their anxieties and prejudices, and occasionally elevated by their idealism. Very little of the "mind of Christ" in it. And Kirby would say he wasn't so sure. After years of listening, he believed there was something of the Spirit even in these less than lofty back-and-forths. He said he didn't look for the Spirit in the exalted, but in the ordinary. John would laugh and tell him he saw good where it wasn't.

Kirby had another quality rare in a pastor, John thought. He did not need to speak. Often a whole meeting passed without a comment from him. Kirby learned a great deal about what was troubling and driving his parishioners by listening to their debates.

The moderator, Catherine Hunter, opened the meeting with a prayer. She was nervous and said she didn't have the temperament of a moderator. She was better at making arguments than refereeing them. She said she tended to blurt things out and so was always trying to restrain herself in order to do her job, never feeling at ease.

She called for a brief report by Vern Keller on the discernment committee on sexual orientation. He summarized its progress and detailed some upcoming meetings. John was curious and made a mental note to ask Vern about the committee.

John was interested to see that the research of the Facilities Committee was the next item and Joe Kurtz was bringing the report. There were three options. One was to keep the church as it presently was, just fixing it to keep it from deteriorating, which to any intelligent observer seemed a hopeless task. The church was old. Soon major repairs would be needed anyway. Standing still was really going backwards.

Option two was to do a major renovation and addition to the present structure. But there were big problems here—not enough space on the lot, not enough parking now, much less in the future. The zoning rules would need exceptions. It would be very expensive. Then what would they have? A partly old, partly new hodgepodge crowded together on land already too small.

Option three seemed almost inescapable—a new church on the west campus, surrounded by lawns, huge parking lots, ball fields, a picnic pavilion, maybe even vegetable plots for gardening members, a labyrinth for the mystics, a large sanctuary enabling growth, a gym, an ample well-equipped educational wing with each room wired for video and Internet. All for about $4 million, not so much more than remodeling, adding on, and staying put. How could anyone argue with that?

John could see that Joe was uneasy with this inevitable conclusion. He admitted it. He said he believed they belonged where they were. He didn't know what to do with the results of this research.

Preston Krunsch rose and spoke in favor of this third option. It was the only wise course. It was good stewardship. Dana Snyder said that the subdivision out there around the west campus had homes worth a half million to a million dollars and the kind of people who would never be interested in "our kind of church." Krunsch said the wealthy needed to be ministered to too. Maud Miller said that a lot of those people were working professionals, both parents, rushing their kids off to ballet lessons and soccer practice, trying to keep up with each other, and sometimes living by the skin of their teeth financially even though they had all those nice things. Their lives were empty and taken up with material things, she said. Maybe they needed ministry more than the poor people down on River Street. Paul Fry said he thought that was a convenient rationalization. Dana reminded everyone that their church was an anchor for the present neighborhood, which was a good neighborhood. Krunsch pointed out that not very many members still lived in the neighborhood. Dana replied that it was still a good neighborhood and they were much closer to the problems of the city than if they were out there among the beautiful homes and wide lawns.

Joe Kurtz, having presented the report, was still standing at the podium ready to answer questions. He broke in to say that maybe it wasn't a question of money and sort of apologized for the fact that his report seemed to say it was, pointing out that his committee's task was simply to look at costs. Wasn't it really a question of ministry? Shouldn't they decide what they wanted to do, or better what they were called to do, and then set out to do it? Be smart about cost, but be willing to spend whatever it took, wherever they needed to be. Krunsch said they weren't doing anything in the present neighborhood anyway. Their service work downtown could be done just as easily from out west. Dana pointed out that the people who came to the Soup Kettle would have to go another four miles farther from where they lived in the poor sections of town. Krunsch said if you came on Saturday night, you'd see that many of them drove cars anyway, and some pretty nice cars and SUV's at that, which made you wonder who the poor were. Kristen Witter rose to ask if you can really follow Jesus when you have a lot of money and a gorgeous church house. Krunsch pointed out that Jesus had rich friends, like Joseph of Arimathea, and Kristen replied that he also told the rich young ruler to sell all that he had and give it to the poor.

Bob Flory rose to speak. John had been watching him. He knew the type. The one who lay back in the grass until all the main lines of the argument had come out into the open. Bob rose and spoke in his lazy southern drawl, which always became thicker and more mesmerizing when he was getting ready to pounce. "It's all very well to discuss this. In fact this discussion is a credit to our commitment to ministry and good stewardship. And there is a lot to be said for all sides. But being realistic, we probably can't do any of these options now, not in this economy. We need to make a long-range plan, begin to do what every congregation has to do—build up a building fund. On the whole, weighing one thing against the other, a long-range plan to move to the west campus makes the most sense if you look not just at now but at the next 50 to 100 years, if you look at the demographics of growth in Selby, if you look at the space needs and technological needs of any growing church in the 21st century. And with the kind of transportation and communication we have and will continue to have and develop, will it really matter where we are in the long run.? Think of what we can accomplish with the kind of state-of-the-art church we can build out there. We can even bus kids out from downtown to use the gym."

At this point Herman Fry rose. He was glad he and his family had a place in the church. He believed they would always have differences in the congregation, but they all had to learn from their differences. He didn't always agree with everyone, but he was learning from others. That was what they needed to do. They needed to keep learning from one another. They couldn't all be alike, but they could be loving. That was what they needed to do. They just needed to love each other. Like the Sunday school class that they used to have. He turned to Joe, who had taught that class. "We didn't always agree, you and I, but you always listened to me. I was always glad you listened to me. I think we respected each other. That was a good class. I miss that class. We just need to love each other."

John could see that people were sort of glad for that speech. They knew it had something to do with the discussion. How could you be against love? It even reminded them that maybe it was something to keep in mind, but people didn't want to be distracted from the questions. There was some impatience with Herman's rambling.

Jack Foster rose. John could see that people paid attention when Jack spoke. He said several months ago he would have supported moving to the west campus in a heartbeat. The sooner the better. As a builder he knew the value of the land could only go up. It was surrounded by rapidly growing subdivisions—some of them being built by his own company. He was one of those over-busy, well-to-do people who could afford to live out there. He hoped his life wasn't as empty as Maud made it sound. Here there was sympathetic rumbling. Then too the cost of construction would only go up. The sooner they built the better.

But he wasn't sure about this reasoning anymore. He wondered if you didn't become what was around you. He said it was hard to be clear-thinking wherever you were in today's world. He said even people of faith were pushed around by money in ways they failed to notice. He said he did not quite know what he was talking about. Some new ideas he was mulling over. He said he wondered if we weren't all a little bit contaminated by the society we lived in. He said he was not even sure how these remarks related to this debate. This was a new role for him. He was complicating things. He believed in making things simple and doing what needed to be done. He said he didn't know what needed to be done here, except that he felt this wasn't simple. He paused. He said it was probably very simple but he had an uneasy feeling that they were all missing the simple answer.

John saw puzzled looks on almost everyone's face, as though the speech struck them as odd and made them uneasy. He wondered—if someone else had made it, would people have just shrugged it off. Probably they had never seen Jack confused.

Kristen stood and said there was a simple answer. Just follow Jesus. If they just prayed about it, the Lord would show them the way.

As the meeting wound down, John thought how alike church meetings are everywhere. He had taken an interest mostly because he knew how deeply concerned Kirby was. But when Bob Flory was offering his oh-so-reasonable comments, he had been amused. He had listened carefully to Jack and was glad he was hooking up with the River Street project. He thought about the integrity Joe had brought to his reluctant report. He smiled to himself. He liked these people—sincere, good-hearted, fair-minded, concerned about others.

Chapter 8 – Connections

With the meeting coming to an end, John's thoughts strayed to Angela. He spoke briefly with Jack in the parking lot after the meeting and then drove to her house. It was a small brick structure with a high-peaked roof and, over the doorway, a smaller roof that swept up to the peak. Flowers and shrubs in asymmetrical patterns festooned the front yard around a curving brick walk from the brick driveway. A sturdy urn-shaped stone planter with red and pink geraniums guarded the front door, which opened as soon as he rang the bell.

The darkened hall, painted in a muted red and carpeted with oriental rugs opened into a sun-filled room that looked out through a solarium into a compact, intimate backyard of winding paths and flowering bushes and a shaded, brick-paved nook with a small glass-topped table and comfortable upholstered lawn chairs. A carafe of coffee and a teapot sat on the table. The house was designed so the visitor could see all this from the hall. Angela took John's hand and led him inside. When the sun struck her hair, it burst into flame and the embroidery on her kimono leapt into brilliance. His eyes strayed from the garden to her eyes and involuntarily to her figure. Her perfume seemed to come from the sun and the greenery and her hair and her body and to be some essence of her. The warmth from her hand passed up his arm. He was enough in control of himself to realize the skill behind this effect.

She led him through to the garden. "It's too cold to sit long out here, but the late afternoon sun is too precious to waste. We can have a mug of something. You came from your congregational meeting. Was it a good meeting?" They chatted until the slanting sun passed behind the trees and no longer warmed them. They went back through the solarium into the main room where Angela turned on the table lamps to make warm circles of light on the rusts and golds and earth greens and stone blues of the furniture and the blond wood floors and red carpets. They sat on the sofa.

"You seem uncomfortable," she remarked.

"That's probably not the right word," he replied.

"Oh?"

"'Enchanted' might be a better word."

"That word can mean 'delighted.' But it can also mean 'cast under a spell'—'in thrall to someone'."

"In your case, probably both."

"You flatter me, I think."

"I'm like a schoolboy with a crush." John leaned forward with his elbows on his knees. "Only when I was a boy, I couldn't even bring myself to talk to the girl. I suppose being 62 instills some courage and confidence."

Angela laughed. "You're so serious. Many men would have tried to make a move on me already. Instead you talk."

John smiled. "This is new territory for me. I was married for thirty-five years to the only woman I ever loved or made love to."

"Are you assuming we are going to make love?"

John reddened. "No."

"But the thought crossed your mind?"

"Yes, I confess."

"You know my reputation?"

"I know that women are sometimes unfairly stigmatized."

"That's a diplomatic answer. Well done. But surely the things people say have piqued your interest."

"So you think that's the only reason I'm here?"

"Is it?"

"I don't know why I'm here. Except that I like your conversation as well as your...other attractions."

"I'm glad you like me for my mind," she said with a dry smile and glint in her eye.

"I've never had a conversation like this with a woman before."

"You never talked this plainly with you wife."

"Oh, yes, we did, but not on the second date." He paused and thoughts of Mary came to him. He could feel her hand on his, her body next to his.

"You are thinking about her. You loved her," Angela said.

"I did."

"She was fortunate."

"Thank you. Are you paying me a compliment? Or remarking on the blessing of a good marriage?"

"Both, perhaps." She looked away then added with a trace of sarcasm, "It's a blessing I've never had."

John found he wanted to comfort her, though she wasn't asking for comfort and certainly not for pity. He felt the affection a brother might have. He reached for her hand and she responded by holding his. He thought he saw sadness in her eyes.

"There is a story behind that look. Maybe many stories."

She nodded. "This is not how I expected this conversation to go."

"Oh, and what did you expect?"

"You remind me of someone else, though you're stronger and have more wisdom than he."

John made no answer.

"He was older than I, by a good bit. A nice man. A married man. He lost his head over me. I was still a student. His student. We would meet in his office, late at night, while he made excuses to his wife that he had to work late. She was, according to him, a woman with no energy or vitality, trapped by her life, depressed, oblivious. Still, I think she knew. Most women do. He was tormented. He belonged to your church, by the way. Still does. You may even know him. He's much older than you are, long retired. No longer holds any church offices. He chaired your church board at the time. He was racked by guilt. Looking back, I see that he couldn't help himself. He found passion he'd never known he had. Like many middle-aged men, he mistook it for something real. Me—I was flattered. And, it was more than that. In a way I loved him. I'd had a rough, working class background. This man was gentle and intelligent. He was the first man who treated me with respect and tenderness. My boyfriends were all tough guys."

"How did it end?"

"He told his wife. She surprised him. Forbade him to have anything to do with me. Insisted he be home before dinner. Actually came and picked him up. I think she found her own strength, when she fought for him. I saw her some years later, and she was a confident woman; she even dressed with a bit of style." Angela smiled. "She was the only one who gained something from that affair. Carl pulled into himself and never showed much life after that. Retired early. When I came back here to teach, we sometimes crossed paths. He seemed a sad and proper man."

John's mind ran over the people he'd met at the church trying to remember if he'd been introduced to a Carl. "And you?" he asked.

"I actually had a fantasy of marrying Carl. I was miserable." She laughed. "I was so dramatic. I was writing horrible, love-sick poetry. I thought I was Sylvia Plath. I thought this angst would make me a great writer. But I was really a heartbroken girl who had terrible taste in men and thought I'd found a good one at last who turned out to be weak and scared. I think I learned three things out of that. I'm drawn to men who are lousy at long-term relationships. I don't have the knack for marriage. And I'm a mediocre poet."

"Painful insights to live a life by. How old were you?"

"Twenty-two."

John pulled his hand back. She took it as a rebuff.

"Does this story disturb you? Have I confirmed your 'woman of the night' fantasies about me?" she asked drily.

John smiled. "I think the story is terribly sad, because you were a lovely young girl who wanted to trust and be loved."

They sat in silence for a moment.

"Actually the whole story made me uncomfortable for another reason. You started it by saying I reminded you of Carl. Which part of this weak, philandering man do I remind you of?"

She laughed, delighted, and took his hand. "I thought you were concerned about me or at least disapproving of me, and you were really just concerned about yourself."

"That's not fair."

"John, you have a typical male ego."

"That's not fair either." He paused. "But I do want to know how I remind you of Carl."

"He was a good man at bottom. He did care in his own way about me. He was kind. He was thoughtful about his own life. He thought about how his actions and his manner of living affected other people." These are qualities many people in your church have. Nancy has them. Her husband has them in spades. You have them. Carl was intelligent. When provoked, his mind was quick.

"There the comparison stops. He was weak. You seem strong. You may be wise. I don't know you well enough to know. You've had a good marriage. Despite your hesitancy, you seem to know something about women."

"Hesitancy?"

She laughed. "Your ego again."

"But by your own self-description, you should have no interest in me. You should not have invited me to sit on your couch and have this conversation. I don't fit the pattern of men you attract."

"Maybe I'm looking for an upgrade. And I'm not so sure you're looking for another marriage. Are you?"

John stopped, surprised. "I don't know. I'm not sure I'm looking for anything."

"Of course you are. Everyone's looking for something."

"Are you being cynical or talking about the general restlessness of humanity?"

"Oh, the second, surely. It sounds so much more profound."

"Why are you interested in mystical literature?"

"It's not the literature I'm interested in, but the experiences behind the words."

"Are you a believer?"

"Does it make a difference to you?"

John smiled. "My first answer is, 'Of course not.' When I was young, I rejected the idea that God disapproves of 'unbelievers.' Being able to love is a better measure of spirit than being able to believe. And, God knows, there are plenty of believers who do not practice love. But the more truthful answer is, yes, I think it does make a difference."

"Really. Why?"

"I misspoke when I asked the question. I should have asked, 'Is any of this experience true? Is God real to you?'" John shrugged. "Belief is not intellectual assent. It's trust. There are 'believers' who don't trust God, and there are 'unbelievers' who trust themselves and the 'universe,' or whatever they call it; they live open, caring lives. I like to be around people who are interested in both questions. When you told me you were talking to college kids about the mystics, I figured you must be someone who is receptive to larger realities, however strange or surprising they might be. So are you?"

Angela laughed, moved closer, and kissed him. All thought, theological or otherwise, fled from his mind. Her lips were soft and warm. An exquisite, nearly painful rush went through his body. Almost involuntarily he put his arms around her and held her close, kissing her back. When she pulled away, she was smiling and he was without words. "Was that a larger reality?" she asked.

He looked into her wide hazel eyes. "I believe you could do anything you want with me," he said simply.

****

John drove home to the Beahms later in the evening in a thoughtful mood, pleasure mixed with uncertainty and anticipation. As he drove to River Street the next morning, he thought how unexpected his new life was. One of his first tasks was to figure out what to do with a tenant who was seriously arrears in her rent. He needed to open up at least three apartments where the remodeling could begin. His plan was to do three at a time, then offer the redone units to people from the old apartments, thus eventually renovating the whole building without having to empty it. Jack had already given notice to the two tenants he suspected of drug-dealing—

something he did as soon as he bought the building. Those apartments were a mess. Day laborers had been hired to clean them out. A dumpster squatted on the front lawn to receive the trash, old carpet, broken pieces of drywall, nail-encrusted two-by-fours, and other detritus of renovation.

The building was long and three-storied. Concrete stairs ran up the outside of the building at each end to balconies that ran the length of the building on the second and third floors. The first floor was partway below ground at garden level, and instead of a balcony a sunken cement walk went the length of the building, edged by a retaining wall, on the other side of which the ragged front lawn rolled at waist-level down to the street. There were eight apartments on each level, their front doors opening onto the balconies or the sunken passage. The building faced east. At the south end near the steps on an incline, a sewer vent was emitting a stream of dirty water and pulpy paper that was flowing down and across the steps and into the gutter.

He gingerly avoided this nameless stream and walked up the stairs to the second-floor and down the balcony to the third door from the end. The window that faced onto the balcony was open, and loud music poured out. He knocked on the door, got no answer. He leaned down and looked through the open window. He could see someone working out on the carpet. The woman obviously had not heard his knock. He called through the window. She jumped up quickly and looked around.

She turned off the music, and in the sudden silence, she came to the door. She was wearing a tattered full-body leotard that hung loose over her emaciated form. The angles of her hips protruded. Though she was delicately boned, her elbows seemed large on painfully thin arms. Her face was drawn, with a haunted look. Her eyes were sad and frightened and in their considerable depth were reservoirs of long-remembered pain.

"Excuse me for interrupting," he said, wishing he didn't have to talk to this ravaged woman. "May I come in for a moment?"

"I'm in my workout," she said with some anxiety, as though there was danger in ending it too soon.

"Perhaps I could come back. I'll be here at the building all morning."

"Are you the new owner?"

"No, I'm his…" John searched for a word—what was he for Jack Foster? "I'm working for him."

"Listen, I know I'm behind in my rent," she said quickly. "I haven't forgotten. I've had some things I've had to deal with, but I've got some money coming in now, soon. I meant to call him—the new owner. I'll be able to give him some money by Friday."

While she was speaking, John saw a boy come out of the bedroom. He was listening closely and alertly to what she was saying. He had a handsome, even beautiful face, the way only nine-year-old boys can be beautiful, round and well-formed, clear skin, a bit of color in his cheeks, and a clear-eyed gaze, though John could see that he was troubled as he heard his mom speak. John was sure this was the woman's son. The boy seemed to know that his mother was covering up and was embarrassed by it and wondering what he, John, would do.

He sighed inwardly. He knew in a moment he would not be able to put this woman and boy out. He ran his mind over possible things to say. "How much do you expect to be able to pay on Friday?" he said, sounding colder than he wished.

A tone of resentment came into her voice. "I will pay," she said. "I'm not blowing you off. I've just had some things I've had to deal with. I'm trying to find a job. It's hard to find work. I've been calling places and putting out my resume."

He nodded, "I'll stop by on Friday." He turned away, feeling vaguely defeated, wondering if he would have the hardness to do this job. This woman was not going to be able to pay. Why did he know that? Gut feeling. She was in trouble. Something was wrong. It was her eyes—at once wise and full of panic.

Chapter 9 – Stuff

Sam looked about his office. His eye lingered on the Chinese brush painting and the cloisonné vase and the rows and rows of books and the leather chair where he liked to read. These would go with him, but the new place wouldn't be as good as this. Then he reminded himself that the last time they moved his new office was nicer than the one before. This time it wouldn't be in the house. It would be in an old office building somewhere—a place he could afford to rent.

He began to miss the house. He pictured himself walking through it empty one last time and then with tears in his eyes pulling the door shut and locking it. He pushed this maudlin fantasy aside and called his attorney. He'd found a buyer without going through a realtor. The realtor's percentage had been a bargaining chip. The buyer had agreed to split what would have been the fee. He had asked his attorney to draw up the sales contract and set a closing date.

He would miss having a house that held guests. No more college students, volunteers, exchange students—the long string of young adults who had taken the place of the kids they had never had. The apartment they had found had three bedrooms, but the living space was small. No family room or extra bedroom upstairs or out-of-the-way basement room where guests could spread out or hide away. Well, he wouldn't miss mowing lawn or shoveling snow.

The sale closed two days later in their attorney's office and went so smoothly that he wondered again if this were all part of God's plan. Thinking like that made him uncomfortable. He didn't like the word "plan." It sounded too much as though God had everything worked out to the last detail, and you either got with it or not. God with the mentality of a CEO? No, God was an artist, a creator. God made things—universes, energies, matter, creatures, people—started them off, set them in motion, pointed them in a direction, gave them essences and potentialities. And gave them freedom. Then they found their way into or along these inner and outer dispositions or they moved away from them. God knew all the choices and all the possibilities that could flow from all the choices but did not know which one each creature would choose. So what part of what plan was this declining money situation? Was there a failure that he somehow needed to live out?

On moving day their furniture looked shabby as their friends helped carry it to the truck he'd rented—mostly pieces they'd picked up at auctions or used furniture stores, with an occasional worn, good piece they'd bought years before. His mother-in-law had once said that he and Eve had the knack for making their house cozy and inviting, but odds and ends artfully arranged appear faded and ratty when scattered on the lawn beside a U-Haul truck. Their life laid bare seemed small and of no consequence. It embarrassed him. He wondered what his friends thought. And then that embarrassed him further. Why should he worry about what others thought!

The stuff of a life together was a lot of stuff, too much for an apartment. He'd been moving extra beds and old furniture to a storage locker and carting desks and files to the rented office space. He'd stored the lawn tools too. He couldn't yet give them up and face never having a yard.

The equity in the house was paying many of their debts. What relief he'd felt writing those checks! Still there was credit card debt, and they still owed some back taxes. If they sold everything— furniture, their few antiques, the car—they would still be in debt. He was past middle age and had nothing. No pension. Poor health insurance. A host of good friends who had no idea and if they did would have no understanding. Until you never had the safety of a salary and benefits and had to live on what you could make day by day, you simply could not know. He had not booked enough business for the next six months. Nor had Eve. His anxiety never wholly disappeared. These thoughts were running through his head a few days later as he sat at his desk in his cubicle in the small collection of rooms they had rented for their office in an old industrial building. Boxes all around him. No shelves up yet. The boxes were labeled, but still, he would lose time trying to find things, not to mention the time needed to put up shelves and get things in working shape.

He took out his journal and began to write. *"Here I am. I always pray when I'm in trouble. When things are going well, I don't. I wonder why that is. Are others like me? Are most people foxhole Christians? Probably not. They must be better at faith than I am, certainly more disciplined. I don't see how I'm going to be able to meet my obligations. We can't pay off all our debts. We don't have enough to live on. We'll be in worse trouble if something doesn't change. I don't know what to do. I need your guidance. I sense that it will be all right. "You do not need to be afraid. I am with you. You will be cared for. Ideas will come to you. The money you need will come." I don't see how. I thought I had faith, but it's wearing thin. I'm wearing out. I can't do this much longer. I wonder if I should take a salaried position somewhere?*

Sam felt the inner change again. Something deep inside was taking shape in his thoughts. He wrote, *"Listen each day. Pay attention to Eve. Show* love to everyone you meet. Trust that the things you need will come to you." But will I be able to pay all my bills? Will we ever get out of this hole? "You know that I love you. Do not live in fear. You are good."

As always, Sam was heartened. A sense of well-being stole through him. The skeptic in him wondered once again where this still small voice came from. Maybe it was just his subconscious. Even so it was a better place than his anxiety-riddled ego.

The inner voice said nothing about how to proceed. Just to trust. What should he do—ramp up his efforts to get business? This wasn't the way. His business seemed to be coming to an end. But how could he possibly tell anyone that. Everyone he knew, even those of deepest faith, believed that you had to do for yourself. Who would counsel him to wait? Then the thought came that there was an active kind of waiting. What was that? To wait on God and trust, yet actively pursue—what? Building his business was not the answer. The days of his business were numbered. Something else was coming. But what?

He sighed. He had to do something! He could not just sit here and write in his prayer journal. For a second the thought flashed through his mind—"Why not?" He shrugged and got up and began to open boxes.

His cell phone rang. He gladly pushed a box aside and answered. It was Hank. He was ridiculously glad to hear his voice. It had been a while. Not for the first time, he wondered why they had drifted apart. A sharp memory of shared moments came back to him. Why hadn't he thought of calling Hank? When Hank asked if he wanted to have lunch, he quickly said yes.

The coffee shop was around the corner from his new office. Eagerly he walked the block and a half. They exchanged the usual pleasantries, but not for long. Neither was inclined to get lost in small talk. But then they never had been, never needed to. Hank had begun his life as a voluble pleaser and had made a steady effort year by year to say less and mean more. Sam admired his gritty resolve.

He wanted to tell Hank, to pour it all out in a rush of words and feelings, but of course he didn't. He spoke slowly and cautiously. Hank smiled when Sam began to talk. Sam felt self-conscious. How many times before had he talked with Hank about money and not having enough of it! Nothing had changed. He was embarrassed. Hank understood, he always did, but things had changed for him. After all those years of trying to make it as a musician and then as a self-employed carpenter and small contractor, he had taken a job as the custodian, the "Facilities Supervisor" in name, at a community rec center and for the first time had a regular salary, employer-provided health insurance, and a small pension plan. Still Sam labored on with his story. Hank listened.

"I admire your courage," Hank said. Sam relaxed. He should have known Hank would never have the typical response. "You stay on your path. Most people would have quit long ago. Hell, I did."

"Most people would say I'm crazy, or worse, irresponsible."

"Well, maybe you are. So what! Do you still believe you're doing the right thing?"

"I don't know any more."

"Do you pray about it?" Hank asked.

Sam smiled. This was such an incongruous question from a lapsed Catholic who avoided church, hated dogma, and thought most religious people were nice at the expense of being honest. Yet he knew Hank prayed daily and often and counted his relation to God to be at the center of his life. Crusty, profane, Hank was a curmudgeon who knew more about God and grace than anyone Sam knew including Kirby, who, it suddenly occurred to Sam, might enjoy meeting Hank.

"Not enough, I don't," Sam said.

Hank shrugged as though the answer was self-evident.

"I can make excuses," Sam said, "but the truth is I'm not much good at it."

"It's not a big deal. You just do it. You just talk to him. Hell, you know that. I'm not saying something we haven't said before."

"I don't do it even though I want to do it and need to do it and feel better when I do it. St. Paul writes in one of his letters, 'I do that which I don't want to do and do not do that which I know to do and want to do.' That's not the exact quote, but it's something like that. I always thought that was nonsense. If you want to do something, you do it. If you know something is good for you, you don't hesitate. But I do understand what he meant. I feel satisfied after I pray, centered, more whole..."

"Yes, that's it!"

"Yet, I find every reason to avoid praying. I simply don't know why."

"You're afraid of what you're gonna hear."

"Do you hear God's voice?" Sam asked.

Hank took out his cigarette pack, laid it on the table, and looked at it longingly. He coughed. "Five times I've tried to quit. One time I made it three months—with the help of the patch. I've got to quit. I know I do. I want to, but I can't. I have to have a smoke."

"Do you want to go outside?"

"No. Hell, I should have enough will power to get through another half hour."

"Do you hear God's voice?" Sam repeated.

"Yes," said Hank.

"An actual voice? Auditory? Real sounds?"

Hank smiled. "Would I be nuts if I did?"

"I don't know. I just want you to tell me what actually happens. You're not nuts. Anyone who knows you knows you're not nuts. Do you hear an actual voice?"

"No." Hank peered at Sam. "You're relieved—I can see it!" He laughed, "You really would think I'm nuts, wouldn't you? Are you afraid you're going to hear a voice?"

"Maybe. There are some real lunatics who hear God's voice."

"You mean like TV preachers and—what was that crowd in Texas years back— Branch Davidians?"

Sam thought for a moment. "I don't know. I used to think I was afraid of what I might hear. But it's not that. You know what it is…?" He paused. "I just want to figure it out on my own. I don't want to be bothered with sitting quietly, praying with pen and notebook, and listening. That's how I pray. I begin to write in my journal and things come to me—first my own questions and needs and thoughts and then something shifts and another stream of words and thoughts that come from deep inside replaces my own thoughts. And I write those things down too, and that's what I think is God's voice. I feel relief and joy. It's like springs bubbling up. It really is. That passage in the scripture about the fountain of living water is not just a metaphor. There is really something like that. It's real and I feel it. It's there. It rises, bubbles, fills, overflows. These water images really work for me. And then there is such a sense of goodness and wholeness and, yes—love. It's great! Some of the best moments of my life."

Sam stopped and looked at Hank, who laughed, and then began to cough. "Ain't it a bitch!" he exclaimed through his coughing and laughter. "You love it and you don't want to do it!"

"Yes. It is a bitch! Does that happen for you too?"

"Used to. But not any more. I love those moments now. I live for them."

"You're a saint!" Sam exclaimed.

"Too bad my mother isn't alive to hear you say that," Hank remarked sardonically.

"Well, I mean it. You're not holding on. You let God in. You've given yourself up."

"I had to. It was the only way I could stay sober."

"I prefer myself to God. I like to be self-contained. I'm proud of my ability to figure it out for myself."

"Is it working?"

Sam laughed. "Of course not. Still I persist. Perverse, isn't it."

When Sam got back to his office, he took out his prayer journal. *I'm going to lay it on the line. That sounds so trite. Can people 'lay it on the line' to you? I'm sick of prevaricating. I want money. That's what I really want to say. I believe money does all kinds of damage to people. I believe money would never be good for me. But the truth is that I want it. I've resisted it because I want it. I'm afraid of how I will spend it. I admit I want beautiful and lavish things. Money has many good purposes, but it has an ill effect. People make too much of it. They measure themselves by it. They waste their lives seeking it. They build lavish homes and buy beautiful cars, while people starve and the homeless sleep under the bridge. They want status. They want to satisfy themselves. They seek it in pride, in lust, even for beauty. They...they...they! They do it for all these human reasons. But it's not 'they.' It's me. I want these things. That's the truth. Yet I have more stuff than I need, now even in my financial crisis. I feel guilty about what I already have. Still, I would like to have a large and beautiful house. I would like to own a BMW because it's a lovely machine, a beautiful piece of craftsmanship. I want digital camera equipment. I want a large summer home on a lake. I want enough money to travel anytime and anywhere. I want rich oriental rugs. I want enough money that I can help anyone I want to help anytime I want to do it. I want to pay off all my bills and debts and back taxes.*

I don't want to follow Jesus or listen to you. Well, that's not true. No one impresses me more than Jesus. I do want to listen to you. But the simple life! A life with just what I need, unburdened, light. No. I like baggage and stuff and complications and struggle. I love you and I love me and I love stuff. And I'm not willing to choose.

Chapter 10 – Life

The alarm rang. It was 6:00 a.m. John rolled out of bed. Old cooking smells and the stale odors of cigarette smoke, peeling paint, and rotting carpet filled his nose, coating the membranes till he wondered if he'd always carry that stench in his nostrils. Why had he ever decided to move into this decaying old building? He asked the question every morning and his answer became less persuasive with each passing day. It had only been two weeks. It seemed an age. Vi had been impressed when he'd told her what he was going to do. It was just the sort of thing she would do. He believed in what he was doing. He just wasn't sure he could do it.

He'd taken to going early to the Athens House on Thursdays. He had to be there by 6:30 to beat Sam and Kurt, and he liked to read and be quiet. He knew the other two were early for the same reasons. Still, once there, they all seemed to feel that they had to talk to one another.

The others straggled in. Jack and Vern were the last. "I'd like to know why the hell we are doing this discernment process, anyway," Jack said as he pulled his coffee cup closer and dumped in some sugar. Sudden silence. John saw Sam glance at Kirby from the corner of his eye. No one tried to answer. It was a rhetorical question anyway. And either you thought it was a good idea or you didn't. Everyone already knew Jack was impatient.

"So we had still another meeting last night. I don't know why I went. We've been at this for a year and a half and no end in sight. We'll get the same vote we would have gotten if we hadn't done it at all. If we ever get to a vote!"

"We learned a lot," said Sam.

"What did we learn? That Ray and Judy are opposed but are good sports anyway. That Homer is upset and will tell us about it in a dozen different ways. That Sally Borden will lose face in the community, but supports the process anyway. That Barbara Nolt thinks we're going to hell. That there are another half dozen or more people who won't say anything, but will nurse their disgruntlement along for the next twenty years, glad to have another reason for saying we are too liberal and never listen to them. I'll tell you. I have some sympathy for them."

John was confused. At first he thought Jack was referring to the debate over what to do with the church building. Then he remembered the brief report on the discernment committee for sexual orientation from Vern at the congregational business meeting. One of the discernment sessions had been scheduled for last night.

"Come on, Jack!" exclaimed Kurt, so loud some people in the booths along the window looked up. "You know those folks would be much more upset if we weren't doing the process. We bend over backwards for them. If anything, it's Jim and Jerry who should be upset."

"Jim and Jerry?" exclaimed Vern. "Do we really know they are gay? Everyone assumes it, but no one says it out loud."

"In their generation, you couldn't say it. Don't you know the story of what happened when they were in school fifty years ago?"

"No, what story?"

"Their story's not the point here," said Kirby. "Jack's saying we're wasting our time. Kurt's wondering if we're spending so much time listening to the conservatives that we're hurting the LGBT people. A lot of people are tired of the whole thing, not just you, Jack. And Homer can't let go of his anger. So where are we really?"

"Is the process a good thing, Kirby—speaking as pastor?" asked Sam.

John was curious what Kirby would say. He knew his friend had strong ideas about the nature of a church community.

"All right, what's it gonna be today?" said the waitress, bulling up to the table, opening her order book, and pulling a pencil from her ear. She became aware of the tension. "Serious bunch today." She inclined her head toward Kurt, "Even you. Not even a smart remark."

"We were just waiting for you, Linda," Kurt said.

They ordered the usual all around, relieved at the interruption, except for Jack, who was impatient to continue. "I don't see that we've gained anything. No one's happy with this."

"Not true," said Sam. "Many of us are. I am. I think we're doing the whole thing with a pretty good spirit. I don't think we're going to lose anyone. Ray and Judy and Homer, even Barb, are not going to leave."

"Homer can't leave," Jack said. "He's been here since the 50s. He has daughters in the congregation."

"So we're bending over backwards to hear him, to make a place for him?"

"Are we really doing that? Does he think we are? He's mad. He can't stop talking about it," said Jack. He turned to Kirby, "Am I right?"

Kirby nodded. "He's upset. I just said so."

"Think about it," Sam said. "Suppose the congregation was going to take a position that offended you. And you've been a member your whole life. How would you feel? What would you do?"

"Exactly!" replied Jack. So why do the whole frigging thing? Will Homer be any less pissed off than if we just go ahead and vote without this dragged-out process?"

"I still want to know what Kirby thinks," said Sam.

Kirby shrugged. "It's a good process. I think we're learning some things about ourselves."

"Like what?"

"That even though we're a liberal congregation, we have a minority of conservatives who often feel left out but still love this church."

"But we knew that before."

"Probably, the thing I learned had nothing to do with sexual orientation," Kirby said.

John got suddenly interested. "What was that?"

"I know what you're going to say," Joe said his eyes alight.

Kirby was taken aback. Vern, who though he was chair of the discernment committee had been uncharacteristically silent, saw Kirby's reaction, turned to Joe and laughed. "A breakfast clairvoyant!"

Joe looked suddenly crestfallen, the sadness returning to his eyes. "I'm sorry. What I really mean is I think I know why this whole thing has value. But Kirby, I interrupted. Go ahead."

"Tell me when I'm finished if we mean the same thing. In my opinion the real value of this process is that we are groping forward to a different way of making decisions and dealing with controversy. I was visiting Bill Swartz. One of the old-timers. We don't see him much these days. He can't get around well enough to come to church. He was remembering the days when this congregation was leading the civil rights work in this town. He said his one regret was that he never had much sympathy for the three realtors in the congregation who took heat and lost business because we had the reputation of buying homes and apartment buildings in white neighborhoods and selling or renting to blacks."

"Did people in the congregation really do that?"

"Yes."

"Good for them!"

"Point is. We cared for one set of people and ignored another."

"But we were on the side of those who were shut out. That's where we should have been."

"True. But the realtors were God's children too."

"So what are you saying?"

"That justice is not the same as love," Kirby replied.

"Say more," said John. "What do you mean?"

"The civil rights movement was about justice. And a measure of justice was achieved. Blacks have opportunities they never had fifty years ago. But we're as racially divided now as we were then. We could have gotten justice for people in our congregation with a different sexual orientation fairly easily. But I think what we've been working on is something much harder. We're trying to find a way to include gays and lesbians *and* those who reject them."

"Why would we want to do that?" asked Jack.

"Because these differences are not going to go away," said Joe quickly. "The way to deal with pain is not to go around it or forget it or ignore it, but to go through it, to take it into yourself and live with it. By trying to do a process that includes Homer and Ray and Judy and Jim and Jerry, we are finally acknowledging that people of faith are always going to fight over something. Deep differences are not going to go away. They will always be with us."

"Exactly," Jack said. "So why pander to the differences. Do what's right and let the chips fall where they may. You can't please everyone."

"It's not about pleasing anyone," said Sam. "It about putting reconciliation before rightness."

"Nice utopian fantasy," said Jack. "When have people ever made room for people who are different! Power always wins, or in our case strength of numbers. The ones who lose just have to snuff it up. Finally gays and lesbians are beginning to win a few. Good for them. Let the other side suffer for a while."

"Looks like we have some differences right here around this table that aren't going away," said Kurt.

"Good point," said Sam. "So what do we do? We go on being friends. We agree to disagree. We may even come to respect and understand one another. But I don't go back to my office convinced that Jack is immoral or stupid or needs to be converted. I'm willing to live with him."

"I'm glad to hear it."

"These are not new ideas," remarked Kirby. "Some Quaker meetings wait until everyone can move forward together or until the ones in opposition are willing to stand aside. Even in our own tradition there was a time when we did things by consensus."

"But you never get anything done," said Jack. "It takes forever to make simple decisions."

"Why are we in a hurry?" asked Joe.

"We have to make money," said Vern cynically.

"Why do we feel this need to get things done? This rush to action? This anxiety?" asked John.

"We value ourselves by what we do," said Sam.

"Of course we do," said Jack. "When we were hunters and gatherers, our lives depended on what we could do."

"Do you think so?" said Sam. You're telling me people got up every morning riddled with anxiety about whether they were going to find enough for the day. Early homo sapiens had ulcers and high blood pressure?"

"People didn't live long enough to get ulcers or high blood pressure," Jack shot back. "They died in their 40s."

"So people developed agriculture," said Vern, "which gave them the means to have food when they could not find food. It also gave them leisure. So we live now in a time when we don't have to work as much as we do. We could live more simply and have more time. Instead, Americans are working more than ever, more than our fathers and grandfathers did. Why is that?"

"What does this have to do with our discernment process?" asked Jack.

"We're trying to figure out why people fight."

"Anxiety and self-protection," Vern said. "That which is different is alien. Get rid of it. Protect the community. In the case of same-sex relations, they threaten the survival of the species. People are afraid that it might catch on and people would stop procreating."

"Hell, that's ridiculous!" Jack exclaimed. "We're drenched in heterosexual sex. It's everywhere. We use it to sell everything from soap to cars. And we're afraid it will go away and be replaced by homosexuality! Hardly!"

"Why are people so afraid of being attracted to the same sex?" Joe asked

"I do really like all of you so much," lisped Kurt, looking longingly around the table with doe eyes and dangling a limp wrist. "See. That's what I mean. You were turned off just for a split second before you caught yourself."

"What the hell does it matter what we feel," said Jack. "It's what we do. We're going to accept and affirm gays and lesbians in our church. It's a done deal. Let Ray and Judy and Homer and Barb take it or leave it."

"Wouldn't you miss Homer if he pulled out?"

"Well, yes, probably, but we can't run the church to please Homer."

"Who are we pleasing?"

"Ourselves. God. I don't know."

John began to laugh.

"So what's funny?"

"Well, you don't know how lucky you are! This conversation would never have happened in the congregation I came from. Personally, I like the idea of making a decision in such a way that there's a place for Homer and the others who oppose it. But I like even better a church that is willing to deal with the whole thing at all. The folks back there would say this congregation is way off base. But I think this's exactly what a church should wrestle with.'

"Well, that's something we can agree on!" said Jack.

****

John had invited Vi to come out and spend the day. He picked her up at the train station in the used van for which he'd traded his car, took her first to the apartment building. She walked around the outside, seeing the scattered construction rubble and the trash piled in the dumpster, commenting on the condition of the structure. She sniffed the air when they entered the apartment and wrinkled her nose, shook her head. "It's a far cry from your beautiful house back home," she remarked.

John shrugged.

She looked around the apartment, at the stained carpets, the badly scuffed floors, the grease-encrusted stove. She opened the refrigerator, then closed it quickly. "Are you okay with all this?"

"No. Yes. It's a learning experience. My job is to clean this up. Gut these dreadful apartments. Make them habitable—and at a rent that's affordable for low-income tenants or those who qualify for Section 8. So it's not going to look like this long. The clean-up guys begin tearing out this carpet tomorrow. That stove can't be saved. I've been eating out. All in all, this has been good for me. But I don't see how people as an act of faith live with the poor day in and day out, people like yourself or Dorothy Day."

"I'm not in her league."

They went out for lunch, then spent the afternoon on the bike path and sitting on a bench over on Durham's Island. John showed her the new library. He kissed her on the cheek as he put her back on the train. The whole time he wondered what he was feeling. He caught her giving him a knowing look, as though she knew what he was thinking and was being patient. As he drove to the Hill Restaurant, the little hole-in-the-wall greasy spoon where he was going to catch supper, he thought, "If I'm wondering what I'm feeling, that's a pretty good indicator of what I'm feeling or not feeling."

After a sandwich and some soup, he could not go back to the sour-smelling apartment, so he found himself straying past Angela's house. Her car was in the driveway. He was suddenly nervous. He grinned, "I guess this tells me something," he thought. Vi was the woman he ought to want, but here he was. He drove around the block, then pulled into the drive-way, got out, and rang the bell.

Angela came to the door in jeans and a baggy shirt stained with some-thing that looked like tomato juice. She wore no make-up, and her face was tired and lined. But her eyes lit up when she saw him.

"You caught me!" she said.

He shrugged. "Probably good to know you aren't always put together."

"Put together! That's an insult," she snapped.

"Well, you do know what to do with what you've got."

"If anyone else said that to me, I'd slap him!"

"Why not me?"

"Don't know. Maybe I like you. Candor becomes you. Come in."

She took him through to the kitchen. "Sit there," she said, indicating a bar stool by the counter. She went back to her work.

"What are you doing?"

"Canning tomato juice."

"You're the last person I'd expect to be doing that."

"Why?"

"You don't look like the domestic sort."

"What's that mean? Loose women don't do kitchen work!"

"Oo, you said that. I didn't."

"Yes, I said that."

"What's up? You're upset. Did something happen?"

"One of the men in my department made a pass at me."

"I'm sorry to hear that."

"Are you?"

"Yes. You're angry!"

"Sometimes I hate men! Present company excluded."

John was quiet.

"You don't know what that is!" she snapped. "You've never hated any-one?"

"Sure I have."

"Who, one of those awful people in your church?" she said sarcastically.

"There were some difficult people back home."

"But not in this one here in Selby."

"No. But I've got a different problem. I don't hate women. I'm afraid of them," he hesitated, "present company excluded."

That brought the first smile of the evening from Angela. "Really? That's a nice thing—for me right now."

"Why?"

"Because in some odd way, it lets me be myself."

"And what's that?"

"Complicated, angry, afraid, confident, insecure, sexy, and sometimes disgusted with myself."

"You left a few things out."

"Oh?"

"Intelligent, sensitive, spiritual."

"Oh, you say the nicest things. Is that how men from your background come on to women?"

"Sure. We usually talk about Jesus on dates."

"You haven't gotten to that yet."

"Come to think of it, I haven't."

They both stopped.

"You know, Angela. I'd like to kiss you right now. But some instinct tells me not to. That that's what men always want to do. Kiss you, fondle you, and take you to bed."

"You don't want that?" She seemed disappointed.

"Sure. But I have a sense that I'd be just like all the rest if I did it."

"So what does this mean? That we are going to have a chaste friendship?"

"Maybe for a while."

"I know how to handle a man who makes a pass. What do I do with you!"

****

John stopped on the way home for coffee and sat thinking about the day. He knew he was avoiding going back to the apartment. When he arrived, the building was dark. The bulbs in the walkway lights had been removed, stolen by tenants he assumed. The building was always eerie at night. But now in the complete dark John hurried to his door expecting someone to jump out of the shadows and seize him. He fumbled for his key, quickly threw on the light, and locked the door behind him as soon as he was inside. He was disappointed in himself for being so frightened. He wondered if the people who lived in this building often felt that way. It made him angry that he—that they—had to live in fear and disquiet. He was just turning away from the door when he heard a soft knock. He leaped away from the door as though it were hot.

"Who's there?" he called through the door.

He heard a soft call that sounded like the voice of a child. He opened the door a crack, still keeping it on the chain, and peered out. It was the son of the woman who was behind in her rent. He quickly opened the door and let the boy in.

"What are you doing out this late? Should you be out alone?" John asked, then caught a closer look.

The boy's thick, dark brown hair fell over his forehead. His soft brown eyes were large and ready to fill with tears. His clear face was clouded with anxiety.

"Something's wrong!" John exclaimed.

"Could you come over and look at my mother. She won't wake up. I think she did something to herself."

John took the boy's hand and they quickly went to the apartment. The door stood open. In the middle of the living room floor lay a mound covered with a quilt. In front of it was a tinfoil pie plate holding a burning candle surrounded by cigarette butts and ash. Scattered on the carpet was a cigarette package, a book of matches, a sheet of art paper covered with writing, an empty quart beer bottle, and two empty Advil containers. A long lock of hair showed under the edge of the quilt. There was no movement.

John knelt at the end with the hair and quickly but gently raised the quilt. The boy's mother lay in utter stillness, the candlelight flickering on the planes and hollows of her sunken cheeks. John stiffened. Alarm ran through him and something in him countered with a reserve so strong it was almost as though he was withdrawing—his instinctive internal resistance to shock. He touched her hand. She was warm. He wanted to touch her neck to see if there was a pulse, but it seemed invasively intimate. Then he thought how ridiculous it was to be wary of touch when she was either dead or dying. He was saved from his dilemma.

"Momma!" cried the boy, whose tears came finally. "I couldn't wake you. I tried. You wouldn't wake up. Oh, please wake up, Momma."

At the sound of the boy's voice the woman stirred slightly. She made a feeble effort to raise her head. She tried to turn toward the boy. She mumbled something thickly. Her head fell back to the carpet.

"She's alive!" John almost shouted. "Your Mom's alive, David. We're going to get her help. Here's what I want you to do. Sit right here and hold her hand. I'm going to call 911."

The fire station was around the corner and the paramedics arrived quickly. Still, it seemed long. John knelt next to the woman and David with his hand on the boy's shoulder. There was nothing he could do for the woman. But the boy—what a horror this must be for him. The fireman who came with the paramedic team asked questions and looked around the apartment, confiscated the beer bottle and the Advil containers, asked if that was what the woman had taken, asked if she was on any other medication. John didn't know the answers to these questions. He hesitated to put David through questions, but knew the boy might know something of use. He told the fire captain who the boy was. David answered stoically.

The captain asked John who he was, why he was there; he seemed suspicious. The paramedics tried to rouse the woman, got no more than a few muttered, slurred, indistinguishable words. While two of the men were putting the woman on a stretcher, another was looking around the room. "Did she leave a note?" he asked. John shrugged and said he didn't know, that he'd called 911 immediately and had not taken time to look around. In less than five minutes she was on the stretcher, out the door, and into the ambulance. David's eyes grew big and tears rolled down his cheeks as he watched the doors close on his mother.

"It's going to be all right," John said, realizing he was giving false assurance, but knowing he must say this to the boy.

"I want to go with my mother," said the boy.

The fire captain spoke to John. "I'm sorry, the boy can't come in the ambulance. Does he have family who can come and get him?"

"I'll take care of you, David. You can stay with me tonight."

"But I want to go with my mother."

"Of course you do. Let's get you out of your pajamas, and we'll drive to the hospital, and you can see your Mom as soon as the doctors say you can."

At the hospital they sat in the ER. It was nearing midnight. The waiting room was almost empty. An old rerun of "Jeopardy" played on the video monitor on the shelf high in the corner. The crass, hyped-up excitement was offensive to John in this moment of trouble and pain for the boy who leaned against him, every so often shuddering with a sob. This boy, who had remained composed and quiet in the car, even now was not falling apart. He seemed to know how to face trouble. John felt a rush of affection. David laid his head on John's shoulder.

After an hour had passed, a nurse came out and said they could go in and see the boy's mother. John was surprised. He thought it would be hours before she would come out of her stupor. She was in one of the curtained cubicles, propped up in the bed. Her teeth and lips were blackened. She held a large plastic cup with flexible straw, black at the tip. When she saw who came in, she had eyes only for David; on her face was a soft, sheepish, loving expression.

"Your Momma really messed up," she said.

David went to her haltingly and touched her arm as though he wasn't sure she was real. Tears rolled down her cheeks and she gathered him in to a hug, her desperately thin arms holding him and caressing him. The boy's shoulders shook as he sobbed again.

After a moment he stepped back and looked at her. "Your mouth's all black," he said.

"They gave your momma some awful stuff, with charcoal in it."

"Why?"

"It stops the stuff your momma took from working."

"What did you take, Mom?"

She hesitated, "I took a lot of pills."

"I saw a beer bottle on the floor."

She nodded sadly, "I drank some beer too."

"Is that bad? The beer and pills together? It's bad, isn't it?"

"Yes."

"Why did you take that stuff?"

"David, I felt really, really sad." To John the woman seemed remarkably composed for just having attempted suicide, as if she were relieved to be there in that bright room with the big plastic cup of charcoal mixture and her blackened lips and the nurses bustling around and her son there with her instead of cooped up in the dark, dreary apartment.

"But...but," the boy's face broke up and tears squeezed from his scrunched-up eyes, "what will happen to me if you die?"

She drew him to her again, staring at the floor as she cupped the back of his head with one hand and patted him lightly on the shoulder with the other, for a long time saying nothing. Then John heard her say softly, "I'm sorry, David. I won't leave you."

It was two in the morning and John felt that boy had been through enough and needed sleep. John asked if there was someone he should call, and the woman shook her head. He offered to take David home and let him sleep in his apartment, saying he'd bring him back right away in the morning to see his mom. The woman agreed. David clung to her, and he was crying again as they said good-bye.

In the car he sat quietly. Again, John was surprised by the boy's composure. He made a bed for David on his couch. He went back to the woman's apartment to make sure all the lights were out and to lock it. When he folded the quilt and put it back on the small loveseat, he noticed the corner of a piece of paper sticking out on the floor. When the quilt had been removed from the woman and crushed against the base of the loveseat, it must have pushed the paper underneath. He picked it up. It was folded. He opened and read it. It was a rambling outpouring of pain and sorrow, and regret for failing people, especially David. It was signed "Momma/Maggie."

John folded the letter and put it in the drawer of his desk when he got back to his apartment. He wondered what those people from Maggie's past were like. He pulled the covers up on David. Despite the horrors of the evening, the boy's face in sleep was clear and beautiful. John's heart went out to him. He wondered if this is what a parent felt—such a mingling of tenderness and affection, even something fierce and protective. He sighed and looked around his dingy, bad-smelling apartment. He nodded his head. This was where he belonged. He was starting the rest of his life.

But he knew something else suddenly. He was going to call a cleaning service first thing in the morning, and even though this apartment like all the others would soon be rehabbed, till then he was going to clean it up and fix it up and make it as light and airy and comfortable as possible. He was pretty sure this experiment did not mean living in dirt and squalor and darkness. For a moment he wondered how Jesus would live in this building. He smiled. He hated the way people asked that question, wearing WWJD bracelets, and making a big deal out of it—What Would Jesus Do? But it was a real question, in some ways it had always been his question. There were a lot of things he wasn't sure of—was there a God, what was God really like, was Jesus divine, was God in Jesus and if so how? But one thing he knew—Jesus really impressed him. It had always been so, since before he could remember. How would Jesus have dealt with this night?

Chapter 11 — Maggie and David

John kept the boy home from school and let him sleep in. Mid-morning he heard the phone ringing in the boy's apartment and went to answer it. The school secretary wanted to know where David was. John explained that he was taking care of the boy while his mother had been taken to the hospital in the night. The secretary asked what was wrong. John hesitated. Should he tell the school staff what had happened? He answered that she'd been taken ill with stomach problems, which was partly true. The secretary wanted to know where David would be staying. John said he was the next door neighbor and he guessed the boy would be staying with him for now.

He hung up and wondered what he should do. Could he take care of a child? He'd never been a father. John had watched the boy. The kid was pretty self-reliant, often seemed to be looking out for his mom. It probably wouldn't be too hard to have the boy with him. But, on the other hand, did he have a responsibility to call someone in authority?

He called Vi, keeping his voice down so as not to wake the boy. She asked if the woman was a good mother when she was able to function. John said she seemed surprisingly good. Vi advised not to call the governmental authorities—the Department of Children and Family Service (DCFS)—not yet anyway. They might take the boy away from his mom, she said, which would intensify his trauma. "I'll come out for the day," Vi offered. John said not today, maybe later. He thought he'd be okay. He'd call if he needed her help.

The boy stirred on the couch and opened his eyes. John asked him how he slept. He wondered what you say to a boy whose mom has just tried to commit suicide. You don't pretend things are alright, but you probably don't talk about it either. He remembered Mary had told him, when she was handling a divorce case, that kids reacted to trauma differently. They didn't talk about it the way adults did; they couldn't process it. You couldn't ask them what they felt. They often didn't know or couldn't say. But it might come pouring out when you weren't looking for it, when you were talking about something else. Sometimes it remained locked away. So John gave David breakfast and let him do the talking. David wanted to know if he could go back to his apartment and play on his computer.

John said yes, then called David back. "I think I need to walk over to your school and tell your teacher and the school social worker what happened."

David shook his head, "Why?"

"They need to understand, in case you have trouble paying attention or you have to miss more school."

"Will they tell everyone at school?"

"I don't think so. We can ask them not to"

"I don't want the other kids to know."

"Maybe the teacher can just tell them your mom's in the hospital and you're worried."

"They'll ask why she's in the hospital. What am I going to say—that my mom just tried to commit suicide!"

"No. I can see how you don't want to have to say that." John paused, in thought. "Okay, for now I'll just tell the teacher and social worker that your mom will be in the hospital for a few days, and you're staying with me."

John left David alone for the half hour he spent at the school, then took him along on some errands and bought him lunch. They went back to the apartment building, and the boy helped John carry some debris to the dumpster from one of the apartments he was getting ready for rehab. David was good company, very bright. He told him in great detail about his favorite computer game. In the evening John took the boy to the hospital to see his mother. They wound their way through the corridors to an isolated elevator in the back of the hospital and took it to the sixth floor, only to find out that he needed Maggie's identity code to get onto the psych ward. But because he was not family, the hospital staff would not give him the code. He said he had Maggie's son with him. He was told they could not give the code to a minor. John asked to talk to Maggie herself. He was told he had to call the phone in the patient lounge. It rang a long time. Finally a thick, flat male voice came on the line. John asked for Maggie, got a blank silence, then a grunted assent. After a long time he finally heard Maggie's voice. She gave him the code. He called it in. A woman staff member, with a waist like a sack of potatoes, abrupt and sober like a prison matron, came to the door. When she saw David, she said he could not come in because minors needed the permission of the psychiatrist to come onto the floor. John sighed, "How do I get that?"

"You have to come back tomorrow when he's in."

"This boy's mother is on this ward. He hasn't seen her since last night. He's worried about her. Can't you let him come in?"

"Not tonight. Not without a psychiatrist's order."

John turned to the boy, who was listening. "David, I'm sorry."

The boy composed his sad face and shrugged, "It's okay."

"No, it's not okay," John exclaimed.

"So what are you going to do? Are you coming in?" the staffer said impatiently.

"I can't leave this boy out here alone. What choice do we have, we'll call the doctor tomorrow and come back then."

John called on the patient phone again, went through the same laborious process until Maggie's voice came on the line again. "That woman is a bitch!" she said. The first anger John heard from her. "Everybody up here says that."

"It doesn't seem just to be her. It's hospital policy."

"Yeah, that's how it is with these places. Doesn't make sense, does it!"

That night John watched a DVD with the boy. They sat side-by-side on John's couch. David kept up a running stream of questions that annoyed John. He reminded himself that kids learn by asking. The boy's questions were not frivolous; they were triggered by the dialogue or action in the movie. So John paused the film each time. He made up some ridiculous answers, which David quickly saw through. The boy appreciated the humor. His mind was quick and he had a precocious sense of irony. Not being used to factoring kids into his environment, John had chosen a film with some adult content and was suddenly embarrassed when profanity and nudity flashed across the screen. He was thinking about how to apologize to a nine-year-old and wondering if he should stop the film, but David seemed not to be fazed. The only thing that grossed him out was when the male and female leads passionately kissed. He covered his eyes and said, "Ugh-h-h."

John laughed and said, "It won't be too many years before you'll want to do that!"

"I don't think so!" David said. But they both laughed, the boy knowing in some uneasy alchemy of fascination and repulsion how true it was.

Maggie stayed in the hospital for six days. She got the psychiatrist's permission and John worked out the arcane hospital system. So each night he took David up to the "sixth floor." Everyone knew what that meant. People said it when they didn't want to say "psych ward." David's mom said this was where they put the "crazy people," but she implied that it was the only really sane place and they were the only ones who were real. In a way, that made sense to John. On the sixth floor when you were depressed, suicidal, psychotic, strung out on drugs or alcohol, you had no reason or energy left to cover up. Maggie seemed more at home there than back in her apartment. When you walked down the corridors, you couldn't be sure who was staff and who was a patient. Maggie asked John to bring her cigarettes, and she hung out with the other patients in the smoking room, drinking bad decaf (they only gave real coffee in the morning), laughing and making hard-edged observations about the rest of the world. She went to the group sessions. Some of them she liked. John realized, listening to her talk, that she was an experienced, well-traveled patient who knew almost as much as the therapists.

When they arrived in her room each night, she hugged David hungrily. On his face John read delight, sadness, disappointment, and eagerness. For a moment he seemed like a younger child, not able to push his mother away like a typical nine-year-old who hates to be hugged by his mom in public especially in front of another male. He was taking care of his mom; she was fragile; but he needed her. They spoke to each other in a slightly infantile shared language. But Maggie quickly turned her attention to John. She seemed to want adult conversation. John talked for a while, then excused himself to give David time alone with his mom.

Maggie refused drugs. The hospital kept her until the psychiatrist felt confident she was stable. Maggie laughed. "That's all they care about. Get the crazy ones stable. Put 'em back on the street. Make sure they don't freak anybody out. God forbid they should actually treat someone. That's what they call treatment! Give 'em drugs. Put 'em back in the situation that screwed 'em up in the first place."

John offered to give her a ride home from the hospital. He asked if the hospital was going to follow up with outpatient services. She said they referred her to a therapist at the community mental health center. He asked if she was going to go there. She laughed, "Yeah, I'll try. The last time I could only get in to see a therapist every two weeks. I fucking try to kill myself and they can only see me every two weeks. As if that's enough! What do they fucking think it's like to try to off yourself! I don't have any money. I have to take what I can get."

John needed to talk to her again about her rent. She was five months behind. She was already two months in arrears when Jack Foster bought the building. Rent collection was in chaos. It had taken John a while to figure out who owed what. He could not carry her any longer. He figured Jack's patience was about two months long. They were way past that. But he couldn't bring up the rent now. He wanted to find her some assistance. She talked tough sometimes, but he knew how fragile she was. She wasn't eating. Her arms were like toothpicks. She hadn't worked since John had moved in.

"Do you have food in the apartment?"

"Some carrots and a little milk. My stash was pretty low."

"Ah, I'm not sure how to ask this...Have you thought about food stamps?"

"Yeah, I was on food stamps till five months ago. When I got a job, I reported it, and they took me off the program."

"You have a job?"

"No, I had to give it up after a month. It wasn't working out. I was waiting tables at Rigatelli's, that Italian restaurant on State Street. I had to lift heavy trays of food. My back went out. I just didn't think it was good place for me. It didn't have a healing atmosphere."

"Why didn't you go back on food stamps?"

"I never got to it. Too much to do."

John wondered what the "too much" was. In the time he'd lived in the building he'd rarely seen her leave the apartment except to take a bus to the supermarket. He wanted to be helpful. He recognized that the rent made him less than disinterested. He needed to help her because she was becoming his problem.

"Does the mental health center have other services?"

"What do you mean?" she asked.

"Uh, like help with rent or utilities?"

"Are you saying I can't handle this myself?"

"Uh, sometimes people get into a bind. It can happen to any of us."

"Yeah, well, a single mom with no car isn't like everybody else. People fucking look down on you. When you don't have money, people think you're shit."

John made no response, leaving an awkward silence. He could feel Maggie's anxiety rising. "I'm sorry," she said. "I'm pretty stressed out."

"Of course you are," John replied quickly, "after what you've been through."

"You mean I'm a nutcase and should be messed up."

"I don't know, Maggie. I'm just trying to find a way to make contact here. Listen, you said you don't have much food in the apartment. Do you want me to stop at Jewel? You can run in. I can wait for you."

Maggie hesitated, then said, "I'm a little short, right now. Thanks. I'll catch a bus to the store later."

"If you have money at the apartment, I'd be willing to take you home and then drive you back to the store."

"No, that's all right."

John pondered that. "Look, I can spot you twenty dollars." Before she could answer, he pulled over, took out his wallet, and handed her a twenty.

She took it reluctantly and eagerly. "Thanks. It's a loan. I'll pay you back."

That afternoon John kept an eye out for David as he came home from school. He saw him go into his apartment, waited a few minutes, then knocked. David came to the door. He smiled when he saw John.

"How're you doing?" John asked.

"I'm good," the boy replied.

"How's your mom?"

"She's good."

"May I talk to her for a moment?"

"Uh, she can't talk right now."

"Well, David, if you need anything, come over and get me."

Chapter 12 – Money

Sam woke to anxiety. He got out of bed in the gray pre-dawn and paced the length of the apartment, past the still unopened boxes. He found the coffeemaker in a box labeled "kitchen" and started a pot of coffee. He stood at the sliding glass door in the small living room and looked out across the corn stubble in the field behind the building. He wondered idly how long it would remain undeveloped. The faint red light of dawn coming from the other side of the building fell across the roof and tinged the tops of the trees that edged the field. He shivered in the cold and went back to the bedroom for his bathrobe. Eve lay sleeping on her side. He slipped back into bed and curled next to her, putting his arms around her, holding her close, and cupping her breasts. She murmured in her sleep and seemed to snuggle closer. For a moment quiet stole over him and he rested. He felt he could almost go back to sleep. Then the deep unease rose again. He tensed. Eve stirred. He was up again, filling his mug with the hot, fresh coffee. He pushed aside some packing blankets and sat on the sofa. He stood again and paced. He went to his case and took out his journal. He went back to the loveseat, pulled a packing blanket around his legs, and began to write.

"I turn away from you and go my own way. Yet I think about you. You are always in my peripheral vision, in sight but not in the center of my view. I stand in the middle of my life, and I cannot see because I am blocking the view. I have lost my way. I don't know what to do next."

He paused, thinking about the credit-card debt and the back taxes. Together their income was not large enough to pay down these obligations, even over time.

"I don't know what I'm doing. I'm not even sure I believe you are personally involved in these everyday matters, yet I have been on this path for so many years. I'm a person of half-faith. I doubt this inner voice that is mine but more than mine. The worst of it is I believe my struggles are my fault. I simply don't have the faith I need. I don't practice the discipline that goes with this kind of faith. I don't even know what success looks like. I'm pretty sure it's not money flowing in and lovely big houses and wealth and security like the evangelical gurus promise. There's no Jabez prayer, at least not for me. But it's not debt and back taxes either. I can't believe you would lead someone down that path, so I have to blame myself. I'm a

washout. I turned away from conventional finance and haven't given myself to radical faith. I am one of those lukewarm people the scripture says you abominate. I don't feel anger and judgment from you. Rather sadness and disappointment. Are you disappointed? I don't want to hear the answer. It's all about me. This is my problem. I'm trapped in myself."

Sam put the pen down. He released the foot rest which was built into the sofa, and it rose under his legs. He leaned back and closed his eyes, resting in half-consciousness somewhere between sleep and prayer. He heard Eve beginning to stir, going into the bathroom. Anxiety ran through his whole body, roiling around in his solar plexus and radiating out through his arms and legs. He sat up and squirmed and wanted to run away—to the shower, to the bedroom to dress, to his office—anywhere but right here with his need and sense of failure.

He seized his journal. *"Dear God! Please help me. I am desperate. I cannot go on like this. Please send me money. Send it! I don't care whether it's good for me or not. I don't care whether you wish it or not. I want it! I need it. I cannot go on without it. It defines me! I wish it didn't, but it does. Please God send it. A lot of it. Let it rain down on me. Let me pay my bills and taxes. Free me from this terrible burden. I give up trying to be good and faithful. I just want money. Please God!"*

He felt acutely embarrassed. This was not the prayer Brother Lawrence would have prayed, or Thomas Merton or Thomas Kelly or St. Teresa of Avila or Mother Teresa or Dorothy Day or George Mueller—or any of the saints he admired and followed and knew he was no match for and not the least bit like. Certainly Jesus would never have prayed such a prayer.

Sam closed his journal and went to the sliding glass door, looking again at the corn stubble, noticing now the tinge of frost in the thin wintry sunshine. Shrugging his shoulders, resigned, no longer hopeful, but oddly at peace, he turned toward the shower and his day.

He was working at his design console later. It had been a productive morning. He always worked better when he stopped caring, stopped trying—just did the work as it came to him. The phone rang. It was the eccentric old man, Oliver Larkspur, offering to take him to lunch. Sam, surprised, accepted and agreed to meet him at Panera's near the tollway.

"The only fast food franchise that doesn't insult the palette or the intelligence," the old man said as they sat down in a booth after picking up their soups and salads. Sam smiled to himself. The old man always surprised him. He could not imagine someone with so much money ordering at the cash register and standing and waiting at the serving counter, however good and fresh the food might be.

"Well now," said the old man, "how's the experiment in faithful finance coming?"

"Are you making fun of me?" Sam asked.

"Maybe a bit. Well, no. Actually no. I find your experiment amusing, I do. And immensely interesting. And admirable, too."

"You admire me!"

The old man tilted his head. He smiled. His eyes twinkled. Later Sam laughed at that memory. The old man's eyes really did twinkle. He seemed to have more good humor than his sophisticated old self could contain, so some of it glittered in his eyes.

"You're laughing at me!" Sam said.

"No, I'm not," said the old man. "Well, maybe I am. Well, actually not. Well, maybe I'm laughing at what I'm about to do."

Sam eyed him thoughtfully. Sam could feel the old man's anticipation. Sam said nothing and began to eat his salad. The old man was quiet too, and Sam noticed that the silence did not make either of them uncomfortable.

"I am going to make an experiment too," the old man said. Sam listened and kept eating. "An action I've never taken before, and it may well be a mistake, though I don't think so or I wouldn't be taking it. But—it is highly unusual. Even for me," he laughed.

There was another silence. Sam smiled, "You've got my attention. But why are you telling me? We've only begun to know each other. Why single me out of all your friends and acquaintances?"

"My experiment involves you."

"Oh!" Sam said in surprise, skepticism slipping into his voice. He thought how little he knew about Oliver Larkspur.

Larkspur reached into the inside pocket of his tweed jacket and took out a blank white envelope. He laid it on the table and pushed it across to Sam.

Sam stared at it, curious and reluctant.

The old man said nothing, but watched Sam with amused interest.

Larkspur's gaze unnerved him. He knew he had no choice really but to open the envelope. It would be impolite if he didn't.

"You may take it with you and open it in private, if you wish," said the old man.

Sam smiled suddenly, shrugged, and picked it up. "You know this is odd, don't you?"

"Of course it is," the old man replied, as though being odd was as natural as eating lunch.

The envelope was unsealed. Sam lifted the flap. Inside was a plain sheet of white paper. He unfolded it. There was a check inside and words were typed on the paper. He glanced quickly at the check. A bolt went through him—only such an electric word could describe the intensity and power of the feeling—a shock of surprise and hope and fear and even anger that this might be a cruel trick. He could not let himself believe what he saw. He turned to the words on the paper. It was a short letter.

> My friend,
>
> You have tried debt and lonely financial disaster. You have learned a bit about money and about yourself. Now, try wealth. What will you learn from that?
>
> This check does not represent real wealth, but it is a start. There are no strings attached. This is yours. You may do whatever you like with it.
>
> If you would be willing to tell me from time to time what you are learning, I would find that engaging and enlightening.
>
> Yours truly,
>
> Oliver Larkspur

Now Sam looked more closely at the check. It was for $500,000—a half million dollars!

He folded the letter, slipped the check into the folds, and carefully put it down on the table, taking care not to put it in a spot of salad dressing. He looked up at the old man and then away, then back again. He noted the old man's quizzical smile, wondering if he was laughing at him, then realizing that the old man must know what an over-mastering moment this was. He knew he was expected to say something, had to say something. The anguish he had lived with for years came rushing back to him—the endless anxiety, the spreading sense of failure, the crush of self-doubt that had returned cruelly after brief moments of conviction. The feelings he had bravely kept at bay in order to go on each day rose in his mind and heart now that he no longer needed to contain them. He looked down dumbly at the folded paper. Tears came to his eyes.

He shook his head and wiped the tears away with his fingers. "I'm sorry," he said. "It's all so…impossible!" He looked off into the middle distance, his face under control, but tears still standing in his eyes. Sadness filled him for a moment, as though he carried the grief of careworn men and women across the generations. He sighed, took a deep breath as if to speak, and then stopped. Nothing he wanted to say seemed to say what he wanted to say. It came to him that he did not need to be polite or proper. This moment called for something more. Stunned silence was maybe the greater eloquence. He did not have to please the old man. What he owed him in this moment was honesty. Amazement, anger, explosive joy, suspicion, sorrow, stillness—the old man deserved his exact and unadulterated candor.

"Do you have any idea what this means!" he said sharply.

The old man shook his head. "I hope to find out."

Sam rubbed his eyes and massaged his temples.

"Are you unwell?" the old man asked.

Sam laughed, "That is hardly the word for it. I am undone! I am grateful...   con-fused...elated...afraid...astonished...distrustful...worried...thankful almost beyond words—for starters."

The old man listened.

"How can I possibly accept such a sum? How can I not be forever beholden to you? How can this not utterly change your relationship to me? How can I ever again feel my independence?"

"A common shortcoming of the middle class. If you haven't earned it, you have no right to it. The sons and daughters of the wealthy don't suffer this malady."

"Perhaps they should."

"As for changing your relations with me—we've only just begun what you call our relationship. There is not yet enough to change."

Sam listened.

"Are you afraid I will begin to call in this favor? Insist on your friendship? Ask you to be my companion or, like in an English novel, make you my secretary or recruit you as my driver? Actually, I had thought about hiring you as my secretary. I think you would make a good one. But I am not interested in your assistance. I am interested in your soul."

"Like the devil in the desert with Jesus?"

"No, his object was to corrupt."

"Then like Satan in the book of Job?"

"Well, hardly. Satan in that story destroyed Job's material happiness. Satan was a cynic. He thought Job was too good to be true. My object is not to twist you or tear down your goodness. I want to see if you will grow more into the man I think you already are. I don't expect this money to corrupt you or do you in. But I do expect it to present another set of troubles and I do, I have to admit, want to see how you meet them."

Sam suddenly picked up the envelope, took out the check again, and looked at it closely. The old man watched him with interest. Sam looked up sheepishly. The old man raised an eyebrow and smiled. "I had to check to be sure it was real," Sam said. "It is real, isn't it? You're not playing with me?"

"Yes, it's real. And, yes, I am playing with you. Money is too serious to be serious about it."

"You can't mean that. People who have money and keep it are not playful. People who play with it, lose it."

"So it's not possible to be lighthearted and rich?"

"Playful maybe in a cavalier or casual way—a dilettante—but truly light in heart and spirit, I doubt it."

"Then I have just burdened you?"

Sam laughed, "I've never been lighthearted anyway. I'm a serious guy. Serious when poor, so I expect I'll be serious when rich."

"Where does this analysis leave me?"

"I can't make you out. You defy classification!"

"Thank you. That's a compliment."

There was a silence. Sam fidgeted. He heard the counterman call out an order. He looked to the side and saw a college student open his laptop and log onto the Internet. He glanced back at the old man who was watching him.

"You don't know how to bring this lunch to an end. But you want it to end, so you can go tell someone."

"I do!"

"Go. Please. This is not a time for restraint." The old man laughed, "It's been a pleasure doing business with you."

****

Sam insisted on paying the bill. The old man laughed at him. They parted outside and Sam almost ran to his car. He dialed his cell phone as he drove. Eve's voice came on the other end. "Where are you? Sam asked. "At the gym?... You're in the shower?...Get out and get dressed. I'll meet you in the parking lot...Why?...You'll know soon enough...No, there's no accident, no emergency...Yes, a great mystery! Just get your clothes on and be outside...I'll be there in ten minutes!...Forget blow-drying your hair!...A crisis?...Well, maybe, but not the sort you think! Just be outside...Yes, I know you have your car. But, I'll pick you up."

Eve was waiting when he pulled up, her damp hair plastered to her head. She looked miffed and alarmed and puzzled and excited all at once. Sam said nothing, drove the car to the corner of the parking lot, and turned off the engine.

"I got ready in record time. This better be good. What's going on?" Eve demanded.

"Here," Sam said, handing her the envelope.

She pulled the check out and looked at it. "Um, a check for $500. Great! We can really use it. Where'd it come from? Who's Oliver T. Larkspur?"

"Look again," Sam said, trying to hide his excitement.

Eve read it, then read it again. She shook her head and brushed back one of her damp curls. "I don't get it. Is this a joke? This is for five hundred thousand dollars!" She waved it in the air. "Where did this come from? Why are you showing me this? What's the point? This is a cashier's check. Did you make this up on the computer? Are you playing a prank? It's not funny. And who is this Larkspur guy?!"

"It's a real check. Oliver Larkspur is the eccentric old man I told you about, Preston's friend."

"No! It can't be real!"

"Why not?"

"Nobody gives away a half million dollars!"

"He just did."

Eve began to shake her head in denial and disbelief. She seemed almost angry. "It's too much," she said. "Too crazy, too unreal, too impossible! Too good to be true! How can I let myself be glad! I've hugged my fear to my heart and schooled myself to have faith! For so long! How can I let go! How will I know myself!"

Sam watched her put the hand with the check in her lap and peer out the window. She turned back and looked at him. She began to tap the hand with the check against her thigh. Suddenly she began to sob. Sam reached out in dismay. The emotion was wrenched from her until her crying eased into a quieter flow. Sam held her.

"I need a Kleenex," she said, rooting for one in her purse and blowing her nose. "It's good I didn't have time to put on mascara," she said, laughing through her tears.

Sam touched her chin and lifted it to look into her eyes. "I love you," he said.

Eve began to cry again. "What are we going to do?"

"We're going to deposit it, for one thing!"

"The bank won't believe it either!"

"Yes, they will. The check's drawn on an account at our bank."

Eve sighed and shook her head. "This better be real! I couldn't stand being disappointed, now. Don't you see what this means!"

"Of course, I do."

"We can get out of debt, pay the back taxes, pay off the credit cards." She paused. "God, we can be out of debt! There no end to what we can do! I wish it had come four months sooner. How's that for instant ingratitude. We wouldn't have had to sell. No, I don't wish that. We needed to get rid of the big house. We're not big-house people! Still, It would have been nice to decide that, though, with graciousness and wisdom. We could have been fine and magnanimous people of faith simplifying our life. Instead we were desperate failures bailing out ahead of bankruptcy. Is all that behind us? Really? We won't know how to live with money!"

"That's the old guy's point. He saw how the lack of money affected me. He wants to see what we do with wealth."

"We're an experiment!"

"Well…yeah…but the money's real. It's ours, whatever we do with it. No strings. He's not demanding that we talk to him, give him reports. We're free and clear. Still he'll know something because he knows so many of our friends, but I like the old guy, and I'll have lunch with him regularly."

Eve sat back, then sat forward, then sat back. She shook her head. "Okay, so what do we do next?"

They drove to the bank and asked to talk to the manager. They were shown to the office of the assistant manager. She was a young woman in a gray business suit and black pumps. Her dark hair was trimmed close to her head with bangs sharply cut across her forehead. Sam recognized her as the loan officer who had dismissed with disdain his application for a business loan a year earlier, when she had seen his credit rating. He saw she remembered him. She smiled with a politely distant and haughty manner and invited them to sit down, speaking with a slight Mexican accent. Unsure how to begin, they told her they had unexpectedly come into a large sum of money, just today as a matter of fact.

"How large?" she asked, her eyes widening slightly.

"Very large," Sam placed the check on the desk in front of her.

She peered at, then picked it up and examined it more closely. She looked up quickly. Sam read suspicion in her eyes and body language. She put the check down beside her computer and tapped the keys rapidly, studying the screen. She turned back to them with an altered manner.

"How can I help you, Mr. & Mrs. Ellerby?"

"You were checking to be sure the check is legitimate," Sam said dryly.

"Yes, and it is. Mr. Larkspur drew the cashier's check this morning on money deposited in this bank. We will be very glad to be of assistance."

"Yes, I expect you will," Sam replied.

There was a silence. It was broken when there was a knock and the door opened. A stocky, dark-haired man came in as though to ask a question, then realized his colleague was in conference. But the young woman asked him to come in and introduced him as the branch manager.

Sam greeted him, then paid him little attention, not being impolite exactly, but enjoying the power to return the casual condescension he'd suffered more than once from this self-important man.

"We don't know what we will do with the money after we've settled debts. We'll probably find a financial consultant," Sam found himself saying. "What we need from you is a place for our money in the short term till we have figured out where to invest it." Sam was full of questions about certificates of deposit and treasury notes and especially he wanted to know when an account became too big to be covered by federal deposit insurance.

It took a long time to set up various accounts and CDs to hold the money yet keep it liquid. When they were finished, Sam's head hurt. They drove home and sat in their living room in silence, weary, elated, and numb.

"You know what we have to do. The first thing," Eve said.

"I know what you're going to say. We should tithe this money."

"How can we not?" Eve replied.

"It's a huge amount. $50,000!"

Eve smiled at him.

"We've had money for only a couple of hours," Sam said ruefully, "and already it's hard to part with it! Is that what you're thinking?"

"Yes, but think of the pleasure we'll have in writing all those checks."

Sam shook his head, then suddenly looked up. "How much should we give to the congregation? You can give too much, you know. How much is too much?" He stopped, then added, "And then everyone will know!"

"They'll know anyway! How can we hide this? Why should we?"

It was harder than Sam expected to pay the back taxes. There were papers and forms to fill out; there was a trip to a tax center far across the metropolitan area; there was a cashier's check needed for each year, which had to be exact to the penny as of the day of payment, so the tax and interest obligations could be fully discharged, without a leftover small balance. Sam was first frustrated and then amused that a government that so badly wanted his money made it so hard to pay it.

Later that week he got rid of his desktop computer and bought a top-of-the-line laptop loaded with software with a docking station an extra keyboard and second monitor. He bought a new cell phone and the digital camera he'd been salivating over. Should they buy a house, now that they could afford the one they'd just sold? Sam liked large interior spaces. Eve missed having lots of people over. There were boxes they still hadn't unpacked. It would be easy to move. Conventional wisdom said you shouldn't rent unless you had to. But their credit was damaged. Even with a huge down payment, they'd never get a loan or if they got one, it would be at high interest. They were getting used to their cozy small apartment. Sam was glad someone else was raking the leaves and mowing the grass.

Eve found a second-floor condo two blocks over. In the down market they were able to get a good price. They bought it outright, paid cash. It was one of the most satisfying transactions of Sam's life. He relished the realtor's surprise. Eve had it redecorated. They bought a gorgeous area carpet for the living room. They paid movers to do everything, including unpacking and putting clothes in closets and drawers and dishes on shelves. It was a relief not to have to impose again on friends.

"People's hearts sink when their friends move," Sam said to Eve, "but they still show up to help. They did for us the last time. They even carried stuff out of the back corners of our basement, ending up covered in cobwebs and dust." So Sam and Eve spared their friends this indignity after so recently putting them through it, but moving day with its precision and efficiency also seemed lonely.

From time to time Sam sent sporadic bursts of gratitude upward or inward to wherever God was. He thought of God with affection and guilt. He felt he should be praying, but he was content. He should need God, but he didn't really. He was glad for God and glad to go confidently on his own way. He had survived. Indeed, it was through nothing he had done. But was it anything God had done? It was hard to imagine God working through an old curmudgeon like Oliver Larkspur. What did it mean for God to "work"? Did God put the idea in the old man's head? Sam was embarrassed even to think of God this way—the God of the universe straightening out his life like a mother fussing over a child.

He talked about it with the old man over lunch.

"Did you feel some sort of nudge to give us the money?"

"Nudge?" exclaimed the old man.

"Yeah, like an inner prompting?"

"God didn't speak to me, Sam," said the old man laughing.

"How do you know?"

"I'm an odd old man, but I don't hear voices, and I will know when I do."

"Not voices. An inner movement. I mean why did you give us the money? Tell me about the moment you decided to do it."

"I'm the one asking the questions," said the old man, laughing. "This is my experiment, not yours."

Sam made no reply, waiting.

"Interesting," said the old man. "Well, I'll try to answer you. I was sitting in my library, in my favorite chair; leather, it sort of envelops me. I was very comfortable. Is that important? Do you have to be comfortable to hear God's voice? Or, on the contrary, is discomfort a precondition? Flagellation. Asceticism. The desert fathers."

"You've read the desert fathers?"

"Not read them really, but I know a little church history. If there's any truth in their experience, then I was far too pleasantly situated to hear God's voice. I had a whiskey in my hand. Now I cannot recall any instance in history where God spoke while someone was imbibing."

"How about wine at the Last Supper?"

The old man shrugged. "So I was sitting in my library thinking about how improbable and intriguing your holy adventure is. I was admiring you actually. And wishing you weren't suffering. You were suffering, of course. You put a good face on it, but financial anxiety is real and debilitating, no matter how strong you say your faith is. I was thinking how easy it would be to relieve you of that, but knowing how important it was that you see your effort through. One should interfere with the trajectory of another's life only with great care and respect. Still I found myself wanting to do something. And it came to me that you were completing only one half of your investigation. To know really the relation of money to faith, you had to know what having money would do to your faith. You see, I'd read a biographical sketch of a wealthy TV preacher. I remembered that he started with nothing and experienced great and seemingly miraculous moments of faith. It was money and fame that led to his downfall. So I wondered if money wouldn't be a greater challenge to your faith than poverty. Ah, I thought, I can have it both ways. I can relieve your suffering and contribute to your education in faith." The old man laughed. "So giving you money suddenly seemed deliciously right."

"There, right there!" exclaimed Sam. "That feeling of rightness. What was that like?"

"You think that was God prompting me?"

"Why not?"

"Sam, there are a lot of poor people, much worse off than you were—and many people far richer than I. Why would God pick me to give money to you?"

Sam thought for a moment. "I don't know. Maybe we were the ones listening."

Chapter 13 – Affinities

John almost did not attend the congregational meeting. It was a beautiful afternoon, and he was tempted to drive out into the country to see the pale green buds on the trees and the furrows of black earth where farmers had begun spring plowing. People took seats, and the semicircles of chairs filled quickly. More chairs had to be set out. The moderator began with her usual disclaimer about not being sure she was up to the job. There was a quick scripture reading and a prayer.

Joe Kurtz reviewed the options presented at the last meeting, summarized the discussion from that session, and invited further comments and questions. Many people spoke.

John, sitting off to the side, leaned forward with his elbows on his knees and listened without looking at the speakers, letting the give-and-take wash over him, sometimes smiling at the predictability of the speeches.

"It's time we made a decision. We've been talking about this long enough."

"If we move out west, we'll be just like all those other churches that desert the city to be safe and comfortable. We don't need a sprawling new building. We belong here in this neighborhood."

"Our ministry isn't to the well-off people who live in their five hundred thousand dollar homes. Those people won't be interested in peace and social justice. Leave them to the mega churches that preach the gospel of prosperity. We're called to stand with the poor people."

"We don't live with the poor. Our neighbors aren't poor. This is still a middle-class neighborhood."

"But we're a lot closer to the problems of the city than we would be out there in Cotswold Court."

"Some of those people are worse off than the poor people downtown." There were murmurs of disagreement. "Well, it's true. People caught in the pressures of keeping up, kids neglected emotionally. People living on the surface of their lives, superficial people who need God and need community."

"We don't know that. How can we know what it's really like to be rich—or poor! We do our thing with Soup Kettle and the homeless shelter, but we don't really connect with those folks. And we have our stereo-types of five-hundred-thousand-dollar living, but we don't know what it's like to have lots of money. This neighborhood is probably where we be-long, close enough to downtown to have to see the poverty, far enough from Cotswold Court to resist getting caught up in that world."

"We're just whistling in the dark here. In this economic downturn we're not going anywhere."

As the arguments went on, there was growing uneasiness and surprise at the depth and intensity of the differences.

"I just think we need to get along with each other."

"We are not going to resolve this today; that seems plain."

"We have different ways of looking at this."

"It's not just different views of what we want or think is right. It's a stewardship question. What do we do with our resources and where do we do it and why."

"We've already had members lose jobs and go a long while till they found work again. How will this economy affect giving over the next few years? We can't risk a building program of any kind now."

John could see that the members of the congregation thought of them-selves as good people who understood and accepted each other and knew how to work things out. They were teachers and social workers and nurses and psychotherapists and mid-level professional people. They were well-educated and knew by training and inclination a good bit about relation-ships. They believed they could handle anything that came along.

John knew of churches with one or two families who dominated the congregation. From what Kirby had told him, he knew this was not true of the Westbrook Church. Only once had they come even close to this, and that apparently ended when Robert and Josey Brandt moved to a retirement center in California to be near family and friends. The church was about 75% "progressive," which meant they could get a strong ma-jority vote on most of the issues that mattered. John knew there were members, some of them his friends from the breakfast group, who were embarrassed to be called Christian because in the popular mind that meant pushy fundamentalists or angry conservatives or members of mega-churches. But he could see there were two matters that carried an explosive load. The one they had just been discussing, whether or not to build a new church, made people uneasy; liberals who otherwise agree with one another were coming out at different places. The other matter was the one coming up.

Vern Keller came to the lectern to give a report from the discernment committee on sexual orientation and to make a recommendation. The committee had been meeting for nearly two years. It had held hearings, discussion sessions, and Bible studies. It had invited psychologists and social workers to talk about the latest research on homosexuality and about their clinical experience. Someone from a church in Indiana had been invited to talk about how they got into trouble with the other more conservative churches in the district.

As Vern went on, John was impressed by how much the congregation had done. The committee had invited a man who had founded a program in inner-city Chicago to try to convert gay and lesbian street people back to heterosexuality. Members of the congregation had actually been surprised at the man's compassion and understanding, though deeply troubled by his conviction that same-sex relations were perverse and LGBT people could and should be brought back to their "true nature" as heterosexuals.

A man who had been a leader and elder in an evangelical congregation had spoken of being a closeted gay man, who cruised the streets in secret while maintaining his proper Christian life. He had talked of his relief when he finally told the truth about himself. He had elected to stay with his wife. He had come to see his homosexuality as real and irrevocable, but he believed his calling was to remain chaste.

A gay couple and a lesbian couple had told the congregation of their long and stable relationships and had described the vilification they had faced when they came out—and of the rejection by their families and their church. They had spoken of how hard it had been to grow up in a world that regarded them as perverse and immoral.

John thought once again how different this was from churches back home. Here people wanted to talk. And no one wanted to appear close-minded, even those few who felt same-sex relations were immoral; they wanted their remarks to be of the "hate-the-sin-love-the-sinner" variety. John wondered briefly why it was so important to people to appear open even when they weren't. Maybe everyone wanted to seem loving. Who could be against love, especially in this congregation! There were a few older people who were uncomfortable with the whole thing, but couldn't admit it and didn't want to be "out-liberaled."

Kirby had told John there were those who wanted to accept homosexuals as members while not dealing with the question of same-sex unions or ordaining gays or lesbians. There was one person who by instinct and feeling was not alarmed by homosexuality but took the Bible seriously enough to think that maybe God did disapprove. There were others who were intent on showing that all the Biblical passages about same-sex sexuality had to be seen in context and could not be applied to our time. They were as determined to reinterpret the scripture as the literalists were to defend it.

John thought how little even the scholars really know about texts written and recopied many times over millennia and based on stories passed from mouth to mouth for years, even centuries. How could anyone know anything? Yet, he thought, don't all people of faith have this deep conviction that they do know about God and that scripture really does reveal something? Still, no one accepts and follows every part, even the most hidebound literalists who say they do. Wouldn't it be better if people didn't fight, if they admitted how little they know and how muddled they really are!

Vern's committee made an intriguing proposal. First a paper would lay out the differences, not just on homosexuality, but on other hot-button issues in the congregation, and would commit members to live with these differences. This nuanced paper would be sent to every member and would be discussed and voted on. If it was approved, then the second step would be to write five specific statements on inclusion ranging from the very conservative to the very liberal. These would be distributed to the congregation. There would be a second meeting. People would vote for as many of the five as they could affirm. If one of the statements received an 80-percent vote, then it along with the nuanced statement would become the position of the congregation.

This proposal was greeted with silence at first. It was involved, creative, and labored. John smiled to himself. He remembered a story Vi had told him of traveling behind the Iron Curtain in the 1980s. She'd been carrying a lot of camera equipment. The customs official was startled and suspicious. He spoke no English and she didn't speak his language. She settled down to a lengthy, patient, and hugely involved explanation, in English and in great detail, of the cameras and lenses and of all the reasons for the huge amount of film. She prepared herself to stand there all day if necessary. The official's eyes began to glaze over. He drummed his fingers in boredom. His patience at an end, he waved her through. John wondered if the committee was trying to mute controversy with excessive thoroughness. But it was a creative effort to dignify all points of view yet reach something the congregation could stand for. John was not surprised that there was little discussion. It was a lot to take in. The congregation approved the plan.

****

John put the congregation out of his mind as he drove out of the church parking lot. He was having his drive after all, going west through the countryside, enjoying the Sunday afternoon sunshine, occasionally pulling off the road to let an impatient driver pass so he could continue his Sunday-driver pace.

The sun warmed his arm resting in the open car window. The breeze ruffled his hair. He leaned back in the seat and drove even more slowly, pulling off by a small stand of trees. A feeling of contentment stole through his body. What did he have to be content about? No real job, not much income to speak of. A rundown apartment in a building being re-habbed. New friends, but none of them close yet. He did have Kirby and Nancy and Vi. He wondered about Vi. Was he interested? He smiled. Sometimes attraction grew slowly. He remembered two people from college who had hated each other at first, then married each other. But for him if the attraction wasn't immediate, it would never come. When he and Nancy were growing up, they had almost every reason to fall in love. In early high school she had had a crush on him. She was smart and pretty. It never entered his mind to go out with her. Mary was a different matter. He was taken by her the moment he saw her. He remembered the sweet agony and heartbreak. He had always loved her. But he gave up hope for years, and then she came cycling back into his life, years after college.

So what was Angela to him? No question he was attracted. But her record with men troubled him. It wasn't that she had all those relation-ships. That would have bothered him when he was younger, but the attrac-tion of virginity had worn off. Maybe Angela liked the chase and didn't know what to do with a man when she caught him. What would she do with a man who wanted a relationship? Maybe she wasn't a good candidate for marriage. What was he doing even thinking about marriage! And did he want marriage? It occurred to him that when you were in your sixties, there might be other alternatives.

He drove back to town. There were still some lazy hours left in this Sunday evening. He drove to Angela's house and knocked. No answer. Her car was in the driveway. He took the brick-paved path around the side of the house to see if she was in the bower in the back. It was empty. Dis-appointed, maybe a bit relieved, he went back to his car, and then, instead of getting in, he looked up the street and started walking. In five blocks he came to the park, strolled down the path beside the golf course till he came to the picnic tables and pavilions. He walked to the left, through an opening in a low stone wall, into a large play area covered in wood chips. He watched an agile girl of about eight scurrying over the climbing equipment, rattling the rubber-encased chains, leaping from rope-hold to rope-hold, then standing triumphant on the highest perch. Little kids were being pushed on the swings yelling "higher" to their parents in both English and Spanish. At the far edge, he stepped back over the low wall and sat on a bench where he could see the whole panorama. The sun dropping low behind him pulled the sharply etched items into a warm, orange-tinted tableau.

He sighed and settled himself to be quiet, to let his eyes open to the widest periphery and take in all that came to them and then to let the outer seeing open his inner eye to all that was passing in his spirit. For a moment he wished he had a book. He released that thought and reminded himself that reading would be an escape from a moment like this. He was moving into a deepening peace when he felt a cool hand on his shoulder. He jumped! His meditation shattered! He turned so abruptly that the hand was yanked back as though he'd been a hot stove.

It was Angela, holding her hand over her heart. "My God, you startle easily! You shocked me! Are you okay? I am sorry."

Whatever evening peace he'd achieved was gone, lost not in the heart-thumping startle reflex, but in Angela's raw presence, unprepared for and undefended-against, seizing him through the openness and vulnerability of his meditative state. His pleasure at seeing her was palpable—and wordless. For a woman as used to men's stares as she was, it was like standing in a spotlight. She smiled, sat down beside him, and took his hand. He still did not speak. "That is one of the highest compliments any man has ever paid me," she said.

"To die of heart failure?"

She smiled again, "No, not that," in a tone implying they both knew that was not what she meant.

John said nothing, but he stood, not letting go of Angela's hand, and they began to walk. It felt amazingly good to hold her hand. He thought he probably ought to say something, but nothing came to mind, and he decided it was okay. He'd enjoy this moment and see what happened. There was nothing else in the world to do but walk through this park and down this street with this woman. Something connected him to her—her trouble, her beauty, her sexuality, her pain, her joy, her bitterness, her irony, her intelligence, her spirit. At the center was a lovely person. He smiled to himself. He wondered if this was love.

He remembered his fascination with Mary when they were college students, later the rising anxiety and intense interest when she came back into his life, finally the love that grew between them. He had known Mary down to the bottom and she him. The knowing had come gradually, as the romance wore off and they began the long and difficult effort to make a life together. There were times when they passed each other by, were perplexed and mystified. There were even moments when they lost sight of each other and despaired. But their love always came back and it grew stronger, until it made the fascination that had drawn him to her seem only a pale beginning.

But this was different. This connection was coming quickly, and so improbably. The romance and the knowing seemed wrapped in the same moments. Was this the way it happened when people were older and travel-worn—and maybe wiser? He felt guilty for comparing Mary to Angela. How could he do that! Mary was the love of his life. He could not remember a time from his sophomore year in college when he had not loved her. He'd known Angela only a few months, had hardly spent any time with her. She was tougher, harder, had lived through things Mary could never have imagined. Was he in love with this woman who was so different? Well, if he was, how could he help himself! Love was a great leveler. Feelings were like breathing. You couldn't choose not to breathe. It was what you did with what you felt—and how you understood it. Was this love he was feeling for Angela? Maybe he was capable of two great loves. He and Mary had had so much in common, same background, same college, nurtured in the same moral climate. He and Angela had none of this. But he knew her. He could intuit what he did not know. He felt a powerful connection to this woman's humanity, as though all the other stuff—experience, lovers, culture, even faith—that seem to define differences, did not matter.

He came out of his reverie, turned to look at her. She was watching him with a smile and an expectant expression. He realized that they had walked all the way back to her house.

"I would give a great deal to know what you've been thinking about," she said.

John laughed and squeezed her hand.

"You're not going to tell me?"

"I don't think so," he said.

She gestured toward his car in front of her house. "You came to see me?"

"I did."

"And then you chased me down in the park?"

"Remember it was you who found me."

"Would you like to come in?"

"I don't know."

"Why is that?"

"I am in some mystery over you."

"That's an odd thing to say. Am I to take it as a compliment?"

"Yes, I think so. Will you join me for dinner?"

At the restaurant John began to tell Angela about Maggie and David. The more he talked about the boy the more animated he became. Angela commented on it. He said he found himself thinking about David often during the day. Angela asked him why.

"I don't know," he said. "He's such a good kid. Bright, sensitive, tuned in. His mom's misery hems him in. Amazing that it hasn't blighted him. He seems remarkably healthy. I sometimes find his mom barricaded in the back room sobbing, while he watches a video and entertains himself. You'd think that would really mess him up. I can't find that it has. Despite her persistent struggles, Maggie has given him good nurture. I'm worried what will happen when he becomes a teenager. David the young man may not be as tolerant as David the school kid. He said the other day that he can't understand why she doesn't just get a job, any job, even a crummy job."

"Does Maggie resent your interest in David? You're more concerned about him than about her. Maybe she needs someone to take care of her, too."

"She's an adult. She has to take hold of her life. He's just a kid," John said.

"Some people never do—own their own lives."

"You say that like you know what you're talking about."

"My brother is an addict. Can't hold a job. In and out of rehab. He always blames someone else—our parents for screwing him up, a boss who was a jerk, his ex-wife. He's partly right. Our parents made a lot of mistakes. He did have some bosses who were jerks or worse. He ex-wife was no prize. But he chose the bosses and the wife. He didn't choose our parents, of course, but he has a choice what to do with the marks they left." Angela paused. John waited. "At some point each of us has to say okay, this is what I'm stuck with. What am I going to do with it? For a long time I was angry with my brother. He wouldn't take hold. Then I began to think that maybe there are some people who can't. They're missing some essential gear wheel. No matter how much they rev their engines, the gears never mesh. Maybe Maggie just doesn't have it."

"If that's so, then someone is going to have to be there for David."

"I agree, but don't shortchange the kid himself. There are children who've come through far worse. And don't dismiss Maggie. She takes care of him. She doesn't abuse him. Maybe there's a lot more she can do. And you don't know what her inner reality really is, what she's up against."

"She needs to get a job, get therapy, take medication—whatever it takes. The boy needs a parent!" John said.

"You're hard on her!"

"A kid's life is at stake."

"Maybe she's still a kid herself."

"I don't think she'd like to hear that!" John replied.

"Why are you so interested in this boy?"

"Are you saying I shouldn't be?"

"Are you getting defensive?"

"Are we having a quarrel?" John asked.

"Maybe. But I want to know what's in this for you?"

"Are you saying I have some hidden agenda?"

Angela shrugged. "Do you?"

"Suppose I do. Are anyone's motives pure? Are you trying to start a fight?"

"Maybe I am."

"Why?" John asked.

"You're too nice. Do you have any hard edges?"

"I thought you were tired of men with hard edges."

"Why are you so interested in this kid?"

"Why do you want to know?"

The waiter arrived with their food, and they ate in uncomfortable silence. The warm feelings from the park were gone. He looked across the table at a stranger.

"What just happened here?" John asked. Angela made no reply. John went on, "I'm not aware of nefarious motives. I never had kids. I guess I wish I did. I suppose I want to father David. But this isn't really about David, is it?"

"It's about us. Do we really have a relationship?"

"What does a relationship look like to you?" John asked.

"You're asking the wrong person. You're the one who had a mate. What would a relationship with me look like to you?"

"What are we talking about here?" John asked. Was it marriage? His anxiety went way up. He was drawn to this woman, but did he want to be married to her or—and this made him squirm—live with her?

"It comes down to this. Are you like other men? You want to sleep with me but not marry me?"

"Are you asking if I want to marry you?"

"No. I want to know if sex is all you want from me."

"I haven't even asked that of you."

"You've thought about it. You're a nice guy. I could fall for you. You want to be a dad. You've got domestic instincts written all over you. You could be a good candidate for a husband. You've already been a good husband. It would be just my luck that the man who could really be a companion only wants to get in my pants!"

"If I wanted only that, I'd have done it already," John replied hotly.

Angela laughed. "You think so! You're pretty confident for someone who's only been a one-woman man."

"Well, I'll say this. You asked me what a relationship looks like. It looks a little like this!"

****

John picked Vi up at the Metra station and took her to Emma's for lunch. Then they went back to his apartment building and John showed her the progress he was making. Two of the apartments were nearly finished. He said he was uncertain how to rent them. He wanted to make them available to people who would not normally be able to afford such units, but he still needed people who could pay some rent. He asked Vi about Section 8, and she explained how it worked.

"You're going to have to get involved with the tenants," Vi said. "You're going to have to get to know their financial situation. You'll have to anticipate their problems so that when they can't pay rent, it doesn't come as a surprise. You're going to have to educate yourself about programs and services that are available to poor people. You're probably going to have to go with them sometimes, advocate for them. Have you ever gone to the state department of public assistance? It's degrading. If I were poor and desperate, I'd give up. You have to make an appointment. You don't have a car so you have to depend on public transportation. It takes an hour for a trip that would be less than ten minutes by car. So you get there. You stand in line. Then you sit for a long time in a waiting room. No one explains anything. You finally see a case worker who asks you insulting questions and tells you about all the paperwork you were supposed to bring that no one told you about when you made the appointment. You realize the case worker is shuffling paper and doesn't really know what she's doing either. Your anxiety rises. You ask some angry questions. She cuts you off. She tells you not to come back until you have all the paperwork. You ask her bitterly, just to make sure, what you need and she cuts you off again and tells you she already explained it.

"When I go with someone, often a single mom, who needs food stamps or public assistance. I dress up so I look like an attorney. I carry a clipboard. I have a pen ready. I ask steady and definite questions. When the caseworker is impatient or insulting, I tell her that I understand how hard her job is and that I just need to know a few more things. When she gives a quick and incomplete explanation, I ask her politely and calmly if she can give me a form or a list. If she cannot, I ask her quietly if she would slowly tell me everything we need so I can write it down. When the mom who is with me begins to steam and is ready to call the caseworker an 'effing idiot,' I quietly put my hand on her arm. I repeat the comment that the caseworker's job must be difficult. I ask her how long she's been doing it. I thank her for being helpful, and I ask politely if she can give us another appointment.

"So, would I be able to do all that if I were that single mom with no money, no self-esteem, on the brink of eviction, without time or energy or knowhow to negotiate the bureaucracy? I don't think so. I can do it because I have an education, a job, reasonable mental health, an apartment, and a community of people who give me support and validation. She has none of that. The public assistance is supposed to help start her back on the road to that kind of a life. But it reinforces her present misery."

"So, offering affordable housing is sort of like peeing into the sea," said John.

Vi laughed, "It's still worth doing. Just expect to put a lot into it and to be frustrated and weary."

They were sitting on John's couch. Vi seemed at home in the Spartan furnishing, with the stale odors oozing from the walls and floors despite John's efforts to get rid of them. There was a knock at the door. It opened and David walked in; he hesitated when he saw John had a guest. John introduced the boy, and Vi took an immediate interest. David lost his cautiousness when Vi asked him about the small electronic game he was carrying. Soon they were talking about school and the neighbors, and John was impressed by how relaxed and talkative David became.

After David went back to his apartment, John and Vi picked up some sandwiches and chips and soft drinks and drove out into the country. They found a forest preserve, where they did some hiking, then spread a blanket and had a picnic supper.

"So what's up with you these days?" John asked. "Are you going to stay at Casa? Or maybe I should ask, do they have money to keep you?"

"'Yes' to the second question. 'I don't know' to the first."

"Are you satisfied with your life?" John asked

"That's a frank question."

"I ask the same question of myself."

"So how do you answer it?"

"I'm in transition. Can you ever be satisfied when you're in between? I'm more content than I thought I'd be. Curious to see what will come next."

"Do you like this work you're doing?"

"As far as it goes. But really, I don't know where it's going. I can't see myself managing real estate. Your talk earlier about having to be like a social worker. I don't think I want to do that, at least not over the long haul. Truthfully, I sort of like not knowing, not being tied down. I'm tired of being responsible."

"You want to be irresponsible at the age of 62?"

"Nothing shocking or ridiculous. I'm just tired of doing the right thing."

"What would doing the wrong thing mean?"

"Doing the wrong thing is not the opposite of doing the right thing."

"Oh."

"I'm weary of trying to do the right thing for other people. Human beings are social creatures. We are made for each other. We do things to build up the community and strengthen our relationships. I'm tired of doing those things. I want to come and go as I please—eat when I want, sleep when I want, travel when I want. I don't want responsibility for anyone or anything."

"Then what are you doing renovating this building, helping David, getting involved in the local congregation?"

"Bad habits die hard."

Vi laughed, "Come on, John. You've never been a free spirit."

"I think I'd like to be, but I keep getting sidetracked into being a good guy."

"So you want to live for yourself?"

"When you put it that way, it sounds pretty bad."

"So back to my question. What are you doing fixing up that run-down apartment building?"

"You tell me. Waiting for the next thing. All right, your turn. Are you satisfied with your life?"

"You really want the truth."

"Why do people ask that question? Of course, I want the truth. Do you think I want you to give me a lovely answer that brings a tear to the eye and a phony lift to the heart?"

"I'm lonely, John. I'm almost 60 and I've never owned an apartment or house that was mine. I've never been married. I have no children. My life has been a great adventure and now I'm left with almost nothing. In another ten or fifteen years I'll go into a retirement home and go through all the stages until I die in the nursing section."

John fell silent. He'd never heard such bitter words from Vi. He'd assumed she was happy with her interesting life.

"I know you and Mary always admired my life." She paused and smiled. "I am grateful. I've had a wonderful life. But I want something different now. I'm done with traveling. I want to settle in one place and put down roots. I like the work I'm doing at Casa. I do need that kind of work. I have no desire to stop. I want to do it *with* someone. I want intimate relations as well as broad community connections."

"You want a mate!"

"Well…yes."

John raised his eyebrows.

Vi looked at him ironically. John knew she knew what he was thinking, and he knew what she wished he was thinking.

Chapter 14 – Grieving

John arrived at the Athens House early and found Sam already there reading a book and not quite ready to be friendly. Kurt Wampler came in a moment later, and John watched as Sam dutifully put his book aside. The others showed up slowly. At first it seemed it would be a small group, but gradually everyone turned up.

John and Jack happened to be sitting next to each other and Kurt turned to them and asked how the rehab work was going.

"Fine, as far as it goes," said Jack.

John frowned.

"The whole economy is screwed up."

"Well, that's not a new idea!" Kurt said.

"I know," Jack replied. "But I'm not talking about this recession and the economic crisis. I saw a statistic yesterday comparing the number of obese children in the US with the number of starving children across the world. What is the correlation? What the hell is going on?"

"Is this conversation going to make me feel guilty?" Vern said. There were smiles around the table.

"Hell, Vern," Jack replied, "we're not talking just about your weight problems. Everyone around this table carries more pounds than they should. Look around this restaurant. You walk into any coffee shop like this anywhere in this country, and I guarantee that 60% of the patrons are overweight, not just a few pounds, but fat. If you go into a beef and hotdog joint, the figure is closer to 80%. Even in the soup and salad places where the lean and mean eat, most people are carrying extra pounds. But the kids! Kids sit around on their butts, eat bad food, and don't get any exercise." He paused for breath. Vern was about to speak, but Jack went on, "This is only part of the problem. What about our carbon footprint! We use so much fucking oil, it's beyond comprehension!"

"Jeez, Jack! You're starting to sound like someone from the Green Party!" Kurt exclaimed. "I mean, this is great, but it's out of character."

"What the hell is my character? Maybe I don't know anymore. This housing project down on River Street is like pissing into the wind. This world is really messed up."

There was silence around the table. John knew something was up, and he could see the others knew it too. As friends, they owed it to Jack to listen, but John figured they all just wanted to have breakfast and, at least until their eggs were eaten, inhabit a world that was okay.

Jack shrugged, "Oh, well, I don't want to talk about it anyway."

"Of course you want to talk about it, or you wouldn't have brought it up," Joe said.

"Maybe I just wanted to let off steam." He turned to Vern. "You don't look so good."

"That's a nasty way to change the subject," Vern said.

"Yeah, well, you guys don't want to talk about this, and I really don't either. But seriously, Vern, are you feeling okay?" Jack said.

"Just a little tired."

"You been to the doctor recently?" Kurt asked.

"I have an appointment for Thursday."

"Well, that's good. You're pale and your lips are blue," Joe said.

****

John lingered after the rest left and asked Jack to stay. He wanted to know what Jack meant with his comment about the River Street project. Jack shrugged. John asked if he was going to back out of it.

Jack said no but without much enthusiasm. "I'm in unfamiliar territory. If this were a regular building project, I'd pull the plug in a minute."

"You're worried about losing money?"

"No. Hell, compared to the size of my company this is small. Things are bad in my business, right now. You know that. New commercial construction is way down. The housing market is down. I've laid off half my work force. But I'm still fine. We're one of the few big construction companies that doesn't borrow for operating capital. I have hardly any debt. But why am I telling you this. The truth is I'm losing interest in my company. I want to sit on my deck and write in my journal. Christ, I'm writing poetry and meditating." He ran his hand through his hair, "Hell, you already know that!"

John laughed.

"You laugh! This is not me! At least not yet. Is this what I'm going to become. A fucking poet?"

"Why not?"

"I don't recognize myself any more. I'm starting to care about fat kids. I come here and I talk about the goddamn news. I critique it! Hell, I never even used to watch it. And it's not like I'm bitching about Fox news. I'm worried that PBS is not getting it right. This frigging world is screwed up! That's what I see. Shit, I sound like a goddamn liberal. Or worse than that, one of those foaming-at-the-mouth fanatics you find on both sides. I want to do something and I don't know what the hell to do.

John laughed again, "I'm glad to hear you say it."

"Yeah?"

"I don't know what to do either."

"Then what are we doing renovating that goddamn apartment building?"

"I don't know. For me—I had to start somewhere."

"You sold out in Pennsylvania and moved here with no idea what you're doing or why?"

"I did."

"You have more balls than I do."

"I'm not sure it was balls that made me do it."

"Well, what did?"

"I was through with what I was."

"Well, maybe that's what happened to me. But where does that leave me? Who the hell am I if I'm not running a company!"

"You're a hardhat poet!"

Jack laughed. "That's good!"

"So are we still on with the River Street project?"

"Why not."

****

Later that morning John got an urgent call from Sam, "Terrible, news! Vern died this morning!"

"I don't believe it!"

"Kirby just called, asked me to call the other guys in our group. He was talking from the emergency room. He and Janet arrived at the same time. The police called Janet. She called Kirby. Apparently Vern left breakfast and went over to the Jerrod Avenue post office. You know that little station in the strip mall. They found him in the parking lot, slumped over the steering wheel of his van. The motor was running. His stereo was playing. A Mozart CD. Someone must have seen him, thought there was something wrong, and called the police. He was dead when they found him, but they rushed him to the ER anyway." Sam stopped.

John was silent for a moment. "I don't know what to say. Vern was your friend for years! It must be unreal!" He paused. "So is Kirby still with Janet?"

"Yeah, and I need to get off the phone and call the other guys."

Later that day John joined the men from the breakfast group in the lounge at the church. He looked at their faces and thought that grief doesn't come easily for men, even ones who think they are in touch with their feelings. Words don't suffice. Feelings are muddled and incomprehensible. John knew that when men don't know what to say, just being together helps. They were sitting in a circle in the easy chairs and sofas of the lounge, not touching—feeling affection across distance. This was how these men were suffering and—though the word would probably embarrass them—loving each other. John knew Sam was comfortable calling it love; certainly Kirby was. But it didn't matter what they called it. They were glad they had each other, and they wanted to talk about Vern. They needed to bring him alive in words and stories. These were the first efforts at accepting that he was gone. They laughed as they remembered his pedanticisms. They almost lovingly recounted how conscious he was of his weight. They remembered how he had looked that morning. Kurt said he'd had the impulse to drive Vern to the hospital. "He looked that bad to me!"

"Hell, Kurt," said Jack," you can't blame yourself. We all saw his bad color and blue lips. But why should we think today would be the day. Vern's been a candidate for a heart attack for a long time. This is not the first day he looked bad."

"Truth is," Joe said, "we could all be more attentive to each other. We should feel some guilt, not because we messed up, but because we cared about Vern and wish we could have helped him. Guilt is a measure of love."

John saw each was grieving in his own way—Joe keenly because he was still in grief himself; Kirby with mixed sorrows, for Vern was a friend and a parishioner. Sam seemed heavy and empty. John found himself remembering when Mary had died and thinking about Vern's wife. Kurt, he could see, was angry, indignant that someone so young and with so much to give was gone. Jack seemed unsettled. Was he thinking he could die like Vern? He pushed himself, carried a lot of stress. He'd already had a heart attack. Sure he exercised—unlike Vern—but John knew he ate bad food and ate it on the run. Jack looked afraid, deeply anxious. What was he thinking? He looked like he wanted to run out of the church and do something.

Jack got to his feet, said he needed to go. He'd see everyone at the visitation and the memorial service. And he was out the door, leaving silence in his wake. "He's taking it hard," said Kurt. "Funny," remarked Sam, "I never thought he was close to Vern."

"Well, we're all taking it hard," said Kirby, sounding pastoral. "How can we not? Vern was part of us. This group's been together a long time, longer than I've been pastor here. Sam and Kurt, it was twenty years ago you started, wasn't it?"

John listened as the men decided to do something as a group at the Saturday morning memorial service. Kirby as pastor was in charge and would do the meditation. They asked Sam to be their spokesman. They each gave him a story or a few phrases and trusted him to put them together into a brief tribute. When the time came in the service, they stood together in the chancel, behind the lectern, with hands on each others' shoulders. It seemed corny, but somehow it expressed male solidarity. Sam talked about how men love each other without saying it and made people laugh when, with a few deft phrases, he brought Vern's gifts and idiosyncrasies to life.

****

After the memorial service John saw Jack quickly leave the Fellowship Hall where people were lingering over coffee and refreshments, offering condolences to family members. When he went outside he found Jack waiting in his car in the parking lot. He pulled up next to John, and asked him to hop in and go to lunch with him. Surprised, John agreed.

"Where's your wife," John asked.

"She drove her own car. But there's a more complicated answer, actually."

They took a booth in the coffee shop near the church, and even before they ordered, Jack said, "You know the streets behind our apartment building on River Street? Not a great neighborhood, but it's in better shape than our building was. A bit run-down but people are still trying to keep the properties up. Those streets could go either way. I bought a small house about a block from the apartment building. Its yard backs on the back yard of our building. One of my crews is fixing it up. I'm going to move in there in two weeks."

He paused. John looked surprised and expectant. Jack went on, "Jenn and I are splitting up. She's moving to New York City."

"New York!"

"Yes. We got married young. She never finished college, had only one year. She's always wanted to be a teacher. She's bright as hell. Columbia University has this program for older returning students. Costs fifty grand, but we can afford it. It's a hell of a school for teachers. And she got in. She wants to finish her bachelor's and get a master's. She leaves in a month and a half. Neither of us have said, 'This is the end,' but we both know it probably is." The kids are grown. We're selling the big house—if we can in this market. If not, we may rent it for a while. I don't need all that space."

"Wait a minute. You're talking about space and houses. What about your feelings! This is huge! The end of a marriage of, what, 30 years. What does that feel like?"

"Well, hell, you know things are up for grabs with me. I don't know what the hell I'm doing or what to think. Or what to feel. I'm a doer, John. When something's not right, I fix it. When something needs to be done, I do it."

"You can't do or fix relationships."

"You're telling me," he paused, looked out the window. "The only thing I know is to do something. When things change, I do something different. So here's the deal. We keep working on the River Street project. I buy this little house, fix it up, see what it's like to live alone."

"Why buy a house there? I thought you had rich guy's tastes."

"I'm going to revitalize that neighborhood. I'm going to start with the apartment building and my little house. I'm going to start a neighborhood association. I know a guy downstate who did this. He bought an old house, redid it, lived in it for five years, and sold it at a reasonable price to a family of moderate income. He built a new house for himself, more house than that neighborhood can support, and he continues to live right there. He has bought and renovated more than twenty buildings, houses and two and four flats. Some he rents. Some he has sold to people of modest means. If people have trouble with financing, he helps them."

"Do you really know how to do all this?"

"I can sure as hell learn."

John laughed. "I like your spirit. But it looks to me like all this frenetic activity is an escape from your own pain and confusion."

"It probably is. But you tell me. Which is better—doing this or sitting on my ass and feeling miserable?"

"People who do one thing when they really should be doing this other thing often screw up."

"Do I look like a guy who's going to screw up?"

"How would I know that, Jack? I'm only getting to know you."

"Are you in with me on this?"

"What do you mean?"

"I'm looking for a partner in crime. My life is falling apart, so I'm going to have the adventure of my life."

"How do you know you won't blow all your money and lose your company?"

Jack looked John in the eye and smiled. "I don't think so. I may be confused. God knows I'm probably not in touch with my deep feelings, whatever the hell they are, but I'm not stupid. I've never lost money, and I don't intend to now."

Chapter 15 – Sam and Friends

Sam got a call from Hank, whose voice was muffled and speech slurred. He was in the hospital, he said, had just been through triple bypass surgery only 24 hours ago. Hank apologized for sounding confused, said he was on heavy medication. He couldn't talk long, but he wanted Sam to know. Sam wanted to know if he could come to visit and insisted he would come right away that night.

Hank was in intensive care in the cardiac care unit, propped up in bed, surrounded by beeping monitors and screens showing moving graphs, entangled in a spaghetti of tubes. He smiled and gave Sam his hand, which was soft and vulnerable under the callouses. His voice was rough from the tube that had just been removed and his throat was sore, but through the groggy speech he sounded like himself and even had a few feisty remarks about the nurses, who seemed to have an affection for him and to be vigilant in their care. Sam was feeling some guilt because Hank had had the operation without his even knowing about it.

Sam visited him regularly during his long hospital stay which included three weeks of rehab necessitated by the fact that Hank's health had been compromised by his years of heavy smoking. Sam went often to his house during the weeks of recuperation at home. One day two months after the surgery when Hank was allowed to begin driving again, they met in the cafeteria back at the hospital where Hank had come for a checkup. They sat in the sun in a large atrium-like area eating food that was better than the average hospital fare.

Sam looked across the table at this man who had been his friend for so long. Hank wanted to talk. "The nurse said when I was coming out of anesthesia, I was talking about people that I saw. I don't remember that. I don't remember anything except a feeling. I think I went somewhere while I was out. Somewhere good. I think I saw people that I know, people I loved."

"A near-death experience?"

"I don't know. I think I was pretty near death. The doctors and nurses aren't saying, but reading between the lines, I think I was in bad shape." Hank had been looking out the window. Now he turned and looked Sam in the eye. "I think I didn't want to come back. Maybe you think I'm crazy."

"You know better than that!" Sam exclaimed.

"I was angry for the next two days. I was too sick to show it, but underneath the pain and all the grogginess I was pissed off."

"Well, who wouldn't be after what you'd just been through?"

"Yeah, but this was more. I came this close!" He held up his thumb and forefinger. "You know there have been times when I wanted to go. You know what I mean. It wasn't wanting suicide. I was just tired of all this shit and wanted to get to the next place and see what that was all about, because it had to be better than this. I wanted to get closer to God.

"So you'd think I'd still feel that way. But now I want to stay here. Everyday has something good in it. I love sitting in the sun porch with my coffee in the morning and just looking out and seeing the wind in the trees and watching the birds crack open seeds and throw the shells on the ground and hear the neighbor's mower in the distance.

"I'm having dreams. I had one the other night where a person came to me and stood at the foot of my bed. She was filled with judgment. I felt like when I was kid and had all that guilt laid on me by the nuns. I was no good, and I was going to hell. No chance of goodness. Only pain and guilt and darkness. I woke feeling god awful. For the first time in years I was afraid of dying. Where the hell did that come from!"

Sam wanted to say something wise and reassuring, but false assurance and quick analysis were not wanted here. "How long ago was this? Are you still feeling frightened?"

"It was a few days ago. It shook me. I'm okay now."

"Let me get this straight. For years you've had a simple faith that God is good and the next life is a place you want to go to. Then you have an encounter under anesthesia that seems to confirm all this but you can't remember it and you're ticked off that you had to come back. And now you're having bad dreams that call all this into question. It doesn't make sense, Hank!"

"God is with me. I know it! I feel it. I write about it in my journal. He's all around me. In me. I can't even think of my life any other way. But why the hell would I have that dream!"

"All of us have bad stuff stuck in our memories and worse buried in our subconscious. That's where that dream came from. God didn't send it."

"It shook me!"

It was Sam's opinion that people involved in formal religious organizations often had no idea of the simple piety sometimes found in those who refuse to enter a church. Sam knew that Hank's Catholic upbringing had soured him forever, that Hank felt physically ill when he had to go to a wedding or christening. Hank believed that his own mother, if she were still living, would refuse to recognize him as a man of faith. The priests who taught him in grammar school and the seminary where he went for a few years wouldn't either, except for a few who had a kind of bone-marrow belief that withstood and lived below the expectations and predilections of the church. Hank hid his faith around religious people and secretly cherished his conviction that a lot of what they had to say was unexamined bullshit. He hated hypocrisy and thought that most actively religious people suffered from it. He was one of the few people Sam could talk to about faith with the sort of grit and candor usually reserved for sports.

"God, Hank, if we can't trust that God has our best interests at heart, then what do we do?' Sam exclaimed.

"The hell of it is that God is God. If he's not the good guy we want him to be, what can we do? We're stuck with him."

"But if he just does what he wants to do, if he messes with us, where does that leave us?"

"An old question. What Job wanted to know," Hank said. "Job's story is a hell of story, not really very reassuring. In the end he bows down and says God is God, who can do what he wants."

"All right," Sam said. "Here's my situation. I struggle for years taking financial risks, trying to practice this idea that still seems crazy to me that God is in the details, that God will provide. But I don't really have that faith so the experiment never works. I don't really know if God is helping me, providing. I muddle through and get deeper in debt. I call out in desperation, and this old guy gives me money to see how this faith thing works on the other side, when I have more money than I need. Where is God in that? Am I just a deluded man who gets lucky? Was God's hand somehow in the gift from this old man who doesn't believe in God?"

"Are you happy?"

"Hell, I don't know, Hank. Sure I am, I guess I have no worries. I'm immensely relieved. But what comes next. I don't know. If God is really moving behind this thing we call the 'real world,' then we are all living in delusion. We happily think we're running our own lives, when something else entirely is happening. We're so far removed, like city people who have lost all connection to the earth. We have no idea what's going on. Most of us really do think we are producing our own reality. A paradox: we talk about reality as though it is something hard and immutable outside of us, yet we believe we can control it and even produce it. We found the job we have. We earn the money we receive. We pay the mortgage, buy the groceries, drive the car, take care of the kids. We believe we have our lives under control. It's a measure of how good we are. The delusion is shattered only when something happens we can't control: death of a child, terminal illness, marriage breakup, loss of a job. Then things spin out of control. We look elsewhere for control. We're all fox-hole Christians, I'm afraid."

Hank shrugged, like this was too intellectual for this moment on this morning.

"You know my friends in the church. Good people, all of them. But we don't talk this way. I just wonder how many of them have this daily sense of providence." Sam paused. "Maybe more than I realize. I don't know. I've wanted to believe for a long time that God is in every minute. But I'm afraid to believe it because it may just be wishful thinking. No intelligent, well-educated person believes it, and even the religious people who do believe it, don't live by it. It's a preposterous idea!"

"Hell! I believe it. Something got me through my surgery."

"Yeah, but that was just good medical practice. God wasn't in that."

"I sure as hell hope he was in the surgeon's fingers and brain."

"How do you know that?"

"Well, maybe the whole fucking shebang has God in it! Every minute and molecule! Maybe God is the energy and life force that makes it all happen."

"So then, how do you pray to a life force?"

"Shit, I don't know. Maybe there is divine intelligence in every particle. We're just too dumb and impressed with our own intelligence to see it in other things. We are too fucking arrogant! Hell, I'm the wrong guy to say anything about this. I don't know a goddamned thing. I nearly died. When I did, I think I saw God, but I can't remember it. And now I'm plagued by these goddamned dreams!"

"Yeah," Sam laughed, "we had answers when we were young. Now we don't know anything."

But Sam was heartened, and he felt quietness stealing through him as he walked with Hank to the parking lot.

This was a day for meals with friends, and his next stop was Emma's where he was meeting Oliver Larkspur.

"I suppose you're tied in knots figuring out how to live with money," said the old man after they had made small talk and given their order to the waitress.

The usual lunch crowd was there, a few city workers, a couple of business people, and a soccer mom with two of her cronies, women whose husbands made enough money to permit them the freedom to do volunteer work and have leisurely lunches.

"People from your tradition, as I understand it," the old man went on, "are uneasy with wealth. Eye-of-the-needle anxiety. Jesus grew up a carpenter, owned nothing, and had some hard things to say about rich people. His disciples were working class guys. It was the rich—his own people and Romans—who wanted to get rid of him. The little people loved him. They're the ones who followed him. Well, there was Nicodemus and Joseph of Arimathea—what do we do with them? But all told, your New Testament is pretty hard on us rich people, which makes it all the more amazing that millions of Christians believe that wealth is how God rewards his followers. Frankly, I prefer honest greed. So how does it feel to be on the side of mammon?"

"You're baiting me. And how do you know so much about Jesus and the New Testament and our tradition?"

"I've told you before I have long conversations with my old friend Preston. He loves your church. He would never say 'love.' Preston doesn't go in for strong feelings, but deep down he has more passion than he admits to…"

"Do you always presume to know more about people than they know about themselves?"

"It's a bad habit, isn't it?" the old man laughed. "But as I was saying, Preston and I talk about these things a lot. He, because he's fascinated by my cheerful agnosticism and because, like anyone deeply rooted in a religious ethos, he needs occasional outside contact. And I, because I like his rock-ribbed integrity. That's one of the marks of your people. You have it too. I believe back a few generations you had the expression, 'Their word is as good as their bond.' You're all a bit serious sometimes, but on the whole pretty good company. But I want to know if the money is corrupting your soul. Did I doom you to live outside the kingdom of God?"

"It's too early to tell. I've spent these first weeks settling back taxes, paying all our bills, and buying some things we were putting off. And, I'm sorry to say that in this day in this economy having a half million is no longer being rich."

The old man laughed, "So you've downgraded my gift a bit."

"Hardly. It's been wonderful. To be free of anxiety. If we're careful the money that is left will go a long way toward preparing for our retirement."

"So you're going to secure your future?"

"That's what every prudent person would do."

"Are you a prudent person?"

"I don't know. No, I'm not if I practice the faith I've been flirting with. Basically, I believe that the whole creation operates on a deeper principle than the one we use to organize our economic life. If we live deeply rooted in God and are attentive and awake and engaged each moment of the day, the money and resources we need will come to us. But I'm afraid to live by that. Even my closest friends, in the church and out, would think I'm nuts. You know all this. We've talked about it before. If I lived by this, I would regard your gift as the resources that came for this day and this time and I would ask how I can use them now, not how I can assure my future security, and I would trust that the resources for that day will be there when I arrive at that future day. But, of course, I am afraid of that future. Eve and I have no children. Who will take care of us when we're old?"

The old man made no reply. There was a silence that grew more obvious.

"I know you're thinking something," Sam said. "You always are. I pour out my deepest soul struggle and you suddenly lose all speech. Is this a sign of disapproval? Or have I stunned you?"

The old man smiled, "The money has done one thing."

"What's that?"

"You speak your mind more."

"You think so?"

"Shouldn't you be 'nicer' to the old man who gave you all that money?"

"You're telling me that your money has made me less nice."

"More direct—a quality I like."

"Is that all you have to say?"

"For the moment, except that it is a privilege to be privy to your thoughts and struggles and that I am delighted to have given you the money."

"I'm living up to your expectations?"

"You are a man of integrity and I'm glad to know you, and I am glad that whatever else this money may do for you, it has lifted you out of your anxiety."

"So are you saying I'm a better person with the money—more honest, less anxious, bolder in speech."

"Those are good qualities, but it remains to be seen if you become a better person. You will have to tell me or show me, and I'm not sure how we judge that. This is not an experiment to see if I can improve your quality of life or your fineness of spirit. I really do want to know how money affects spirit. I have money and enjoy it and do not feel guilty about it, but I know enough of human history that there are people who eschewed money for very good reasons and became magnificent human beings because they did. I may seem to be an eccentric old man indulging his whims, but I do hope to learn something."

"Well, here I am, Sam Ellerby reporting in. I am afraid of this desire to create security. Can you really live with God if you are trying to ensure your future? You live in that future moment, not this one. The richness and possibility of the present is missed, and you really won't need God in the future either. You will have a good pension and fine investments."

"So God can't be in pensions and investments?"

"I don't know! I don't know! I want to find that out. Trouble is, the only way I can find it out is either to make the investments and see what happens now while I'm doing it and then when I reap the benefits. Or to use all your money up now in projects, good work, creative work, helping others—whatever I am led to do in each moment—and then see what I can find in those future moments when I'm old and have no retirement funds."

"I appreciate your dilemma."

Later that afternoon Sam drove to O'Hare to pick up Will who had a layover on a flight from Seattle to New York, one of those dogleg flights that save money. They went to a restaurant near the airport. Sam, full from lunch and thinking about the dinner still to come, only had coffee, while Will ordered salmon. As soon as the waitress left with their order, Sam took an envelope from his pocket and gave it to Will, who slit it open with the dinner knife, and looked up in surprise.

"It's twice what we lent you!"

"You were generous, and you trusted us when we needed generosity and trust. Meant a lot to both of us."

"Thank you very much for giving the $2,000 back, but I don't need a loan of another $2,000."

"It's not a loan. It's a gift."

"Why?"

Sam shrugged, "I don't know exactly. You know we came into a good bit of money. Frankly, I don't know what to do with it, but I have this sense that it's a mistake to hoard it. I think we need to give it away. Some of it, at least. I don't know how much of it. But I think we need to start and see where it takes us."

"Well, give it to someone who needs it."

"We will. We are. But I am thinking that money is not just a matter of meeting need. It's also a matter of fearless and even sometimes indiscriminate generosity. I know about your beautiful woodshop in your garage. Eve and I want you and Rae to spend this on something that will feed your creativity—woodworking, concerts, books. We are paying you back, but we are also seeing if spontaneous giving may be a lifestyle, may even be the way God intends human beings to live."

"What about saving for retirement?"

"Yeah, what about it!"

"Are you putting money aside for it?"

"I don't know."

"Are you serious?"

"I don't know."

"Doesn't this scare you?"

"Yes."

"What does Eve think?"

"I don't know that either. We are talking, but we are both unsure, feeling our way."

"You know how utterly peculiar this is!"

"So what are you saying?"

"I don't know whether to applaud or give you a careful warning."

"I think that's your call. It's the same question I have. How are we really meant to live?" Sam paused. "Here's my question? When is it good to hold on to money and when is it good to use it all up or give it all away and trust that more will come?"

Will shook his head.

"Have you ever wondered why people take risks with money? Think about the people who go bust, build a business back up, and then go bust again. Why do they do that? Most of us would say they like to live dangerously, but why would they want that? Maybe it's not a sickness. Maybe they know something we don't know—that life was meant to be lived without a safety net. Money was never meant to be hoarded and protected. Money was meant to be put into action. I know there's pathology in those who take crazy risks. Maybe they need to self-destruct. But aren't we all more alive when we risk everything for a larger purpose. That's the telling thing. We need a purpose. A big purpose. But even if it's a small purpose, like climbing a mountain or running a marathon, aren't we more alive when we put our money and energy into something rather than guarding and conserving it? So what's a big purpose? What is worth risking all?"

"You tell me."

"That's the answer," Sam said suddenly. "It's not whether I use the money or protect it. It's what to do with the rest of my life. When that's clear, won't the money question shake itself out?"

"Yeah, I agree. But what if the thing you want to do demands that you use up every penny you have? What then? That answer doesn't get you off this hook you're on."

Conversation flagged when the food arrived. After a bit, Will looked up from his salmon and gave Sam an intense, questioning look. "I should probably tell you something," he said. "Last week I was diagnosed with prostate cancer. My PSA is off the charts. It's an aggressive form of the cancer."

Sam put down his fork. He had an urge to reach across the table and take Will's hand. All the clichés ran through his head. Suddenly it was terribly important not to utter any of them. "I don't know what to say," he said lamely. "That's bad! Terrible news! You seem so chipper. You say it was only last week. Not enough time really to begin to deal with it. It's a damn shame! An aggressive form—what does that mean?"

"I won't die next month,"

"Well, that's a blessing," Sam said. "Can I ask—it is bad form to ask— is this terminal? I thought prostate cancer was treatable. Uh...have the doctors told you how long you have?"

"There are new treatments coming online all the time and new research going on. I could have anywhere from two years to fifteen. I'm starting a new drug next week. I'm flying to New York to attend a conference on the latest research. The conference is not for patients, but I talked my doctor into getting me in."

"You seem hopeful."

"If treatment can buy me two years or more, who knows what the research may produce."

"But what is this doing to you and to Rae? How are you handling it?"

"I don't really know how I'm handling it. Rae's worried, of course. I think she's putting on a brave face. I suppose the most honest thing to say is that it's not real yet. I'm trying to pay attention to myself. So far my body doesn't feel any different. I don't feel like I have cancer. I ride my bike every day. My appetite is good. I'm not afraid, except sometimes when I wake up in the morning."

"Do you think about dying? Do you think about what lies beyond death?"

"Not much. No, to the second question. Yes, to the first. I think about the people I love. I think about leaving them behind. My children and grandchildren—I'm afraid they will miss me. I think they still need me." Will shook himself, and let out a short, sharp laugh. "I'm not dead yet. This research is moving fast. I could end up living into my nineties."

Sam took out his checkbook and quickly scribbled a check. He tore it from the book and handed it to Will, who looked at it with astonishment.

"What is this! This is a lot of money!"

"I don't know what you're going through. How could I?" Sam said. "And God knows money has almost nothing to do with something like this. When people are facing death, they don't say, 'I wish I had more money'—unless they are leaving a burden of medical bills on their family, which you'll not be doing. They say simple clichéd things like 'I wish I'd spent more time with my family.' Or they think about the friend they've lost touch with. Or they remember the book they once wanted to write. Really, Will, I don't know what you think about when you face the possibility of your own death. And, yes, you could live to be ninety, and God knows, I hope you do. But this cancer will make you think about such things. When you do, use this money. Don't spend it on medical treatments—well, do, if you really want to. Do something that feeds your spirit. Anything. Throw a huge party for your family and friends. Go up in a balloon. Take Rae on a sybaritic vacation in the Caribbean. Do a silent retreat at a Trappist monastery. Barricade yourself in your den with stacks of books and DVDs and don't come out for a month. Fly to India and spend a month in an ashram. Take a leave from your job and volunteer at a homeless shelter. Go on a trip with all your grandchildren. Take your closest buddies backpacking in the Sierras or fly fishing in Montana. Anything that you've put in those compartments we all have that are labeled 'not enough time to do that' or 'not enough money' or 'too crazy.' Do those things."

Will laughed again. "This is crazy. I can't accept this."

"Why not?"

"I don't know. It's too much."

"So there's a sort of cosmic limit on gifts?"

"Well, maybe an emotional limit. Past a certain point the gift is embarrassing."

"You mean you feel undeserving?"

"Well, yeah. It's like it skews the friendship. So I suddenly feel beholden, and you become my benefactor, and no longer my friend. And we start to feel awkward with each other."

"Hell, Will, we only see each other about once a year, and that's after many years of not seeing each other at all. You can put up with that level of awkwardness."

Will stared at the check, shaking his head.

"Would you feel this way if I gave you a gift of $25?"

"There's a difference."

"Yes, because we measure everything by the amount of money it represents. The larger the amount the more impressed, even daunted, we are. I'm trying to change how I think about money."

"It's easier to do that when you have money."

"Yes, it is. But the reality is I have money now. So I'm going to find out. This check is coming from a far larger sum that was given to me. In just this unexpected and overwhelming way. Look at it as me passing on a much larger awkwardness and asking you to share in it."

"All right! I think I can live with that! Share the misery of money." Will laughed.

Sam had just enough time after taking Will back to the airport to drive home and pick up Eve and their casserole dish and head over to the Kurtzes'. This was Joe and Anne's first effort to entertain since the death of their son. The men from the breakfast group and their wives were invited. The women all knew each other and some were close friends. It was an easy crowd. Sam was looking forward to it. But there was just a little edge of anxiety because no one quite knew what this would be like for Joe and Anne. The first thing they saw in the Kurtzes' living room was a newly framed photo of Michael. Below it was small bronze plaque that read, "The speaking of Michael's name will always be welcome in this house."

Sam noticed that very soon after arriving, the men found themselves on the deck while the women gravitated to the kitchen and dining room laying out the various dishes. Sam smiled. These were all professional women, and their husbands were all, more or less, men who did not insist on old, conventional male roles. Still, invariably, the women ended up managing the food. They thought things would be done in a slapdash way if they didn't do them. Sam pointed this out to Eve one time and reminded her that, when the men went on one of their retreats, which they did from time to time, they somehow managed to put food on the table, and sometimes it was gourmet fare. Still there was this tacit agreement that if the women could not sit still and wait for the men to get around to helping, the men would be glad to take advantage of the food-prep gene that pot-lucks seemed to trigger in their wives and let them do the work.

Sam overheard the women, who seemed more at ease talking of grief, ask Anne about the large photo of Michael and the bronze plaque. She answered that many people didn't realize bereaved parents wanted to hear people talk about the child who died. Friends and family sometimes said nothing, and it was as if the child never existed. Anne began to cry and the women gathered around her. She looked up at Janet Keller who had been invited because Vern had been a member of the breakfast group. Suddenly surfacing from her own grief, she went to Janet and embraced her. The two women cried in each other's arms while the other women gathered in close in sort of a large embrace. Sam and the other men heard the sobs and saw the women through the glass deck doors. They stopped talking, and to break the silence, Kirby asked Joe about the photo and he said much the same things Anne had said.

"What do you do to get through your days?" Sam asked.

"A friend I met in our bereaved parents group says he has to do so many units of grief every day. He says if he doesn't, he gets sick, loses focus, can't work, gets depressed. I know it probably sounds odd, but I try to make room for my grief. I spend some time every morning. I write about my feelings. I look at pictures of Michael. I give space to even the worst feelings of emptiness and despair and anger. There is a vast yearning. I cry a lot. There is this relentless feeling that this is all wrong. It should not have happened! I have this old CD from *Les Miserables*. I put it on when I'm driving, when I'm alone, and I cry and I pound the steering wheel. I watch my driving. Yeah, I'm doubly careful because I'm not driving well. I don't care sometimes. I'd just as soon be dead so I could be with Michael, so I try to compensate, drive slower, look more carefully."

The guys were listening so intently they did not hear the doorbell, and only realized that Jack Foster had arrived when they heard his voice through the doorway. When he stepped onto the deck they saw that Jenn had come with him and was inside with the women. Sam could not hide his surprise.

"What! You think it's weird that we came together? Well, we're not going to divide up our friends, and say you get the breakfast guys, you get the church people. You're stuck with both of us. We're separating, not planning mutual mayhem. We get along better, actually, since Jenn decided to move to New York. We thought it might be awkward to come here together, but hell, why not? Once you make yourself painfully public, which a separation always does, what do you have to lose?"

"That's good," Joe said. "Let there be no bullshit in death or divorce!"

The men laughed, but a bit self-consciously.

"Really," Joe went on, "I am miserable most of the time, but I can still laugh. It may seem strange, but all the other emotions don't really go away. They are buried sometimes, swamped really, but they are still there. So don't handle me with kid gloves and don't pussyfoot around Jack and his separation or divorce or whatever it ends up being."

"All right," boomed Kurt.

"That's not license to be assholes," Joe snapped back with a smile.

"By God, it's good to see you smile!"

Sam was watching John Engelsinger, who was the only one other than Janet Keller without a mate or date, and he was the new guy as well, wondering if John felt left out. He glanced at the women through the doorway who were still surrounding Anne and Janet.

"John, you know something about grief, yourself," Sam said.

"How could I forget that?" Joe exclaimed.

"We do forget it," said Kurt. "We know you as a single guy. We never knew your wife. It's like out of sight, out of mind. I just don't think about the fact that you are a widower."

John smiled and shrugged. "That's an old-fashioned word. Do we say Janet is a widow? Somehow that doesn't capture the reality. It feels different to lose your mate in the 21st century."

"Really," Jack exclaimed. "How is that?"

"Those terms, 'widow' and 'widower' came from a time when people died in a community. You had a role in that community. You had to be identified as the one whose mate died. That became your identity. But Janet works in a real estate office. Her colleagues and customers didn't know Vern and won't call her a widow, though they're probably aware of her loss and may offer condolences. Some don't even care as long as she does her job. After my wife died, I sold everything, pulled up roots, and moved out here. You don't think of me as a widower. I'm the new guy who's on this late-in-life search. There's no social context for me, at least not yet."

"Still, I wish I'd known your wife," Joe said. "Then we'd know you better and could understand what you've lost, instead of not even thinking about it."

"I wish you had known her too. You would have liked her. She was beautiful. Well, I thought so. I think others might have called her cute.

Smart, full of energy. Good figure." John paused, almost blushed. "I mean she had the right things in the right places. You know what I mean."

The men smiled and nodded.

"She was my only love. I fell for her in college. It didn't work out. I was miserable. I ran away to Chicago. Came back home. Took over the family farm. Years passed and then our paths crossed again. This time I knew a little bit more about wooing and had a little more confidence. To tell you the truth, I think I was always a bit more crazy about her than she for me."

"John, that's not true!" Kirby jumped in. He looked around the circle, "I knew both of them from college days." Turning back to John, he said, "You can be dense sometimes. That woman adored you."

John smiled, obviously pleased. "I'll take your word for it. I miss her every day. It's been three years and it's gotten a little easier."

"Tough question but someone's got to ask it" said Kurt, "Have you begun to date anyone?"

John laughed a bit nervously. "Not dating exactly."

"What do you mean 'not exactly'?

"There are two women I see from time to time. Nothing serious."

"Oh. Do we know either of them?"

"Maybe, maybe not," John laughed. "But I don't think I want to tell you and listen to your wisecracks!"

"It's someone we'd wisecrack about?"

"That's not what I meant."

"Let the poor guy alone," Sam said with a smile. "We've moved him from widower to playboy in under five minutes."

"We love you, John. You know we do." Kurt said. Everyone laughed, and Sam thought to himself that John really was in.

The men drifted back inside and people queued up for food and spread out in the living room and dining room and out on the deck in small mixed groups of men and women.

Sam made a point of finding a chair next to John. "I'm glad you're out here in Selby, glad you're in our group."

John gave a short laugh. "You don't know how glad I am to be here."

"Really. I thought you valued your roots."

"My roots, yes. But not the rest. I didn't belong any more. I could have moved to another congregation, one of the progressive churches in the area. But that would have seemed odd. I confess I'd have had trouble explaining it to people. I didn't have the courage. It would have been a rejection. Pulling up stakes and moving out here is too, but it doesn't look like it. People can believe I wanted a change of place. I did—do—want that, but I wanted to get away from a church life that was stifling me. It's hard to say that to people you've known all your life, or I should say the next generation, the kids of people you've known, who in a curious way have become more conservative than their parents and grandparents. Nancy Beahm's dad is a prime example. One of my all-time favorite people. A farmer. One of the most open-minded people I know. His kids, Nancy's siblings, are more conservative, more uptight about the 'family values' issues, more worried about getting the Bible right than he is. Nancy's the only one like her dad. He's 94, still as sharp as ever. He's coming out for a visit with Kirby and Nancy. He was like a dad to me after my own dad died when I was sixteen. I miss him."

Sam listened to this with great interest. He wanted to know more about John's break with his own people—what he thought about "getting the Bible right," what he thought about God, which is not a question you bring up at a potluck, even one where the people are all members of a church that prides itself on having an open spirit. But Sam felt bold and without thinking much, he suddenly asked, "Are you a person of faith?"

"Christ!" Sam heard John mutter under his breath.

"Was that an imprecation or a prayer?" Sam asked.

"I don't know. I don't make a habit of swearing like that. A 'damn' or even an 's-o-b' now and then, but I have too much respect for Jesus to, as they used to say, take his name in vain. I don't know where that came from."

"Did my sudden question offend you?"

"No, just the opposite. It was immensely appropriate."

"Really. Maybe we need to talk."

"Maybe we do.

"How about coffee, tomorrow, say, 4 p.m."

"Sounds good."

The two men turned to others nearby. The party ran on until almost midnight. Everyone was at least middle-aged, so their kids were either grown or old enough to be at home without a sitter. Sam was grateful for this circle of friends. He watched Joe and Anne. He could see that just being themselves with others, in an ordinary way was healing. He thought the people in the group were especially free and comfortable that night and he thought it had something to do with the fact that they'd started the evening with tears and words about grief and separation. Even good and sensitive people could stay on the surface, unless something pushed them deeper. Life was richer, Sam thought, when it was lived on a deeper and more honest level. How easy, almost natural, it was to avoid this.

Chapter 16 – John's Decisions

The next morning John had just gotten out of the shower and was dressing. He'd turned the air conditioner off and opened the windows and doors, and he was enjoying the fresh morning breeze which carried away some of the stale odor. He had just gone into the kitchen, which was like an alcove off the livingroom, to make some breakfast when there was a knock on the screen door. It was David. He asked the boy in, who said his mother has sent him over to invite John to come next door for breakfast.

John smiled to himself. Maggie had an uncanny ability to sense trouble and to divert it by redirecting attention. Later in the morning John was going to have to tell her that if she didn't pay her rent, she would have to leave. She was still five months behind. He did not want to do this. He'd put her in touch with the township office, which made small grants to people facing eviction.

"Tell your mom thank you and that I'll be right over," he said. David lingered in the doorway. John sat on the arm of the sofa and asked him how he was. He gave his standard answer, "I'm okay. I'm good." John said he had not seen him yesterday and asked what he'd been doing. David answered that he'd been watching *Star Wars*. David had put all six movies on his birthday list. John had been planning to get him the six-volume set, but Maggie had bought it for him. John wondered at the time where she'd gotten the money. He knew that if she had any money at all, she would spend it on David. John knew enough about the movies to ask a few questions, and David was eager to talk. When John's questions showed his ignorance, David corrected him in a tone that indicated he could hardly imagine how anyone could not know. John said, "If your mom is making breakfast, she's expecting us. We'd better go." John stepped by him and opened the screen door. David seemed reluctant to follow.

The screen on Maggie's door had a rip in it that had not been there before. The inner door stood open. John could smell toast and saw that a plate of scrambled eggs stood on the table congealing. Beside it on a smaller plate were two pieces of burnt toast. The table had been set. Milk had been poured for David. Two mismatched kitchen chairs had been pulled up to the makeshift table.

"Where's your Mom?" John asked.

David shrugged and looked down the short hallway to the closed bedroom door. In the silence John heard something. He was not sure what it was. And then he realized it was sobbing.

"Is your mom okay?" he asked David.

In the look he gave John there was understanding beyond his years. "She's in the bedroom."

John wanted to ask the boy if there was something he could do. He knew David had been through this many times before. But he was unwilling to place that burden on the boy.

"I'll go back there and talk to her."

"She won't let you in."

"I think I have to try." John walked back to the door and knocked lightly, "Maggie, are you alright? Is there anything I can do?"

"No, nothing."

"What happened?"

"It's nothing," Maggie answered in a small voice. "Please go away. I'm sorry." She sobbed. "I can't do it today. I'm sorry I asked you to come over. I'll make you breakfast another day. Please go away and leave me alone."

"Maggie. Can't I help? It sounds like you need help."

"No! I don't need help!" she said, suddenly angry." Go away and leave me alone." Then she became contrite and apologized. "I'm sorry. I'm sorry. This is a really bad day for me. I have to get myself together. I can't talk to you right now. I'm sorry," She sobbed.

"Maggie, what happened?"

"Can't you see that I don't want to talk?"

"I do see that, but sometimes that's when someone needs another person to talk to. What happened?"

Maggie went into a series of heart-wrenching sobs. "I wanted it to be right. I just couldn't get it right."

"What?"

"I burned the toast and the eggs are soggy. I just couldn't get it right."

David whispered to John, "She gets stuck sometimes."

"David, is that you?"

"Yes, Mom."

"David, eat some of the eggs that are on table. I'm sorry about the toast. I'll fix you some more later."

"Maggie, let me help," John said.

"No, no, please just let me alone," she said in a pleading voice, sniffing and inhaling in bursts as she tried to control her sobbing.

"I can't just go away, Maggie. David needs someone to be with him."

"I'll be all right," David said manfully.

John thought for a moment. "Maggie, I'm going to take David into my apartment. We'll take some of the eggs so he can have breakfast. I'll keep him there until you're feeling better. Okay?"

Maggie answered in a voice full of sadness and defeat.

Next door, John made some toast. David sat at the table and ate the eggs and toast. "My mom makes really good eggs," he said. "They're good even when they're cold."

"I should have warmed them up in the microwave."

"It's okay. My mom doesn't like microwaves. Your toast is good, too," David said, as if remembering his manners.

"You don't have to say that," John said laughing. "You don't have to like my toast."

"It's good. It really is," David repeated.

John laughed again and then he began to laugh harder. His laughter was infectious and David had to smile and then chuckle. "Why are you laughing?"

"This conversation seems so"—John hesitated, searching for the word—"inconsequential. You probably don't know what that means, do you? Stupid and meaningless, small. You're Mom's over there sobbing and we're talking about toast!" As he said it, he thought he was talking over the boy's head, but David seemed to get the irony and he gave John a big smile and took a large and obvious bite of his toast.

John and David went out on the second floor porch that ran the length of the building. They sat on two old molded gray plastic chairs and propped their feet on the metal railing. With his shirt open to show his t-shirt David looked very adult slouching in the chair and resting his heels on the metal. All he needed was a cigarette and a hard hat, John thought, to look like a shop steward taking a break on the factory floor.

"So, what are we going to talk about?" David said.

"What do you want to talk about?"

"I don't know."

"Well, that doesn't help much."

David gave John a withering look that made him smile.

"Are you a tough guy?" John asked.

David, suddenly sober, shook his head. "Quentin thinks *he* is."

Quentin was David's close friend from the neighborhood. "Is he being nasty to you again?" John asked.

"Not really. He called me a girl because I cried a little when I fell off my bike and skinned my knee. My mom says that's what Quentin's big brothers say to him and he's just passing it down. My mother says it's all right to cry."

"What do you think?"

David thought for a moment. "It's okay, I guess. But I don't want Quentin to see me."

"Well, your Mom's right," John said.

"When am I right?" came a voice from inside the apartment. The door opened and Maggie stepped out. She was so thin her collar bones stood out against her tank top straps. Her drawn face was red and splotchy from crying. She had pulled her hair back and pinned it up.

"David was saying that you tell him it's all right to cry and I was agreeing."

"Good," said Maggie tussling David's hair. "I'm glad your momma can do something right." David leaned into this mother's caress and then pulled away.

There was an awkward silence before Maggie said, "I really am sorry. This is just not a good day for me. I'm better now. I need some time today to get my shit together. I know you want your rent money. I'm working on it. I'll have some of it soon."

John was pretty sure that Maggie had no money and no plan, but he was not going to say that. "Can you give me an idea how soon?"

"Friday. I'll have something Friday."

"Well, then, okay. Friday it is."

John offered to take David with him on some errands later in the afternoon. David seemed to want to come, but Maggie thanked John and said they had things to do.

****

It was 10 a.m. and John still had not had breakfast, except for the piece of toast he'd eaten with David. He was looking forward to picking up Nancy's dad and taking him to lunch. He decided to take a chance and go early. Eagerly he drove over to the Beahm's. Kirby was at the church, and Nancy had to be in her office to get ready for school to start, so it was Wilbur who came to the door.

"Vell, Chon, come in," said Wilbur, his Pennsylvania Dutch accent particularly strong. John thought Wilbur sometimes turned the accent on for effect. John stepped in and stood awkwardly for a moment. He wanted to hug Wilbur and leap with pleasure. He gave Wilbur his hand instead, trying to put into the handshake all this conscious and unconscious joy. The old man smiled. As always, John felt that Wilbur knew more than he let on.

"Are you hungry? I am. I never had breakfast. Are you ready to go?" The old man nodded and they drove in companionable silence. "What are you hungry for? Hamburgers? A sub? Pizza? Italian? Chinese? There's a place that has the best malts in the world."

"Sounds goodt to me."

"Which?"

"Vhy the malts, I believe."

At Emma's after they ordered, Wilbur said, "Nancy toldt me you have a girlfriend."

John laughed. "Did she say that? What else did she say?" "Vell, she didn't exactly say, but I believe the girl must be a looker."

John laughed again, "I don't think Nancy quite approves. It's not the woman she tried to set me up with."

"Yes, vell, Nancy likes to manage people a little."

John could hear the humor and appreciation in this remark.

"So tell me about her."

"First, she's not a girlfriend."

"Nancy thinks she is"

"And she's not a girl. She's in her early 50s."

The food arrived and John saw that Wilbur had not lost his farmer's appetite. John had read somewhere that people eat less when they get really old and he'd seen that with his own mother. Wilbur was 94, though he looked ten years younger. He had ordered a Reuben sandwich like he knew what he was doing, and this surprised John. He wondered when Wilbur had developed a taste for deli food. The old man was tucking away the corned beef, the dark rye, the French fries, and a malt like he was a teenager.

"Isn't that heavy food bad for you?" John asked.

"If I eat it every day."

"So you're on a vacation from your diet."

"No diet. I chust eat vegetables mostly at home and some chicken and fish."

"No beef?"

"Not much."

"Wilbur, the vegetarian! Who would believe that!"

"The girl, Chon. I vant to hear about the girl."

"Woman?" John said and Wilbur smiled.

John described Angela to Wilbur, and he stumbled when he tried to say what she looked like. It was like discussing sex with your dad.

"So she's got it vhere she shouldt?" Wilbur said helpfully.

"Yes, I think you could say that."

"Is she nice?"

John talked about her teaching and her unusual interest in mysticism. He ended up telling Wilbur about her history with men, his intense attraction, his uncertainty. It all poured out of him, surprising him. He felt like a kid.

"Did you go to bedt with her?"

"Wilbur! What kind of question is that?"

"Vell, did you?"

John laughed. "I'm sixty-two years old, Wilbur. Does it matter?"

"It does to you."

"Does it to you?"

"Maybe."

"What do you mean 'maybe'?"

"Vhat do you mean?"

"Wilbur, we're going in circles."

"Chon, does this matter to you?"

"Yes, but you didn't ask me if I want to marry her. Shouldn't someone from your generation be asking *that* of someone still young enough to be your son?"

"Things change, Chon."

"Are you saying I should have sex with her?"

"Vhat do you vant?"

John hesitated. "Yes, I want to have sex with Angela. I admit it. The kids today would say she's hot. Did you ever want a woman just because she turned you on."

"Miriam."

"Miriam? Nancy's mom?"

"Chon, when she was a girl, she was…" he hesitated, "she was 'hot'." John had never seen Wilbur blush. The old man seemed to take pride in never showing any sort of discomfiture. But he did pause here. "Chon, you only saw Mim when she vas wore out and used up. She was beautiful once. Remember Nancy when she was a girl. Mim was even more beautiful."

John had never heard Wilbur talk about his wife. He assumed he bore her weakness and depression like a saint.

"I shoulda treated her better," the old man said flatly.

"Wilbur, you never mistreated your wife. Just the opposite. We all knew how you took care of her."

"Ve hadt to get married," the old man said. "I bet you never knew that."

John laughed, "When I was fifteen, just before he died, my dad said one time that I'd be surprised how many people in the church had to get married. For a long time I thought it was Melinda and Fred, because I knew how wild Geraldine, their daughter was. So it was you that dad was talking about.

"Others too."

"Wilbur, you're breaking my heart!" John laughed. "You're telling me the church was a hotbed of sex."

"Chust being human."

"Wilbur, do you regret your marriage?" John thought how brazen that question was.

"No. Not the sex. Not being together before we got married."

"Do you mean there is something you regret?"

"I didn't love Mim enough."

"Wilbur, you can't blame yourself."

"Ve hadt four kids right in a row. I was working day and night. I chust didn't see what Mim needed. Until it was too late. She never came back." He stopped, and for the first time John saw tears in this tough old man's eyes. "She was a pistol vhen I met her. I vas crazy about her. I couldn't get enough of her. I chust didn't know how to help her become a woman. She never didt. She chust faded avay."

"Wilbur." John reached across the table and put his hand on the old man's thick work-hardened hand. He was filled with wonder and affection. How he loved this old man! It was a privilege to hear this tender confession—from this man whose strength seemed to come from the hills and fields and from God himself.

"Chon, sex is goodt. It's wonderful. It's okay one way or another. It's the love that matters."

"I know that. I do."

"Vell, do you love this girl?"

"The truth, Wilbur? You want the truth? I've been saying to myself that I don't want to be just another lover, like those other guys who loved her and left her. Truth is, I'm afraid she'll leave *me*. She's had all those men. Wilbur, Mary is the only woman I've been with. I knew she would be faithful. It was in her bones to have only one man. Angela's never had a relationship like that."

"Do you like everything else about her?"

"I think I do."

"Vell."

"Well, what."

"Chon, I'm oldt."

"Yes."

"Church people like me like to make small things big and big things small."

"Yes."

"Vell, we make sex too big. And we don't love enough."

"So what are you saying here? That I should have sex with her and not worry? That I should wait till I am sure I love her? That if I love her, I should not worry whether she will leave me?"

Wilbur shrugged. "Chust don't be afraid."

They left the restaurant and John drove into Chicago. He took Wilbur to the top of the Willis Tower. They looked out over the city. It was a clear day and they could see all the way to O'Hare, where they could make out the landing patterns, the planes going in lines as many as seven planes long. He walked around and looked at the vista at each compass point. "It's a lot of life," was the only thing he said. They walked up to Millennium Park. He walked stiffly and with a bowlegged gait, bending his knees carefully. He insisted on walking, saying that the air and exercise were good for him. He stood and watched the five-story-high video images change and grinned when the water spouted from their mouths. When he looked at the skyline reflected and distorted in the great silver "bean," he remarked that he knew people who saw the world that way. They drove to Hyde Park and looked at the University of Chicago campus, where Wilbur surprised John by saying that he'd like to know what went on in the heads of the people there.

"Did you ever wish you'd studied at a place like this?"

Wilbur smiled and made no reply and continued to peer out the car window at the gray gothic buildings. John wondered, as he often had through the years, what Wilbur was thinking.

Wilbur's grown grandchildren, Nancy & Kirby's children, had arrived while John and Wilbur were on their Chicago jaunt, and they greeted their grandfather enthusiastically when John brought him back to the Beahm home. John made a hurried good-bye and was turning to the door when he felt Wilbur's hand on his arm. The old man said nothing but he held John's arm in his powerful grip, looked into his eyes with just the whisper of a smile, let go his grip, and gave John's arm a small pat.

****

John had enough time to drive to the Athens House where he and Sam were to meet for coffee. They were just seated in the booth and the waitress had taken their order when Sam asked John why he pulled up stakes and came to the Chicago area. John started to give his usual explanation, which was beginning to bore him. He stopped and said to tell the truth he wasn't sure anymore why he'd come.

"You know how you can do something and you're sure you know why and then when you get fully into it you find yourself doing things and thinking things and feeling things that you never expected and you begin to wonder if those don't show you hidden reasons you'd never considered."

"Like what."

"I thought I was coming here because I no longer felt I belonged at home. But I'm wondering now if I really wanted to find another mate. I can't tell how important that is to me, but it's more than I thought when I moved. I thought I was glad to get rid of property, and now I'm helping renovate and manage an apartment building. I thought I wanted to be free of community, but here I am getting involved in your church, maybe being pulled into Jack's idea for community living."

John saw that Sam was surprised. He said he hadn't heard about this. He wanted to know more. John told him how Jack seemed to have a new idea every day and explained Jack's plan to move into the neighborhood where the apartment building was and try to redevelop that whole community.

"Last week he started talking about co-housing,' John went on. "Do you know the concept— where people own their own place but have land and property in common? They do some things together like sharing lawn equipment and laundry facilities or even a community van. There's generally a large common space where they meet once or twice a week for common meals. They even have guest rooms and entertainment areas that everyone may use.

"The idea interests and intrigues me," John said, "but it makes me uneasy."

"It's one thing to be good friends and fellow congregants," Sam commented, "it's another to share property and money. And you say Jack, of all people, is considering this!"

"Yes, he's serious. For myself, I don't know. I'm not sure I want to live so close to other people," John said, "but I like the thought that when I get really old, there would be people around to keep an eye on me. Maybe I won't have to go to a retirement home."

Sam asked how the co-housing thing worked, and John explained that Jack was "retrofitting." "The community will be created with already existing homes. Some co-housing groups begin by buying property and designing independent living units, which surround the common area and are connected to it. The buildings are put on one section of the larger site, so there's plenty of green space left. In an older neighborhood like Jack's, the members buy homes on the same street or around a cul-de-sac. They open up the yards to make large green spaces; and they own one house together that holds the guest rooms and shared areas.

"Jack already owns the apartment building and a small house he bought for himself," John continued.

"Does Jack have any interested families?" Sam wanted to know.

"No, not yet. Why? Are you interested?"

"I might be. I want to see what Eve thinks. Would Jack talk to us?"

"He's talking to me. Why not ask?"

****

This conversation puzzled John because it ended quickly, and Sam never seemed to get to what he had said the night before he wanted to talk about. John pulled out of the restaurant parking lot, and instead of driving home, he headed west into the countryside. Living closely with other people—how would that work? He pictured endless meetings to make community decisions. Did he really want to share a common meal or two every week? Did Jack have any idea what he was doing? He was a babe in the woods when it came to community building. Jack was a bricks-and-mortar man.

And what was he himself doing, John wondered, living in a rundown, foul-smelling apartment building which was nothing like the farm and the stone house where he and Mary had lived? What was he doing flirting with Angela? When he was with Wilbur, he'd felt out of sync, his old life and his new life intersecting.

"I'm an old guy. Past 60," John thought to himself. "I don't get nervous about myself. I've earned the right never again to feel scared. I can be what I am and whatever I want to be. I know who I am. Why do I have this anxiety? I feel like a college student again. I don't need this. I can stay here. I can have sex with Angela. Or not. Or a relationship with Vi, for that matter, if she'd have me. I can move back home. I can live in this god-forsaken apartment. I am free. I can get in my van and head out and never come back here or anywhere. So why am I disturbed?"

The thought of getting into his van and driving away came just as he found himself among the cornfields of northern Illinois, and it launched a fantasy of buying a camper and heading out across country like Steinbeck did so long ago or like Jesus. Become an itinerant. He smiled at the ridiculousness of that. Jesus in an RV. Why did he want to run away? For a brief moment he felt real desperation. He had to get a grip. He reminded himself who he was. John Engelsinger. Good guy. Deep roots. Steady. Dependable. Able to commit. Bereaved husband. Someone people liked and trusted. Wise. He paused in this inner flow. Yes, he had wisdom. That wasn't tooting his own horn. He was smart about people, honest about himself. He began to calm down. He pulled off into a small forest preserve along the highway and stopped under the trees. He got out and sat on a bench, hunched over, his arms dangling between his legs. He took some deep breaths and tried to relax. Slowly the tension drained out of him. He sighed and got back into his van. He felt empty as he drove back into town, but at least the anxiety was gone.

He had no sooner gotten to his apartment than David rapped on the screen door.

"My mom asked if you would come over; she wants to talk to you."

"How come she sent you and didn't come herself?"

David shrugged.

John followed the boy out and into the next-door apartment. Clothes and school papers and Lego pieces were scattered on the floor. Dishes were in the sink. The makeshift table had a bowl of grapes and a half-eaten sandwich. The TV was on and Maggie was sitting on the loveseat, which was the only real piece of furniture, watching a movie on DVD. Maggie switched off the TV and DVD player with the remote and got to her feet.

"I'm sorry. It's a little messy. I've had a lot to deal with and I got a little behind."

"What's up?" John asked.

"Uh, I have something to ask you. Uh, I know it's asking a lot, and it's okay if you say no. See, I have this job possibility at this place in Arizona. It's called Nature's Alternatives. They grow everything organically and they give workshops on how to use only organic and raw vegetables and fruits and herbs. And this is tied in with meditation and yoga. I am using some of their methods and it's really helping me get my head on straight.

They have a job working in the garden and helping to prepare the food in the kitchen. It's only for four weeks, but it pays pretty well and I can take the workshops for free. I've been talking with them on the phone and they told me I can have the job. It starts next week. I'll be able to earn enough to pay two months back rent.

"Uh, so I wondered can I move out of this apartment and store my stuff in the basement. I'd need more space than my storage area down there. But then you could get into the apartment and start working on it, and I'm not falling behind another month in rent and you'd be getting two months' rent which puts me three months behind, not five. Maybe when I get back I can move temporarily back into one of the other empty apartments until I can find something else."

Maggie said this with the earnestness and seeming good sense that made talking to her confusing. She walked back and forth in her bare feet on the ratty carpet, her face alight with possibility, though her eyes were sad. John stood, somewhat awkwardly, because there really was no place to sit down except on a pillow on the floor. That's where David sat, watching his mother intently and every so often giving John an inquiring look.

"Maggie, I have to think about it. I guess it seems like a good plan. "How are you getting to Arizona?"

"I'm going to drive."

John knew the state of Maggie's old Honda. "Can your car make it that far? What are you going to do if it breaks down?"

"I don't think it will. I'm going to have a guy I know at the garage down the street check it out. He said he'd do it for $25 if I bring it in early before the place opens."

John said nothing, thinking.

"Uh, there's something else," Maggie said. "I don't know how to ask. I know this is asking a lot. And it's okay, it's really okay if you can't do it." John happened to look at David and saw that he was watching him intently. "You see, David doesn't want to come to Arizona, and there really isn't a place for him there. They don't want someone with a kid. Which is really shitty." Maggie launched into a rant about how no one knows how hard it is to be a single parent. "But you don't want to hear all that," she said, "Uh, what I really want to ask is if…and I know this is asking a lot, a lot…but I wanted to ask if David could stay with you while I'm gone. Before you say anything, I want you to know that this was David's idea, not just mine."

John felt David's eyes on him, and he knew that how he reacted, what he showed on his face was really important to this boy.

"We talked about David staying with one of his friends, but that really wouldn't work out. David feels that he wouldn't be welcome for that long. He feels bad about imposing on people. He likes you a lot and trusts you. And he'd be able to stay right here so it would be like still being in his own home, and I wouldn't have to worry because I know you and trust you and know that you care about David."

Instead of showing his dismay, he turned to David and smiled, "So you'd like to stay with me? Do you think you could stand me all the time, not just now and then? I'm a tough guy to live with, you know."

David breathed out as though he'd been holding his breath and grinned. He nodded and then looked quickly at his mom, checking to be sure it was okay to show enthusiasm.

"Maggie, this is a lot to digest. I'd love to have David stay with me, but," he turned to David, "I'm old enough to be your grandpa. I have to think about whether I have enough energy to keep up with you."

"I won't be any trouble," David said.

John laughed, "I know that. You're a really good guy. I think I'll be able to do it, but you have to give me a little time to think about whether I can. Maggie, let me think about this, and about your proposal for what to do with your things while you're gone. I'll let you know tomorrow. Oh, and David, thank you. It's a compliment that you think enough of me to want to stay with me."

Back in his own apartment John sighed and sat down to digest what had just happened. Maggie had neatly maneuvered him. Now, the decision wasn't just about saying yes or no to her leaving and going to Arizona. He really had no illusions about that. It was about disappointing a sensitive young boy. He was pretty sure Maggie would go anyway, and that she knew he knew that. He would not put David through being dragged along to Arizona. He could not say no because he could not break trust with this boy he'd come to care about.

Now, his earlier anxieties seemed academic. He laughed at the idea that he had the luxury to be confused. Taking care of a child certainly focused your self-understanding. He shrugged at the thought that he was free. Was anybody ever really free when you lived with others? That late afternoon flirtation with going on the road—what a false view of freedom! Was he free or not? Did it matter? There were people all over the world who would never have the leisure even to ask the question.

John walked out onto the porch. He heard the sounds of a Star Wars movie through the torn screen next door. He looked at the moon through the tree branches. It was a pleasant night. The humidity of past days had dropped. He went to the end of the porch and down the steps to the sidewalk. He turned west and began to walk. He crossed the river on the George Street Bridge and wandered aimlessly along the streets. This part of town was safe but he stayed on the main thoroughfares with bright streetlights until he was far away from the river and in the neighborhoods of well-kept bungalows and large old frame houses. His eyes saw the flower beds and well-trimmed bushes, the neat driveways and the trees carefully circled with mulch, and here and there he caught a glimpse of decks at the sides of houses with deck furniture and umbrellas and gas-fired grills under protective gray coverings. The moon silhouetted the trees and the street lamps threw patterns of light and shadow on the sidewalks and driveways. His eye took all this in, but it did not really register. Much of the time he just looked at the sidewalk in front of him. He'd been walking for an hour when he realized he was at the end of Angela's street. Peering down the block he could see that her light was still on. He looked at his watch. It was only ten o'clock. It seemed later. He knew she was often up late reading student papers. He was drawn to the house like a moth to a flame. He hesitated on the step, suddenly uneasy. He almost turned and ran. He shook himself, shrugged to loosen his shoulders, and rang the doorbell.

He heard Angela coming to the door. It opened a crack, and he saw it was still on the chain. He could see half her face through the opening. Her eyebrow lifted in surprise, and then she smiled, undid the chain, and opened the door. She took him by the arm and ushered him in and closed the door. She looked at him carefully, then reached up and kissed him. His arms went around her almost of their own volition and he held her close. He remembered how good it felt to be held. She was wearing only a dressing gown and he could feel every part of her through the clothing.

"Why are you here?" she asked.

"I don't know. I started walking and I ended up on your doorstep."

She smiled, "Well, come in." She turned to take him into the back of the house to her den where she'd been working.

"Wait," he said and turned her to him, taking her in an embrace and touching his lips to hers, at first lightly and then with sudden energy and desire.

She returned the kiss with quick interest, then pulled back a bit and peered at him. She said nothing but her eyes held a question.

He made no answer but he gently traced her lips with the tip of his finger and let it trail over her cheek, around her ear, and down the side of her neck. He kissed her on her brow and then bent down and very delicately kissed the soft place where her neck and shoulder met. She closed her eyes and arched her body. Very softly she extricated herself, took his hand, and led him to her bedroom.

Later, they lay side by side, in silence. John was utterly relaxed. All the puzzlement and anxiety of the day seemed to have left him. In its place was a deep and life-giving sadness. He was glad to be human. He belonged to everyone who had ever felt desire, who had hoped for fullness and satisfaction, who had wanted to love and be loved. He had fallen somewhere below morality, not in the sense that what had just happened was immoral, but that he'd come into a deeper communion that morality pointed to but missed because it got tangled up in dos and don'ts. There was something good and whole about what he and Angela had just shared that cut below the question of whether they were married or not, that could only have happened because they had a deep connection.

He was surprised at the tenderness and affection that had poured from him as they made love. How could he miss Mary and at the same time be so completely absorbed in Angela? This was a mystery. For a moment he felt guilty. He had broken faith with Mary. Then he knew he had not. He had entered once again into the gift of love that was greater than any two people. He and Mary had known it, and now he knew it again. People apportion love in bursts of passion and possessiveness, he thought, when it is given in deeper flowing streams. It had been wonderful to be inside Angela, and he felt he had caught a glimpse of her soul in the mix of forward, confident love-making and hesitant, hopeful desire. He was grateful.

He turned to Angela and began to trace meaningless patterns on her body with the tips of his fingers. She took his hand and looked at him carefully.

"So, is this going to be a problem for you?"

John laughed and rolled onto his back again, but he kept hold of her hand. "You're the least of my problems."

He told her about the whole day. She was very interested in Wilbur and said she wanted to meet him. She was sure she would like him. She thought they would have a lot in common. John laughed at that, but then he remembered what Wilbur had said about Miriam. Angela grew thoughtful when John told her about Maggie's request and the possibility that David would stay with him. She wanted to know what he was going to do.

"I think I'm going to say yes," John answered. "I don't see how I can say no, but really I think I want to do this."

Angela shook her head slightly. "I couldn't do it," she said.

"You're great with kids. Nancy told me how you inspire her grade-schoolers when you visit. You work with young people every day."

"But I can come home to my own house and my own space. It's different taking care of someone, being responsible for him around the clock."

John did not want to talk anymore and he began to caress Angela with more interest and intent, which quickly brought them into each other's arms again.

When John awoke, the sun was slanting through the blinds and laying strips of light across the bedclothes. Angela came out of the bathroom wrapped in a towel. "Did you say you walked here last night? You crazy man. That's several miles." Angela offered to give John a lift home before going to her classes, but John said he wanted to walk. He showered quickly and joined her in the sun room for breakfast. It was good to have company and to be sitting in a fresh, well-appointed room eating food he had not prepared himself. He looked at her across the table. Angela had not yet put on her make-up. She looked her age. John was glad.

BOOK TWO

Prologue

Samantha Jones and Marianne Svoboda walked into the Westbrook Church one Sunday with three children, two girls and a small boy four years old. They lived four blocks away on Allen Street and were looking for a church. Samantha was slender with beautiful, thick, carefully trimmed gray hair, wearing dark slacks and a tailored blazer. She carried herself with quiet elegance. She was slow to speak, and when she did, it was in a soft articulate voice. Marianne was short and stocky with no waist and hair that was chopped off at the shoulder and cut straight across her forehead in unruly bangs. She wore baggy gray trousers, running shoes, and a colorful tunic with an African batik design. She spoke with pugnacious energy and peered at people with knowing eyes and a cautious, ironic smile.

Maud Miller was a greeter that morning and she shook their hands including the two girls, kneeling down to say hello to the little boy, and introducing them to Kirby. A short, full-bodied woman in her early seventies, Maud, with her brusque ways, was never at a loss for conversation, and she soon knew their address, what each of the adults did, the names of the three kids, and how they found the church. If they were taken back by her forward manner, they didn't show it. They had often passed the church, but because of its plain architecture, they thought it was a non-denominational Baptist offshoot. One day they happened to come across the church's website, and they realized it might be a church where they could be at home. Maud took them to an usher who gave them bulletins and the kids the special children's bulletin and showed them to a seat. When her greeting duties were finished, Maud, instead of finding her husband, bustled down the aisle and sat with the newcomers. During the time for introductions she asked them to stand up and told everyone who they were. She escorted the kids up front with the other children for the children's story. Later in the service she took the small boy downstairs for children's church. That next week when Kirby visited them, they commented on how thoroughly they'd been welcomed.

The two girls, who were the same age and in middle school, quickly found a place in the junior high class. Gradually members of the congregation came to know the circumstances of the two women. Both of them were divorced and each had a daughter from her former marriage. People were not sure where the boy came from and at first were reluctant to ask, but people soon came to understand that Marianne and Samantha had adopted him.

When something was not spoken of openly in the congregation, the people who would be comfortable with the unspoken truth often knew it and those who would be uncomfortable with it, didn't. For a time this was how it was with Samantha and Marianne, who were lesbians and had been partners since their daughters were toddlers. Everyone liked them and hardly anyone referred to their family arrangement, the ones who knew because they did not want to make it the defining thing and the ones who did not know because they really did not want to know. For three months the family came regularly.

Samantha taught English in the nearby high school and Marianne was a social worker in a shelter for battered women in Chicago and rode the Metra to work every day. Very soon Samantha was asked to be on the worship committee because the church made a point of putting new people on committees even if they were not yet members. Marianne agreed to serve on the witness commission, which worked on the congregation's social outreach. Joey, Samantha's daughter, who was pretty and popular, was soon part of the junior high in-crowd. Kaylie, Marianne's daughter, who was quiet unlike her mother, was tall and lean and gawky and uncomfortable in her own skin as only a 13-year-old girl who has grown too fast can be. But she had a quick tongue when she spoke, her cutting humor could throw the other kids into paroxysms of laugher. The four-year-old Sonny, which was a nickname for the improbable name of Solomon, which his birth mother had given him before giving him up for adoption, was having trouble and often hung on Marianne's slacks or Samantha's skirt or hid behind their legs. The one person he warmed up to was Preston Krunsch, which surprised everyone because Preston was so erect and reserved and proper.

Sonny became a member of the Sunday school class for four and five-year-olds. He sat quietly in class each Sunday, saying very little. Carrianne Witter-Olson, an energetic young woman who taught science at the same high school as Samantha and enjoyed her Sunday sojourn with the little kids after all week with adolescents, worked hard to bring Sonny out.

When Carrianne found out about the pageant the Christian Education Commission was planning for the Christmas Eve candlelighting service, she volunteered her class to be the sheep. She found thirteen light pink sleepers, the kind usually worn by much smaller children for bedtime that zip up in front and have feet in them. The moms and dads came in one evening and painstakingly glued hundreds of cotton balls to each outfit. They made masks they hoped looked like little lamb faces.

The big night came. The chancel was decorated as a stable with a manger and some hay. Chairs were placed in the back draped in black for the angels to stand on. Mary and Joseph, played by two kids from the senior high youth group, came down the center aisle followed by a boy in a donkey costume. Instead of risking a real baby, the director had given Mary a doll, which she placed in the manger, while Joseph tied the donkey to the pulpit. They took their positions as the holy family. The wise men walked in stately procession, bearing their gifts before them. The angels came in from the sides and perched on the chairs, flexing their wings, as though suspended in the night sky.

Then the sheep came, thirteen wooly preschoolers herded down the aisle by a tall pimply-faced ninth grader in a bathrobe, carrying a crook. They swarmed up the chancel steps and spread out aimlessly as sheep do. Chuckles could be heard from the audience. People craned their necks with heightened interest. The organist was playing "Joy to the World."

Perhaps the pink sleeper, the mask, and the cotton balls gave Sonny anonymity and released some hidden boldness and energy. When everyone was in place and a few more shepherds had come from the wings followed by two girls with burlap humps playing camels, Sonny came scooting out of the flock behind the manger, gamboled around to the front, and poked his woolly head over the side for a quick look at the Savior. He nodded as if he approved, then scampered over to the donkey and gave him an interested sniff. As he headed to the front of the chancel he rubbed against the leg of a wise man who jumped like he'd been stung and dropped his Frankincense. The contact loosed some cotton balls which scattered in Sonny's wake as he leaped down the chancel steps and began to frisk about like all the lambs he'd ever seen in cartoons, throwing off more cotton balls. The actors in the tableau turned distracted eyes toward the action and forgot their roles. Mary stopped gazing rapturously at the Baby Jesus and stared transfixed. The wise men began to snicker. The rest of the sheep crowded forward to see what was happening. Polite chuckles in the audience grew to incredulity and then to outright laughter. People leaned one way or another to see past those in front of them. The kids who were not in the pageant stood up on the benches where they had been sitting. Sonny rose up on his hind legs, cotton balls flying, threw out his arms and began to dance. He danced like Snoopy, flinging his joy to the stars, as though all the firmament or at least the high-peaked sanctuary were full of the glory of God and the song of the angels. Laughter turned to astonishment and then to silence. The organist who was still playing "Joy to the World," dropped down into a quiet register. It was a holy moment—this shy little boy dancing his heart out!

As he gyrated his arms about his head, Sonny caught the edge of his mask and knocked it off. He saw three hundred pairs of eyes glued to his every movement. He stopped. His face fell. He dropped to all fours as though shot, shock and misery on his small face. He looked desperately about for some refuge, some place to hide. He spied his mothers in the third row and scurried there at top speed and buried his face in Marianne's lap—just as the organist came to the end. There was a moment of complete silence. Then someone clapped and then another and the sanctuary erupted in applause and whoops of pleasure.

The pageant was never the same after that. It went on, but worshippers and actors alike never really got back to a proper spirit. The service ended as always when the lights were turned off. A flame was passed from candle to candle until the sanctuary was filled with the orange glow of more than 300 candles. Everyone sang "Silent Night." Even the most cynical could not help feeling the mystery. Usually after the candlelighting, people would quietly go home, not staying to talk or visit. But that night, as soon as the lights came on and the candles were blown out, people wanted to talk to Sonny. They crowded up front. He had pulled off the denuded pink sleeper as soon as he was hidden between Marianne and Samantha. People told him how much they enjoyed his performance. He would have none of it. He buried his face in the lap of the parent closest to him and wouldn't even look at people. They nevertheless patted his shoulder and said what a great job he had done.

Chapter 17 – Controversy

One morning five weeks after Christmas, John stopped at the church to see if Kirby was free for coffee. His friend was just coming from his office, saying good-bye to Samantha Jones and Marianne Svoboda. When they were settled at the nearby Starbucks, John said, "That looked like an interesting meeting. What's up?"

"I got a call from Marianne and Samantha yesterday. They said they wanted to talk. Very serious about it, as they sat down in my office. They told me they've been together for almost ten years. They've always hoped one day to have a public ceremony. They know our denomination doesn't condone same-sex relationships, but they said they thought I might be of a different mind." Kirby paused and smiled. "As you probably know, John, a few weeks ago the state legislature approved civil unions for same-sex couples. It's not quite marriage, but it's a real legal recognition of the relationship. They asked me to perform a public ceremony of union for them."

John whistled. "That's no small thing!"

"I said I was honored they asked. I would consider it a privilege." Kirby was quiet for a long moment. "But I had to admit that I'm not sure I can do it. I told them about the discernment process we're in the middle of, and they said they already knew all about it. I said we could probably get a strong vote on including LGBT people. But I explained that we were working hard to reach a decision that included both LGBT people and those who disapproved. I laid out the stages of the process: first including LGBT people as members, which we are already doing, but have not stated publicly, then putting LGBT people in leadership, which again already has the tacit approval of many, and finally performing union ceremonies. We're only in the first stage.

"I'd perform the service in a heartbeat. But I can't impose my own position on the congregation. I told them that. I gave them some history to explain the denomination's official position. But, of course they already knew most of that. They've really done their homework on us. I confessed that performing the ceremony might get me and the congregation into trouble with the district and the denomination. John, the risk to me is mine to weigh, but I am not free to put the congregation at risk without congregational discussion."

John nodded. He didn't like seeing his old friend upset. Kirby was speaking with pained deliberateness.

Kirby went on derisively, "I certainly looked less than courageous. It bothered me and I told them so. I said I would have to discuss this with the church board and probably it would have to go to the congregational business meeting.

"John, I'm embarrassed! To have to ask the board and the congregation about this! It's a private thing between me as pastor and two people in my church. A good thing, John! I shouldn't have to discuss it! But I do!

"I asked them if they were willing to put themselves through a public discussion. They looked at each other and hardly paused. Marianne said, 'If we say yes, are you willing to take this as far as the congregation will let you?' Of course I had to say 'Yes,' I wanted to say yes, and I did! Then Samantha said in that soft voice of hers, 'Give us a few days to think about it.'

Kirby stayed on John's mind and two days later he called him.

"They came back yesterday already," Kirby said. "They discussed it as a family. They even included the little guy, Sonny. They said they want to go forward with their request. They want me to find a way to hold a ceremony. I asked them what their kids said about it. Joey, Samantha's daughter, is nervous. She doesn't like to rock the boat. Kaylie, Marianne's daughter, apparently is tougher than she looks, a bit of a crusader, which, given her mom, makes sense. But Sonny was a surprise. He apparently gets it, at least as much as a four-and-a-half-year-old can. He said the church has nice people. I figure that's pretty good coming from a kid who was mortified not long ago in front of everyone. Kids at that age forget an embarrassing moment more quickly than we do. Marianne said he thinks all the time about Christmas Eve in all its," Kirby paused and John heard a smile in his voice, "... it's fleecy splendor. Marianne said that when the embarrassment wore off, he remembered what people had said. Someone told him he was the best dancing sheep they'd ever seen. She said she sometimes hears him jabbering about it when he's playing and thinks he's out of earshot."

Kirby brought the request to the church board. John asked if he could sit in as an observer, partly to support Kirby and partly to see how the board handled it. Some were uneasy about going against the denomination. Rory Neff, a young computer programmer who commuted to the Loop, said he didn't think it mattered much what the denomination said. The congregation just needed to do what was right. Maud Miller looked troubled and kept moving her notepad around, making nervous doodles. Joe

Kurtz, who was chairing the meeting, turned to her. "Maud, you aren't talking."

"I think Marianne and Samantha are nice people. We need more new members like them. They took hold right from the start. They're doing more than our old members. And their kids are great kids. That little one, Sonny…well! Those women are good mothers." She gave everyone around the table a hard look. "I guess they're both mothers. I don't know. Does one of them do the father thing? I don't know about this lesbian stuff. And what does LGBT stand for anyway? But you know, I don't care what they do in their bedroom. In the world I grew up in no woman ever married another woman. But you know something else—there were old maids that lived together. And we just accepted it. No one ever asked what they did when they were alone. Sometimes they even raised kids if something happened to the parents, and those kids turned out okay. So if Marianne and Samantha want to get married or have a public ceremony of union or whatever you call it, why not! I mean what is wrong with that? You tell me! I don't know what to do about the rest of the denomination. Of course, we want to respect the decisions that have been made, but why should some people in some other congregation that is all uptight say what we should do? Do we try to tell them they have to accept these gbtl people, or whatever that stupid acronym is?"

Joe reminded the board of what had happened to a congregation in another district when they performed a union service. The district conference censored them and blocked members from serving on district committees. "They could revoke Kirby's ordination," he added. "This is not a speech against doing it. I support holding the union ceremony and accepting the repercussions, but we owe it to the congregation to tell them what to expect. That's the reason we're talking here. It really isn't our decision. It's a congregational decision. We have to discuss this in open meeting. Do I hear a motion to bring this request to the congregation?"

The vote was 8 to 1. The next congregational business meeting was scheduled for three weeks. Word went through the congregation. John watched and listened and stayed in close touch with Kirby, who reported a few conversations, but not as many as he expected. Herman Fry, who was the one board member who voted against it, came to Kirby. He said there were people in the congregation who were against it, but they didn't want to talk. He said he always liked that people had different ideas and that they shared them and he was thankful that people always listened to him even though he never had any education. He said Joe always took his ideas seriously in the Sunday school class. But he just couldn't support this holy union. The Bible said homosexuality was wrong. Kirby replied that some people felt those three or four passages quoted against homosexuality could be interpreted differently. Herman said he had read the paper that was passed around, and he just couldn't see it. He said the Bible was right and there was no getting around it.

Kirby told John about another visit with Samantha and Marianne. They said they felt awkward at church. Some people went out of their way to be nice, and others gave them embarrassed looks. No one was nasty or unpleasant. "It's about what I expected," Marianne had told Kirby.

"They've been through this before." Kirby said to John with a small smile.

****

John was looking forward to this congregational business meeting. He was curious to see what would happen. But he had to admit what was really at stake for him—he had high hopes. He wanted to see this congregation do the right thing. And he was uneasy with his eagerness.

To begin the business, Joe Kurtz brought a recommendation from the Facilities Development Task Force that plans for building on the west property or renovating the present church be put on hold as long as the economy was so bad. Joe expected the members would quickly agree, but Jack Foster objected. He began with an apology. He said he was not prepared to speak. He did not know this was going to be on the agenda. "The west campus is a resource," he said. "We can't just let it lie out there. We should do something with it. If we're serious about moving out there, now would be a good time. We own the property free and clear. We don't have to come up with money to buy it. Builders are crying for work. We could get a good deal, maybe build something for 25 or 30% less than in boom times."

"Are you really saying we should build?" someone exclaimed.

"Actually, no. That would have been my choice a year ago, but not now. I think we should sell that property and rebuild right here. Tear down this old building. Build a new one. Stay here and continue to anchor this neighborhood. But whatever we do, we should do something! People are scared. That's what's causing the downturn. Let's show some courage!"

Members were silent. Surprise was on some faces. Uncertainty on others. A few looked around to see what others were feeling. Jack's speech had not been expected.

Bob Flory rose. It was early for him to speak, which meant that the discussion had not taken the direction he expected. He prided himself on knowing what people were going to say. Jack's speech had thrown him off. He knew members respected Jack for his business acumen.

"Brother Jack makes some interesting points," he began. Bob laid on the folksy, older form of address—brother this or sister that—when he was not sure of himself and wanted to buy a little time and space, "but we really don't want to embark on a major building program in this economy. I know, I know, Brother Jack said just the opposite. And he's right that fear is driving this recession. Fear of investing, fear of risk, anxiety about not having enough money. And theoretically if everyone cut loose and started building and buying, we would come out of it quickly. But people don't work that way. People move slowly, recessions turn around slowly. Everyone wants to put a toe in the water first, then a little bit of leg. No one wants to plunge in unless everyone else is going to do it. Brother Jack is, in effect, asking us to be among the first. Now, I like that. I like courage. But it's one thing for Jack to do it or for me to do it. But we can't ask the congregation to do it. Suppose we start a building program, and the economy takes a further nose dive. Some more members lose their jobs. Suddenly we have construction loans, and our giving is down because people don't have as much to give. We've taken the plunge and we're in over our heads."

Several people called out quick comments.

"Aren't we people of faith. What about stepping out in faith?'

"True. But we're talking about reality here."

"Jack, why are you interested in rebuilding? Why not fix up a few things and wait out this recession?"

"Let's make a building that fits the 21st century," Jack replied. "Get a permit to build up higher. Dig out and put a two-deck parking garage, one floor below street level. Open the upper deck into a gym and meeting and activity rooms. Use these for community activities during the week, church school classes on Sunday." Jack paused and looked around the room at all the people seated in neat rows. He had an odd look in his eyes, as though he was confused about something and at the same time it was coming clear. John leaned forward to hear what Jack would say next. "I thought I'd never be making this speech. It's not about building a damn church—excuse my language. It's about community. What kind of community are we going to be? Think about it!"

Kurt Wampler stood. "Jack, on one level that is a cockamamie idea. Full of problems...and maybe something else." There were some chuckles.

"Will the city allow us to build up? Where do we worship while this build-ing is being razed and the new one built? The financial risks are huge. But it's a good idea! Absolute nuts, though. In this financial climate! It makes me as nervous as a long-tailed cat in a room full of rocking chairs."

"Why are we even talking about this? This is not what we really need to deal with. This financial risk is small potatoes beside the risk we're be-ing asked to consider in our next agenda item."

"Maybe these two things are connected. What kind of congregation are we going to be? Bold, with the courage of our faith or…"

"Or dumb, in hock to our ears, with everyone ticked off at us!"

"We don't know that!"

"Well, it happened in Indiana!"

The moderator stepped in. "People. Let me pull you back to the item before us. This is a report from the Facilities Development Task Force. It requires no action. Do I hear a motion for some action? Jack, do you want to put your ideas into a motion."

"No, Sister Moderator. It's too soon. The idea needs work. I'd like to ask the task force to consider it, but I'm not going to put it in a motion. We're friends here. We do listen to each other, most of the time. Joe, I know you'll take this discussion back to the task force. Maybe I'll come to your next meeting and lay out my idea. That's enough for now."

There were some internal sighs of relief, people glad to be taken off the hook. No one wanted to be accused of lack of courage.

The moderator thanked Joe and moved on. Vern had always reported for the Discernment Committee. She said how much he would be missed, that he brought a spirit of intelligence and fair-mindedness to these discus-sions. The next item normally would come from him and the Discernment Committee. Instead it came from the board. Joe Kurtz went to the mike again and presented the recommendation that the congregation consider a service of commitment for Marianne Svoboda and Samantha Jones. Some-one asked if it was a motion. Joe said it was, and since it came from the board, it did not need a second. The board members felt it required care-ful consideration by the whole membership.

"Are you for it or against it?" came a blunt question.

"Board members by a vote of 8 to 1 support the recommendation," Joe answered. "Let me word it as a formal motion. I move that we accept the board's recommendation and agree as the Westbrook Church to authorize our pastor Kirby Beahm to perform a service of holy union for Marianne Svoboda and Samantha Jones."

There it was! John sat up intently, watching Kirby in the front row. John saw him tense up, move slightly, and then stop. He knew Kirby wanted to turn around to see the expressions on his people's faces but was resisting the temptation. John's gaze traveled around the room. Sam Ellerby was leaning forward in his seat. Maud Miller fidgeted and played with the strap on her handbag. Jack Foster looked down at his hands and then up at Joe. Kurt Wampler was peering keenly at the microphone, his body ready to move, on the edge of speech. Bob Flory sat back in his seat trying to appear cool, but his tapping foot gave him away. Eve Ellerby had a very intent and purposeful look. John caught Sam glancing at her with curiosity and maybe some uneasiness. Marianne and Samantha sat in the back. People seemed to be avoiding looking at them. Their daughters sat with them, looking conspicuously uncomfortable. John knew Sonny was playing in the toddler room with the other small kids, watched over by a sitter from the youth group. Herman Fry had a frown on his face. The moderator looked as though she wanted to be somewhere else. Joe seemed resolute, fully aware that the next few minutes might be hard. Was he was preparing himself to be a target? Dana Snyder had her eyes closed. John wondered if she was praying, and what the prayer might be. It occurred to him that maybe he ought to pray. If not now, then when? But he was badly out of practice. He figured his prayers wouldn't get much farther than the bones of his skull.

For discussions like these, members were asked to come to a mike that was set up in the center. Kurt Wampler went to the mike first.

"It's time we did this. We've spent enough time in discernment. It's all been good. Don't get me wrong. But we know where most of us are. This is a good family. We love Marianne and Samantha. Let's do this. I support this motion."

"I don't know how to say things as good as some people," said Herman Fry. "I don't have a lot of education. What I mean to say is I am glad that I can speak, and, Joe, I always liked your Sunday school class because we could have different opinions and we could learn from each other. We need to learn from each other. We need to listen to each other. I mean I try to listen. We need to do that. And I like Marianne and Samantha. I do. Marianne, you have some good things to say in Sunday school class. I learn when I hear you. I don't want to hurt no one's feelings. Doesn't the Bible tell us that we can't do this? What I mean to say is we can't just go against the Bible. And we can't go against our denomination."

A line was forming behind the mike. Gerard Kurtz, an older man, distantly related to Joe, was next in line. He was a retired guidance counselor who rarely spoke in public meeting. "I hear what Herman is saying, and I have sympathy with his position. For a long time I thought along similar lines. Do you remember this four-page study of the Biblical passages about homosexuality?" He lifted a copy for all to see, "We were given it some months ago. I'm pretty sure the writer is correct about how we have to read those passages. They were written in a different time. We don't keep slaves or have multiple wives, so why hang on to those few passages. I think I am ready to support this motion."

"I support it too, but we don't stand alone," Anna Firebaugh said when she got to the mike. "We don't practice the extreme individualism of the mega churches. We interpret scripture in the community. There are many people in other churches in our denomination who disagree with what Gerald just said. What about them? And there are a lot more of them than there are of us. They say the expression of homosexual love is a sin. They think homosexual marriage is an abomination." Several members reacted audibly. Someone called out, "Is that what you think?" "No, of course not, but, that's what they think," she said defensively. "We are not free just to do what we want."

"Point of order!" Eve Ellerby called out. John saw the surprise on Sam's face and thought actions like that were probably not typical of Eve. "I think we should be careful of our language. It must be keenly uncomfortable for Marianne and Samantha."

Marianne rose where she was sitting, did not come to the mike, but spoke with a strong enough voice that everyone could hear. "There is probably nothing you could say today that we have not already heard. I'm not afraid of words." She added dryly, "I have heard us called an abomination before."

"I'd like to say that this is okay," said Barbara Nolt who was next in line. "These two women look so friendly and normal with their kids and their church work. But let's just name it. This is unnatural. God made us male and female to cleave to each other. That's what it says in Genesis. I don't care how normal it looks. Sometimes Satan looks very fine…"

Many stirred and muttered or involuntarily called, "No!"

Maud Miller leapt to her feet and spoke out of turn from where she had been sitting. "Barb Nolt, you should be ashamed of yourself! That's a terrible thing to say. And you of all people! Who are you to say that Marianne and Samantha are the devil disguised!"

"What do you mean 'me of all people'? What are you insinuating, Maud Miller?"

"You know very well what I'm talking about. Look to the beam in your own eye, before you point out the mote in someone else's!"

The moderator cut in with a sharp voice. "Here! We will have none of that. We can disagree. We do disagree. But there'll be no name calling. There is room for differences."

"Not on this. This is not opinion. This is truth. We have to draw a line somewhere." Barbara Nolt was leaning in and hanging onto the mike as though she never intended to let go.

"Sister Barb, I think it's time you gave someone else a chance at the mike," the moderator said softly, but with enough force that everyone heard it.

Meanwhile more people had gotten in line for the mike, including Maud. The line now snaked around the back of the Fellowship Hall and over toward the kitchen.

Sam was next at the mike. John noticed that he had gotten up as soon as the discussion began, putting himself in position to speak. "I have something to say, but first I think we should hear from Kirby. He has the most to lose. If the congregation is censured by the district, the worst that can happen is they won't let us serve on the board and committees, which will hurt the district more than it will hurt us. They need our money. We give more to the district budget than any other congregation. They won't kick us out of the district. But Kirby could lose his ordination."

John was glad someone was paying attention to what this meant for Kirby. He watched as Sam looked to the left where Kirby was sitting. "I guess I'm putting you on the spot, but we need to know what you think we should do and how it will affect you."

Kirby stood and instead of going to the mike that had the line, he stepped to the mike where Joe Kurtz and the moderator stood and looked out at his parishioners with sadness. "I wish I had some great wisdom. I don't see a way through this that won't cause someone pain. If we say no, we hurt five people—Marianne, Samantha, and their kids—and a lot more who feel deeply about this, and LGBT people everywhere who have been hurt by rejection over and over. If we say yes, we trouble Herman and Barb—and there are others who are reluctant to speak up—and we upset people in our local community who are deeply convinced that same-sex relations are immoral. And, if we say yes, we upset people in the district and the denomination. There simply is no peace on this matter. People on both sides don't want to talk to each other. We're all sure we're right. So my ordination and my ministry are only a small part of this larger picture of woe. I am going to step out of the pastor's role and speak more candidly than usual. I am weary of all this! We are like the birds from mythology that tear at the guts of their victims and then do it again the next day. We tear at each other's guts. We stop seeing each other as human beings. I'll tell you, whether homosexual relations are a sin or a blessing from God—either way—what we are doing to one another is a far deeper matter than getting our sexuality right. Jesus reserved his harshest words for the Pharisees, the good people full of pride in their rightness. So I say to you, I would perform this ceremony because I see the goodness and humanity of these two people not because I am certain that I'm right. I would stand by the action before God and the district and the denomination because I believe that God's deepest reality is love not judgment. But..." he paused, "this is not just my choice. I will not perform the ceremony in this church building unless we can come together. I don't mean that we all agree to do it. I mean that we make an honest decision and then find it in ourselves to respect each other and more importantly to reach out to each other across this divide. I'm saying this to you Kurt and you Herman—I single you out because both of you have spoken clearly and out of conviction—what is at issue here is not whether Marianne and Samantha are moral beings, but whether all of us are loving beings."

John was smiling with pride and affection when Kirby finished and sat down.

Kurt spoke from where he had gotten back in line after his earlier speech. "Sam, may I ask to claim your space in line to answer Kirby?" Sam nodded and Kurt moved forward.

"Kirby, I hear what you're saying. I really do. But this is an issue of justice. It's not enough to try to love both sides. LGBT people have been rejected over and over again, excluded from leadership, made to feel that they are vile and disgusting. It's time they are given the opportunities of all of us and, more than that, treated as valued and beloved fellow humans and fellow people of faith. It's time their relationships are respected and cherished. You can't have this both ways. You can't have me and Herman in some sort of illusory harmony. What he is saying hurts Marianne and Samantha and their kids and perpetuates an injustice. You have to make a decision. Is it the justice that I and others want or is it Herman's position which simply denies them their due as human beings? Herman, I don't like saying this, but there is not any middle ground here. You've been clear. So have I. I'm sorry." Kurt left the microphone and went to his seat.

There was a pained silence. Sam stepped back into his place at the mike. "So, Kurt, you've said that you and Herman cannot pretend to harmony. It's your way or his. Clear cut. One way or the other. So here's a question for both of you. Can you be in the same congregation? Herman, if we vote to support a service for Marianne and Samantha, will you leave? Kurt, are you saying that if we decide not to do this, you'll leave. Or here's a question for all of us—are we able to stay in good fellowship regardless of today's vote? Or maybe an even more painful question— should we ask Marianne and Samantha and Herman and Barb to live in the same congregation? Why put them through that—on either side? I know, I know. I'm just asking questions. I have no answers. So what do I know? Not much. But I do know that I value Herman." He turned to him, "For what it's worth, Herman, I really appreciate you. You bring a lot to this church. I also know that I love and value this new family. And for me it's a family with or without a ceremony." He turned to where they were sitting and smiled at Marianne, Samantha, and their daughters.

Gil Smith, a slender man with long, black, shoulder-length hair, a moustache, and bright intelligent eyes, who was wearing blue jeans and a t-shirt, and who had been standing patiently in line behind Sam, came to the mike. "Sometimes we can't be nice. We have to do the right thing. Even if we like someone, if what they are doing is wrong, we have to do something. We can do it in a nice way. Christians often hurt each other by being harsh. We should never be that way. But sometimes we have to say what is true and then do it. I want this family to stay in the church, but I can't say what they are doing is right. I can't read the Bible and then say that."

With each speech Maud Miller seemed more impatient. When she finally reached the microphone, she blurted out, "What is wrong with you people! We are talking about human beings here. I am disgusted! With all of us!" She swept her arm in an arc to include everyone in the room. "I don't care anymore if you think Marianne and Samantha are sinners or saints. They are people! God's children! We're talking about them like ...like they're another species. Put yourself in their shoes. Think about it. I've been in this church almost 50 years, and this is the first time I've been ashamed to be a member!"

Barb Nolt leaped to her feet, "That's unfair! That is so unfair! I care about these people just as much as you do. I care about their souls. What about our immortal souls? All of us—we will have to stand before God someday."

"Sister Barb," said the moderator, interrupting, "if you want to speak, please take a place in the line for the microphone."

Gerald Kurtz had been standing patiently in line behind Maud. He gripped the mike, "This matter is too divisive. We are just a speech or two away from being at each other's throats. We need time. I don't think we're ready to vote. I want to make a motion." He lifted a sheet of yellow lined paper he was holding and was about to read from it.

"Point of order," said Paul Fry who was in line behind Gerald and had been waiting a long time to speak. "We already have a motion on the floor."

"Gerald, that is correct," said the moderator.

"This is a motion that has priority over the motion on the floor. Let me read it and you will see. I move that we lay this motion on the table until our next meeting and that in the meantime we ask the discernment committee to help us find a way to bring understanding and reconciliation."

Bob Flory promptly rose where he was sitting. "I second that."

"Sister Moderator," Gerald said quickly, "May I say a word about this motion. We are not ready to vote. We need to cool off. We could return the motion to the board for further thought, but we already have the discernment committee. They haven't finished their work. This motion from the board jumped the gun. Let's give it back to the committee and let them do their work."

"Gerald's motion does take priority," said the moderator. Those of you in line, if you want to speak to the motion to table, then come to the mike. If not, then stand aside please, and let those who want to speak to this motion do so."

Kurt Wampler rose to go to the mike. The others who were waiting stepped aside. "I speak against the motion to table. We cannot leave these two women, our sisters, hanging. Let's vote this motion down and return to the main motion."

No one else seemed to want to speak on the motion to table. John saw that members seemed relieved. Bob Flory rose deliberately and went to the mike. He was shaking his head. "Friends, we're in a pickle, aren't we! There's no easy way out. Brother Gerald makes a lot of sense. We already have the machinery set up for discussing and dealing with matters pertaining to sexual orientation. Let's let those processes play out. Remanding this to the discernment committee makes eminent sense. You know, back in the day of our great grandfathers...and mothers...people sometimes voted to do nothing. You should read those old minutes sometime. They had a lot of wisdom. We could learn from them. This matter is not going away. With all due respect to Marianne and Samantha and appreciation for their uncomfortable position, this matter can wait a bit longer."

Herman Fry stood up. "I don't know about these things…about parliamentary procedure and all that, but I think we should go back and vote on whether this here ceremony is right. We need to do that."

"Call for the question!' someone called out.

"That means we must stop and vote, if we are agreed," said the moderator. "Are we ready to vote on the motion to table?" I see many heads nodding. "Is the motion understood?" Again heads nodded. "Then those in favor of the motion to table signify by saying 'aye.'" There were many voices. "Those opposed?" There were only a few voices. "Those abstaining?" There was one voice. "The motion to table has been approved by a clear majority, clear enough that we don't need to count. The motion carries."

Talking broke out all over the room. Kurt Wampler put his head down and leaned his elbows on his knees. Maud was shaking her head and looked really angry. Herman Fry was nodding his head slightly, an involuntary condition that had come on him with age and was triggered by stress, disappointment and anger on his face. There was no more business and the meeting was quickly adjourned.

John stayed in his seat as others got up to leave. He took a deep breath and exhaled slowly. He watched the people as they got up from their seats. Bob Flory and Gerald Kurtz stood on one side talking. Eve leaned over to Sam and said, "Let's get out of here!" Kirby walked back to Marianne and Samantha, who were quickly putting on their coats. Maud and Barb walked past and would not even look at one another. Kurt got up and left the building without talking to anyone. Gil Smith, who had janitorial duties, began to fold the chairs and put them on the holding cart. John saw Nancy Beahm, who had said nothing all afternoon, go up to Catherine, the moderator, place her hand on her arm, and quietly tell her she had done a good job under trying circumstances. Slowly the room cleared out, though there was none of the usual laughter or good fellowship. John waited until Kirby was free and then went up to him. Joe was wearily putting some papers together. Jack Foster was still there too. The four friends stood together.

"Not much to be said, is there?" Jack remarked.

"You're in a difficult spot," John said to Kirby. "And you too, as board chair," he added, looking at Joe.

"It's a hell of a thing!" Jack said as he turned to leave.

Chapter 18 – Relationships

The men were talking about computers, laughing a little too loudly, and falling into awkward pauses, when John arrived. He had just taken his seat when Sam said, "We have to talk about Sunday. You know we do."

The waitress came at that moment and fell into her usual vaguely suggestive banter. The men seemed glad to join the empty reparteé. When she moved away, Jack said, "Okay, who's going to start?"

John watched Sam's face, as Sam looked around the table and then commented, "We really don't want to talk about this, do we?"

"There's not much to say," said Kurt

"We're acting like we're on opposite sides," Sam said. "The last time I checked, we were all pretty much on the same page."

"Basic ideas maybe, but not on what to do," Kurt replied.

"Hell, I'll jump in," Jack said. "You want to know what I think? I really don't care. I don't want to have to deal with this right now. What's the big deal? If these two women want to marry or have a union or whatever you call it, why not? It's between them."

"I wish it were that simple," said Kirby with a sigh.

"You're the one with his balls on the line," Jack replied. "I do get that. I'm glad I'm not in your shoes."

"I'm sure that helps Kirby," said Joe.

Jack turned suddenly to John. "You're still the new guy here. Not as much at stake. What do you think?"

"You should feel good about what happened," John said.

"Just what we need to hear," said Kurt sarcastically. "Are you one of those God-never-gives-you-more-than-you-can-handle guys who thinks he has to find a blessing in every pile of shit?"

"Hear, hear! Enough of that evangelical language!"

John laughed, "Where I come from, we don't even talk about homosexuality. I thought that was a pretty healthy discussion on Sunday."

"So, Kirby, are you counting your blessings?"

"John's right you know. Nancy's from the same congregation. There are maybe ten of our churches on the whole Eastern seaboard where Sunday's discussion could happen."

"So what good does that do us?"

"I'm just angry," said Kurt. "I'm done with waiting. I say we back Kirby to perform the ceremony and let the chips fall."

They went back and forth. Sam and Jack and Kurt did most of the talking. Finally, Kirby said, "I think I'm ready to do this, but there will be strong reactions in the district."

"You asked me as the new guy what I think," John remarked. "But I'm not new when it comes to Kirby. I've known him since college. If he says he'll do something, he will, and once his mind is made up, he'll risk whatever is necessary."

John had to leave early to go back to the apartment and get David off to school. Maggie had come back after four weeks in Arizona, paid one month's rent, and asked to move back into her old apartment. John and Jack had decided to carry her awhile longer. Now she was on another four-week trip to the nature farm, and David was with John again. The boy was old enough to be alone for an hour or so and probably could get himself ready if he had to, but John wanted him to feel cared for, and he liked making him breakfast, packing his lunch, and making sure he had all his books in his backpack. David was just stirring as John let himself into the apartment. The boy stumbled into the shower and in a few minutes he was combing his wet hair and sitting down at John's small table, while John scrambled some eggs.

"Is my Mom coming back?" David asked.

"She said she was. Why do you ask?"

The boy shrugged, "I don't know."

"Are you worried she won't?

David shrugged and began to eat his eggs. "These are almost as good as my Mom's," he said.

"That's high praise. Listen, your Mom has her struggles, but she is usually there for you, isn't she?"

"Yeah."

"So why would this be different?"

"I don't know."

"She calls you every day. That reminds me. I thought I'd get you a cell phone, one of those phones that I can put money on whenever you need it. That way she can call you directly and you won't have to use my phone. How does that sound?"

"Cool."

"So why are you wondering if she's coming back?"

"She sounds happy out there. She doesn't like living here in Selby."

"How do you know that?"

"She complains about it a lot. She wants to move down to Chicago, but I don't want to move. I like the friends I have here. She really wants to go to New York, but I don't think she can get a job there."

John had this conversation on his mind as he went through the morning. He talked to the plumbers and electricians who were in one of the downstairs apartments. Then he went to the upper level apartment down at the end where he was tearing out an old kitchen, work he hated because the walls and broken old appliances were covered with grease and he kept finding dead cockroaches, and some live ones. He stopped work at 11:30 to clean up. He was having lunch with Angela.

They met in a small Italian restaurant that had just been opened by one of Angela's cousins. It was a little more upscale than John liked when he was in work clothes, but the cousin, Vince, gave them an enthusiastic welcome, and there were other men in faded jeans and flannel shirts at the tables, which were laid out with brisk white tablecloths and cloth napkins tucked in the wine glasses.

Angela had come from her morning classes and was wearing a form-fitting burgundy turtleneck with a scarf pinned around her neck, dark green with subtle blue stripes. The colors accented the tints in her complexion and her red hair and the blue in the scarf bought out the blue in her eyes.

Vince went out of his way to be friendly to John, standing by their table and chatting. "The family tells me you're different. We all love Angie, but we don't approve of most of her boyfriends."

"Angie?" John laughed, looking at Angela.

"You can tell the family what they can do with their gossip," said Angela.

"You know there's nothing you can do about it. You should hear what they think of me starting a restaurant at my age," said Vince. He turned to John, "Our family is big and sloppy affectionate, but we are hard on each other."

After their order was taken, Angela noticed that John seemed preoccupied. "What's up with you today?" she asked. "Are you all right?"

"Huh. Oh, yes. I suppose." John told her about his breakfast conversation with David. "My heart goes out to this boy. I almost wish I could adopt him."

Angela listened with a wrinkled brow. "Do you think we, you and I, have a future together?"

John shifted in his chair, suddenly uneasy. "Why do you ask that question on this Thursday afternoon? And what connection does it have with David?"

"I might have room in my life for a man, but probably not for a man and a boy."

"Are you saying we are going to have a life together? Is this a left-handed proposal?" John asked with a slight smile.

"Did I mention marriage?"

"Are you suggesting we live together?"

"Is that even possible in your moral universe?"

"Let's bracket my 'moral universe' for a moment and talk about yours. Have you ever lived with someone before?"

"No."

"So you are paying me a compliment?"

"I suppose you could put it that way."

Angela looked away. He knew he had to do something or she would quickly retreat behind her wall of determined self-possession. He reached across the table and took her hand. She closed her fingers on his. "I don't know what to say," he said

"You'd better say something quickly, buster," she replied.

John took a deep breath. "I think I want something more."

"But if I didn't have all this sex appeal, would you be interested? See, that's the question I always have with men." She laughed bitterly, "Do you love me for my mind?"

"Actually, the answer is yes. I do like the way your mind works. I don't think I could love a woman who was not interested in ideas. As for what you would be like without your 'sex appeal.' That's like wondering what the sun would be like without its heat."

Angela looked up at him, with the old spirit back in her eyes. "Thank you for that. I'll settle for being like the sun."

"But what are you saying about David? That you can't love me if I take a role in his life?"

"No. It has nothing to do with love. It has to do with making a life to-gether. I have no idea how to be a parent."

"You're an aunt to your nieces and nephews. You live in a big family."

"That's just it. I know all about how hard it is to take care of children. I see aunts and uncles and cousins, some doing a bad job. My parents were at best disappointing. I know myself. I couldn't do it."

"There are two big assumptions here," John said, "that I'm going to end up with responsibility for David, and that we are going to end up together."

"As for the first, I think you have already decided on David."

John was surprised. "How do you know that?"

Angela shrugged. "You're really a fairly simple guy. Your loyalties are strong. I think you love that kid."

John sat back. She was right.

"As for the other assumption," she went on. "I am tempted to offer myself to you, to take you anyway I can have you. There! I've admitted it, though I am sure I'll regret it."

John laughed out loud.

Angela pulled back.

"No, no. Don't be offended. You just have to understand how astonishing this is. When I was a young man, before Mary and I got married, I never believed a woman could love me, especially an attractive one, and now the loveliest woman I know has thrown herself at me."

"Did I just do that?" said Angela.

"No, no," said John still smiling. "I'm not saying anything about you. I am saying that I am amazed that someone as beautiful and accomplished as you could want me."

"So where does that leave us?"

"I don't know." This conversation had taken place while they were eating bread and having salad. Now the main course was brought and they ate in silence. John put down his fork and said, "Angela, I have no idea what the future holds."

"I think we'll have to be satisfied with that for the moment," she replied.

John went through the rest of the afternoon in a confused, pleasurable, uncomfortable daze. Angela's comments about David ran through his mind. He did love this boy. He liked the kid's wide open gaze and his thoughtful manner. He got a kick out of the big words David occasionally used. He wondered if the boy ever let down. He hardly ever goofed around. It bothered John to see him escaping into the TV. His mother could not afford cable, but people had given him a lot of old videos and DVDs, which David watched over and over. What would the boy be like when he grew older? Sometimes when John put his head in the door to say hello after school, he could hear Maggie in the back room weeping. One day he suggested therapy and she swore at him. Then she turned suddenly contrite and apologized and said she was still going to the local mental health clinic, but they could fit her in only every other week. Sometimes David didn't have his supper until 8 or 9 in the evening. Other times John would find Maggie and David having a picnic on the living room floor sur-rounded by plates of cheese and fruit and popcorn. Some days John want-ed to take the boy to a good store and buy him new clothes, install a better computer, pay for Internet. He wanted to take Maggie's place. Then when he thought further, he figured he should probably help Maggie be a better mother. He saw how she tried and how she suffered and he wanted to make it easier for her. But he had no claims on her. He was just the next door neighbor and, worse, the surrogate for the landlord.

When his heart had exhausted itself with these unprofitable thoughts about David and Maggie, it turned to Angela. And he thought of Mary. Then he went back over the women who had been his friends, in college, in his business relationships. He was not naïve or without experience in the world beyond his community and church. But his close relationships had always been with people who had come from the same roots. Mary's work as an attorney had given her a diverse circle of connections, but she had grown up in a family and church like his. Vi was as widely traveled as any big city sophisticate, yet she had come from a farm in Indiana. There was nothing in Angela's family that was like his: old Italian neighborhood at Taylor and Western in Chicago, then a move to Elmwood Park and then to Selby when Angela was a teenager. Large, noisy. Drinkers. Quick to love. Quick to hate. Earthy, profane. Lovers of too much food. Multiple marriages. Mechanics, factory workers. Angela was the only one of her siblings to go to college. So why did Angela want him? Could she commit to a guy like him? Would she get tired of him? She had moved from man to man. Was that because the guys were jerks or because she just got restless and wanted a different man?

Chapter 19 – Finding What's Right

Sam was sitting at the breakfast table in their new condo, watching his wife. The morning sun was on the other side of the building, but still plenty of light flowed in the windows and the sliding glass door that led to their deck. Sam was in his bathrobe and pajamas. Eve had wrapped herself in the Japanese kimono her sister had sent her many years earlier while she was living in the Far East. Though she'd just gotten up, Eve had brushed her hair neatly and already rubbed herself with the slightly coconut-smelling body lotion. Sam appreciated the great care Eve took in her appearance and the constant effort she made to keep herself in shape. She had the body of someone twenty years younger. She was pouring tea for herself and chattering away about the things she needed to do that day, reminding him of some things she wanted him to do. Sometimes this annoyed him. He liked to keep his responsibilities contained to the times when he was at work and not be reminded of them when he was at ease at home, but this morning he was enjoying her energetic early morning activity. She was turning, with tea in hand, to go back to the bedroom to dress and then be off to her car and her lengthy agenda for the day.

He pushed a chair toward her, "Sit down for a bit. Forget what you have to do. Have your tea with me, rather than scurrying about the house. All that stuff can wait. I want to talk to you." He smiled, "That is if you can you spare me a few minutes."

She sat down, smiled, and raised her eyebrows.

Sam took her hand and leaned forward. "What are we going to do with this money?"

"Yes, I've been worrying, too."

"Did I say I was worried?"

"Well, I am."

"Why?"

"It's going so fast. We've used more than half of it already."

"But it's not gone. We bought this condo. A lot of it is in the equity."

"But the money is tied up."

"Yes, and I wonder if we should have bought it," Sam said. "It also ties us down."

"We have to live somewhere. It's nice to own our own place again."

"Do you know about Jack Foster's idea?" Sam asked.

"The co-housing thing. Yes, Jenn told me Jack was talking to John Englesinger about doing something like that in the neighborhood behind his apartment building on River Street."

"I think I'm interested. I've been doing some research."

Sam sketched out what he'd learned about the hundred or so co-housing efforts in the United States. He became animated, and Eve picked up some of his excitement. They remembered when they were younger, flirting with the idea of living in some kind of community. The thought of doing this with friends was appealing. In the co-housing set-up they could still own their own living unit. It was the land and a central common area that were owned together. Eve thought it might be a good way to get old without having to go to a retirement center. Sam commented that it would have been easier if they hadn't just bought the condo. Still with what was left of the money, they had more liquidity than most of their friends.

"I don't know about that neighborhood, though," Eve commented. "It's pretty dicey."

"In principle we believe we should be willing to live with people who are different from us, or in this case poorer. Are we really willing to do that? Frankly I don't know. We have to find out what Jack and John are thinking. I'll call them and see if we can get together."

The next day Sam and Eve listened over lunch as Jack sketched out his idea, while John looked on. There was a cul-de-sac behind the apartment building, and the backyards of the houses at the end adjoined the back of the apartment building lot. There were six homes on the cul-de-sac and five homes on each side of the street that led into the cul-de-sac. That made 16 single family dwellings and 24 apartments that were all connected or contiguous. The house Jack had bought and was fixing up was in the middle at the end of the cul-de-sac and thus adjoining the apartment building property, so that Jack already owned that much of the neighborhood. Two more homes were up for sale. The apartments were being renovated as small one-bedroom units, but some of them could be combined to make larger flats. Jack had checked and the average turnover for homes in that neighborhood was five years. He'd also gone up and down the street and around the cul-de-sac and talked to all the homeowners, telling them he was a developer and might be interested in buying up the homes in the neighborhood. He found that many of the owners were interested in selling.

Sam interrupted Jack to say that his research showed that co-housing groups generally needed 15 to 30 units to make the project work. Fewer families and the work and the costs of the common area were heavy. More than 30 families and people could not know each other.

Jack agreed and said that's why he thought this neighborhood was a good location.

Eve said, "I drove through there this morning. Most of those homes are in sad shape."

"True," Jack said, "but they're older homes which means they're on larger lots and have good space inside. A number of them have been divided into apartments and are being used as rental units."

"My research showed me there are two ways of doing this," Sam said. "One is for the group to buy land and start from scratch, design the common areas and the living units for a compact section of the land and keep the rest of the property for gardens and green space. The other way is to retrofit an old neighborhood. That's what you're doing, Jack. Frankly, I like the idea of starting new. I saw some great co-housing communities on the Internet. The living units were energy-efficient. There were walkways and glassed-in patios that connected the units. The common areas had gleaming, commercial-grade kitchens and large open eating and recreation spaces. There were fireplaces and windows facing south for solar heating. They even incorporated some office-sized rooms for members who wanted to run small businesses. One community built up, with three floors of units, all opening onto a courtyard, with a basement parking garage."

"Yeah, I know. I like those places too. But look at this." Jack took out a sketch of the neighborhood. "Here is the house I'm fixing up. It's one of the smallest. Right next to it is this large old Victorian home. Admittedly rundown, but it's got five bedrooms and a lot of kitchen space. The large dining and living rooms could be opened up to make a common area of about 20 by 25. There's a fireplace, and there's enough room on the side of the house to build out and double or triple the common room as we grow. The bedrooms can be used as guest rooms. The basement could be converted to a common workshop. There is a two-car garage that would be winterized for office space or used to house a community van if we wanted to have one. It would cost a lot to renovate that big old house, but structurally it's good. The place is for sale, and I've made an offer."

"But what about the people who don't want to sell and what about the tenants in the apartment building?" Eve asked. "Do co-housing groups have people living with them who are not members?"

"Well, yes and no. Mostly, no. The point is for people to live in closer community. You have to buy into that idea and be a member, share in the decision making and community tasks, and become joint owner of the common space. But in reality, some co-housing groups have rental units for people who want to try it out before joining in. Sometimes they have a unit or two just for people who need housing. The ones that retrofit a neighborhood cultivate good relations with their neighbors who do not belong."

John had said nothing until now. "Jack's idea is to put into practice some of the things we've been saying over the years about living across racial, cultural, and economic lines. His idea is to mix well-off, well-organized white middle-class professional people with a racially diverse working-class community."

"Is that your idea too?" Eve asked.

John shrugged. "It sounds good on paper. Will it work? I don't know. Think of the people in our church. We talk a good line, but how many of us want to live in this River Street neighborhood?"

"Maybe the so-called working-class people of other races and cultures won't want to live with us," Sam said.

"Yeah, yeah, I know. This is a stretch for me! I have no experience." Jack said. "But," he shrugged, "what do I have to lose! I'm ready to put the apartment building, the little house I'm renovating, and the big Victorian house (I think the seller's going to take my offer) into the deal."

"Say Eve and I are interested, what do we do? And by the way, are you interested, John?"

"I am, but I don't have enough capital to buy a unit."

"Here's what we do," Jack said. "We start meeting. Anyone who is remotely interested. We talk. We imagine possibilities. We raise questions. We deal with fears. We talk about the kind of community we want. As for retrofitting as opposed to starting new—I'm committed to this neighborhood, so I guess if you're talking to me, you're stuck with this project. Do we want to incorporate the apartment building? If we go forward, what's our long-term vision? Do we hope all the homes on the cul-de-sac and entering street will become part of the community? We discuss what might be common land and buildings. We place a value on this and divide the cost, based on how many units are in our final goal."

"This is like a condo setup? All the land is held in common? The members hold deed to their own units?"

"Yeah, that's the idea. So as homes go up for sale in the cul-de-sac, the co-housing group buys the home and then deeds the structure to the member who wants to join and live there."

"So to begin, the earlier members have to be willing to own more than their own share in order to raise the capital necessary to get the thing started?"

"As you said, most co-housing people say you should have about 15 family units even to start. Because I have some money to put in, we don't have to wait for that number."

Afterwards Sam and Eve sat in their car in the restaurant parking lot. Jack's energy and fearlessness had left Sam feeling tired. Eve was filled with anxiety. "How do we know this is a good idea? Who do we talk to? Wouldn't people want the appeal and excitement of new land and new buildings? People love new stuff. But to rehab old houses in that neighborhood. What is Jack thinking?"

At home Sam went into the study he was making in the third bedroom. There were still some boxes stacked in one corner. He took out his journal. *Is this a crazy idea or is this a direction? You created us to live in community. Instead we live separated from one another. It's our own choosing, not yours. What would human life look like if we had not fallen away from you? It's beyond imagination. We get into all kinds of trouble because we can't imagine a different life. A world of cooperation and unity. We think it would be boring. Our best stories have painful, exciting, and dramatic conflict. We thrive on conflict.*

I like living on my own, not having to consult others or try to live with them. On the other hand, I am drawn to other people. Eve and I have always been. What am I trying to say? I want to have my life to myself, but I see there is a richness that comes from living with others. What is it? Support? Love? Shared struggles? Less financial anxiety? When we live close, we know others will be there for us. The Amish understand that. They don't have insurance. If a barn burns down, they get together and build a new one. Is this even possible in this world? Are we too far gone?

What am I trying to find? My way back to you? Is that what this is about? Most of the time I don't even know why I want to be closer to you. My heart burns when I feel your presence. Fear is lifted. I am suffused with love for others, even people I don't like. Think of that! Is that how you want us to live? Is that agape?

I always thought that was agape. Love that runs counter to everything we feel or are taught. Maybe it's something even deeper. There are times, very rare, when I actually feel love for someone I abhor. Loving my enemies has got to be the craziest and most counter-intuitive thing! But in that moment it's not just an act of will, it's a reality of heart and spirit. I only feel it when I am centered in you.

Is this what you hope for from each of us? The answer's got to be yes. But how to live that way? Most of the time I'm not centered. I'm preoccupied with myself, as I am right now. So are we to live in this co-housing thing? It'll be with people we already know and love. You remind me that Jack wants to include some low-income people. That means people with ragged, messy lives. I'm not far from retirement age. Why would I want to live with those people? Yes, I know the obvious answer. They are your children.

Do you know how impossible this all seems? Is there a payoff? Joy and peace? It seems like struggle and irritation. Is this something you hope for everyone? "That is not your question."

Sam called to Eve. "I think this might be the direction for us, well, for me at least. Are you feeling anything?"

"I'm trying not to think about it. I have this sinking feeling that we're going to do it."

"Because you think it's the right direction or because I think it is?"

"I have all this resistance. Does that mean it's something I have to look at and don't want to?"

"It could mean it's the wrong way."

"Yeah, I wish! I'm going to pray about it, but I'm afraid we're going to have to do it."

Sam and Eve joined several couples who gathered in the living room of the small home Jack was renovating. The work wasn't done. There was no furniture, but Jack had his men bring in some folding tables and chairs. The fresh smell of sawdust, new drywall, and paint met them as they entered. It was pretty much the same folks who had been at the party. Sam was surprised to see Janet Keller there. He assumed someone who was into traditional real estate would not be interested. He was even more surprised to see Jenn, who must have been back from New York for a visit. The men were looking at the tools that were stacked in the dining room. The women were in a group in the living room, making small talk.

Jack didn't say much but took them on a tour. He had gutted the house. Everything was new. The women expressed pleasure over the kitchen fixtures and appliances which were top of the line. He'd even had his painters do some stenciling along the living room walls. Jenn said of all the things Jack had done, the stenciling surprised her most. Sam was tempted to ask her if she knew Jack was writing poetry. Floors were carpet or hardwood. He'd put a large glass door in the south wall that opened into a small glass garden room-cum-greenhouse. Upstairs he'd opened two small bedrooms into one master bedroom with bath and whirlpool. The third bedroom he'd turned into a study/guest room.

The group gathered back down in the living room. There was an excited hum. Sam stood talking to John, peering out through the greenhouse room into the large open area formed by the backyard of this house, the backyard of the next house, which was the big Victorian one, and the lot behind the apartment building. Jack came up and stood beside them. When they looked at him, he just winked.

He told them all to sit around the two large folding tables that were put side by side. He went to the kitchen and pulled out a large plate of cheese and crackers and another of fruit pieces with a cream dip. He brought in carafes of tea and coffee. Jenn watched with interest. The other women were impressed. The men kidded Jack about becoming domestic.

But Sam noticed that he was all business again when he began to outline the project. He brought out a plat drawing of the whole neighborhood, which showed the different options it afforded: some large homes, some smaller homes, units in the apartment building converted to condos. He stressed that a co-housing community needed to offer different sizes and designs to fit different people. Then he brought out a drawing he'd commissioned from an architect—a design of the community if all the houses on the cul-de-sac and the feeding street as well as the apartment building had been redone. The drawing especially highlighted the common areas with gardens, lawn space, flowers, trees, and play areas with playground equipment.

People got up to lean over and look more closely. Jack pulled out a drawing of the large Victorian house next door. It was painted a muted green with the trim in three different colors in the red and rust pallet. A large peaked addition with a stone chimney was built out from the side. The inside drawing showed an activity/lounge/dining area with cathedral ceiling and a gleaming industrial-grade community kitchen. There was a state-of-the-art entertainment center with digital projection for community meetings and events. The upstairs rooms were outfitted as community guest rooms and there was a community shop in the basement.

Then Jack ushered everyone next door to show them the present state of the building. With the image of its future lingering in their minds, the rundown building didn't look so bad. Jack took them across the back yard strewn with construction materials and through the back way into the apartment building. Sam was interested to see that Jack asked John to conduct this part of the tour and noticed that John looked up as they approached the building at the face of a woman peering out of a window.

John showed them the apartments that were finished, and two unfinished units side by side that could be opened up into one larger condo unit. They asked to see John's apartment. He showed them and explained that he was living in one of the old ones before renovation and that it was not in the greatest shape. He commented on the smell that he could not get out of the units until they were gutted.

Looking ahead, Sam saw a boy standing in the doorway of one of the apartments. John introduced him as David, and Sam remembered he was the boy John talked about at their breakfasts. As they passed the door to the apartment, Sam saw the woman he'd seen at the window scurry into the back bedroom and close the door.

Finally everyone trooped back to Jack's house and sat down around the table again. Jack outlined how co-housing was usually done, how he saw this project starting, and how he was going to use his money to get it going. Then he invited questions. They ranged from skepticism to enthusiasm, but they shook down into three main concerns. How would decisions be made about the common areas, which would be considerable; how would it all be financed; and how could any of them join if they wanted to when the housing market was so bad?

When Sam and Eve came home that evening, there was a message from Will asking Sam to call back right away. It seemed urgent and Sam dialed anxiously, but Will sounded good, even energized when he answered.

"I'm going to follow your instructions and use that money you gave me for something I want to do. Right now I'd like a few days with you. How soon can you free up a few days—that is, if the idea appeals to you?"

Sam laughed and said it sounded good to him. He needed a couple of days away. Will said he would fly east to meet Sam, anywhere he chose. Sam suggested they go to the city. "People always retreat to the country. Not this time. How about next weekend? I'll meet you at the airport. We'll take the train into the Loop and stay in one of the hotels. We'll go to the Art Institute, wander through Millennium Park, and walk along the lakefront. If you don't have a job to do or somewhere you have to be, the city can actually be restful."

Sam put Will on hold to discuss the plan with Eve. This was a rare chance to be with Will. He could see Eve was a bit jealous that he would be enjoying himself in the city. It was agreed Will would fly into O'Hare Friday afternoon and fly back Monday afternoon.

Sam had just put the phone down when it rang again. It was Hank's wife Melissa saying Hank had been in the hospital again. Doctors had been worried about his heart rhythms and had installed a defibrillator. She said he was back home now and wasn't doing so well. Sam wanted to know what that meant. She said Hank was tired and weak and had lost almost all the conditioning he'd built up since his open-heart surgery. Sam said he would come over to visit in the morning.

Next day when Sam arrived, Hank was in pajamas and slippers, propped up in his chair.

"I'd get up if I had the energy, but I'm so goddamned tired. Beyond tired! I'll tell you this was worse than everything else, worse even than the open-heart surgery. I was lying in that hospital bed and I prayed to die. I was done with it. It's been one damn thing right after another."

Sam shook his head and didn't know what to say.

"I'm wondering what the hell my purpose is. Why am I still here? I thought I knew what I was going to do in my retirement. I don't even know that anymore!"

Sam listened, but it was hard for him to shift gears from his anticipation of Will's visit. He composed himself to pay attention. As Hank talked, his heart quieted, and he began to have the feeling of coming home to himself he always had with Hank. Anything could be put into words, no matter how lofty or crude, impossible or ordinary, heartening or troubling.

A thought occurred to Sam. "Hank, is the fear of dying still bugging you?"

Hank looked sharply at Sam. "You're damn right it is! It feels like hell, too. I was in that goddamned bed, and at the same time I wanted to die and I was scared I might. Hell, you know I've never had a strong attachment to life..."

"Wait! I don't know that! It's not true. You like your life."

"Sometimes I'd be glad to be done with it all. Even hope for the end, look forward to what comes next, figure it has to be better than this. I've never been afraid of dying. Now, I'm not sure."

"Have you changed your image of what's on the other side—hell, purgatory, some kind of awful judgment—all that stuff from your childhood?"

"No, I still think that's all bullshit. I don't like this life I have now. My body has not readjusted. Nothing feels right inside. I'm tired all the time. I did all that rehab work. Hard work! And now I have to do it all again. I can't get comfortable. I want it to end. But I don't feel I can ask for that. I'm stuck in this life until it's over. How I live this life I no longer want will have something to do with how I go into whatever comes next. I'm afraid if I screw it up here, it will be harder there."

"You're not telling me God is going to be hard on you if you don't handle this illness well?"

"I don't know what I'm saying. These are feelings. There's no sense in them. I'm stuck here in a life I don't like. I'm afraid it will get worse and I'll just be miserable for the rest of my time here. And I'm a hell of a lot less certain about what comes next. But I want to get to it because I'm tired of all this."

Sam laughed.

"Why do you laugh?" Hank asked.

"You're in a hell of position!"

"You're telling me!"

"And there's nothing you can do about it."

"That the God's truth. Well, I can get up every day. And that's what I'm doing. That's what I've been doing my whole life. I write in my journal. I talk to God in that damn journal and I do still feel that God listens."

"Do you think God cares about you?"

"You're damn right I do!"

"Well then."

"Well then what?"

"I don't know. I don't have any profound wisdom here."

"We're a frigging pair. In our sixties, and we know less than we knew when we were thirty."

"Yeah, but at least we can laugh about it."

"Ain't that the truth!"

****

Sam found Will at the airport, and via train and cab they made their way to the Marriott on North Michigan Avenue. Comfortable hotel. Not exclusive, but good. At $190 a night, not bad for the loop, but Sam was used to paying $75 for a Days Inn. Will had arrived first and secured the room. He insisted on paying for Sam. He said either way it was Sam's money. They ate dinner in the hotel and sat up late talking. Sam told him about the co-housing possibility, and Will was intensely interested and asked many questions.

The next day, which was Saturday, they walked for hours down Michigan Avenue to the Field Museum, then back along the lakeshore, then over past the Art Institute to Millennium Park where they sat and contemplated the "Bean," which offered endlessly entertaining and misshaped images of young parents with kids in high-tech strollers that the Bean stretched out to look like limos and well-dressed young professionals, some of the women with short skirts, long legs and impossibly high heels, which the Bean foreshortened, completely destroying the sleek elevated look the shoes were supposed to produce. A bag lady passed in front of the Bean pushing a small utility cart overflowing with plastic bags and odds and ends of clothing. As she passed around the end of the Bean it lengthened her and for a brief moment she looked lean and elegant and her cart looked like a piece of Louis Vuitton luggage.

Will laughed when Sam pointed this out. "Is that what great art does? Makes the high low and the low high?"

"I thought Jesus did that."

"Maybe it's God's humanity that infuses great art."

"Is the Bean great art?"

Will shrugged. They had settled into a mode of conversation where neither had to answer the other and any tangent, however much of a non sequitur it was, was welcomed. Sam could not remember when he had felt so relaxed, inside, down deep.

Sunday afternoon they were sitting in the Chicago Shakespeare Theater engrossed in "The Taming of the Shrew" done as a play within a contemporary play in which the actress playing the shrew that needed taming was in a lesbian relationship with the director who could not seem to tame her. It came to Sam how unimportant money was, far less important than he had ever imagined. The ideas came in fleeting bursts, and he had to focus to keep them from disappearing the way dream images fade as you come awake. An interior dialogue. Like prayer, but not. *How could I be so blind? Yet how could it all be true? I was meant to live in joy and freedom, not to worry. Never to worry. Live and let the things you need come to you. I don't believe that will happen. It's already been happening. I've been lucky. So is that the choice—luck or hard work? Nothing else? Those actors on stage—are they there because they worked hard? Do they know divine energy is flowing through them? Some of them do. Artists and creative ones often know. But they still believe they're there because they put out their own effort. This is true. You have to show up, Sam. You have to put in everything you've got. But you don't produce the moment. Something larger does that. You can get with it or not. Your life is a gift, Sam. All of it. Eve. The money. The old man. Will. Hank. Your friends. This co-housing adventure. What have you done to produce any of it? You are free, Sam. Do the next thing. Don't be afraid. Think big. You are part of the universe. This is God's creation. Enjoy it. Spend yourself. Spend your money. Don't hold back. Spend your love. Dance, Sam. Like peering into the Bean, watch the fleeting images and know they point to a great mystery. Embrace its beauty and inscrutability. You can trust it, Sam. You know what it is at its heart. You know.* Tears ran down Sam's face.

Afterwards, walking back to the hotel in the late afternoon Sam tried to tell Will what had happened, but the images were already moving into the mist.

The next day they rode the El to the airport and Sam thanked Will as they parted at airport security. Will laughed, "It was your money that made this possible. Thank yourself."

"It was your idea."

"Well, we can be glad for our friendship," Will said and took his place in the line that snaked toward the conveyor belts and scanners.

Sam took a limo back to Selby and found Eve sunning herself on the small deck at the back of their condo. "I know what I want to do," he said. "I want to throw in with Jack and John (if he's in it) and anyone else who's interested."

"Why does that not surprise me?" Eve asked.

"Something broke free, Eve. I know above all else that I love you. If you don't want to do this, it's okay. We'll do something else. You don't *have* to do anything. We'll figure it out."

Chapter 20 – Decisions

Sam woke early, went around to Eve's side, and sat on the edge of the bed gazing down at her, reaching out to stroke her face. She opened her eyes and gave him a sleepy smile, leaning her face into his hand. "Anything else, and you'd be in trouble for waking me up."

"I'm heading to breakfast, going to talk about the co-housing thing. Any further thoughts?"

"At 6:30 in the morning! I don't think so. Are you pressuring me?"

"Just full of energy. Don't know where this is coming from. I'll talk to you later this morning." He kissed her on the forehead and headed out the door.

Sam was the first one there. He'd brought a book, but instead of reading he watched people through the windows as they climbed out of their cars, came through the door, shed their coats, and took seats—actions as ordinary as the coffee cup the busboy put in front of him, but they seemed beautiful. He greeted each friend with noticeable enthusiasm. He thought he should probably curb this unseemly spirit, keep his interest level appropriate to a gloomy mid-week morning in March, but he didn't care. Kurt tipped his head in Sam's direction as the others sat down and said someone must have spiked Sam's coffee.

"I have some news," John said before he got his coat off.

"You got some last night," Kurt blurted out. The rest of the men laughed the obligatory male laugh that such a comment demands. By now, they all knew about Angela. Sam for a moment was jarred out of his cloud of purity and simplicity.

John looked uncomfortable and gave Kurt an ungrateful glance. "Not that, and I sure as hell wouldn't tell you if I did. You know the boy who lives in the apartment next to mine? His mother has been offered a job on this nature farm in Arizona she's visited twice before. She's just back from the second visit. Her son David has stayed with me. This time she'll be working in the gardens and the drying rooms and the kitchen where they prepare herbs and vegetables to make various organic and herbal mixes and the vegetarian meals for the people who come there for courses and classes. She'll be leaving again in two months. David doesn't want to go with her. This time it's for five or six months. She's asked if David can stay with me again."

"Jeez!" exclaimed Kurt. "That's huge! What can she be thinking? To ask that!"

"It's not as crazy as it sounds. I spend a lot of time with the boy. He's lived with me twice. I like him—a lot. He feels comfortable with me. She knows that. He has a lot of friends at school."

"Is she thinking about David or herself?"

"Some of both. She thinks it will be better for David to stay here. She loves him fiercely, but she knows sometimes she can't take care of him. It's more than she can manage to take care of herself. She knows this about herself. I'm getting to know her better, and I have to say, I can see how immensely difficult her life is. Just getting through her day—it's almost heroic! Thing is, she can't bring herself to talk to David. She hasn't told him yet."

"Can you do this?" Kirby asked quietly.

John smiled, "Actually, I think I can."

Sam, who had been watching John keenly, said suddenly, "You want to do it, don't you?"

John paused, "I do. I've never had kids. At my age! Doing this for the first time! Crazy, huh?"

"Let me see," Sam said. "You're taking on responsibility for a boy. You're starting a relationship with a woman. You're joining Jack in this co-housing thing. My hat's off to you!"

"You're doing the co-housing thing?" Kurt broke in. "For sure?"

John looked at Jack. "Yes and no. I don't have the capital to buy in, but I'd like to rent a unit." He looked across the table. "Jack is hoping the group can have a few rental units available. The apartment building makes that option pretty easy. I'll continue to manage the apartments."

"I'm ready," Sam said. "Eve is still thinking, and we won't do it unless she's 100 percent. But I've made up my mind."

"Anne and I are interested," Joe said. "But we don't see how we can sell our home in this market."

"That's my predicament," said Kurt.

"I may have that covered," said Jack, who'd been quiet. I can make some short-term, unsecured loans, sort of bridge loans, to carry you through until you can sell your homes."

"You would do that?" Kurt said in surprise. "Take that kind of risk. People don't do that anymore."

Jack shrugged, "You're my friends. I think I can trust you."

"Is this a good idea?" Joe asked. "Friends and money don't always mix."

"They're going to have to if this thing is going to work. We'll be holding land together. Like in any condo set-up we'll be collecting a monthly maintenance fee from each other."

"Isn't that the point of co-housing?" said Kirby. "You mingle some of your resources. You build community."

"You've been quiet this morning," Sam said to Kirby. "Are you and Nancy going to come into this venture?'

"We're intrigued, but we can't right now. Our future is uncertain."

"Why?" Joe asked, "Though I think I know."

Kirby smiled, "Our financial situation could change."

"Why?" John asked quickly. "What's going on, Kirby? Is Nancy in trouble? I can't image that she is. She's the best principal in the district."

"No, Nancy is fine—fortunately. We may really need her principal's salary. I've decided to perform the union Samantha and Marianne have asked for."

Joe nodded his head.

"I told the board last night that I am going ahead with it as a matter of conscience. But I won't do it in the church. Won't force that decision on the congregation. I'm talking with the folks at the Unitarian Universalist church about renting their facility. I've told the executive for our district, Daryl Bender, that I'm doing this so he won't be blind-sided."

"What did he say?"

Kirby smiled, "I think he has sympathy for what I'm doing, but he can't say that publicly."

"Why not?"

"You know there are churches downstate whose members deeply disapprove of same-sex relations. I expect those churches to press for action against me. Daryl expects it too. He has to maintain some neutrality."

"Neutrality! When does neutrality become fellow-traveling?" Kurt asked

Kirby sighed, "I know it looks like that. But with Daryl it's not. But I don't need to know the reasons for someone else's actions. I just need to account for my own...and try to respect those who disagree...and have compassion for those who are hurt."

"Kirby, I don't get this," Kurt said. "Those narrow-minded bastards downstate cause all kinds of hurt for people like Samantha and Marianne. What about that!"

"Well, I'm doing something about that by performing this ceremony. I can't undo that pain. But I can be on the side of something different for the future. But I'm not going to treat the people who reject or even hate homosexuals as the new 'abomination.' They're human beings too. It'd be easy to write them off. On my bad days I'd like to tell them all where to go. But I know most of those downstate folks. The hate stops here, all of it. There are no good guys or bad buys here, just human beings." Kirby paused for a moment. "Too much said. I didn't intend to make a speech. I'm not preaching. I'm not trying to set an example. I'm not trying to convince you. Here's the long and short of it—I'll perform the ceremony. If the district comes after me, I'll resign to protect the congregation."

"Kirby, how the hell can we let you do that!" Jack exclaimed. "Think about it! What kind of friends would we be if we let you take the whole rap!"

"I've been reading our constitution and bylaws," Joe said, "then checking the district's bylaws, and looking into the denomination's polity. The district ordains a minister, but the congregation employs him. There is nothing anywhere that says a congregation has to employ only an ordained minister. Congregations can and do employ custodial staff, secretaries, organists, choir directors. A congregation can ask anyone to preach. Plenty of our members, non-ordained members, have filled our pulpit, when Kirby's been out of town."

"I see where you're going with this," Sam said. "We can still employ Kirby, even if he's defrocked. He can still preach. But what about the things that necessitate an ordained person? Kirby won't be able to baptize or lead communion or perform marriages."

"We have two retired ministers in the congregation, whose ordinations are in good standing—I checked. We can ask them. Or, if need be, we can ask for help from a minister in one of the other congregations in the metropolitan area."

Kirby smiled again, "Well, I think employing me even in that way may become a problem. But I appreciate your creativity."

The men fell into an uncharacteristic silence, which Sam finally broke. "There's a lot happening. John taking on David, the co-housing thing, Kirby's decision. All risky."

"What are you saying," Joe asked.

"I don't know. Big changes ahead, I guess, touching all of us."

Kurt laughed, "You forgot one, Sam. I mentioned it at the beginning. John conveniently sidestepped it. Probably hopes we've forgotten. Staying quiet there in his seat, Still playing the new guy. Come on, John, spill the beans. We all know about Angela. We're all envious."

"We're all happily married too," said Joe.

"No harm in vicarious participation in our brother's good fortune."

"I don't know what you're talking about," John protested. "And I'm not the new guy anymore."

There was an expectant silence. They waited for John to say something. He threw up his hands. "My lips are sealed. I will say she is a very intelligent and thoughtful lady."

There was laughter.

"You have to know something about John," said Kirby. "He was a bashful young man when he was pursuing Mary, the girl who became his wife. What you see before you now is a man who has made great strides. He's a lothario compared to what he was. We should toast his conquest."

"Let's hear it for John's conquest!" said Kurt. "And for Kirby. When was the last time you heard a pastor endorse a conquest?"

"Poor word choice," said Kirby with a smile. "Let's toast John's maturing relationship."

****

On a whim Sam stopped at Oliver Larkspur's house after he left the restaurant. It was still early, but he knew the old man was an early riser. He lived in a two-story gray stone house. A brick path curved from the driveway to a slightly raised flagstone platform surrounded by low bushes and flowers. The red front door was set in a round stone turret topped by a round pointed roof rising a few feet above the main roof that was broken up by dormer windows. Sam had admired the house long before he realized that the old man lived in it. Larkspur came to the door. He was in a burgundy-colored paisley robe and leather slippers. He was smoking a pipe, which Sam commented on since he'd never seen the old man using tobacco. He said he only smoked it in the morning with his first cup of coffee. It was an indulgence that had never risen to the level of a vice. He invited Sam in and ushered him through a richly comfortable living room carpeted with oriental rugs to a small breakfast room that looked out into a landscaped backyard, all the time keeping up a steady stream of talk. Sam was amused and pleased by the old man's easy hospitality. He sank into a padded breakfast chair and, though he was already awash in caffeine and sugar from his breakfast, accepted a fresh mug of coffee and some coffee cake that made him look up with admiration and ask where it came from. The old man asked if Sam would believe him if he said he'd made it himself. Sam said he was long past being surprised. Larkspur smiled.

"I had an epiphany," Sam said, and he told him about it.

"So you're free now of the power of money?"

"Is anybody ever? Certainly Jesus was free, though he was tempted in the wilderness. Maybe St. Francis. I'm not making a once-and-forever statement. But for the first time I felt deeply what I've been toying with intellectually."

"And?"

"It's like…It's hard to express it without saying what it's not. It's no longer being anxious. It's being freed from the feeling that having that next new thing will bring joy. It's no longer worrying about the future."

"Is it turning you into an ascetic?"

"The opposite. I find myself relishing the physical realities around me. I can enjoy the beautiful things others have, like your house, for instance, and have no desire to have them for myself. I'm living in the present. Things actually look brighter and the colors more vivid. Things that once might have made me reluctant and uneasy now look like adventures."

For the first time in Sam's experience, the old man seemed non-plussed. Sam stopped talking and watched him, waiting for him to say something. "You surprise me, Sam. This is a breakthrough! Something rare! Will it be sustained? Probably depends on your spiritual practice. But now that you've tasted this, you'll find it hard to go back."

Sam heard something in the old man's voice. He was about to ask him if he'd had a similar experience when Larkspur said, "I have always carried my wealth lightly, but not with this level of freedom. I celebrate this. I'm a bit envious." He paused. "I'm not able to go where you're going. I'm unwilling to let go of my wealth. You have put me to shame."

Sam leaned forward across the glass-topped breakfast table, pushing aside his mug and plate. "I want to put the rest of the capital you gave me into an experiment in community living." He told him about the co-housing thing and explained that they would need around 15 families to move ahead, unless they had an infusion of capital. He wanted to use the rest of the money to buy a unit and invest in the process, adding their capital to Jack Foster's. He looked away and his intensity faltered, then he seemed to gather resolution and looked the old man straight in the eye. "Would you consider helping to finance this venture?" The old man sat back and for the first time Sam saw his face close. It was as if he had dropped a curtain behind his lively eyes. Sam wanted to back up, to apologize, but he seemed to find himself firm and unwavering and he continued. "It is way too presumptuous to ask this, but I had to do it."

The old man nodded. "Yes, I see that. I've been toying with you, playing with fire. Now am I to get burned? I think I probably deserve this."

"You have to understand that nothing rides on your saying yes or no. You will not disappoint me if you say no."

"Maybe not, but I might disappoint myself. You have turned the tables on me, young man."

"I'm in my sixties," Sam said. "How am I young?"

"I cannot give you an answer. I have to think and talk it over."

"I know it's none of my business, but I'm curious. Whom do you turn to if you need advice?"

"Someone you know. Preston Krunsch."

Sam laughed, "I'd like to be a fly on the wall for that conversation." The old man raised an eyebrow. "Nothing against Preston," Sam said quickly. "I like him. I've known him for years. He's solid, but...ah...conventional. He just doesn't...You're an odd..." The old man let Sam be hoisted on his own petard. "He's...ah...a good man," Sam concluded lamely.

"Of course he is. You think I'm exotic and eccentric and he's plain and proper. Well, Preston has good sense, and sometimes the conventional is appropriate, even right."

"Well, I've done my part in asking you to consider. It's out of my hands now."

"So...whose hands is it in?"

"I put this idea out to test the possibility. I'm letting it go to see what develops. That's all."

Sam drove to his office. Eve was gone for the afternoon. He took out his journal. *Well, I am grateful for this burst of energy and hope. I have no idea where it will lead. Should I care? I don't. I don't want to care again. You know what I mean. I don't want to be anxious. I don't want to angst over anything ever again. I'm free and it's good.*

Are my brain chemicals producing a false euphoria? A lot of people would say yes. I've either stumbled into a profound reality, or I've joined a grand fantasy.

What am I doing? Do I really want to live in this co-housing community? Lord, we will spend hours making decisions together. I've read the material. Many communities work by consensus. Do you have any idea how hard it is to reach consensus—on anything in this post-modern world!

What is "post-modern" anyway? Just a word that makes people sound intelligent. Are you beyond absolutes? Are there no absolutes because you are so absolute that you are eternally shrouded in mystery? So we can never know you in your entirety. Truth eludes us because you elude us. The great "I am"! The Jews get this. They won't even say your name. You are incomprehensible.

Still, I feel like I know you. How is that? You have a heart. Heart-knowing does not produce clarity, but it produces trust and love. So how can something so incomprehensible that none of us can ever know you, love us? That's probably the greatest incomprehensibility. The absolute that cannot be spoken because it cannot be known, only experienced.

Is this kind of rumination of any value? I'm babbling on and not listening. What do you have to say to me?

Sam found he could not listen. His soul was filled with his own swirling thoughts. So he closed his journal and was putting on his coat when he heard the outer door open and Eve appeared. She was not smiling. Her mouth was set. She took off her coat and went into her room and asked Sam if she could talk to him, in a quiet voice that carried elements of both uneasiness and resolution. Sam sat down in the loveseat that took up one corner across from her desk. "You look very serious," he said nervously, feeling defensive though there was no reason.

"I can't do this co-housing thing," she said.

"Okay," Sam said slowly.

She told him how she had started worrying about money again. After paying off debts and back taxes, tithing, buying the condo, and making all the other purchases they had been putting off, they had only $200,000 left toward their retirement. "Most people don't have that amount in savings," she said, "but most people have pension plans. That money and some social security are all we are going to have. Our income has never been great, so our social security payments will be low, and who knows what's going to happen to that whole system as the baby boomers retire. I can't put our money at risk."

Sam nodded.

"I'm sorry. I know how much you want to do this," she said.

"Have you prayed about it?"

"I'm drawing a blank. Maybe my anxiety is so high I can't hear."

Sam was silent.

"Say something, Sam. I don't want this to come between us."

"I need some time to think," Sam said. He stood and walked toward the door, then came back and softly stroked her cheek. "You know I love you," he said.

He got in his car and drove over to the cul-de-sac. Jack's car was in his driveway. He parked in front of the rundown Victorian house. Apart from the little house Jack had rehabbed, the whole neighborhood was shabby. The bright plans Jack had showed everyone seemed far away—wishful thinking. Say they did retrofit this whole street and cul-de-sac. It was still in a shabby neighborhood. They'd never get their money out if they decided to sell their homes.

A kid with a bat and ball came out of one of the homes, took the porch steps in a single bound and went tearing down the street toward the open area between the cul-de-sac homes and the apartment building. Boys came out of several other homes, and even a girl showed up carrying a first baseman's mitt. Sam watched them choose sides. The girl appeared to be in demand. As her team spread out and the other team got ready to bat, she took her place at first, pounded her hand into the glove and began to shout standard baseball patter. Sam smiled and walked over to watch the game.

He could picture this whole large area with gardens at one end and flower beds and play equipment and a baseball backstop at this end and even a few benches. He could see the space behind the apartment building landscaped and brick and flagstone paths crossing from the building to the backyards of the homes which melded into each other and were planted with fruit trees. He saw scattered lawn furniture and sandboxes, a large communal gas grill, and an open fire pit. He saw tables with umbrellas.

He pictured the addition to the old Victorian house and he could visualize through floor-to-ceiling windows adults and kids gathering around a large table with a fire blazing in a huge stone fireplace. The people were laughing and someone brought out a guitar and another sat at a keyboard and they sang. The scene shifted and it was Christmas and the great room glistened with lights and a tall tree in front of the windows. All the houses of the street glowed with Christmas decorations.

The scene shifted again and he pictured the adults of the community gathered in a large circle in the great room. Tension in the air. They were talking and talking and talking, trying to resolve some matter. Everyone was frustrated and just wanted to be done with it, but they could not reach consensus and everyone went home disappointed and wondering why they'd ever gotten themselves into this.

Sadness came over him and a yearning. He wanted to live in a place like that fantasy, but he wasn't sure he'd be good at it, or that it was even possible. He loved his friends, but would they be able to do the hard work of community? Once upon a time people had to live more closely and depend on each other. Now, if you were middle class or better, you could be self-sufficient, have everything you needed, even down to your own hedge clipper and snow blower. Would any of them really be willing to give that up?

He heard footsteps and turned to see Jack walking toward him. "So, what do you think?" Jack asked.

Sam sighed. "Eve doesn't want to do it."

"Why? Is it the people issues? Or the money?"

"On the surface, it's the money."

"Suppose I could show you a way to do it for no more than you have tied up in your new condo?"

"Jack, is this going to work? Say we get five or six families to start. We're all friends, so we have a good basis. We have a great vision, but are we all really going to want the reality? It's hard work to live in closer community."

"Are you getting cold feet?"

"Just being honest with myself. I've been standing here, and I've had a shining fantasy. A community that is almost idyllic. But are we kidding ourselves?"

"I don't care," Jack said.

"Really?"

"I'm up for an adventure. What the hell!"

"Jack, you can't do something as complicated and difficult as all this on a whim."

"It's not a whim."

"Well then—so unconcerned about failure."

"Why not? What do I have to lose but money!"

Sam shook his head.

"What does that mean?"

"If I'd have told you three years ago you would be talking like this, what would you have said?"

Jack laughed. "You know the answer to that!"

Sam made no reply.

"So you don't believe people can change?" Jack said.

"No, I know people can change, but this…"

"Is what? Beyond belief? Jack Foster, the last man in the world to be trying to talk people into some kind of hippie experiment!"

"You said it."

"I just wish I'd done it sooner. Jenn and I might still be together."

"You think so?"

"Who knows! It is what it is. So where does this leave you, Sam? You can't do this if Eve isn't with you."

Sam nodded and said nothing.

Chapter 21 – Unions

Sam and Eve went with Samantha and Marianne and others from the Westbrook Church to decorate the Unitarian Universalist church. It was a new structure built from the remnants of an old barn that had been painstakingly dismantled into numbered pieces, hauled to the site, and reconstructed. The sanctuary ceiling rose like a cathedral, supported by thick soaring barn timbers instead of stone vaulting. Wood beams also ran across, adding intimacy to the sense of uplift. The women appliquéd banners and hung them from the beams. Sam and several men fastened vertical posts to every third pew and attached vases of wildflowers. They draped the lectern with garlands and covered the altar with a richly brocaded golden cloth on which they placed an earthenware chalice with wine and a large, colorful ceramic platter with loaves of freshly baked bread.

The Westbrook congregation turned out in full complement. Some of the people surprised Sam. He wondered if it was curiosity that drove them or a desire to be in solidarity despite their reservations about same-sex unions. Joey, Samantha's daughter, stood up with Marianne, and Kaylie, Marianne's daughter, stood up with Samantha. Sonny was flower boy and ring bearer. People watched him as he walked down the aisle scattering rose petals, hoping he might do something unexpected. The two women wore white gowns in different styles designed to fit their different personalities, but each wore a thin elegant strip of rainbow-colored fabric from right shoulder to left hip. The service was simple, music interwoven with vows written by each woman and a short meditation by Kirby, after which he officiated at a communion service in which the two women acted as servers, breaking the loaves and passing chunks of bread down each aisle for participants to break off a piece and passing trays of wine in small ceramic communion cups that had been made especially for the service as mementos to be taken home. A video camera set on a high tripod in the back recorded the service, and throughout there were flashes from the cameras of the wedding photographer and others anxious to capture the moment.

Sam and Eve sat three-quarters of the way back, a position Sam chose so he could see the action up front and also see most of the wedding guests. There were many people he did not know; some he recognized as UU members. He knew their congregation supported same-sex unions, but he also knew this ceremony was a first for them, and he assumed they had come in support and curiosity. He also saw male couples and female couples and he assumed these were Samantha's and Marianne's gay friends. During the service Eve leaned over to Sam and whispered comments about lovely little touches she especially liked. As Samantha and Marianne said their vows, Eve took Sam's hand in both of hers.

Downstairs after the service during the reception Sam saw a young woman he did not recognize talking to Kirby and making notes on a stenographer's pad. He glided over just as the young woman moved on and corralled Maud Miller.

"Someone tipped off the press," Kirby said. "This is the first service of this kind in Selby. The paper seems to think it's big news."

Sam snorted, "It will be, I'm afraid! What angle did she take?"

"She wanted to know why I performed the service and why we didn't do it in our own church. She asked what the people in our congregation think."

"Was she hostile?"

"I don't think so. She gave me the impression that she liked the service and was sympathetic. But she was interested in the controversy. She knows this will make a dramatic story and stir up a fuss."

The next morning Sam saw the 100-point headlines in the Sunday paper glaring through the pink plastic even before he removed the wrapper: "Lesbian Civil Union—A Selby First." Kirby's name and the name of the church figured prominently in the sub-headline. A large photo above the fold showed Samantha and Marianne embracing and exchanging the kiss, with Kirby looking on with a smile. The article included Kirby's explanation of why the service was at the UU church and not in the one he pastored, making Kirby seem at once like a courageous man following his conscience and a rebel unwilling to follow his congregation's guidance. It included quotes from members of the UU church in support and a small boxed sidebar with excerpts from an interview with the pastor of the largest Baptist church in town who sternly disapproved and remarks by the pastor of a nearby nondenominational megachurch who expressed his dismay and said this was why the mainline churches like the Westbrook congregation were losing members. The only thing about the article that made Sam smile was a quote from Maud Miller, who told the reporter, "I didn't get this gay and lesbian thing either. I thought it was wrong and weird. But then I took another look. And I met these two women and their families. There's no way what happened here today is wrong. You tell the people of Selby that. You tell them it's time to lighten up!"

Sam turned on his computer and Googled "Lesbian Civil Union, Selby." Already there were many references. The local paper's website headed the list. Both Chicago papers had picked up the story, as well as some downstate journals. He checked Facebook and found many postings.

At church that morning Sam saw several people he knew did not approve of Kirby's action talking in a corner of the lounge. He noticed that Herman Fry was not with them. A small group of people were gathered around Maud Miller in the narthex, and he saw Kurt slap her on the back with a hardy laugh of approval. He found Kirby in his office, briefing Kristen Witter, who was the worship leader. He caught Joe's eye across the narthex, who shrugged and raised his eyebrows. During the service Kirby made no reference to the Saturday ceremony or the press coverage, but Maud stood up during the sharing time and said she was proud of "our pastor." Sam thought how sometimes the most unlikely champions emerge. After the service Herman was standing by himself in the narthex, and Sam made a point of greeting him, shaking his hand, standing next to him, yet not saying anything. After a bit, Herman said, "I saw the paper today."

Sam nodded.

"Just don't seem right."

"Does it embarrass you or make you ashamed of our congregation?" Sam asked.

"No. What I mean to say is people can have different opinions. Kirby is doing what he thinks is right. I just can't go along with it. But I ain't one to stir up trouble." He glanced at the group in the lounge. "But I just can't go against what the Bible says. What I mean to say is, you can find different things in the Bible, and we don't always have to agree. I know Samantha and Marianne are nice people, but it just don't seem right. We have to learn to listen and understand each other. I just can't go along with this."

"I know, Herman. This is a hard one. Some of us on the other side feel as strongly as you do."

"Will this put Kirby in trouble?"

"It might. We have to wait and see."

"Well, I don't want that. I've always respected him. What I mean to say, we have to get along in the church. I just don't know how."

On Thursday at breakfast the first words from Sam and everybody else were questions to Kirby, who told the men the district ministerial commission had called already and asked to meet with him the following Monday evening. He would have to drive downstate.

"That was quick!" Kurt exclaimed.

Kirby shrugged. "Sunday afternoon someone in our congregation faxed the newspaper article to Fred Vogel, pastor of the Effingham congregation, but he'd already seen it online. Apparently ministers from ten downstate congregations met Monday night at the Tutorville church and formulated a petition asking the ministerial commission to review my ordination. Fred Vogel chairs the commission. He e-mailed the members and persuaded them to summon me to a special meeting next Monday."

"How do you know all this?"

"They sent their request through Daryl Bender. He gave me all the background."

"What did he say? Does he support this...this witch hunt?"

"His hands are tied, Kurt. You know in our polity, the district executive's power is mostly persuasion. Decisions are made by the membership, in this case other ministers. He was candid with me. He thinks Fred has the votes to censure me or even rescind my ordination."

"Is their decision final?"

"No, the district board has to approve it, but he thinks there aren't enough votes there to stop it."

"Is he just going to stand by and watch it happen?"

Kirby shrugged. "I don't know."

"You're remarkably sanguine about it."

"If you want the truth, I feel some anger, but mostly I'm just sad and out of sorts. I was always one of the good guys, someone people were proud of. It's a new experience to be vilified. Apparently the language at the meeting at Tutorville was pretty nasty. I'm not surprised. I expected this. But no amount of preparation can get you ready for the raw reality."

"Kirby, you know we're with you," Sam said.

He smiled, "Yes, thank you."

"You know we have a plan," Sam went on. "Joe, remember what you said. Are you working on that?"

Joe nodded.

"We're loaded for bear!" Kurt said.

"We're not hunters stalking prey," Kirby paused. "We're good people. But we are driven by motives and feelings we don't even fully understand ourselves, whether it's Fred Vogel's angry campaign or your aggressive advocacy."

"You're being nicer about this than I would be."

****

Sam knew the process for questioning a minister's suitability was laid out in the denomination's polity manual. He made a point of going online and reading it, then dropping by the church to talk to Kirby, who was sitting in his office with John. Fred Vogel had apparently read the manual carefully and had based his arguments to the commission on the claims that Kirby had not been true to the scriptures and had not supported the beliefs of the church. The process for discontinuing an ordination was lengthy, designed to protect the minister from precipitous attack. It required the appointment of an assessment team and a series of hearings before a recommendation could be presented to the district board. Kirby told Sam that Vogel's strategy was to create the assessment team and start the process but in the meantime he was going to call for Kirby's ordination to be temporarily suspended until the final determination had been made. Fred had read the manual closely enough to know that the polity did not provide for or prohibit a temporary suspension. Kirby smiled grimly, glancing at John and then back at Sam. "It looks fair," he said. "My ordination will not be rescinded without due process, but it achieves Vogel's goal of punishing me and indirectly the congregation."

Joe Kurtz, as board chair, went with Kirby to the meeting of the ministerial commission. Sam also went, as an interested board member and friend. John asked to go along too, and Kirby smiled, nodded, and said with uncharacteristic sarcasm, "The commission still permits friendship."

At the hearing, Kirby gave a careful exegesis of the passages of scripture people quoted to show that those passages were rooted in a different culture and referred to somewhat different matters than appeared on their surface. Several members of the commission argued heatedly that Kirby was wrong and was ignoring the plain truth of the Bible. One, a woman from downstate, said nothing but listened carefully. Two members argued that Kirby's exegesis had to be acknowledged as having merit and pushed for room in the district for active ministers to disagree. Joe described the care and thoughtfulness with which Kirby made his decision and emphasized his effort to respect the position of the denomination while staying true to his own conscience. The woman who had been quiet asked Kirby if he had considered the effect it would have on the other churches in the district and the denomination. Fred Vogel said it came down to a matter of simple truth. What did scripture say and what did the church say?

Sam said nothing, but he watched the members of the commission, storing away in his memory little details of language and demeanor. He watched Kirby and Joe, too, and especially John, who kept a keen eye on Kirby and seemed to be willing him to acquit himself well. Several times

Sam was on the point of asking to speak, but each time he felt a slight inner check. He could see that minds seemed to be made up.

The commission was composed of six members plus the chair. It split three/three on the vote to appoint the assessment committee and suspend Kirby's ordination in the interim, pending a final determination. To break the tie, Fred, as chair, cast the deciding vote, which gave them a four-vote majority to put Kirby under investigation.

Several weeks later in the district board meeting, Sam noticed that the discussion was more cordial. Again Joe, Sam, and John accompanied Kirby, but this time Maud Miller came along too. Fred Vogel presented the recommendation of the ministerial commission. Sam noticed that some of the board members were surprised at Fred's restraint. Both Kirby and Joe spoke. Daryl Bender risked the ire of the downstate pastors by saying that Kirby's act of conscience should be respected. He pointed out that there were other congregations in the district that did not follow every part of the polity. Fred's church, for instance, was not willing to ordain women or have them serve in ministry even though the denomination had recognized the ordination of women for many years. "We need to find ways to tolerate one another's differences," he said.

The board sessions were open, and visitors could ask to speak. Maud Miller made a ringing speech that rankled some of the members and made others smile. In the end one of the moderate board members said she agreed with Daryl, but the board had a responsibility to support the ministerial commission. The process had to be initiated. She turned to Kirby, "I'm sorry, but I think this is such a 'hot-button' issue downstate that the suspension of your ordination while the assessment committee works is probably necessary. I personally will argue in support of your ordination, but I think we have to let this process run its course." The recommendation carried by a small 5 to 4 majority.

Joe called a special meeting of the Westbrook board the next day. Sam saw as soon as he entered the room that feelings were running high. He also noticed that John had again asked to sit in and listen. Some members were angry, some sad, some confused. Did this mean Kirby could no longer be their minister? Did he have to take a leave of absence? Joe let the talk run for a while, until people vented their feelings, and the meeting made a turn and members began to ask what to do.

Sam cleared his throat and said, "Some of us have been thinking about this possibility for a long time. Joe's taken the lead, and I think he has something to say."

"In our polity the district controls ordination, but we control employment. We can hire Kirby to preach and do his pastoral duties, even if his ordination is suspended. And that's mostly what he does anyway. We can find other people, retired ministers in our congregations or a pastor from a nearby congregation, to do the things only an ordained person can do."

There was immediate interest. Board members wanted to be sure they could really do that. They discussed whether the district could do anything to the congregation. Joe said he thought the downstate churches would not like it, but he could find no grounds in the polity for them to push for action against the congregation. The mood of the board meeting lightened. What went unsaid but assumed was that the congregation wanted to keep Kirby.

Sam noticed that Kirby, as he always did at board meetings, sat quietly and listened. Board members were accustomed to this and knew that when he needed to speak he would and that what he would have to say would be helpful, sometimes exactly what was needed. He was not the kind of pastor who tried to dominate meetings. Board members rarely turned to him for approval, but they often turned to him for his wisdom. So on this night their discussions went on like usual and they almost forgot they were discussing Kirby himself, until John interrupted, asked if an observer could speak, and pointed this out. Everyone stopped.

"For a moment," Joe said, turning apologetically to Kirby, "We were talking about you as if you're not here. So, what shall we do that is best for you?"

"Your question must be what is best for the congregation," Kirby replied.

"But what do you want?" Sam asked

"I want to continue to pastor this church, as I have been doing. But that is no longer possible."

"Doesn't Joe's proposal make that possible?" Maud asked.

"Maybe, but I'm not so sure. Will people feel the same about my leadership if they know I'm under scrutiny by the district?"

"Our people know your character," Sam said. "They know that has not changed."

"But they see how my actions have affected the congregation. Some are already upset."

"But that's a small minority."

"They are members too. Can I pastor a divided congregation? I'm not talking about what I cannot do because ordination is suspended. I'm talking about the underlying relationship of trust that exists between a pastor and the congregation. Isn't that broken?" He looked at Herman Fry. "And won't people somehow know and remember that as long as I am under this suspension, I am in a sense neutered, a good guy maybe, but no longer with any spiritual potency? What subtle effect will that have?"

"I think you're underestimating our congregation," Sam said.

"If you follow this course of action, the downstate churches may ask district conference to sanction the congregation," Kirby replied.

"Joe says there are no grounds."

"People can always find grounds."

"Do you really think the district would do that?

"It happened in Indiana."

There was silence. People knew about what had happened in that district.

"Do you want to risk putting the congregation through that?" Kirby asked.

Joe, speaking softly, said, "What are you saying, Kirby?"

"I'm thinking that the best thing may be for me to resign."

People around the table immediately shook their heads and some blurted, "No."

"We're in uncharted waters here," Joe said quietly, "but I don't think we can let Kirby take this all on himself. I think we have to give the congregation a say in how we move forward."

"Before we even think of accepting a resignation from Kirby, we need to put forward a recommendation for keeping him. Let the congregation wrestle with this," Sam said. "Kirby, you've always preached that we must listen to each other and trust that the spirit speaks through the community. You often say that's one of the strengths of our tradition. It's part of our genius. So let's trust it and let it work."

"Amen!" said Maud enthusiastically. "I move that we bring Joe's ideas as a recommendation to the congregation."

Joe asked Maud to hold off on the motion while they worked out the wording of the recommendation. When they got it where they wanted it, she made a formal motion. It was seconded and passed with only one no vote and that was Herman Fry, who had listened and said nothing.

Chapter 22 – Domestic Arrangements

The next day Jack wanted details from John about the meeting. He already knew something since he'd run into Joe and Kirby having lunch at Emma's, but he wanted a full report, and he had some keen observations. So the church was on John's mind later as he was sitting at his kitchen table in the afternoon, taking a break and waiting for David to come home from school. He was looking around proudly at his new apartment. This morning he'd moved three doors down into one of the finished units. He told David to be sure not to go to the old apartment. He had moved only his clothes, personal stuff, and two pieces of furniture—the table where he sat and the sofa he'd purchased. He had left behind all the ratty used furniture. Pieces that still had some use he had moved to the storage area in the basement to be available for new tenants who might need quick furnishings. Anything else he had put out to be picked up by the trash hauler. In the dismal old apartment, he'd never put up pictures or made it his own so there was little to move, and he'd brought west only what he had been able to put in his car. The rest he'd left in storage in Pennsylvania. He liked being unencumbered, or at least liked the idea of it, but these few things seemed meager for a man his age.

The white walls glistened. The taupe carpet balanced all-purpose firmness with living-room softness. He'd spent $1,500 of his small savings to buy a loveseat and matching recliner, which had been delivered that morning. They sat in the middle of the living room next to the sofa; he was not sure yet where to put them. Except for the sofa he'd acquired in desperation, he'd never bought furniture before. Mary had always done that. He was not sure the earth browns, greens, and rusts were a good color scheme, but he liked it. Everything smelled new. He didn't mind that chemical smell of new carpet, actually kind of liked it, wondered if it was good for David to be inhaling it. He was going to find some sort of entertainment center and, yes, he admitted it, he was going to buy a large screen TV. He missed watching news and escaping into bad movies. He wondered what cable cost in Selby. He was surprised at how much he enjoyed setting up this new apartment. He'd already lived in Selby for a while, but this felt like settling in.

He was thinking about something Jack has said. The people in this Selby church were sitting ducks for people like Fred Vogel. When keeping an open mind is an article of faith and a character trait, you're powerless in the face of "God-inspired" certainty. He remembered how the voices of tolerance were slowly silenced back home. People who had been raised in a spirit of patience grew hard and certain as changes and pressures flooded into the church. A kind of naïve trust in the accuracy of the Bible became a hardened literalism. People who once had a bit of forbearance for one another began to judge and defend against each other.

The door opened and David came in. He banged it shut, shrugged off his backpack, and flopped it on the new sofa. "Looks good," he said offhandedly, glancing around and then heading for the refrigerator and pouring himself a glass of milk. Maggie had not yet left, but David took to hanging out in John's apartment more than his mom's. He sat down across from John. "So what's up?" he said.

John inclined his head to indicate the whole room, "It's pretty obvious, isn't it."

"Yeah, it's cool."

"Come with me. I want to show you something. The apartment I was in before had only one bedroom, just like the one you and your mom have, but this one has two." John led the boy to a small room with a large window that looked out on the backyard and the yards of the cul-de-sac. The air mattress that David had used on John's living room floor in the old apartment was lying on the carpet. "This is your room. I ordered a bed that will be delivered tomorrow. We'll find a dresser for you."

"This is nice. This is my room?"

"Yes."

"Is my mom going away for good and not coming back?" David's voice was anxious.

John put his hand on David's shoulder. "No, nothing like that. Your mom will be back after six months. But you already know that. This…" John moved his hand to indicate the room. "This is yours whenever you need it. You will always have a room in my house."

The boy took that in but did not say anything.

They heard a bell tone, and for a moment John did not know what it was. The old apartment hadn't had a doorbell that worked. John was used to people knocking. He went to the door. He saw through the glass that it was Angela. He was glad to see her. She stepped in and kissed him, and he blushed and felt awkward and turned to David. Before he could speak, Angela walked to the boy and said, "You must be David. John has told me all about you. I'm glad I can finally meet you." The boy was pleased with this attention, and John thought ruefully that Angela had an effect even on boys. "You know, John wouldn't let me come to see him in his old apartment. He said it was rundown and smelled bad."

"It was pretty bad," David said. "I like this one better."

"I brought a house-warming gift." Angela handed John the plant she was carrying.

"He's not good with plants," David said, glancing slyly at Angela. "My mom asked him to take care of her plants and he almost let them die. But I remembered and watered them."

"I didn't know you did that!" said John in surprise.

"Will you remember to water this one?" Angela said to David. "Or maybe I'll have to come over every other day and do it."

"I'll do it," David said, pleased with the trust.

"Do you have homework?" John asked. The boy said he didn't have much, so John suggested he go out and see if he could find Quentin and play for a while. "I want to spend some time with Angela."

"I see why you like him," she said after the boy went through the door.

"I'm turning the second bedroom into a room for him. When I told him, he wanted to know if his mom wasn't coming back."

"Is that a possibility?"

"No, I don't think so, but I continue to wonder about her ability to care for him."

Angela peered at him, "I think David is going to be in and out of your life for a long time."

"You still don't like that?" John said.

"I wonder if it's a good thing for someone at...your stage in life."

"So I'm too old to take care of a boy?"

"Did I say that?"

"What are you saying?"

"How's your co-housing project going?"

"You deliberately changed the subject."

Angela laughed, "I did."

"How do you do that!" John exclaimed. "I can never do it. Mary's grandmother came from a proper mainline Philadelphia family. When she didn't want to talk about something, she just politely changed the subject. It was blatant. And the family went along with it. It was as obvious as a burp at a dinner party, and everyone pretended it didn't happen. Me, I'm the sort of dutiful person who feels responsible to try to answer an awkward question even if I don't want to."

They had moved to the table and were sitting across from each other. John had poured her some coffee.

"I do want to know about this co-housing thing."

"I thought you weren't interested."

"Not for myself. But I want to know about it because it's your thing right now."

"You say that as though you think it's a passing fancy."

"I think it will be hard to carry off."

"Aren't you usually in class right now?"

Angela laughed, "You just did it too—changed the subject."

"Okay, so what do you want to know?"

"People like their own stuff and their own space." Angela said. She didn't see how it could work over time. It was hard enough for families to live together. How would it work if a large group of people had to make decisions about the common property and space? Who would mow the lawns and rake the leaves? How would they decide how much to spend when something needed to be fixed? Who would straighten up the common rooms? Who would keep the common kitchen clean and orderly? How would they share washers and dryers and storage space? Each family would have its own complete unit, but there would be all this common space and common life. Wouldn't people get tired of the weekly common meal? Angela wanted to know what anyone would gain by going through all that hassle.

John replied it was the experience of living in community. Angela said that has always been hard. John asked what about the fact that for millennia, people have lived in tribes and villages and more recently small towns. "It's only been the rise of cities that has isolated people from one another, though in the poorer city neighborhoods people still live pretty close to each other." He said the rise of a middle class gave large numbers of people enough money to buy their own space and fill it with their own stuff.

"That's a good thing, isn't it!" Angela exclaimed.

"People living in boxes surrounded by green, working their butts off to keep it all nice, never knowing their neighbors, feeling protective and anxious about their stuff?"

"You make it sound so bad. I like my little house and my privacy. I don't need to know all my neighbors. I got a fill of 'community' in my big family. I like space and silence and being alone."

"So where does that leave us?"

"I don't know, John. You love David and want to take care of him. You have friends you care enough about to go into a cooperative living arrangement with them. But these are not my inclinations. This is not my life."

"So I live my life? You live yours? We spend time together? I sleep over when I want to or you come here now that I have a decent space?"

"Put that way, it seems very clipped and cold. But, yes, I've known couples who made that work. Well, one couple."

"Who was that?

"I have a proper grandmother, too. About five years after my grandfather died, she met a man who led a much more Spartan life than hers. They liked each other's company, but she was not willing to give up her lifestyle, nor he his. They spent several evenings each week together. They went to each other's family gatherings. They traveled together. But they never married and they actually never 'lived together'."

"So I can have my David 'thing' and my co-housing 'thing'? You can have your 'thing'? And we can have our together 'thing' too? Is that it?"

Angela got up, came to his side of the table, put her hand on his shoulder, and stroked his hair. Her perfume flooded his senses. He gently pushed her hands away and stood up. He put his hands on her shoulders. "It's not fair. You know the effect you have on me. I'd like to think about this without your attractions clouding my mind."

She backed up a step to look at him more clearly, "But John, this is about my attractions—and yours. Why would you want to be with me if you weren't drawn to me? But that's never been the only thing with you. One of the reasons I trust you," she paused, "though I guess it's okay for you to be in my life so we can have sex."

"Do you really think that's the main thing?"

"I just said it isn't, but if it were, would that be a bad thing for you?"

"I think so, but I don't know. I've never had sex just for the sake of sex."

"Well, I've heard people extol the virtues of recreational sex. Certainly the movies and TV make it look appealing. Frankly, I think it's overrated. It's pretty empty. John, whatever we do, there will be nothing casual or shallow about our relationship."

John stepped forward and put his arms around her. Just at that moment David burst through the door, and John jumped back from Angela.

"It's all right," David said. "I know all about that."

"All about what?"

"See, David is okay with it," Angela said with a smile and wink at the boy.

"With what? What is 'it'?"

"You take care of your friend John here," Angela said as she moved toward the door. "He's a good guy, but he needs someone to look after him."

"She's cool," David said after she was gone. "Do you like her?"

"Yes," he said and then grabbed David as though to wrestle. "But what do you know about anything? What is it you know all about? You're just a kid. You don't know squat."

"Yes, I do. And I'm smarter than you are," the boy said laughing and squirming out of the pretend hammerlock John had on him.

"So why are you back so soon?"

"Quentin and I want to get some pizza at Sammy's, but I don't have any money."

****

The next day John drove down into the city to have lunch with Vi. He met her at a pricey restaurant called Russian Tea Time. They usually had lunch at burger joints that fit their budgets, but Vi had invited him and said she wanted to treat him. The place was small, decorated in an unprepossessing old world style. Most of the tables were full, working executives, some young, some old. Vi suggested the "Russian Peasant's Lunch," sausage sautéed with sauerkraut, boiled potatoes, onion, and caraway seed.

"You've been here before?"

"I hear the surprise in your voice. Yes, I splurge. Once a month, I put aside my guilt about hunger and the neglect of the poor and have a great meal."

"I think I should say 'good for you.' Why double your expense and include me?"

"For all those years you and Mary took me in and lavished hospitality on me. Those were wonderful times. I'll never forget."

"Vi, we've been getting together every month or so since I arrived in the area. Is there something special now?"

"No, not really. I'm grateful for your friendship. And I want to catch up with you. Especially with your co-housing project."

John told her about it as they ate. She listened closely and asked a lot of questions. John looked at her, "Are you interested?"

"I am. That shouldn't surprise you. It's nearer to the way people live in the villages of Central America. Think about it. It's a good way to retire. Twenty-five years from now when I'm pushing 80, I can still live independently, but the neighbors can check on me now and then. If I need nursing care, I can get it in my home. The other people won't have to take care of me, just make sure the caretakers are doing their job. I'd rather live like that as long as I can than go into a retirement home."

"You're a long way from that."

"Of course, but I'm alone. There's no one to take me in or take care of me, and I don't want to go live in a home with old people. For a lonely spinster, it's time to think ahead."

"Spinster! Terrible word. I thought it died years ago. You're not a spinster!"

"Of course, I am. I'm an aging single lady."

"What does than make me? I'm older than you are."

"Well, it's more acceptable for a man to be single. Harder emotionally, probably. Notice how quickly men get married after death or divorce. You're an exception."

"I'm not ready to think of myself as old."

"Well, I am. I don't have enough capital to buy a unit, but I am interested in one of the rentals. Can someone rent with a plan for buying?"

"Yes, Jack Foster's the one to talk to about that."

"How's Angela?" Vi asked with a wry smile.

"She's good," John answered self-consciously.

John fell into a brown study as he drove home. Why was Vi thinking about moving to Selby? He didn't like her question about Angela. It wasn't like Vi to be jealous. He'd not given her any grounds for jealousy. How would he handle this? Vi must know he had a relationship with Angela. She was not naïve about sex. She'd seen plenty in the villages in Central America and among the staff members of the NGO's who worked there. He knew she'd had an affair with an AID worker that ended painfully. She had dragged herself back and stayed with him and Mary for two months. They would find her curled up in her room, crying inconsolably. She'd come out of that tougher. He smiled to himself. Vi could never really be called hard. She had too much innate empathy and compassion. But she had never regained her youthful enthusiasm. She'd become cautious and always had a speculative look in her eyes when men were mentioned. As far as he knew, there had been no relationships since then.

A thought came to him. Suppose they became friends, Vi and Angela. That would be awkward. Vi might appeal to Angela for the same reason she liked what she once called John's "good guyness." Both women had a broad understanding of people, though earned in very different ways. Neither was prudish, though Vi, like himself, had been more straightlaced at the start of adult life than now. He almost liked the idea. Vi and Angela sitting on Angela's patio, drinking tea and laughing together. But he could not see himself in that picture.

A picture of Angela lying on her bed partly covered by the sheet looking at him with her bemused expression intruded on his thoughts. He sighed. He was making an interesting life for himself, and sometimes it seemed strange. He'd spent his time except for his college years in one community on the same piece of land where his father and grandfather and great grandfather had lived. What was he doing in a suburb of Chicago with an Italian girlfriend, a ten-year-old kid depending on him, living in a small, second-floor apartment, and about to join something they would call a "commune" back home, participating in a congregation that could come apart over a matter that wouldn't even be on the radar of his old church, and supporting his longtime friend the pastor of that church who had been suspended for taking a stand that would be abhorred by many back home! And how was it possible that most of this was still within the denomination he'd grown up in. Two congregations, so different, still in the same church. If it didn't always fit together, was it no surprise that the denomination no longer made sense and sometimes seemed ready to split? His girlfriend didn't fit in his old church or his new church. He sighed again and realized he actually liked this ambiguity. He wondered if he really had slipped morally, as he knew many people back home would think. On the other hand he felt more at home with himself than he could ever remember. What did that say about him, about his roots, about his future?

Chapter 23 – Struggle

"Frankly, I'm conflicted," said Preston Krunsch, standing at the mike at the congregational business meeting. "The board's proposal gives support to Kirby as our pastor, and it indirectly supports the majority view in this congregation that the union ceremony was a good thing, but it will seem to the downstate churches like a direct challenge to the district's authority. It will look like a clever way to get around the district."

John was sitting to one side at the congregational meeting in a position where he could watch the members and especially Kirby. He found Preston's speech interesting and was curious as Kurt Wampler went to the mike.

"It *is* a way to get around the district," Kurt exclaimed. "Let's name it for what it is."

"Well, put yourself in the shoes of people downstate," Preston replied. "Let's say the situation is reversed. Let's say the ministerial commission suspends a pastor pending an investigation for preaching fire and brimstone and putting people out of the church if they don't follow his line. But he has the support of the majority of the congregation, and they vote to continue to employ him. Would you support their right to do that?"

"Yes. I wouldn't like it, but I would recognize their right."

Kurt and Preston were standing together at the mike. Preston stepped away, and Anna Firebaugh took his place. "I'm with Preston. We are not free to do what we want. We need to listen to the other churches. We have to let this process run its course."

"But the process will take time," Kurt said. "In the meantime, we need a pastor. We need him to preach and visit people and administer the work of the church. Kirby can do that even if his ordination is temporarily suspended. If he doesn't do it, who will? Suppose we get an interim. What happens to Kirby during that time? What will the congregation be like at the end of that time? This is not just about supporting Kirby. It's about doing what's best for the congregation."

Maud Miller, who was in line behind Anna, stepped up and pulled the mike close, tipping the stand forward. John smiled. He looked forward to Maud's speeches. "You're right it's not just about supporting Kirby," Maud said. "And it's not just about doing what's best for our congregation, either. It's about standing with two women and three kids who will be left standing alone if we don't stand with them. Have you asked Marianne or Samantha or the kids how they feel about all this? The church and society has hurt these two women and others like them year in and year out until recently, and now when we finally do something to support them, we get the jitters at the first sign of opposition. You think about that! We owe it to *them* to support Kirby."

Barbara Nolt stood in line behind Maud, who gave her a long look as she let go of the mike and stepped back. She did not go to her seat and sit down.

"Kirby has been a wonderful pastor," Barbara began, "but he did not do the right thing and he is paying for it and so are those who supported him. He should not have performed that service to begin with, but he did it. Remember we never voted to support it. We tabled that motion, and it's a good thing we did. Samantha and Marianne are good people, but they've been given bad guidance. They are listening to the world. The Word of God is being ignored, and we are turning away from the values of our parents and grandparents. I don't think Kirby can continue as our pastor, unless he repents of what he has done."

An audible rustle of speech ran through the congregation; there was the sound of people shifting uncomfortably in their chairs. "Careful, sister," called out Jack Foster, to the surprise of most members who never associated him with radical causes and knew he rarely spoke in congregational meetings. "When you call for repentance, be sure of yourself."

"What are you implying?" said Barbara, turning to get a good look at him where he sat over on the far right side.

"Only that none of us is pure," Jack replied.

"I'm going to ask you all that you only speak when you're at the microphone," the moderator said. "Don't call out a response like that. Jack, I have to ask you to refrain from these outbursts."

"Yes, I hear you," said Jack. "I'll keep a lid on it next time."

Maud was still standing near the mike. She glanced at Barbara, leaned in close to the mike, and asked, "May I step back to the mike and say something?"

"Maud," the moderator said, "I think we have to let others have their say."

Maud nodded and reluctantly returned to her seat.

Herman Fry was next in line to speak. He shook his head. "We don't need to fight. What I mean to say is we just have to listen to each other.

We have to help each other find the true meaning of the scripture. We have to help each other so we don't go astray. Brother Kirby, I appreciate you, but I just can't go along with you."

Kristen Witter was the next person in line. When she moved to the mike, she leaned in and put her lips close to the rounded wire mesh and then closed her eyes and sighed deeply. "Aren't we trying to make this decision with our own energy? What does God want from us? We just need to pray and try to follow Jesus, and we will know what to do. God will give it to us. We're making this too hard. God is always close. He always wants to give us what is best for us. Herman said we need to listen to each other, but we really need to listen to the Lord."

"But Kristen, that doesn't help us," Kurt said, who was back in line and right behind her. "The ministerial commission thinks they are listening to the Lord. Kirby listened to the Lord. Herman listens to the Lord. So do Barb and Maud and Anna and Preston. Either the Lord is saying different things or we're hearing what we want to hear. Maybe we're hearing our own thoughts. Maybe God is standing back a pace or two and trusting us to use the wits God gave us to find our way through this."

The next person in line was Bob Flory. He stepped up and looked around with a benevolent and confident air, shrugging his shoulders slightly to settle his well-fitting sports jacket into place. "If you think about it, there isn't much more any of us can say. Pretty much all the possible points of view have been expressed. Isn't it time to vote?"

At that point, Kirby stood up and walked to the front mike where the moderator stood. "May I speak?" he asked.

"Of course," the moderator replied. Bob Flory looked a bit pained that his carefully orchestrated comment didn't have its intended consequence. John leaned forward to hear.

"In a sense," Kirby said, "this discussion is not just about what I did for Samantha and Marianne. It's about my ministry. You are debating the consequences of my action, but you cannot avoid asking yourself if you really want me to continue as your pastor. And that's a discussion you need to have without my presence. I'm going to step out and go to my office so you can speak candidly." He turned to the moderator, "Catherine, you can send someone to get me when you're ready."

John watched Kirby walk out of the room and up the stairs to his office. He knew his friend had done the right thing, but he was sorry to see him take himself out of the discussion. He wondered if he should speak on Kirby's behalf.

There was a silence after the pastor left. Sam rose at his seat, "Sister Moderator, I'm not in the mike line, but may I speak?" The moderator looked at the people in line and saw no objection. "Yes, Sam. I take it you want to say something about what Kirby just said."

"I do. I think Kirby's speech just upped the ante. He's saying this is really a referendum on his leadership. Maybe, Kirby's exaggerating a bit…"

John stood suddenly. "Sam, may I interrupt." Sam nodded. "I'm still new to this congregation. I think this is the first time I've spoken in public meeting. I don't know what's right for the congregation. Well, I do think I know, but I'm not speaking about that. Kirby has been one of my closest friends since we roomed together in college. I can tell you that he always means what he says. If Kirby thinks this is a referendum on his leadership, then you can be sure that's exactly how he views it, and you can also trust his judgment that this vote may have larger implications than this one matter."

"What do you mean?" Sam asked.

"I think Kirby is afraid that this may be the end of his pastorate here, whichever way the vote goes. He has a very fine sense of what it takes for a pastor/congregation relationship to thrive. He's worried that this action has damaged that beyond repair."

Again there were murmurs; people seemed to be thinking out loud. "Are you offering us advice?" Sam asked.

"I think we need to think carefully not just about this matter, but about this pastor and his ministry. Do we want him to continue to be our pastor and to what lengths are we willing to go to see that that happens?" When John sat down, his hands were trembling.

Sam looked around at the congregation seated in semicircular rows. "John's right, I think. This is no longer about whether we support Kirby during this period of suspension and investigation. Do we want him as pastor when this has all been settled? My answer is: yes, absolutely. But what will yours be? I think he was trying to say by leaving the room that he wants us to think carefully about this."

The moderator spoke up. "Bob Flory was trying to move us toward a vote, but we now find ourselves thinking about this proposal in a new way. So I am saying that we will continue this discussion. The motion before us remains the same, but I'll accept speeches that include this larger question of whether we want to continue with Kirby as our pastor. I caution you that we are really voting only on a motion to provide a way to keep Kirby as pastor during this time of suspension. But I think we have to take into account that Kirby sees it also as a vote on his leadership. So both the specific motion and this larger view of it are open for discussion."

She paused for a moment to let people in the mike line sit if they wished. No one did. Several people got up and joined the line. Bob Flory was still at the mike. "Bob, do you have more to say?"

"I'll reserve my comments," he said and stepped aside but did not go to the end of the line.

The next person in line was Gerald Kurtz. "You all know that I've been changing my mind on homosexuality. I support what Kirby did." He turned to where Marianne and Samantha were sitting quietly. "I'm glad you and your kids are in our congregation. I'm sorry you have to suffer through this. I do hear what Kirby is asking us to think about. He's a fine man and a fine leader to be able to put his own interests aside and ask us to think about this. I believe Kirby really likes this church. I think he likes serving here. There are only a few other churches like ours in the whole denomination. Where would he go from here? Think about the risk he takes. Instead of fighting for his job, he's trying to do the right thing for us. But I really understand the concern he raises. After this can he really be the pastor for all of us? Barbara, can he be your pastor? I don't mean to put you on the spot. I'm not asking you to answer. I'm just pointing out the problem."

"No pastor ever satisfies everyone," Kurt blurted out from his seat.

"People, I have to ask you to move to the mike if you want to speak. I ask you not to call out from your seats. Kurt?"

Kurt nodded with a mixture of sheepishness and pique.

"Gerald, were you finished?" the moderator asked.

"Well, this is not an easy thing. My vote is for Kirby, but I see his concern and our problem. Yes, I'm finished, Catherine."

Gil Smith was next at the mike. "I respect Kirby, but I disagree with him. He has courage and he has faith. Can he still be my pastor? I think so, but can he be the pastor for everyone? You know I don't believe that homosexual relations are right in God's eyes, but I don't believe this is the only or most important sin. Sin is when you turn from God and do things for yourself, on your own steam and for your own purposes. Can any of us say we never turn away? Can any of us say we are always or even most of the time turned toward God? Now, in this matter, I believe our pastor is turned toward his own ideas and not following God's way, but is he any worse than any of us when we get set in our own ideas? Kirby thinks he is following God's way, but so do some of the rest of us. I guess we are all pretty human and I can live with my pastor's humanness even if he has disappointed me, but I'm not sure everybody can."

Rory Neff was next in line. "As one of the younger members with a young family, I support Kirby completely. And I'm disappointed in what I'm hearing. Not with those of you who think what Kirby did was wrong. I understand where you're coming from. I respect it. Though I think you're way off base and out of touch. I'm disappointed in those of you who support Kirby, but are worried about what it will mean in the district or even in our congregation. Isn't the right thing the right thing? If you think Kirby did the right thing, then what is there to do but vote for this motion? You can't please everyone. You have to do what's right."

During the entire discussion, Joe, as the one who brought the motion from the board, continued to stand at the podium beside Catherine, the moderator. Now he stepped forward to the mike at the podium and said, while looking over at Catherine, "May I say something?"

Catherine nodded.

"Rory, thinking about others in the congregation or the district is not a sign of weakness or lack of courage. The board supports Kirby and thinks he did the right thing, but we did not and cannot ignore this action's possible effect. We ought not. Whatever action we take, it will disappoint and upset someone. I think we can take the action and have compassion and understanding for those it affects."

Barbara Nolt had gotten back in line and came to the mike again. "If we approve this motion, we will be going against the Bible. We love Kirby, but he went too far. He has allowed the homosexual issue to take over his ministry."

Maud Miller was on her feet. "It's not an 'issue'! It's about people who have been hurt and continue to be hurt!"

"Please, Maud," said Catherine. "Come to the mike if you want to speak."

Maud sat down and Kristen Witter moved to the mike. "We are making this too hard. I think it's time to stop talking and pray. Let the Lord guide us and show us the way. Catherine, why don't you lead us in a time of prayer?"

"You know that I'm not good at leading public prayer." She looked out across the people and saw Sally Bordan. "Sally, would you lead us? I suggest a time of silence and then you bring us to a close with a few words."

Heads bowed. A deep and uneasy silence settled on the group. John had the feeling he always had when prayer was being used as a tool. How could anyone pray with integrity on cue in the midst of turmoil and distress? How could God possibly be helpful when people were each praying with their own agenda stirred up and fueled by controversy and strong feeling?

Sally brought the prayer time to an end with a few words that John could hardly hear. Her voice was quivering. Then he remembered something Sam had told him. Months earlier in one of the discernment sessions, Sally had confessed that her younger brother had come out of the closet last year, after twenty years of marriage. She had said how hard it was for her sister-in-law and their kids. He briefly wondered how many people in the audience had gay or lesbian family members, and if they did, did they know about them.

Catherine thanked Sally and said, "I wonder if we are moving toward a vote."

Bob Flory, who was still standing to the side of the mike where he'd stepped when Kirby had spoken and left the room, now stepped back to the mike. "Sister Moderator, we have given this a good airing. Maybe we're not finished. These are difficult matters," he said shaking his head in sympathy and understanding. "But I'm with you. I believe we're ready to vote. I call for the question."

Catherine asked Herman Fry and Maud Miller to pass out ballots. The only sound was paper rustling and the soft scratching of pen or pencil. Herman and Maud collected the ballots and carried them to a table at the end of the room. Catherine called for a hymn while the votes were counted. Soon Maud came and placed a tally sheet in Catherine's hand.

She cleared her throat. "There were 72 people voting. Of that number 58 voted for the motion. Ten voted against it, and four abstained. The motion carries."

John saw Rory start to raise a triumphant fist and then look around and think better of it. Kurt was smiling broadly. Herman was looking down at the floor. Sam was watching people's reactions. Maud was trying to hold back her look of pleasure. Bob Flory had a look of satisfaction on his face. Gerald Kurtz seemed at once pleased and troubled. Barbara Nolt got up and left the room. Gil Smith seemed to be watching people with an especially alert and attentive eye, staring for a long moment at Rory, who looked back in surprise and shrugged.

Catherine was relieved. She turned to John, "Will you bring Kirby back from his office?" she said.

As John and Kirby walked down to the fellowship hall, there was only time for John to report the results. When Kirby came into the room, he was greeted by smiles. One person began to applaud and then stopped when no one joined in and instead there was an awkward silence.

"The congregation has voted to keep you as our pastor even though you cannot carry out all the functions of ministry," Catherine said.

Kirby came to the podium. He looked at the people for a long moment. He eyes were sad. He looked tired and uncharacteristically dispirited. "Thank you," he said simply. "May I ask what the vote count was?"

When Catherine repeated the totals, he took a pen from his pocket and did a quiet calculation on a sheet of paper he found on the podium. "That's a hair over 80%." He sighed. "When you called me to come here, the vote was 99%. Seventy-four out of 75 votes. The other vote was an abstention. Frank Cashen told me later that he was the abstention. He said he just wanted to keep me from getting a swelled head."

There were smiles. Frank had died two years earlier and people remembered his light spirit.

"But I would never have accepted your call if the vote had been 80%. I wouldn't have accepted a 90% vote. A pastor needs a strong affirmation to begin. I know that no pastor can please everyone all the time. One's approval rating is never as high as the first day on the job. But I don't think 80% is high enough. And remember that the percentage is only of people who are here. Some of the less active members or those who stay away from congregational business meetings are people who disapproved of my action. If you polled everyone, the number would be lower still."

Kurt stood at his seat, "Kirby, a politician would kill for an 80% approval rating!"

Kirby smiled, "This isn't politics, Kurt. I have to do more than represent your wishes. I have to be there when you are suffering. I sit with you when someone dies. I listen when I'm the only one you feel you can trust. I have to be a teacher. I have to be an example. I have to say something each Sunday that asks you to think and hopefully lifts your spirits. Kurt, if my action were something you deeply disagreed with, would you be able to accept me as pastor?"

Joe, as board chair, came back to the podium. "What are you saying, Kirby?"

John was shaking his head. He knew what Kirby was going to say.

"I don't think I can continue as your pastor."

Maud stood and spoke, stumbling over her words. "But we want you as our pastor. At least most of us do. We just went through all this arguing and discussing. What was the point if you were going to say no anyway?"

"We had to find out where we all stood. I had to know what I'd be working with. You all needed to see and hear each other. I was hoping for a stronger vote. I'm sorry."

Gil Smith stood, "Pastor Kirby, I disagree with what you did, but I respect you for doing it. Don't you think you owe it to yourself and us to stay as our pastor?"

Kirby looked at Gil will sadness and appreciation. "Thank you, Gil. That's exactly the speech I would have expected from you. I appreciate it. But there are many who are not where you are, Gil. I have to think of them too."

Kirby stepped back from the podium mike and Joe took his place. He turned to the moderator, holding his mouth close enough to the side of the mike to be heard. "Catherine, there are still people standing in line to speak. I don't know how long you intend to allow these reactions to continue, but there is a process for taking Kirby at his word and moving forward." He turned to the other side toward Kirby. "Kirby, I think you know what we need from you." The pastor nodded. "It would be good if you put your resignation in writing to the board. I think I can speak for the board in saying that we'd like a chance to discuss it further with you. I know you well enough to know that this is not a spur-of-the-moment decision. I'm sure you had already thought before today what you would do if the level of support was not what you need. Still, will you give us all a few days to think about this and pray about it? I'll call a special board meeting for Tuesday night. We'll talk further then." He turned back to the congregation. "There are many things to discuss; most of them come into play if and when Kirby's resignation is final."

Catherine came back to the mike. "I am going to exercise the moderator's prerogative and bring this discussion to a close. There is much to be said, but I think we can say it to one another and to Kirby informally after the meeting and in the weeks ahead."

As the people who had been in line began to move back to their seats, Sam stood and walked to the mike. "Catherine, may I say something? It's about the congregation and what may be ahead."

"Yes, Sam, I'll allow it."

"I mention one thing now that's really the unmentionable, but it's better to say it out loud than be caught off guard. This could cause a rift. I hope not, but we have a better chance of its not happening if we are smart about the possibility. There are things we can do to help ourselves. I ask you all to think about that."

The meeting adjourned and people were leaving when John walked over and put his arm around Kirby's shoulder. "You are too good to be true, but, by God, it's what I love about you!"

Chapter 24 – Introspection

It was Monday morning and Sam sat at his desk with his journal. His mind was running over yesterday's meeting; he was thinking how sad he felt and wondering what part of it made him saddest. His sorrow spread out across the events and moments of his life as they came to mind and filled him with a pervasive low-grade grief. The congregation really was not going to handle this well. There were fissures that would open wider, not big divisions fueled by anger, but persistent differences that people had come to live with uneasily, aggravated by unacknowledged irritations. Did people care enough about each other to stay together? How would they find another pastor as good as Kirby? How would the congregation hold together during a search process? Could they really accept a new pastor without doing some work at reconciliation? How would they agree on that?

Why was he worried? Where was his faith? Where was God in all this? What right did he even have to think of himself as a person of faith? He paid God too little attention. God lurked in the background, always there, but not consulted enough. He lived a kind of parallel existence with God. With Eve, too. She was always there. He loved her, but how often did he give her his full attention? It surprised him that she loved him. He began to write.

As always I pray when I'm in trouble. You know what's happening. I don't need to detail it here, unless I need to put it into words for myself and I've already been doing that. I really don't know what to do. I'm not in a position to do much. But do I even want to do anything? I was sitting in the balcony during worship two Sundays ago, in the front row, and I leaned forward and looked out over the congregation. Kirby was just getting started with his sermon. The choir had finished its anthem. Jessica Witter had read the scripture. Her mother Kristen had done the children's story. Janet Keller was at the piano, and she looked sad. I could see the backs of Joe and Anne's heads. They both were looking down and their shoulders were hunched forward. I remembered the memorial service for Michael and how the kids from the youth group joined the choir and sang "And He shall raise you up on Eagle's wings." And I thought of Vern and his tendency to pontificate and of all the committees he served on. And for a moment I was overwhelmed by gratitude. There was nothing extraordinary about the moment. In fact it was not one of Kirby's best sermons, but I felt so profoundly grateful for this ordinary group of people with whom I have gone through so much. I don't know where that love came from because it had nothing to do with anything any of us have done. No one in the picture was famous or particularly important, but for that moment I think I saw the essential value of each of us. I don't know quite how to put it. Maybe I saw with your eyes. But each of us and each moment we have lived became precious. And our coming together in that place Sunday after Sunday honored that goodness and bound us together with ties that we only fleetingly know for their true value.

So what am I saying? That I live most of my life paying attention to its surface and missing its deepest worth? That there are no ordinary people? That we only appear unremarkable to each other because we don't see each other?

The co-housing thing may not happen. Eve and I won't be part of it. She doesn't want to do it. I thought it was anxiety, but I think she feels she would have to give up too much. I'm disappointed, and I admit, maybe a little relieved. "There may be other ways you can be involved. You don't have to live there to support the idea." How is that possible? You can't be part of a community when you're not a part of it. "Why not? You only have to do the next thing. Now that you know Eve is not ready for it, what's the next thing?" You mean give Jack and John moral support, help them where I can? "You've already begun that. Is that what you think you should do?" Aren't you supposed to tell me? "Am I?"

Sam put down his pen and rubbed his eyes. He looked down at his awkward, un-even penmanship, which had grown worse in the years since computers. He moved over to his keyboard and continued his thoughts digitally. The words flowed across the screen. It was easier. He smiled to himself remembering how in the days before computers he had never been able to compose at the typewriter keyboard. Now it was the pen that felt stiff and ungainly and stymied the stream of thought.

*Money. Money. The old guy is watching me. I wasn't very good at not having money and I'm not very good at having money. There's no grace in the way I relate to money. Can you relate to money? Can you have a relationship with **money**? No, you have relationships with people. How obvious can it be! But some people do put their money above their relationships. All of us do to a certain extent. Otherwise, we would not be so anxious about it. But can there be grace in the having and handling of money? Jesus seemed to doubt it. Well, I feel a little freer of it than I once was. The moment in the theater lifted me up and I've not sunk back to where I was. Some days I can actually trust. Doesn't last for long, but it's good when it happens.*

Sam felt better. He formatted the material he'd written on the computer, printed it out, and pasted it into his journal behind the handwritten part. He got into his car and drove to River Street and went hunting for

John among the apartments. He found him in one of the first floor apartments helping the drywaller hoist a sheet into place and holding it while he nailed it. He waited until John was finished. They walked up the stairs to John's new apartment where they found Jack knocking on the door. "This is good," Sam said. "Both of the men I wanted to talk to."

Inside John motioned to them to sit at the table and poured coffee from a coffee maker he kept going all day.

"Eve and I can't join the co-housing experiment," Sam said. "I'm ready but Eve isn't. I think I could probably pressure her, but I'm not willing to do that. I'm sorry."

John and Jack looked at each other and Jack shrugged his shoulders. "They're dropping like flies."

"To be fair," John said, "no one was ever fully committed."

"True, but in addition to you and Eve, I thought there was a good chance Kurt and Cynthia would come in, and maybe even Joe and Ann."

"I talked with them," Sam said. "It's selling their houses. In this market they can't get anywhere near what they were worth several years ago. They're unwilling to take a hit."

"Yeah, but the cost of the properties here on the cul-de-sac is way down too," Jack said. "And the cost of renovation is down, because small contractors don't have enough work and are cutting their prices. I told them I have enough capital to carry them, even if it takes them a year or more to sell their homes."

"I was with you on that," Sam said. "I even asked my friend the old rich guy, Oliver Larkspur, to consider investing some money in our project. I think he wanted to, but couldn't. Saying no violated some personal code of generosity and risk, but he couldn't bring himself to do it. I think he was disappointed in himself. I was willing to put our money into it, not just to buy a unit, but as capital to make it possible for others, but Eve wasn't willing."

"It doesn't affect me much," John said. "I never had enough to buy into the project. I was always a renter, hopefully with the possibility in the future sometime of buying a unit. But Jack, what does this do to you?"

Sam broke in, "Let me say something before you speak, Jack. Why not continue with what you've started. You said you can afford to own this apartment building, your little house, and the Victorian house next to you. So finish the renovations here. You must be three-quarters done anyway. Rent the units. Try to find people like John who are drawn to the community idea.

"Then let some of us who are interested, but can't join or aren't ready, to be sort of satellite members. Like me. I want to be connected. I'll do whatever I can to help. Keep the people who were or are interested connected by having monthly meetings. I think I can ask Eve to go to a monthly meeting. Don't do the big redo on the Victorian house. Start using it as is. Let some of us come in and help clean it and start fixing it up in small ways. Let it be a place for those who are renting and for those of us still interested to hang out, maybe even eat together and even do an occasional program, a sing-along or some such.

"As other houses along the cul-de-sac go on the market, see if you can buy them. Or maybe some of us will be ready by that time. And let people know across Selby. Extend the base." Sam felt himself getting excited. "I know the research says you need 15 to 30 families to do a co-housing thing right, but there have got to be other, smaller, step-by-step ways to do it.

"I figure, Jack, the key is you. You have resources. You had the crazy idea in the first place. Are you still committed? John, you caught the vision. You've been the onsite coordinator for the apartment building. You continue to live here and work with Jack and manage the mix of whatever develops. I'm in it as far as I can be without actually buying a unit and a share of the common property. Maybe ten years down the road when the market has changed and things are different for all of us, this might morph into a real co-housing community. But for now we can start working at the community part without having the money and property worked out."

Jack listened at first with a poker face and then with slow smile. "Damn! You just laid out my whole program and a hell of a lot better than I could have! Yeah, that's what we'll do, all of it!" He turned to John, "Engelsinger, are you in?"

John laughed, "I am."

"Why do you laugh?" Sam asked.

"I am feeling at home."

"Why is that funny?"

"I left the only home my family and I had known because I no longer felt at home there. So I came out here. I was looking for a place with people who are more like me. But I didn't expect to find a couple of adventurers or find out that I was one too. So this is good. I don't need a physical home, though this place is a good place. Home is where the spirit is. So I am in! I'm an old guy, or almost. I have my health. I have nothing to lose. I am up for this!"

"All right!" Sam exclaimed.

They sat for a time in silence. What more was there to say! John got up and filled their coffee cups.

Jack declined, saying he needed to be going.

Sam suddenly said, "I hate to bring us down from this mountain top, but this is not the only community we're a part of. What are we going to do about the church and Kirby?"

"What do you mean 'we'?" Jack asked. "It's the whole church's problem, not just ours."

"Of course, but the congregation needs some creative ideas, or we're all going to be in trouble."

"I think it will blow over."

Sam shrugged, "Maybe, but I doubt it."

"I spent some time with Kirby and Nancy Sunday night after the meeting," John said. "That session was hard on Nancy. She felt she couldn't speak. She thinks Kirby's being too squeamish about the 80% vote. She's only a few years from retirement. It's not a good time for them to move. Kirby thinks he might be able to get some adjunct teaching jobs at the community college and the university. It doesn't pay much, but it's something. We forget that he got a Ph.D. in history before he changed course and went to theological school. He can teach American history and theology at the university level."

Sam sighed, "I'm glad Kirby has options. I wish I could be confident of the congregation's options."

"If you asked me, which you haven't," Jack said, "I'd tell you to lighten up. Do the best you can. Offer the best you have. Then let it go. You can't make everything right."

"True, but someone's got to do something or we'll just drift apart. People will slowly stop coming. We'll diminish."

"You don't know that."

"Well, that's my gloomy thought on this Monday."

"Maybe the congregation should go ahead, persuade Kirby to come back , and let the folks who don't like it, leave," Jack said. "Why try to hold it together?"

"Good question. I'm not interested in holding it together just to save the congregation. Somewhere, somehow people, all of us, have to stop pushing away those we don't agree with. In this world are we ever going to have agreement on matters of faith, on sexual practice, on politics? No! We're growing even more diverse. If this small congregation of remarkably similar middle-class people can't find the ability to live together with our differences, then what hope is there for the real trouble spots in the world?"

"Sam! Don't load the whole goddamn world onto this! If we can't work this out, it doesn't mean the Middle East is screwed." Jack put his jacket on, "I'll see you guys around."

John raised his eyebrows and smiled, "More coffee?"

Sam declined. His next stop was the home of Oliver Larkspur. The old man took him into his study which was off the living room and continued the theme of polished hardwood floors with oriental rugs. The walls were covered floor to ceiling on three sides by hardwood bookshelves of oak, stained lightly so they caught the light that came from the broad window on the fourth wall which looked out on the trees and flowers in the back yard and kept the room from being dark and overwhelming with its thousands of volumes. Let into the middle of one of the book-lined walls was a small fireplace of gray and brown fieldstone that jutted into the room about a foot, with a broad, low stone slab for a hearth. Except for the section taken up by the stone, which ran to the ceiling and was interrupted by a narrow mantel cut into the stone, that wall was also covered with books. A broad oak desk littered with papers and books sat in the end away from the fireplace, and two burgundy-colored leather chairs faced the fireplace and were draped with throws of dark fabric richly embroidered. The ceiling was painted red and Chinese lamps with burgundy lampshades stood on small tables in three corners. An exclamation of pleasure escaped Sam's lips.

"You like it! Good!" the old man said and ushered Sam to one of the chairs. He disappeared for a few minutes, coming back with two mugs of coffee. "I didn't ask. I assumed coffee would not be unwelcome."

Sam was standing at the bookshelves when the old man came back. "This wall is filled with Westerns!" Sam exclaimed.

"One of my vices. I hope this doesn't lower your opinion of me."

"I stopped forming opinions of you," Sam replied.

"Good. Good. Otherwise, surely our last conversation would have lowered whatever regard you had for me."

Sam shrugged, smiled, and answered without taking his eyes from the books. "I enjoyed it actually. You've been too good to be true."

"So you were pleased to see the mercenary side you always knew was there. I never convinced you that I'm as lighthearted and eccentric about money as I was pretending to be?"

"Was it pretending?"

"You can hardly expect me to answer that."

Sam sat down and took the mug of coffee the old man offered him. "So what brings you here this morning?"

"I don't always know these days why I do what I do."

"Well, I like people who stop by for no apparent reason. It's good for the soul, you know, to idle away time with friends."

"Yeah, I like putting it that way. Maybe that's my true calling. Find the best friends I can and idle away time with them."

"Well, I hope I'm one of them. Speaking of your friends, I hear that one of them is in a spot of trouble."

"Oh?"

"Your pastor, Kirby Beahm."

"You know about that?"

"Preston's been talking of nothing else."

"Oh, yes, of course."

"I believe you are on the church board. Is that right?"

"Yes."

"May I offer a bit of advice?"

Sam smiled. The old man smiled back. "I can see you are preparing to indulge me. You're wondering what an old reprobate like me could possibly have to say about a matter of faith and polity."

"Actually, I was thinking that you might have a particularly peculiar and interesting take on the matter."

The old man laughed, "But not one with much real value. It's okay, you know. I'd rather be peculiar and interesting than..."

"Proper and religious?" Sam laughed. "Please, go on. I really do want to hear."

"How can I possibly say something now that will do anything but entertain you?"

"I'd welcome some diversion. Please go on."

"I think your pastor is being overscrupulous!" said the old man bluntly. "Oh, I admire the fineness and delicacy of his respect for the congregation and the larger church. But he should fight those thoughtless ones downstate. Take an aggressive stance. Use all his considerable knowledge of church history and polity to show how utterly misguided your district ministerial commission is. You folks are just afraid to fight!"

Sam had never seen this side of the old man. He sat forward with interest.

"Preston told me all about the congregational meeting. What a wonderful gesture it was to withdraw because 20% of the congregation was too large a minority for him to continue his successful ministry! And what a load of poppycock! My God, an 80% percent approval rating anywhere else would be called a mandate! Your forbearance with one another is one of your greatest gifts and one of your most astonishing weaknesses!"

"But that kind of aggressiveness is exactly what the downstate people are practicing."

"Well then, fight them with their own methods!"

"Then we're no better than they are. The conservatives across the denomination are pushing for what they want and don't care who they hurt."

"Isn't that the nature of political struggle?"

"I thought we were trying to live a different way. I thought we were trying to love our enemies."

"Well, I admire that sentiment, but…"

"It's not a sentiment!"

"Well, I admire that idea, that approach, but what exactly does it mean? Forget the downstate people. What does your pastor know about the 20% who voted against him or the silent people who weren't there? How angry are they? Some may want to get rid of him. My guess is, not many. Some may be willing to live with him even though they disagree. Frankly, I'm surprised at your pastor. A man of his intellect and experience basing a decision on so little accurate data!"

Sam sat back in his chair.

"And another thing! A pastor worth his salt *ought* to have at least 20% of his congregation disagreeing with him. If not, then he's not standing for anything!" The old man stopped and smiled suddenly. "Well, what do I know about life in a religious community! There are mysteries there I'm sure I'll never fathom. But sometimes you folks would be better off if you'd just fight it out."

Sam laughed and shook his head.

"You laugh, but you have to see that I have a point."

"I admit that I'd like to fight. Go after the conservatives. Match them! Force with force! Judgment with judgment! Biblical quote with biblical quote! I'd like to shred their arguments!" Sam paused, "You know, of course, that a liberal like me is at a disadvantage. I can see the point of the other side; I see where they're coming from; I understand why they're upset. I'm willing to make a place for them. I'll treat them as brother and sister, take communion with them, etc. They're not bad people. But they won't give me the same respect. They have to convert people like Kirby and me and especially Samantha and Marianne."

"But don't you want to do the same, if not convert, at least change them so they accept Samantha and Marianne? Aren't you like them in this way?"

"I suppose, but I'm willing to live and let live as long as they don't attack Samantha and Marianne and other LGBT people."

"You're too kind!"

"You would say that," Sam remarked.

"I'm an old man. I can say what I think!"

Chapter 25 – More Decisions

John got a phone call that Monday afternoon from Vi, asking many questions about the co-housing experiment. John told her where things stood. She was still interested, even if it meant simply renting a unit in the apartment building. She thought, being bi-lingual, she would be able to find work in one of the community agencies in Selby.

John had only just put the phone down and was asking himself if he really wanted Vi to move in next door, when there was a knock on his door. Maggie was standing there, crying and asking to come in. He let her in and gestured toward the sofa. He asked her if she wanted coffee. She nodded and continued to cry. He gave her a mug and sat in a chair across from her.

"I'm such a screw-up," she said. "David must hate me. I'm not a good mother."

"Why are you saying this?" John asked.

Maggie broke into a fresh burst of crying. "I sent him to school this morning without a lunch. I don't have any money. I don't have any food in my house."

"I thought you had a part-time job, a couple days a week, until you leave for Arizona?"

Her face contorted with pain, her sobs became angry and desperate. "I quit. I had to."

"Why?"

"I just couldn't handle it. The pressure was too much. Yesterday, I just couldn't get out the door. When I called later in the day to say I was sick, they told me I didn't need to come in at all this week. I asked why, and they said I was unreliable and they were putting me on probation. I got pissed off and told them I quit." She sobbed now not in anger but as though she were a little girl whose heart was broken. Then she turned hard and furious. "Those fucking people! They don't care. You should see how they treat their other employees."

"What are you going to do?"

Maggie continued to cry, deep wracking sobs. For a brief moment John thought he saw all the way to the bottom of her soul. Something was missing, some basic element of self-affirmation that she could hold on to and build on. "I need time. I have to think about some things. I have to get my head on straight."

John waited as her sobbing wound down. For the moment she was purged of her torment, clean and free of all the passionate misery that swirled through her and colored every thought and feeling.

"I've been meditating and doing my exercises." She sighed. "I need to go back to Arizona. The job I told you about is still waiting. They're ready for me to come. I have to do this for myself. But it's for six months! Remember, I talked to you about keeping David again, but I really want to take him with me. I've been trying to figure out a way. But he doesn't want to go. If I bring it up, he doesn't even want to hear about it." She began to cry again. "What kind of mother leaves her kid behind that long in the hands of a friend! But I have to go. I can't breathe here. I can't get work. I have to go."

There was a pause in her torrent of words. "I know this is too much to ask. You're not even David's relative, but he likes you and trusts you, and you are really good with him."

"Maggie, it's okay. You are really up against a lot! You are doing the best you can right now."

"You think so?"

"Yes."

"I've already asked you, but I have to ask again, just to be sure. Could you...would you be willing to take care of him for maybe as much as six months so I can take this job and get myself back together?"

"You know I will, but you have to talk to David! How does he feel? Have you told him? I don't mean hinted at it. Have you laid it out to him?"

"Not yet. I've been putting it off. I feel so bad! I wanted to talk to you again."

John smiled, looked away and out the window. "So you have. You asked me before. Now you've asked me again!"

"I know. I know," said Maggie. "But it's too much. I had no right to ask. I'm a terrible person even to think about asking."

"I said yes, Maggie, twice!"

"Of course. Of course. I'm such a loser."

"It doesn't help to call yourself that! May I talk to David about it?"

"Yes. Yes. Certainly."

"Is he home from school?" John looked at his watch. "He should be. Please tell him about this and then ask him to come over and talk to me."

Maggie got up and put her mug on the table. "I'll do it. Right now. I'll talk to him and then send him over. Thank you."

John waited. Four weeks was one thing. Six months was another. Did he really know what he'd be letting himself in for? His only experience with kids was the few weeks David had stayed with him before. That had gone well. But for six months! Would the kid become bored or difficult? Did he have an unpleasant side that hadn't come out? Fifteen minutes passed and there was a quiet knock at the door.

The boy entered and John motioned toward the couch and asked if he wanted some milk. The boy said yes, drank, and set the glass on the end table.

"Well, your mom told me what she has in mind. How does that feel to you?"

David shrugged, "It's okay."

"Is it really? I mean do you really want to stay with me that long?"

"I'll miss my mom."

"Of course, you will. You always have."

"But I like living with you."

"Why?"

"You take good care of me." He smiled, "And I like your food. You have more junk food than my mom."

John laughed, "Probably not a good reason. I may have to fix that."

"My mom said it was okay."

"You talked about my junk food."

"Uh-huh."

"Is there anything else you talked about?"

"My mom lets me stay up late. When I stayed before, you made me go to bed early. Will I have a bedtime?"

"Yup. Nine o'clock on school nights. Later on Friday night when you can sleep in the next day."

David made no protest and nodded, almost in relief. "Will I go to church with you?"

"Well, that's a more difficult question. I believe when kids reach a certain age, they should be able to make up their own minds about church. But until that time they must go along with their family."

"What age is that?"

"At least 16, maybe older."

"So I have to go?"

"Well, it's a little different because we're not family. I don't want to impose something your mom might not agree with."

"My mom doesn't go to church because people make her anxious."

"Well, if you live with me, we will be like family together, so my answer is yes, you have to come along to church with me. Can you live with that?"

The boy nodded. "That's cool. I liked it when I went with you before."

"Anything else?"

"How often do I have to take a shower?"

"Every other night."

David thought about that. "Okay, I'll stay with you. Will I really have my own room?"

"Yes, you already know that. It's the room I showed you. The new bed has been delivered. We'll make the room really cool. You can use that air mattress as an extra bed when you have friends over."

David nodded and smiled.

In the evening John went to Angela's house for dinner, and he told her what he had done. She wasn't surprised. She offered the proper words of support, saying that he was doing a really good thing for the boy, but John knew she did not like it. He could see that she felt these were uncharitable feelings. She was usually so surefooted, so clear about what she felt, what she believed, what she was willing to do and not willing to do.

"I'm sorry," he said.

"Why should you be sorry?" she said shortly.

"We both know why."

"I'm suddenly the bad guy here. I can't help my feelings. You will be the father of a 10-year-old. Do you really know what that means?"

"Well, it means I'm not free to do what I want with my evenings. It certainly puts a limit on our time together."

"Yes, it does. And what about when we want to go somewhere for the day or for a weekend?"

John smiled, "I'm glad you're assuming you'll go away with me."

"Oh, John. You know how I feel about you. I don't see how this is going to work. I just don't know if I want to share you with this child. I don't think I'm up to the role of being an adult around a kid."

"You won't have to do anything. I'll do the parenting. I'm the one who's responsible for David, not you."

"John, you don't bring a kid along on a date."

"I can get sitters."

"Really."

"Look!" John found himself getting angry. "I'll find a way to keep David out of our times together. You don't even need to know he's in my life."

Angela smiled sadly, "John, you know that won't be possible. This is a big thing for you. You'll begin to resent me if I'm the reason David can't join us or you're always having to pay a sitter because your girlfriend hates kids. I don't hate kids, but I'm not ready for one in my life. And he will be, if you and I keep seeing each other."

"Are you saying we're finished?"

She thought about the question and shook her head, "No, not that."

****

Angela was on John's mind almost constantly for the next few days. He was sad. He was angry. He decided he could do without her. He missed her.

Now that Maggie's decision was made, she burst into action. She asked if she could move her things—everything except David's clothes, books, videos, and toys—into a storage unit in the basement again. She promised to send her back rent in installments once she got to Arizona and was making money. She would send the extra $25 per month for the storage space. John smiled, though he was careful not to let Maggie see it. She was hypersensitive and would know he didn't believe she would send money. He had resigned himself to the fact that Jack would have to write off Maggie's unpaid rent. She seemed to be filled with resolve and energy and hope. In two days she had everything moved downstairs and David's things moved into John's extra bedroom. By Saturday morning she had packed her battered old vehicle—John doubted it would make it to Arizona—and at 9:30 a.m. she pulled out after hugging David and telling him how much she loved him. This leave-taking was different from when she went for a few weeks. The boy cried hard, a clean honest grief at parting, but no desperate sobs or clinging histrionics. David watched as his mother's car disappeared around the corner. He snuffed up his tears and looked at John.

"Well, David, let's go out for breakfast. What do you say?"

The boy nodded, lifted his arm, wiped his eyes on the shoulder of his t-shirt, gave John a small smile and said, "Can we go to the pancake house and get some of that stuffed French toast?"

In the evening John and David went for a walk. They found themselves moving away from the river and up over the low river bluff, through several neighborhoods, ending up at the park. John sat on the stone wall and watched David clambering over the play equipment. As they left the park, they walked down the street where Angela lived. It was a lovely evening and she happened to be in her front yard, weeding the flowerbeds. John called out, and Angela moved toward them across the grass. He wondered how she would greet them. She smiled at David and said how nice it was to see him again. David stepped toward her, gave her a quick smile, and said, "Hi." She threw John an ironic look. As a boy who was missing his mother, David was an easy touch for Angela's warmth and charm. John watched as Angela asked David questions about his school and told him that she was a teacher. She soon had him talking about his favorite subject, which was math. When he told her that he didn't like to write, she smiled and said she hoped when they had more time he would let her show him why writing was a great thing to do and something that he might find he really did like. David looked as though he might change his mind right there on the spot.

Later, after they had said goodbye and walked back in the apartment, and David was asleep in his new bedroom, John called Angela. "What were you doing?" he wanted to know. "I thought you didn't want anything to do with David."

"I never said that. I don't hate kids, you know. I like them. I'm a teacher, remember. Of course, it's college kids I work with now, but I do like grade school kids. Believe it or not, I taught fourth grade a long time ago before I went back to grad school. I especially like kids in late grade school. The psychologists used to call it the 'latency period.' The child begins to have the intelligence of an older kid but without the hormonal complications of adolescence. David fits that to a tee—intelligent, thoughtful, well-behaved, intellectually curious. He's remarkable, really, given what he's been through."

"So you've changed you mind?"

"How so?"

"You're willing to have David in my life and by extension in yours—in ours if there is an 'ours'?"

Angela sighed, "This was one night. I like this boy. I'd enjoy seeing him on occasion. I'm not ready to have a child in my life."

"I wonder," said John.

"What's that supposed to mean?"

John said nothing in reply.

"Oh, you think you know me now." Angela laughed. "You think I secretly want a kid and I'll come around."

"I never said that."

"You were thinking it or hoping for it. Well, listen, buster, don't make assumptions about me. You won't like it when you find out what happens when you're wrong!"

John laughed, "Are you threatening me? I don't know why, but I feel better. I think maybe I can put up with you."

"Thank you for that lovely and romantic affirmation! Good night, John!" And Angela hung up, but John did feel better.

****

A few days later John finished a project, and it was too late in the morning to do any more work, so, on a whim he called Angela's cell phone and happened to catch her as she was coming out of her last class of the morning. Without thinking, he invited her to come over for lunch. Surprised, she said yes. John hurriedly made a spinach and cheese omelet and some roast turkey sandwiches. He was just finishing setting the table and pouring some fresh apple juice when he heard her heels on the porch and her knock at the storm door. She was impressed at how quickly he'd put the lunch together.

"So what's the occasion?" she asked as they sat down.

"I just wanted to see you." He reached across the table and took her hand. "I'm not going to let this end over David."

"When did you decide this?"

"This morning. It just came over me."

"What came over you?"

"I think I'm in love with you."

"You only figured that out this morning!"

"Is that bad?"

"Well, I had the idea you were more than just partial to me. I'm a bit surprised that you only just figured that out. You're not as smart as I thought you were."

"You're playing with me now."

"I thought you were further along."

"I hadn't made a commitment."

"A commitment. Are you proposing?"

"No. Maybe the word is 'affirmation'." I had not solidly and unequivocally affirmed that I'm in love with you."

"I thought love was more a matter of the heart than the head or the moral sense. You either are or you aren't."

"Well, you can parse it however you want. I'm telling you that this morning I realized that I love you and that I'm not willing to let you go."

Angela smiled.

"Oh stop! Women are sometimes so superior and supercilious about love. You think you know all there is to know about it, and that we men don't have a clue."

"You said that. I didn't."

"I have had the opposite experience—falling in love at first sight and being overwhelmed by it. I was in agony."

"So you're telling me that you did not fall in love with me right away, that it took a while, and that you are not in agony and glad you're not."

"Yes."

"I seem to remember one evening in the park. I remember your look."

John blushed. "I'm not sure that was love."

"Oh, so you're separating love and desire. And you're only now getting around to loving me?"

"You are determined to put me in a bad light. Here's the thing. I want you in my life, and I want David too. On Monday, I thought I would have to choose. I'm telling you now something different, something very specific. If you pull away because of David, I'm going to pursue you. You can't make me choose. I'm not going to let you get away."

Angela stopped her teasing and gazed for a long minute into John's eyes. He stood, walked to her side of the table, pulled her chair back, lifted her to her feet and kissed her. In a moment they were moving toward the bedroom.

Later they were lying close side by side, holding hands. Angela was stroking John's cheek. "By inviting me over and enticing me into your bed, are you trying to make me comfortable in space you and David share?"

"Not consciously, but that's a good idea."

"You know we can't do this when he's in his bedroom next door."

"What do you think couples who have kids do?" John replied.

"But we're not other couples. At least I'm not, and I've never understood how married people do that."

Chapter 26 – Action

Sam woke and suddenly knew what to do. He showered, dressed, ate a quick breakfast, kissed Eve, jumped into his car, and was off. His first stop was Joe Kurtz's house. He knew Joe happened to have the day off. "I want you to come with me. I'll tell you why later," he said. He was not going to take no for an answer, but Joe came with surprising docility. Next he pulled up in front of the building on River Street and ran up to John's second-floor apartment. David was just going out the door for school. John had his work clothes on and was headed to a downstairs apartment to begin tearing out old carpet. Sam had no trouble convincing him that he had something more interesting to do.

"So what's up? Are you going to tell us?" Joe asked, as John crawled into the back seat.

"We're going to find Jack now. John, do you know where he is?"

"I saw him early this morning, making measurements in the backyard of the old Victorian house," John said.

Sam drove over there, and the three men clambered out of the car and walked around the big old house, where they found Jack tearing out the back steps. "Jack," Sam said. "I'm working on an idea. I want you to come with us."

"Right now. Right here. Just like that?"

"Yes."

"Are you going to tell me what this is about?"

"In the car," Sam said and began walking back toward the van.

Jack looked at Joe and John, who just shrugged. And the three men patiently followed Sam.

When they were all back in the van, Sam turned around so he could see everyone. "Here's the deal. We are going to go over to the church and find Kirby, and we're going to talk him into staying. We're not taking no for an answer. We won't leave until we get his agreement."

Jack laughed, "I like it."

John smiled, "I'm in."

Joe hesitated only for a moment. "Why not? What do we have to lose?"

They pulled into the church parking lot and got out of the van like crusaders. Someone should have been playing "Onward Christian Soldiers" on the organ. They went up the steps to the main floor, marched past the secretary's office, and pounded on Kirby's door. It was a good thing Kirby was there. Their reckless energy might not have survived a long search. They were catching him at the height of their resolution.

They trooped in and stood around Kirby's desk like agents in some TV police-procedural. He leaned back in his chair, surprised, amused, and a bit intimidated. Before he could say anything, Sam burst out, "You can't leave. We're not going to hear any more about resignation. We're here to put a stop to it."

Kirby smiled, "Do you have authority I don't know about?"

"Yes, the authority of friendship. When a man is about to do something stupid, it's the job of his friends to stop him."

"You think you can strong-arm me?"

"We thought about slashing your tires," Jack said, "but we didn't have the guts to do it in broad daylight in the church parking lot." They all laughed.

Kirby turned to Joe, "You seem to be part of this. Are you in your official capacity, or are you on your own recognizance?"

"I was drafted, but I came willingly."

"Where's Kurt? This kind of thing is more his style."

"He's out of town," Sam said, "so I didn't try to pick him up."

"So you're the ringleader?"

"No, I'm just the one pulling the finger out of the dike."

"I haven't talked to anyone who wants you to go," said Joe.

"You're only talking to people who agree with you."

"Oh, come on, Beahm," said Jack. "You know you have plenty of support. It was 80% in open meeting. How many pastors would get that in any church after seven years? Everybody makes some enemies. Amazingly you haven't. Even the people who don't like you, like you."

"That's nonsense," Kirby replied, smiling.

"Christ, Kirby, you know what I mean. You're just a hard guy to dislike. People who disagree with you 180 degrees, still respect you and feel good about you. In my business a guy who is trying to get everyone to like him is a lily-livered pansy-ass who's not much use to anyone. I don't know how you do it—and you don't even seem to be trying—but somehow people just trust you and appreciate you."

"It was an 80% vote!" Sam said in exasperation. "Anywhere else, politics, government, the non-profit sector—that's a landslide, a mandate."

"What about the other 20%? How can I pastor them?"

"Most pastors have to pastor some people who disagree with them or don't like them."

John, who had not said anything, leaned forward on Kirby's desk so their faces were on the same level only about two feet apart. "You've always been a bit over-scrupulous. Back in college, everyone knew this about you. No one ever made fun of you, because you were never self-righteous, never a prude. People smiled at you, maybe thought you were a little naïve, a little hard to believe, but you always had people's respect and trust. Face it, Kirby, you're a rare species, a genuine good guy, with no bullshit or pretense. Believe me, you can still be our pastor."

"Suppose you're right. What about the rest of the district? Right now it's only me the district can come after. If you continue to hire me after my ordination has been suspended or eventually revoked, then the district will have cause to come after the whole congregation. Then the 20% minority will be dragged into something official that is deeply offensive to them."

"Well, the action against you has to be completed by the ministerial commission and then go before the district board," said Sam. "We will argue for you in front of both groups. If you're still defrocked and they come after the congregation, then we'll have to decide what to do. I'm not afraid of that."

Jack backed away from the desk and sat in one of the comfortable chairs, making a show of making himself comfortable. Sam grinned when he realized what Jack was doing and followed suit. Joe took the third and last chair, and John moved away from the desk, leaned against the wall, crossed his arms as though he planned to stay a while. Kirby laughed, "What is this? You're not leaving till you have my word?"

The four men looked at each other and back at Kirby, smiling and saying nothing.

"All right," Kirby said. "I hear you. I'll think about it. That's the best I can do."

"Kirby," Sam said, "all posturing aside, we really think we can make this work. We really want you to stay."

"Yeah, we love you, man!" said Jack with mock seriousness, and everyone laughed the way men do when they are uncomfortable with how much they feel for one another.

There was an awkward moment. Then Sam said, "Well, we should get out of your hair, let you do your work, whatever you do in this office— work on your sermon, think deep thoughts, commune with the Lord, shoot out into vast celestial spaces of spirit and wisdom."

"Nothing that exalted. I'm getting ready to visit Maud who's in the hospital to have her hernia fixed."

"Too much information."

John was the last to leave. "We've been friends for a long time. I don't usually give advice, but you really should stay. These people love you."

****

Sam dropped the men off in reverse order. Leaving John at the apartment building, he took out his cell phone and called Hank and invited him to meet at the Athens House for lunch. When they were settled in a booth, he asked Hank a question.

"If I am out of line, please say so. Are you still thinking about dying?"

"Yes, I think about it all the time. I'm only half glad to be here. Yeah, I've wanted to check out."

"I'm not asking if you've had suicidal thoughts. Haven't all of us had those at some time or other in our lives? I'm talking about thinking that you might die from…here's where I probably don't have the right to ask…from your heart disease. Are you afraid of that?"

"Hell, yes, I am. My heart has been damaged, weakened. It's still only working at about half capacity. I have to be careful for the rest of my life, however much I have left. I can't ever again do anything full out. So yes, I think about it. What would happen if I worked too hard in the garden and fell over in the dirt? Or suppose I'm in my shop reaching up for something on the top shelf, something heavy, and my heart suddenly gives out. I fall back and hit my head and die either of heart failure or a concussion. Realistically, how much time do I have left? I'm sixty five. Will I make it to eighty? I doubt it. Suppose I have only ten years left. Are you asking me how I feel about that?"

"Yes, I guess I am."

"It feels like shit. But—I don't want to live to a doddering old age, drooling in some nursing home where I can't remember who I am and some orderly has to wipe my ass."

"So how do you face either possibility?"

"Why are you asking?"

"Well, I'm the same age you are."

"Yeah, but your health is good, and your old man lived into his nineties."

"We're all in your situation. We just don't realize it. When we're young, we think we're immortal. Even at 66, if our health is good, we somehow think we're just going to be able to keep going indefinitely. The only difference between you and me is that your heart has got your attention and forced you to think about dying."

"You said it's only partly for yourself that you want to know."

"Yeah, I have a longtime friend in Seattle, who got the news that he has prostate cancer. He could live two years or ten years or many more if the present research gets ahead of the disease. He has a good attitude. I'm not all that worried about him, but I'm trying to understand. Truthfully, I don't know what to say to him—or to you."

"Hell, I don't know, Sam. Sometimes I don't want anyone to say anything. I don't want to think about it! Other times I'm scared and I need to talk. On any given day, I never know which it's going to be. So with me basically, you're screwed. If you try to talk about it, and I'm in denial, I'm not going to be happy. If I'm desperate to talk, and you're trying to be extra sensitive and careful, you'll drive me nuts. Hell, you probably ought to just ask."

"The truth is I'd rather not talk about it," Sam paused. "I'd hate to lose you."

A small smile crossed Hank's lips. "That's nice to know. That's something you can say any time." He raised his eyebrows. "Your Seattle friend probably wouldn't mind hearing that either."

"Lately I've been having these strong feelings. Like right now. I'm just plain glad you are in my life. Think of all we've been through together. We started out forty years ago, both of us just married, talking about our wives and how hard it was. Here we are, two old farts, talking about dying. Damn, friendship is a blessing, you know that! To have that much shared history!"

"So who's going to be at whose funeral?"

Sam laughed, "Well, by God, if you go first, I'm going to make one hell of a speech at yours!"

"If you're first, I'll write a song for you."

"It better be good! I'll be listening in from the other side."

"So what has made you all soft and fuzzy today? What's going on?"

"This morning four of us, all guys, went over to our pastor—you know I told you about the trouble he's in for doing a lesbian union service—to tell him how much we love him and want him to stay."

"You told him you loved him!"

"Well, not in so many words. But, yes, it was clear we were there not just because we think he's a hell of a pastor, but because we're his friends and we care about him and more than that, we really like him and want him to stay around."

"Sounds like you had trouble saying the L word."

"We did, except in a joking way, but we got the message across. I know he felt loved."

"What is it with men? I've known you for forty years, and I've never told you I love you."

Sam looked around the restaurant to see if anyone was listening. "You might not want to say that too loud." He laughed.

"Okay, how's this. It's been a privilege."

"Thank you. But you know, you don't have to say it for me to know it. That's the thing about men that women don't get. We can care deeply about one another, and we don't have to say it to know it!"

"Does it make a difference if we do say it?"

"You tell me."

Chapter 27 – Letter

All morning John wondered what Kirby was thinking after the strong-arm visit from his four friends. A few hours after lunch he took a break and drove over to the church. Geraldine stopped him as he headed to Kirby's office, telling him that Kirby had asked her to hold all calls and visitors. John convinced her at least to tell Kirby he was there, and Kirby told her to send him in. He found his friend staring out the window. He had his Bible in his hand.

"Listen to this," Kirby said. "'Blessed are those who are persecuted for righteousness' sake, for theirs is the kingdom of heaven. Blessed are you when people revile you and persecute you and utter all kinds of evil against you falsely on my account. Rejoice and be glad, for your reward is great in heaven, for in the same way they persecuted the prophets who were before you.'"

Kirby closed the book and laughed. "Persecution? I wish! This silliness in the district doesn't rise to that level. There's no higher ground here I can claim. That's all on Fred's side."

He closed his eyes. A certain peace seemed to steal over his features, and John wondered if he was praying. Then a troubled look returned. John said nothing.

"I called Nancy after the four of you left. I was overdue to talk to her. I do that, you know. I carry things inside as if it's only my burden to bear. I cut her out too often. We had lunch over at the Athens House. In fact, I saw Sam and his friend Hank there. I told her about the visit from you guys this morning, and she laughed and said I was lucky to have such friends.

"I said to her, 'Don't you see the position I put the congregation in if I accept this offer?' She just smiled at me and said in that slightly conde-scending voice she uses when she think she has to humor me, 'I've always loved your almost exquisite sense of fair play (she was really saying she's weary of it), the way you bend over backwards to take into account every-one else's point of view. But this time you can't do it. You have a large majority who want you to stay, and if you don't, you break trust with them. You have a small minority who may want you to go (we don't know that for sure), and you want to honor their desires. Why?'

"I told her, 'You know my answer. The minority deserves considera-tion. Minorities are always ignored and pushed aside.'

"John, in a democratic culture we think that's how the game is played. When the majority wins, the losers have to snuff it up and suffer, disenfranchised until the next issue and vote."

John spoke for the first time, "But isn't that how the democratic system works?"

"That's what Nancy said. I told her it's always been my desire to care about everyone, the winners and the losers. And she said, 'So you would make a decision that supports the small minority here, even though you think they're wrong?' I said, 'No, I am trying to make a decision that does not deepen the rift, the possibility of polarization in the congregation.'

"'Well, either way, the rift will grow,' Nancy said bluntly. 'Maybe your job is to make the decision that's right for you whichever it is and then figure out how to bring people who can't agree together. Either way that task is the same.'

"I had to admit that was good advice.

"So I dropped Nancy at her school, came back here, and here I am. You may or may not know that I gave the board my letter of resignation on Tuesday night, two days after the congregational meeting. The board asked for some time to consider it before accepting it.

"Anyway, when I got back here to my office after talking with Nancy, I called Joe and left a message on his voicemail. I wrote a short e-mail to the board members saying I am reconsidering my resignation. Then I wrote this letter to the congregation." He took a two-page computer printout off his desk and handed it to John.

Dear Friends,

Thank you for your vote at congregational business meeting to keep me on the church staff even during this time when my ordination has been suspended. I took it as a measure of your appreciation of my ministry and your affection for me as a person. I said at that time that I could not accept your offer because I would not be able to be pastor to the 20% minority who opposed the action. The question of same-sex unions is such a powerful and divisive matter that I felt I would not be able to be a good pastor to those who are strongly against the action I took in performing the union ceremony for Samantha Jones and Marianne Svoboda.

I have changed my mind. I hope you will forgive me for this vacillation. Several people have pointed out to me that no pastor after many years of ministry retains the support of every member. There are bound to be those who do not approve of all of my actions, and there are likely people who do not even like me. Of course, this is not a new insight. I am experienced enough certainly to know this, but I have always retained the perhaps impossible hope that everyone would find my ministry effective and useful and people in general would like me. I have always balanced my conscience and calling against this goal to keep myself in good relationship to all of you.

This is the first time in my ministry with you where one of my actions clearly puts my relationship to some of you at risk. I thought this is a big enough matter that I owed it to you, the minority who are displeased or disappointed or even offended, to remove myself as your pastor. But I see now that by doing that I abandon those of you, the majority, who deeply support my action in performing the union service, and in a way I abandon Samantha and Marianne. Further, maybe I was running away from trouble. We all know that acts of conscience can get you into trouble, and this one has.

So I have a dilemma. I may not be able to be a good pastor to all of you. What do I do with that? Well, let me say this. I am not angry at those of you who do not approve of my action. I don't judge you. You might ask me, how is that possible on a matter where we all feel so deeply. I don't know. I think it's a bit of grace. I can't claim any goodness of character here. But I really do love all of you, and in some cases I like those of you who are against what I did more than those who support it. Don't start guessing here about who are favorites and who are not. Like any ordinary human, I like some people better than others, but I do really feel a connection to and love for all of you that is deeper than mere liking.

So here's the thing. I am ready to proceed with this unorthodox plan for me to go on pastoring you without official ordination. I will do my best to be there for each of you whether you approve of my actions or thoroughly dislike them. May the spirit of God be present in each of us, reconciling us to one another and showing us the love that cuts deeper than any apparent brokenness.

Now, there is one more thing that I have wrestled with and am taking into account, and I think each of you and all of us as a congregation will have to do the same. If I were to resign, it would save you as a congregation from being out of order with the district. But people in the district can construe your action in keeping me on your staff as an unwillingness to be in compliance. You are indirectly approving of my action to perform a same-sex union. There is a possibility that district conference might sanction our congregation, just as happened over in Indiana several years ago. We must be prepared for this possibility.

I have thought long and hard about whether I have any right to ask the congregation to put itself in this position. I've concluded that I don't have this right. So before we can go forward with this plan for me to be your pastor but not quite your pastor, I urge you as a congregation to count the cost of this action. Are you ready to put yourself in a difficult position? If your answer is no, I will again offer my resignation.

One last reflection. I've said nothing yet in this letter about prayer and the will of God. If I were to tell you that I am certain it is God's will that we move forward, then I would be implying that those of you who cannot support this direction are outside of God's will. That is offensive and I am not willing to do that. I have prayed about this, and I've concluded that the things I've written in this letter grow out of God's will for me, but I do not subscribe to the corollary that if you disagree, you are outside God's will. There is a mystery here, and I have to say that I sometimes think God can be on both sides of what seems to us to be irreconcilable differences. Please don't ask me how. I simply have the sense that this is true. God is with all of us and God's grace can bring us through. So I will not get into a spitting match about who is doing God's will here. We are all muddling through, doing the best we can with prayer, with careful discernment, with efforts to understand one another, and with the conviction that God is with us, all of us.

In Christ's name,

Kirby Beahm

When John finished reading the letter, he put it gently back on Kirby's desk, almost as if it were a holy object. He had tears in his eyes.

****

John was at the meeting as an observer when the board accepted Kirby's change of direction. Everyone was glad. Even Herman Fry seemed relieved. Kirby read them the letter to the congregation, and their feedback was positive. The letter went out, not by e-mail, but by regular post. John learned from Sam that somehow through the mysteries and inevitabilities of the grapevine, a copy quickly made its way to one of the downstate churches and from there to the hands of Fred Vogel who brought it to the ministerial commission. It didn't change the position of anyone on the commission. But, Sam told John, those who admired and supported Kirby thought it was a strong letter, and it increased their respect. Three of those who had voted against him, including Fred, thought it was further indication of Kirby's unwillingness to follow the scripture and the discipline of the church. The fourth said the letter gave her pause.

A week later John learned from Kirby who got it from the district executive Daryl Bender that Fred had brought together an ad hoc group of downstate pastors and laypeople who had drafted a recommendation that the Westbrook congregation be censured. It asked that members of the congregation be prohibited from holding any district office and that its delegates to district conference not be seated. It further called for Kirby Beahm to be censured as an action separate from the ministerial commission's efforts to revoke his ordination. Fred Vogel's next step was to bring this recommendation to the district board where he argued passionately for its approval. But there were some sober and thoughtful heads around that table, people who did not approve of what Kirby had done, but who had known him for years, had liked and respected him, and had understood the spirit of his action. They were as dismayed by the vehemence and harshness of Fred Vogel and his supporters as they were by the actions of Kirby and his congregation. They refused to approve the recommendation and send it on to district conference.

John dropped by Kirby's office every few days to hear if there were new developments. One day, about three weeks after the letter had gone out, Kirby told John, "Vogel and the downstate coalition are not willing to accept the district board's decision. They have appealed directly to the moderator to have the recommendation placed on the agenda of district conference. Fred claims to have the support of most of the downstate churches. The moderator is a layperson who was been elected because she has served on the camp board for many years. She's a nice woman. She was a guidance counselor at a downstate high school. But she has little savvy about polity and no stomach for politics. She hates conflict and was intimidated by Fred. She says since this is such a troubling and disturbing matter that it needs public airing. She used her prerogative as moderator to put it on the conference agenda."

Chapter 28 – Sam's Vision

It was late afternoon. The sunlight warmed Sam's face. He was sitting on the deck in a chair surrounded by flowers and grasses in various-sized wooden boxes and ceramic planters, his nostrils filled with many fragrances. The sun grew large and orange as it sank toward the horizon. He peered at it a moment too long. He lay back, in the chair fully relaxed, not caring that his vision had darkened, watching the pinpricks of exploding light that surrounded the dusky center where the sun had bathed his retina. His eyes closed. His body seemed to float off the chair. The points of light grew and came together and gathered themselves into a white and distant brilliance. He felt himself rise out of his body and move toward the light. He glanced back and saw himself sprawled at rest in the chair, his head back as though he'd fallen asleep. He had a sudden sensation of vertigo as he moved up and away while looking back. Then he turned forward toward the growing radiance.

He heard many voices speaking softly and over each other, a gentle cacophony both disturbing and soothing. As he drew closer to the light, it began to resolve itself into a figure. He sensed that he was being accompanied and turned to his side looking for the one moving with him, but there was no figure. He wondered if it were his grandfather and then he wondered why he thought that. If he supposed it, maybe it really was. These thoughts moved rapidly through his mind. Time seemed to be moving very fast and at the same time standing still. He turned back to the figure of light. It was all so utterly strange. He was surprised he was not afraid. The lighted one laughed as though he had read his thoughts. Sam could not see a face, so how did he know the figure laughed. But he knew. Again he sensed the other's laughter. He was now close enough to see that the being of light did have a face. But it was not like any face he'd ever seen. Light streamed from the eyes and the forehead and seemed to fly off every angle and plane of the features. Yet in another way it was like every face. It was very human, as if all the billions of human faces now and always were contained in this one glowing visage. He felt he was in the presence of all history. He saw the suffering and joy, the anger and energy, the imagination and love that had ever been in any face. It was suffused with compassion. Everything that had ever happened was somehow understood and forgiven in that face.

Sam wanted to stand at attention, filled with awe and reverence, ready to carry out any request or order, wanting to speak the being's praise and honor his excellence At the same time he wanted to sit down, lie back, and lounge and luxuriate in the intimacy of this presence, listen to his stories, hang on his words, be washed in his attention and love. A smile formed. Sam could feel it before he saw it spread on the radiant face—a smile of all smiles. It was there in the air between them. It was deep in his spirit.

Sam's mind filled with questions. The figure seemed to welcome this. It seemed to Sam that this was the purpose of the moment.

"Are you Christ?" formed in Sam's mind and he knew immediately that the lighted one heard the question. The realization that the being knew his every thought disturbed Sam. He was naked and exposed. Embarrassing, even lewd thoughts perversely crowded his mind against his will, anything that he would be ashamed to admit to another person or that would be inappropriate or crude. This unruly behavior of his mind brought another smile from the being, who seemed to say this was typical. There was nothing to fear. He already knew all this anyway.

"Are you Jesus?" Sam found himself saying again.

"For some that is a different question from your first question. Who do you say that I am?"

Sam did not answer, but the lighted one read his unspoken reply "You are the Christ."

"You are troubled when you say that?"

"Only because when Christians say it, they often use it to exclude others."

"Do you think that only Christians can see me?"

"I don't know. Who can see you?"

"Those with eyes to see."

Sam thought he should have known that. He felt chastised. And then immediately as though the second feeling was layered with the first, he felt understood and accepted.

"You are still troubled?" came the words from the figure.

Sam knew he had to come clean. He did not even try not to. His actual thoughts were right there in plain view. "I don't believe you exclude people who don't know you or believe in you or who have other cherished beliefs. I believe that they are somehow right too."

"Do you suppose that I value being right?"

"Being righteous, maybe."

"Are they different?"

"One has to do with correct thoughts and words. The other has to do with living a correct life."

The radiant face smiled and seemed to raise a brilliant eyebrow, though Sam had not before noticed eyebrows behind the light. "*You* have used the word 'correct'."

Sam found he didn't want to talk anymore. His thoughts seemed small and limited He had the sense, rare for him, that nothing needed to be said. All was understood.

"Are you wondering why you are here?"

Sam realized he was.

The figure pointed to a wide empty space where images began to form. Sam saw his mother as a very young woman, in a small rural hospital, and he realized he was seeing his own birth. In blindingly rapid succession, scenes from his childhood appeared. They reminded him of the holographic images on the Star Trek holodeck. They had the appearance of being as real as if they were happening now. He was amazed he could take them all in. They moved so fast. Each instant came on top of the one before so that the whole sequence was stacked up in one moment, yet he could see and think about and feel each instant in its entirety. He saw everything in his life, every embarrassing incident, every proud moment, every petty or angry word, every shameful action, every loving effort—his creativity, his stupidity, his selfishness, his selflessness. He saw exactly the kind of man he was. There was judgment in every moment that called for it. There was no escape from the truth. He felt pride and shame, but the strongest feeling was chagrin. He was so much less than he wanted to think he was. But there was the most extraordinary current of compassion and love coming from the being of light. All was known, all was weighed and judged, all was accepted. It left him breathless, grateful, and humbled. Tears came to his eyes and ran down his cheeks.

The stream of images seemed to slow as they came closer to the present, and the moments that showed him wrestling and struggling seemed to come into higher relief. Sam found himself very tired, as though he'd been on a long journey. He could hardly stand. The lighted one asked if he wanted to sit. A chair of some bright white fabric formed behind him, nudging him in the back of the knees. He sat. "Is this why you have brought me here?" he asked.

"Come," said the lighted one. Sam's hand was taken gently but firmly. The two of them began to move through space. Sam was surprised that the chair was moving too and he could stay seated, but then he realized that it was all a matter of perception. He could sit, recline, or stand. His hand would still be in the hand of the figure of light. They would still be moving through space.

They were high above a huge city. They rapidly settled closer to ground level. They moved through the wall of an exclusive office building into the boardroom with luxurious carpet, a thick polished mahogany table, and plush upholstered chairs. Men and women, handsomely and expensively dressed, sat around the table, deep in consultation. They were talking about business activities involving billions of dollars. Sam could see into their thoughts as well as hear their words. Behind the talk were unspoken images. Power to do what they wished, power over others. Clothes, jewelry, good food, travel, luxury cars, the best schools for their children, beautiful, spacious homes, the latest electronic equipment, concerts, expensive works of art, philanthropies that would bring them notice. Sam understood these desires; he had felt them himself. The people around the table seemed to know all this about one another, but not to know each other. They were sure of their status, but anxious. They seemed to want more and not know what it was.

Sam and the being of light began to move again, through the walls and into the air, in the direction of uptown. They settled briefly into a small, dark apartment on a street of rundown four and six flats. A mother, already weary from caring for her kids, was saying good-bye, giving instructions to the oldest who was 12 to care for the little ones, getting ready to take the subway down to the office building where she would put in a long night shift, cleaning the carpets, dusting the rich furniture, and cleaning the toilets of the people who were just leaving for the night. Her thoughts were heavy. She trudged down the stairs, across two blocks, and down the subway stairs. She never stopped worrying about her kids. She was thinking about the store run she would make in the morning so they would have breakfast food. She didn't have enough money for all the groceries she needed.

They lifted into the air again and moved at light-speed across the country, stopping to look at broad fields, grain elevators, freight trains with boxcars carrying vegetables, tank cars full of grain, thousands of semis carrying packaged food. They saw the miles and miles of truck farms in the West. Sam saw a staggering abundance of food and everything essential for life. They continued west past the coast and across the ocean. In a heartbeat they were somewhere in Asia, passing cities teaming with people, country sides feeding more people that he could have thought possible.

They came in low over a vast city near the sea. They slowed as they passed over people dying in the streets, pyres where bodies were being burned, a population crowded into impossibly small spaces, tiny, emaciated children left to roam the streets. He heard the thoughts of these desperate people, but he could not understand their language. Their life was beyond his comprehension.

Then he was pulled back, moving over his own town. He saw his friends at work or at home. He saw comfort and safety and goodness—and half-acknowledged anxieties. He could hear their thoughts. Their efforts to love and to live joyfully were cluttered with thought of things they had to do, houses and businesses they had to take care of, groceries, clothing, sundries they needed, and gadgets they were planning to buy. This was familiar. He recognized his own struggles.

In an instant he found himself back where they had started, wondering whether they had ever really left and why he had been shown all this. The being beside him sensed the question and put it into words, "Do you know why?"

Sam's mind ran over several possible reasons, before he spoke. Then he remembered the being of light could read his thoughts and had already done so. He shrugged his shoulders. "Those are guesses," he said. "I don't really know."

The figure laughed and said, "There is enough." Then the radiant face turned sober and the light streamed in different directions as the facial planes changed. "It is a great sadness—that men and women don't believe this."

Words and questions tumbled through Sam's mind: enough food, enough water, enough energy, enough medicine, enough good will, enough love? Where were these words coming from? This being of light? Yes. But Sam knew his own mind was supplying these ideas too as he slowly took in what the being meant. "But as you said," Sam countered, "no one believes there is enough. Scarcity is the basis for all war and competition.

"Children suffered and died in that city," Sam went on in protest. "Saying there is enough brings them no comfort."

"That is true."

Sam remembered his social justice analysis. "They are starving because some of us consume a disproportionate part of the world's resources."

"That is true also..." the being said, as though there was more to be said and it was Sam's job to say it.

"You want me to say it's a problem of spirit. You want me to say that people get what they believe is possible, that it's a problem of hope."

"Is that what you want to say?"

"For myself, yes, I would say that. But I have no right to say that for starving people in Asia." Sam paused. "I always thought a vision like this would answer my questions."

Now the lighted one laughed outright, deep resonant laughter that seemed to wash through Sam and the universe, filling him with buoyant energy and good humor.

"That felt wonderful, but you still leave me with more questions than answers."

"You will find you have what you need," came the words.

"But not what I want. Is that it?"

"You have said it."

Sam wondered how this conversation could be at once puzzling, yet satisfying. He knew it was coming to an end.

"Will I see you again?" he asked.

"Do you have eyes to see?"

Sam said nothing. No one had ever made him feel so profoundly himself—sad, wise, joyful, deeply in the moment. He wanted to kneel before this figure. He had always thought people who talked about glorifying God and kneeling in God's presence had misunderstood the holy. God wanted strong, forceful people who could stand up, not sycophants.

"It is not self-abasement or the denial of strength," the lighted one said. "It is love, like kneeling to wash another's feet."

A desire rose to the surface of Sam's mind, and he quickly pushed it down.

"It is natural to want to stay," said the lighted one, reading his thoughts. "But what is here is also there. You pushed the desire away."

"I had no right. My wife and my friends—I'm not finished with them."

"Then you choose to return?"

"Yes. Do I have a choice? I'm not near death."

"You never know when you are near death. You can always choose life or choose death."

Sam felt himself moving away from the light, moving into darkness. He saw his body below him and then he was in it. He could feel the crick in his neck where his head had fallen back against the patio chair. The sun had set. There were a few streaks of pink and gray near the horizon. The yard below the deck was in darkness. The temperature had dropped. He was chilled. He wondered how long he'd been sitting there. Had he been asleep? The light, the one, the words they'd exchanged—he would never forget, not a word or thought. He was filled with longing. He went inside to find a jacket, came back out, and sat for a long time gazing into the sky as the stars came out. What did this mean? What was he to do now?

He heard the front door open and he knew Eve was home. He went into the living room, asked her to sit down, and told her the whole thing. He could recall it down to the last word, thought, and feeling. She listened with keen attention. When he finished, she smiled and took his hand.

"Why are you smiling?" he asked.

"It's a good thing. I would like to have a vision like that."

Sam was pensive for the rest of the evening. He ate dinner. He and Eve talked, read, checked the news on TV, and went to bed. He was only partly there. The next day he woke and it felt as though he was starting a new life. Everything was different, yet if he had been asked to say how it was different, he could not have said. In one sense he never needed to do another thing. His life was complete. He could stay in this moment forever. In another sense there were things to do that he had never considered. And they were to be done in a different way. He wasn't sure what the way was, but he knew he would find out. He'd never cared for the idea that believers underwent a second birth. He always felt that faith was a matter of steady growth, not disjunctive moments that seemed to deny all that had gone before. His vision did not cut him off from his former life, as though it had no value, but it gave him a new life that felt different. It seemed to encompass the best of the old and something more that he'd never guessed at. What should he do—the question came without anxiety. He knew he would know as he went along.

Chapter 29 – John and Wilbur

John heard from Kirby that Nancy's father was coming for another visit. John called Nancy and asked eagerly if he could pick Wilbur up and bring him back to his apartment for an afternoon and evening, to include dinner, or supper as Wilbur would call it. John could hear the grin in Nancy's voice.

"He's the only old man left in my life," John said. "You know what a great man your dad is!"

"I know, I know. But even Dad might get a big head if you say that to him. He thinks of himself as an old farmer with a tenth-grade education."

"He does think that, but he also knows he's a step or two ahead of even the smartest people, and he enjoys surprising people."

"That's Dad," Nancy replied. "So I'm going to have to share him with you?"

"I hope so."

On her way to school Nancy dropped Wilbur off at John's apartment early on the second morning after his arrival. He walked creakily up the outside stairs and across the porch, opened the door, and stepped in, this stocky old farmer wearing a clean pair of bibbed overalls, a plaid flannel shirt and brown work shoes. He still had most of his hair and there were a few streaks of black left. It was combed back and his beard was gray and closely cropped

John was packing lunch for David who had not yet left for school. Wilbur smiled and said nothing when John introduced them. He put out his thick, still work-hardened hand, and David took it and shook it, giving Wilbur a quiet smile. He put his lunch in his backpack and slung it over one shoulder and went out the door.

"Always thought you'd make a goodt dadt," Wilbur said.

"Well, I do like it. So how are you?"

"About as goodt as I ought to be at 95."

"You don't look a day over 80."

"Vell, Chon, that's a nice thing to say, but how about you? My days are pretty much the same every day, but you—you're still young."

"Wilbur, I'm past 60!"

"What do they say—60 is the new 40? You're only chust in middle age. I want to know about that woman. You know, the one. You talkt a lot about her when I was here before."

"Suppose I got married again?"

"Ho. It's gone that far. Vell, Chon, do you want to?"

"I'm not sure."

"Vell, ve got the whole day to talk about it."

John showed him through the apartment building. Wilbur tapped walls, looked at the plumbing and wiring, shuffled his feet on the new carpets, checked out the new kitchen appliances. He nodded from time to time indicating his approval of the workmanship, which made John happy. He'd used Jack's subcontractors, who were first-rate, and had insisted on good materials, and Jack had backed him up, so he was not in doubt about the quality of the rehab. Still Wilbur's approval pleased him. He was a boy again, eagerly seeking praise. Wilbur really got interested when they walked through the backyard and into the backyards of Jack's house and the big Victorian house. He wanted to know all about the co-housing idea.

"You know, Chon, that's a little bit like they did in Acts where they all lived together and shared their goodts."

"Yes, but a little different because here we would share only some things. We'd still own our own units, but share the common areas."

"People live better when they share."

"Well, we think so, but we'll only know when we do it."

"So if you get married, will you and she live here?"

"She's not crazy about the idea, and," he paused, "she's doesn't want to have responsibility for a boy."

Wilbur blew air through his rounded lips. "That ain't so goodt. So you think David is going to stay with you?"

"His mother wants to be a good mother, but someone needs to be there for David, when she can't be. I think I'm the guy."

"Suppose David's mother moves away and takes David vith her?"

"I'll cross that bridge when I come to it."

"And this co-housing thing—you said your woman doesn't want that either?"

"She's has her own place. Living that close to other people, making decisions with them, she doesn't see the need. It just doesn't appeal to her. She has many friends. She has lots of nephews and nieces. She's from a big family. She teaches college kids all day. She doesn't need more people in her life, and she's just not ready to take on a soon-to-be teenager."

Wilbur nodded and smiled.

"You think this is good?"

"Vell, it's stretching you a bit, isn't it?"

"Maybe we don't have to get married. We can each keep our own place. Be together a couple times a week. There's nothing that says a relationship has to look like every other relationship."

"You could get married and do that too."

"Yes, I could. But, Wilbur, I'm past 60. Why would I want to get married?"

"Do you love her?"

"Yes, I think I do."

"You think?" The old man smiled.

"I enjoy her company."

"Is that all?"

In spite of himself John reddened. "We talked about this when you were here before. No that's not all."

"And is it good?"

John continued to blush. "Yes, it's good."

"You know, Chon, it's all right. It's not like you're catting aroundt."

John laughed. "Yes, we are only involved with each other. How did you come to be such a freethinker? Wilbur, you've lived your whole life in the church."

"Well, Chon, people chust don't fit into the molds church people would like. Some think Chesus vas very proper. I wonder. Maybe he accepts the way people are better than we think."

"So here are the options: marry Angela and live with her; marry her, but live separately; live with her, but not marry her; have relations with her, but not marry or live with her; break up with her."

Wilbur thought for a long time, then nodded his head. "Yup, that about covers it."

"You're not going to tell me which you think I should do."

"Nope."

John laughed. "You run true to form."

"Chon, which way lets you love each other best? That's the question."

John pushed himself away from the backyard fence where they'd been leaning. "I'll take you for a drive, show you Selby. Maybe Kirby and Nancy have already done that."

"Let's do it again."

John knew that Wilbur liked to see farms and cemeteries. First he drove to Selby Bluffs Cemetery. Back home Wilbur liked to read the headstones and see how the people were connected to people he knew or had known. Out here, there would be no connections like that, but he knew

Wilbur would just enjoy seeing who was buried and what their last names and nationalities might be. He also knew that some members of the Westwood Church were buried there, and some of the early members had come from Pennsylvania and might be related to people Wilbur knew. The old man spent an enjoyable hour walking the grassy corridors. He found a Flory and a Firebaugh he was sure were related to Florys and Firebaughs he knew back home.

As they were getting back into the car to drive out into the farm country, John asked him, "Did you ever think about remarrying after Mim died?"

"Ach, Chon, who wouldt vant me?"

"Wilbur, I happen to know from Nancy that you are a very eligible catch and that there are ladies at the retirement village who have tried to snap you up."

Wilbur's smile was somewhere between being pleased and faintly dismayed. "Chon, have you ever looked at ladies who are in their 80s or 90s?"

"You mean they're old and shriveled and stooped with wrinkles and hair above their lips and smell of powder."

Wilbur laughed outright. "Chon, I'm surprised at you. That's not nice."

"Isn't that what you meant?"

"No. Some of those ladies are on the hunt. They want someone they can trap and housebreak."

John smiled. "Haven't you ever wanted someone to spend time with, to…ah, well…be intimate with?"

"Vell, Chon. I'm in my nineties. Some things chust don't verk so vell anymore."

"Do you never get lonely?"

"I read. I garden. I watch television. I play cards once a week. I still drive to church on Sunday. I play water volleyball. I see people every day." Wilbur paused, thinking about something. Then he continued, "Chon, I'm going to tell you something I haven't even told Nancy. I don't miss Mim. I loved her, but she was a burden sometimes. I like living alone."

They drove west of town 15 miles to visit a farm Herman Fry had suggested to John. The farmer knew they were coming and seemed pleased to give Wilbur a tour, especially when he realized that the old man had been a farmer and was very sharp for 95. With few words Wilbur conveyed a lot—through occasional nods, a grunt now and then, and some monosyllabic questions. John again marveled at the old man's ability to say so much with so little. They looked at the farmer's steers, walked through his cornfield, viewed his silage operation. They were invited inside for coffee, and Wilbur gave his promise to visit again the next time he came out to see his daughter.

John had told Nancy he would bring Wilbur home late. They drove back to John's place to check on the day's construction work and use the restroom. The plan was to go to Emma's for dinner. John had made arrangements for David to go to the home of one of his friends after school and eat dinner there. John saw a familiar car parked out front. He looked up at the porch and saw Angela moving away from his door. As her eyes turned toward the street, they caught sight of John and her face lit up. John's heart turned over. Wilbur saw this exchange, grinned, and said, "So, this is the one."

Angela waited at John's door as John and Wilbur came up the steps and along the porch. She took in Wilbur's bib overalls and flannel shirt. For a reason he could not fathom, John felt awkward, but he introduced Angela and Wilbur to each other. Wilbur took Angela's hand between his two work-hardened hands and looked her up and down and then peered deep into her eyes. He smiled and without taking his eyes off Angela, he said, "Vell, Chon, I see now. This is a good one! You're a real looker," he said to Angela. Then back to John, "She's a keeper."

Angela was used to males admiring her, but not rustic old men who spoke plainly. She seemed unsure of herself, as she said, "Thank you, I think."

Wilbur let go of her hand and, looking at John, motioned with his head. John knew immediately what he was saying. "Wilbur is inviting you to join us for dinner. Are you free?"

Angela, regaining her self-possession, took the old man's hand. "How could I say no after such a fine compliment?" She leaned forward and kissed Wilbur on the cheek.

It was so unexpected. It so completely surprised Wilbur, that his face turned red. John burst out laughing. "Wilbur, I've known you all my life, and I've never seen you blush!"

"Come," said Angela, taking his arm, and he allowed her to lead him to the car.

At dinner she seemed to have a knack for asking questions Wilbur wanted to answer. He talked more than John had ever heard him do. If it had been anyone other than this 95-year-old man, John might have been jealous. Instead he sat back and watched. As the evening progressed, he found himself feeling grateful. Angela was going to great pains to make friends with this old man she knew was so important to him. Even in a state of enchantment, Wilbur was still the best judge of people John had ever known. It pleased him inordinately that Wilbur liked her.

At one point the conversation lagged, and Wilbur suddenly said, "Kids are goodt for you."

"You're talking to me?" Angela said.

"In general, but maybe for you."

"I work with kids, well young adults, every day. I know kids can be good for you."

"I mean having kids."

"Wilbur, you flatter me, but I'm past the time a woman should be bearing children." She looked over at John who seemed embarrassed. "Oh, I see. You're talking about David. John, how much have you told Wilbur?"

"It's all right," Wilbur said. "Chon said nothing badt about you. I'm an oldt man. I can say what I want. Sometimes it's a goodt thing to have a kid aroundt."

"Are you trying to persuade me, Wilbur?"

"If the shoe fits, wear it."

She smiled and looked at John.

"Don't look at me," he said. "I had nothing to do with this. This is a side of Wilbur I've never seen before."

Wilbur reached out and placed his hand over Angela's. "You're a wery goodt woman."

"How can you know that!" Angela exclaimed.

"I can see it," Wilbur replied.

Angela paused, looking at him. "You're an interesting old man," she said.

Angela had driven her own car and drove herself home. John took Wilbur to Kirby and Nancy's house. He didn't go in because he wanted to be on time to pick up David. "It was a great day, Wilbur," he said as he pulled up.

"Yup, it was," Wilbur replied with a smile.

"Wilbur Rutt, I've never seen you like this. That's a smug smile, like you know something I don't."

"Maybe I do."

"I'll ask Nancy if I can borrow you one more time before you go back to Pennsylvania. Sleep well. Despite all we've done today, you don't look tired. You're a tough old guy."

Wilbur leaned down to look in through the window and rapped twice on the car roof, turned and walked stiffly but energetically to the house, almost as though he was trying to prove what John had just said.

As he drove back to his neighborhood, parked his car, and walked the half block to the house where David was playing with a friend, he thought about all Wilbur had said. The old man seemed to think that he should grab hold of her. Angela was as different as night and day from Wilbur or Nancy or Mary. What did he see that made him so sure she was what John needed?

David was glad to see him and chattered the whole way as they walked home. It was a clear night and they could see the stars despite the glow from the street lights. John felt good. He ruffled David's hair and kidded him about talking too much. David said he was hungry. John asked him if his friend's mom hadn't given him supper. "Oh, yeah, we had a big supper, but I'm still hungry."

"Now that you mention it, so am I. How hungry are you?"

"Hungry enough to eat Selby."

"I'm hungry enough to eat Chicago."

"I'm hungry enough to eat the United States."

"I could eat the earth."

"I could eat the solar system."

"I could eat the universe."

They liked to play this game, but of course, whoever ate the universe ended the game.

John went to bed thinking with appreciation about his new life and his new friends, about David and Jack and the opportunity to work on the apartment building, about the co-housing thing and the church community, about his old friend Kirby and this lovely old man who was like a father to him—and about Angela. And then he felt a burst of anxiety that left him restless and wanting to get up and walk it off.

Chapter 30 – Before District Conference

Sam made some calls to people he knew across the district and compiled a list of ten people who were strongly supporting the effort to sanction the Westbrook congregation. He cleared his calendar, packed a bag for at least a week of travel, and drove downstate. His first stop was Effingham, where he called Fred Vogel and asked if he could stop by his office to talk.

Fred asked him why.

"I'm a member at Westbrook. I'd like to talk to you about your action against our congregation."

"There's nothing to talk about. We have made the recommendation and the moderator has put it on the agenda of district conference."

"I know. We are on opposite sides. I doubt I could change your mind, nor could you change mine. But we are still brothers in the faith. Wouldn't Jesus want us to try to stay in good fellowship? I'm coming in the spirit of Matthew 18."

Sam knew that was an argument Vogel could not counter. He agreed reluctantly to see Sam. The Effingham church was a trim, well-cared-for building with a high peaked roof and some middling stained glass. It was situated on several sloping acres of well-mown grass, interspersed with shrubs and trees. Sam came through the front door and was immediately caught by the usual church scent—carpet, wall and floor cleanser, books, and candles. He found the pastor's office down a side hall. The church secretary in the outer office greeted him brightly, and Sam had the distinct feeling that she knew who he was and why he was there and might even be secretly sympathetic. She called through the open door to the pastor's study and told Sam to go on in.

It was a Spartan office with a few books on shelves on one wall, a bank of windows on the opposite wall with plants on the sill, and some knick knacks that seemed out of character. Sam wondered if they had been put there by Vogel's wife. The other walls were mostly blank except for a large reproduction of Jesus praying in the Garden of Gethsemane. Vogel's desk faced the door and behind the desk chair below the bookshelves was a long credenza with neat piles of papers. The books were mostly Biblical commentaries, and Sam recognized an ancient set by Matthew Henry that he knew was popular among some pastors.

Sam had never met Vogel. He was a small man, slightly overweight, with a round head, bald on top with graying hair combed back along the sides, small widely spaced gray eyes peering at him with anxiety and defensiveness, and a mouth set with nervous determination. Sam had expected to find someone in attack mode and instead found a man who seemed afraid. Sam tried to allay his fear. He asked him about the congregation and how long he'd been pastor and what were his greatest challenges and deepest satisfactions. Fred Vogel seemed surprised and began to thaw a bit under Sam's questions. This was part of Sam's strategy, though the questions also came from real interest. Sam had often wondered if something you did naturally could also be manipulative if you knew it was serving a strategic purpose. In this case he didn't care. He knew it was important for him to make a connection with Fred Vogel. As Vogel seemed to relax, he actually seemed to grow a bit larger, straighten up a bit from his cramped, stooped posture. He did not ask Sam a similar set of questions about his own life and congregation. This Sam noted, but he didn't care. His purpose was to be at ease with Vogel, not begin a friendship.

Both men knew, however, that this congenial small talk was beside the purpose. Vogel suddenly stiffened a bit, as though catching himself at being too friendly with a man who was on the other side, and asked Sam what brought him down to Effingham.

"I wanted to be face to face with you."

"Why? Are you here to influence me?"

"Well, I wish I could."

"When something is either right or wrong, it isn't necessary for Christians to try to influence one another. The truth can speak for itself."

"Perhaps, but wouldn't you like to influence me to change my mind?"

"I want to correct your thinking."

"And that is different?"

"I have to think of your eternal soul."

"Are you saying that because I believe differently from you, I will be damned?"

"Only God knows that. But I am responsible for doing all I can toward your salvation."

"Do you see how hard that is? You are saying that even though I am acting in good conscience and believe that same-sex relations are part of the humanity God has given us, my soul is at risk."

"The Bible is clear that homosexuality is wrong."

"But there are many things that the Bible says that no longer apply." Sam saw that Fred was poised for an argument from scripture. "Look, I don't want to debate scripture. I know your arguments, and you may know mine. What I really want to know is if you can find anywhere in scripture a place for persons of faith, followers of Jesus, to be in good standing with God and each other and still deeply disagree about an important matter of faith."

Fred gave that some real thought. "No, I can't. I can see how people might disagree, but if they search the scripture together, they have to agree eventually. There is only one truth."

"Do you think God might sometimes allow for ambiguity, maybe even want it, so that people of faith cannot build theologies to fight over and use against each other?"

"No, God is a God of truth and certainty."

"But doesn't Jesus show us that relationships are more important than righteousness? Aren't we called to love rather than to be right?"

"Perfect love is right. It has no error."

"Are you sure that's love?"

"Are you saying that if two men really love each other, it's okay?"

Sam stopped to think. "Yes, I think I am saying that. At least that's part of what I'm saying."

"It's an abomination."

"Is there no common ground between us?"

Now Fred paused. "It's my duty to treat you with courtesy and kindness. It's my duty to pray for you."

"Yes, that is my duty as well. Would you extend that far enough to say it's our duty to try to understand each other, no matter how wrong we think the other is? Would you say it's our duty to show respect and Christian love?"

"Yes, but not to permit wrongdoing. We cannot allow a pastor to perform a ceremony for lesbians. Respect can never go that far."

"I understand what you're saying. I see why you have to do what you are doing to our pastor. I would ask you to understand him and show him respect and love, even as you do what you have to do. Can we agree on that?"

Fred looked as though he might have been pulled into something he did not want to agree to but had to because of the logic.

"Brother Fred, it's okay," Sam said. "I'm not trying to corner you. I'm asking you to show the compassion I think I see in you as you seek to discipline our congregation, and I will try to do the same as I try to counter your efforts."

Sam visited the other members of the ministerial commission who had voted to revoke Kirby's ordination, and he found people who were uneasy, caught between their own convictions and the gravity of moving against a pastor's ordination and censuring a congregation. They all knew Kirby or knew of him, and they knew he was held in high respect. They knew him to be a man of deep faith and high integrity. It was clear to Sam that Fred Vogel, by playing on their fears and their deep respect for scripture, had influenced them. When he visited Brian Hollinger, Sam found a man with no fixed biblical position who was made so anxious by the whole reality of homosexuality that he could hardly talk. Sam stayed only a few minutes, asking him for forbearance in the upcoming action at district conference.

One of the members, George Fry, who was a distant cousin of Herman Fry, wanted to talk about all the New Testament verses that seemed to refer to homosexuality. Sam sensed that George wanted an honest discussion, was willing to be open, so they engaged in a long exchange in which Sam argued forcefully that these were references to specific social realities, not always even what we now call homosexuality, in a pre-scientific era when people knew much less about human sexuality. George argued that these passages must be taken in their plain meaning, that the Bible was the Word of God. It was unchanging. It applied to all times and conditions.

Sam remembered that George was an ardent teetotaler who argued on religious grounds against the use of alcohol. He asked him how he reconciled that with the fact that Jesus drank wine. He said that in our day alcohol had become an evil that destroyed families and killed people on the highway. No believer should ever imbibe. Sam answered that he was arguing this because of different social conditions and wondered how that was different from arguing for a different attitude toward homosexuality because social conditions had changed. George admitted that Sam had a point, but he just shook his head and said that homosexuality was a deeper sin than alcohol consumption. He quoted the Apostle Paul.

Sam made one more try by asking why Jesus had so little to say about sexuality and so much to say about spiritual pride. George replied that God made man and woman for each other and never intended anything else. Sam was tempted to point out that there were many instances of same-sex attraction in other species, but figured that further argument would drive them further apart.

"George, thank you for your time," Sam said as he stood to leave. "I am glad we could talk. I know you have taken the position that Kirby must be disciplined. And I know you support the ad hoc group that wants to censure our congregation. I am asking that when you make these arguments at district conference you do it with kindness and respect, remembering that those of us at Westbrook are people of good conscience, even though you think we are misguided and wrong. Please don't make this a matter that sows bitterness and hatred in our district."

George looked surprised.

"People feel deeply about this, on both sides. It's a short step to angry judgment, condemnation, abhorrence, even the threat of damnation on your side and angry accusations of stupidity, narrow-mindedness, self-righteousness, and lack of Christian love on ours."

"Do you think it could go that far?"

"I do, brother," shaking his hand, and then suddenly, surprising himself, embracing him.

The seven-member ministerial commission had voted four to three to discipline Kirby and censure the Westbrook congregation. Of the three women on the commission, only one voted with Fred. Her name was Almeda Shank, a retired schoolteacher from downstate Union County. It took him another three hours from George's home to get to her bungalow on the edge of the small town of Jonesboro. He found a lean, energetic, outspoken woman in her mid-seventies. He'd met her a time or two at district gatherings. She apparently knew him. When he'd phoned ahead, she'd said she supposed she'd have to talk to him.

"I know why you're here, young man," she said as soon as she opened the door to his knock.

Sam laughed. "I'm only 10 years younger than you are."

"You remind me of one of my students. A long time ago. He was smart. Too smart for his own britches."

"Well, I hope he has gained some wisdom through the years."

"Well, well. More to the point, let's hope you have."

She invited him in and ushered him to the small dining room just off the kitchen. It was in the back of the house and looked out on a sunny yard with flower beds and a small pagoda in the far corner. It was October, mums were still blooming, and leaves carpeted the ground. Sam remarked how pretty it was.

Almeda humphed and said he was just trying to soften her up. She indicated his place at the table where she had laid out plates of freshly baked cookies, slices of lemon cake, small chicken salad sandwiches, a carafe of coffee, embroidered napkins, and a silver cream and sugar set. Sam smiled. For someone who didn't want to see him, she had gone to a lot of trouble.

When he was seated, she served him, poured his coffee, then sat down across from him, folded her hands, and said, "So what do you have to say for yourself?"

Sam, enjoying one of the best sugar cookies he'd ever tasted, decided to meet her in her own plainspoken style. "I believe if we weren't on different sides on human sexuality, we'd be friends."

"What makes you think we are on different sides?"

"You voted to discipline our pastor and to censure our congregation."

"Yes, I did the first. The second action was taken by a group I had nothing to do with, but I support putting the censure motion on the district conference agenda."

"Why?"

"Three reasons," she said briskly without elaborating. There was a pause.

"Well, are you going to tell me what they are?"

"First, the denomination opposes homosexual marriage. You pastor violated that position."

"But you must know that in our polity a local congregation is not absolutely bound by the denomination."

"True, but that's changing. You know this, as well as I do. It's been clear in recent years that on this matter congregations are expected to follow the denomination's line. Your congregation went too far."

"It was our pastor's individual decision. He did not hold the union service in our own church building."

"Your congregation supported him by employing him even when he was suspended."

"The review process on his ordination is still ongoing. It has not been revoked. Isn't it an admirable and understandable act of support to give him employment at least until the final decision?"

"It is, but that's not all you've done. You've made it clear you stand with him whatever the district does."

"So do you agree with the denomination's position?"

"Doesn't matter. I'm obligated to uphold it until it's changed."

"Does the Jonesboro congregation follow everything the denomination decides?"

"As far as we know."

"So you would have voted differently, if the polity were different."

"I don't know."

"What's the second reason?"

"The churches of the district are not ready for this. The downstate churches are all rural and small. Your Westbrook congregation is a city church that has lost touch with small-town American life. People down here just don't get this homosexual issue."

"It's not an issue. It has to do with real people."

"That's my third reason. I don't care whether someone's gay or lesbian or bi-sexual or transgender. I don't care about that, but I do care about what they do with each other."

"So you personally are against a union between two same-sex people."

"Well, I'm not ready for it and neither is the district."

"Could someone change your mind?"

"You told me on the phone you weren't coming down here to change my mind."

"Fair enough. Are you willing to admit that this is not just a debate? The two women for whom our pastor performed the service are good people. They are the mothers of three good kids. Are you aware of how deeply this has hurt them?"

For the first time Almeda paused, and Sam could see that she was a compassionate woman behind her starchy morality. "I don't see how that can be helped," she said finally.

"Are you also aware of how bringing this before district conference could enflame us all and create bitter division?"

Again she paused, "Yes, I see that."

"I told you I was not coming down here to change your mind. But I am going to ask you to make me a promise."

There was a pause. Almeda Shank sat primly in her chair with her hands folded in her lap, waiting.

"I am going to ask you to do everything in your power to show respect and restraint. However wrong you may think we are at Westbrook, will you use your influence to see that we are not attacked and demonized?"

Almeda Shank looked hard at Sam and he returned her gaze. "Will you do the same, young man? Make sure we are not treated like downstate, small-minded bigots?"

"Yes," Sam said.

"Then I will do what you ask. I would have done it anyway, but I wanted to see if you are as fair-minded as you seem to think I should be."

Sam stood to leave.

"I read your pastor's letter to the congregation," Almeda said abruptly. Sam nodded, "What did you think?"

"It was instructive."

"Is that all you have to say about it?"

"It is, young man."

Sam thanked her for the lovely spread and shook her hand. Her grasp was strong. "It's been good to talk. I think I like you."

"Pshaw. You just like my cookies. That's all."

The next man on Sam's list scared him. He was not on the ministerial commission, but he was one of Fred Vogel's allies. His congregation was too small to have a full-time pastor. He ran a small handyman business and was a quarter-time pastor. He had been called by the congregation when they could not find a pastor. He'd moved to Illinois from Kentucky and had been an itinerant southern Baptist minister. He'd never heard of the denomination until the Rush Creek congregation persuaded him to be their part-time pastor. He agreed with great reluctance to see Sam and was so angry that he could hardly talk. He said flatly that homosexuals should straighten themselves out by talking to the right Bible-believing pastors and counselors, and that if they didn't, they would go to hell. He said he found it disgusting that there were churches in the district that allowed this.

Sam asked if he had ever met Kirby Beahm, the Westbrook pastor, and he said no and he hoped he never would. Sam asked if he was going to be at district conference. He said he considered it a call from God to be there and to oppose such sacrilege. Sam didn't even try to ask him to be respectful. He thanked him for his time and went on to the next person.

As he visited the other five on his list, finding in them the varying spirit he'd already encountered, he decided to spend a few more days and call on some of the downstate and mid-state people who might support Westbrook and Kirby. It was a relief to find people who were sympathetic. Once again he realized how unreliable stereotypes are. Most of these folks were ordinary people in congregations that were conservative. None of them were crusaders, and for the most part they were reluctant to speak up, but Sam found them sincere, thoughtful people who in their own way, usually against their own upbringing and feeling, had arrived at an open and accepting view. They would have trouble speaking up in public gatherings, giving vocal support to Kirby and Westbrook. All the same he was heartened.

He was tired when he got home. He'd been gone ten days. Eve wanted to know all about it. As he talked, he wondered if he'd done any good.

He'd not changed anyone's mind. Would anything change anyone's mind? Probably not for people older than forty. The hope lay with the young people. Even if they thought that homosexuality was wrong, their convictions were not loaded with so much fear and judgment. They had all known kids at school who were gay. They'd seen gay people on TV. They were not afraid of homosexuality or grossed out by it. Maybe hope lay in the possibility that his own generation might learn to live together until they were too old to fight and then pass away. As he finished his account for Eve, he sat down with his journal. Slowly and quietly came the conviction that what he'd done had a purpose he might never know.

Chapter 31 – District Conference

On Saturday morning John was watching as people came from all over the state, delegates from each congregation, district board members, people who served on the various district committees, commissions, and ministry groups, and many who were interested in the conference business or who just wanted to see old friends and enjoy the worship and fellowship—about 300 people in all. They gathered in a middle school gymnasium in Mattoon, a small city in the middle of the state. Those who lived within an hour of so of Mattoon drove in. Those who came from the northern or southern parts of the state were staying in the homes of members of the Mattoon church or the nearby Windsor congregation or they had made reservations at a local motel. John had arrived early that morning and had missed the opening worship the night before. Now at 9 a.m. business would begin, but most attendees had come as early as 7:45 to have breakfast in the middle school cafeteria and to visit.

John knew no one, yet he knew these people. Connections of family, of common experience, of tradition bound him across congregational, district, and geographical lines. And if he knew anything, he knew these were people who liked to get together. Many had known each other for years, keeping in touch through these district events. Until recent decades, the ties between the congregations had been strong. Members had had a solid sense of community, which had eroded in recent years, as it had all over the country. John knew this the way he knew the air he breathed. People moved away from their birthplace. Families moved around while kids were growing up. The family unit had shrunk to just parents and kids. Families no longer lived near uncles, aunts, grandparents, and cousins. But people in this district still felt many of the old connections. Their kids all went to the district's summer camp, and district conference had always been more than a business affair.

The gym had a small stage at one end. The table for the moderator and other officers was up on this stage with two table mikes that could be passed up and down the line. Next to the table was a lectern with a stand-ing mike for presentations. Folding chairs were set up on the gym floor for conference-goers with an aisle in the middle.

As the time neared for the meeting to begin, people moved over from the cafeteria, and more people came in from the parking lot. It seemed the attendance would go well over the typical 300, and people scrambled to set up more chairs, until the gym was filled all the way to the back.

John was sitting with Sam and Kirby, who had both come the night before so they would be fresh. The three of them were in the middle of the large Westbrook contingent. Nancy and Eve had gotten up at 4 a.m. to make the 4-hour drive in Nancy's van and had given rides to John and Maud Miller. Joe and Anne Kurtz had carpooled with Kurt and Cynthia Wampler. Sam had saved a section of seats so they could all sit together. They were joined by Gerald Kurtz and Preston Krunsch and their wives, and Kristen Witter and Anna Firebaugh, who had also come down the night before. They saw Barbara Nolt and Herman Fry sitting across the way, and Maud Miller waved and motioned them over. They hesitated and then joined the Westbrook group. "Did you think because we don't agree with you, we didn't want to sit with you!" asked Maud in a loud whisper that made the Westbook people up and down the section smile and caused Kirby to turn around and greet them. Just as the meeting was beginning, they all got a jolt when Jack and Jenn Foster walked in and took seats in their section.

Later than day, John got the story from Jack. He'd found out from their grown children that Jenn had made a quick trip back from New York for the weekend, not knowing that everyone would be gone to district conference. She was staying in the hotel at the north end of Selby, just off the tollway. Jack stopped by her hotel on Friday afternoon.

"She came down to the lobby," he told John. "There I was, sitting in a lounge chair. I don't mind telling you I was nervous, and for a moment I wondered what the hell I was doing there. She was completely surprised. It almost freaked her out, and honest to God, John, I didn't know what the hell to say. I drew a complete blank. I was without words! That made her laugh. She said it was the first time she'd ever seen me speechless. I stood up and the only thing I could think to do was to shake her hand. That was so weird we both started laughing. 'Look,' I said, 'I heard about your visit. The kids told me. And I know most of your friends have already gone down to Mattoon or will be going tomorrow. I'm going too, leaving very early in the morning.' I started to tell her about the business with Kirby, but she already knew. I said we needed to do something to keep the district from chewing him up.

"So I looked her in the eye and I said, 'Here's the deal. If you don't have something scheduled tomorrow, since your friends are gone, would you like to drive to Mattoon with me?'

"Well, she wasn't expecting that. She was shocked. 'Look,' I said, 'This is nothing more than an offer to ride together. I'm not looking for something, and I assume, if you say yes, you're not wanting something either. But we used to be pretty good company. It's a long drive.'

"'Why aren't you going with Kurt or Joe or Sam or John?' she wanted to know.

"'They all have rides,' I told her.

"'So I'm your last resort?' she said. She smiled at me.

"'No, I would have driven it alone. I like long stretches of being alone. You know that. I wouldn't have asked any of my friends anyway, and I think they knew that and didn't ask me.'

"'Then why ask me,' she wanted to know, 'if I'm going to interrupt your alone time?'

"I reminded her she used to be the quiet one. I was always the one with the big ideas, full of myself and my projects. I said I wasn't worried she'd talk the whole way to Mattoon. I told her she should probably worry that I might."

"Then she said something that surprised me, though why I don't know. She said 'You know, I've changed.'

"I exploded at her, 'Damn it, Jenn, I'd like to spend time with you. That's all! Take it or leave it!'

"She shrugged and said, 'Okay, I'm game.'"

They all scooted down two seats to make room, and Kurt gave Jack the high sign and boomed out, "Good man!" which caused Jenn to glare at him and made Eve and Nancy turn anxiously to see who else might have heard.

The meeting began at 9 a.m. with routine matters—announce-ments, minutes, review of the agenda. Then the moderator, Louise Gingrich, in-troduced the first item on the agenda which was old business. There were four of these items, all reports or motions to take some routine action. Still there were some who felt they needed to put in an opinion, so the morning dragged. John laughed. It was so typical. He almost felt affection for these long-winded ones. He saw the other attendees were getting im-patient. Everyone knew what the big items were, and most people were anxious to get to them. He figured the people who had gotten up early and driven to Mattoon were wishing they had remembered that the early hours of the conference would be so routine. It took all the rest of the morning for reports from the ministry teams, the camps and the district retirement center, and other associated agencies. It was only after lunch that the moderator turned to new business, which began with the recommendation from the ad hoc downstate group.

The moderator began with an apology. "I know some of you think I should not have put this matter on the agenda. This doesn't come from the board, which voted not to pass these recommendations on to you—there are two, or maybe I should say there are two parts to the recommendation. We are going to take each one separately, so there really are two separate recommendations." She paused. "I felt this is such an important issue, and one that people all over the district disagree on, that it needed to come before all of us. I checked and figured out that the district moderator does have the right to decide to put items on the agenda. Not everything has to come through the district board. Fred Vogel came to me and urged me—I admit he was pretty insistent—that I use my power to do this." She looked over at Daryl Bender, the district executive, who was sitting next to the district board chairperson. "You can check the polity manual. I looked at it, and I can do this. So let's move ahead. Fred Vogel wanted to bring this as one motion, but I insisted he separate the two parts into two motions. He is going to present both motions because they relate to each other, but we're going to take them one at a time. Brother Fred."

Fred Vogel stood, walked down the aisle, climbed the four steps at the side of the stage, and went to the lectern, clutching some papers. Though no one else, on stage or in the audience, was dressed up, he wore a gray suit, slightly rumpled, a white shirt, and a thin black tie that was not fully pulled up into his collar. He laid his papers on the lectern. At that moment Samantha and Marianne came down the aisle and found a place where the Westbook Avenue folks sat, surprising them. Fred looked up and saw them and turned back to his notes. John, who watched this, realized Fred didn't know who they were. Fred's hands shook as he adjusted the mike stand and pulled the mike closer. Sweat glistened on his forehead, and his voice quavered as he began.

"Brothers and sisters, we stand at a crossroads. Are we going to go down the road the world is going down or are we going to stay true to the Bible, to all those Christians who have gone before us and kept the true faith, and to almighty God? I ask you, which road are we going to travel?"

Louise leaned forward and looked over at Fred anxiously; she got to her feet hesitantly as though she didn't want to be seen and walked the few short steps to the lectern. She covered the mike with her hand so she would not be heard and spoke very intently to Fred, then walked back and took her seat.

Fred looked down at his papers then looked up and readjusted the mike. "Sister Louise reminded me that I am not to preach a sermon, but to give the background and make the motions. I thought I was giving background, but maybe not. I'll try to do better." He cleared his throat and reached for the glass of water that stood next to the lectern. "Here in our district, one of our pastors performed a homosexual union. This is against the Bible, against the teachings of the church, against our denomination's statement on human sexuality, against all common sense, and an offense against the sacred institution of marriage, which can only be between a man and a woman."

Fred saw out of the corner of his eye that Louise was staring at him. He hesitated as though revising his remarks and went on. "The minister who did this has always been in good standing and is respected by many in the district, but what he did is wrong. Because it is against the polity and practices of our denomination, it puts him against our whole church, and it is grounds for his ordination to be reviewed and revoked. This is what the ministerial commission is recommending. We are following our denominational guidelines, so we have appointed a separate committee to examine this pastor. That committee is working but has not completed its work. During this time the ministerial commission has suspended his ordination. All this has been done and is within our prerogative to do, with the approval of the district board, which they have given…"

A woman called out, "Point of order!"

The moderator recognized her.

"This is a report. Those of us who have followed this know all this. This belongs in a report from the ministerial commission. This item of business was supposed to have two motions. Where are the motions?"

Louise turned to Fred Vogel and replied. "The sister has a point. Proceed, Brother Fred."

"Some of us think this matter goes beyond the ministerial commission and the special assessment committee. In a moment I will give both motions, but I need to give a little more background. When this pastor's congregation found out about our action, they had a meeting and they voted to keep employing their pastor, not just during this time of examination, but even if his ordination was revoked. Legally they can do that, but it's a definite slap in the face of the district, and, of course, this pastor cannot do the things an ordained minister would normally do. At first this pastor did not agree to this and gave his resignation, but then he changed his mind, so that now both the pastor and the congregation are out of order, the proper order of the church. Some us from the concerned congregations felt that action needed to be taken in addition to the slow process of evaluating the ordination. We came to Sister Louise and asked for this to be put on the agenda."

Fred Vogel paused, partly for effect, partly to gather his strength. "So we are proposing two motions. They are close in purpose, but the moderator felt they needed to be dealt with separately. The first is this: We move for the district conference to publically censure Kirby Beahm, pastor of the Westbrook congregation, for performing the immoral union of two homosexual women and to restrict him from serving in any leadership capacity in the district."

The same woman, who was still on her feet, said she had a question.

The moderator asked her to wait until Fred Vogel was finished and asked him to continue.

"The second motion is this." Fred looked down at his paper and read, "We move for the district conference to publically censure the Westbrook congregation for promising to support and employ their pastor, Kirby Beahm, despite the outcome of the process by the ministerial commission to discipline him for performing the immoral union of two homosexual women and, therefore, blatantly going against the district; and to rule that until the Westbrook congregation retracts its action, it may not be represented on the district board and its delegates may not be seated at district conference."

The woman, who had raised the point of order and wanted to ask a question, moved to the microphone that was set up in the center aisle. John leaned over to Sam and learned she was Lila Weaver from one of the other progressive congregations. Now, she again asked to be recognized, and the moderator did so.

"These are terribly garbled motions," she said. "The first one is not necessary. If the ministerial commission finds against Kirby Beahm, that will amount to censure. I can find nowhere in our polity or practice that a district has the right to censure an individual. I've never heard of a district doing it. Back in the days when a person was put under the ban or put out of the church, this was always done by a congregation, not a district. In fact in those days, districts did not even exist."

John heard Sam whisper to Kirby, "Good for Lila. I had no idea that she knew so much about polity!"

Lila went on, "Sister Moderator, I argue that this motion has no standing and ought to be ruled out of order."

Several people got up and moved to the mike. There was silence. Louise seemed rattled. She said nothing, but turned to the other officers who gathered in a huddle. The conferees grew restless. Finally she turned back to the table and pulled the mike close. "I'm going to let this motion—both motions—stand for now. We will take them one by one. Is there a second for the first motion?" Someone called out a second. "The floor is now open for discussion of the first motion."

"Then before I give the mike to someone else," Lila continued, "I have one more thing to say. Then I'll sit down. This is about the second motion, which you say is not up for discussion yet, though it's been placed before the body. So since we're already not following Robert's Rules of Order, nor our own polity, I'll say this, and then I really will sit down. Can we really censure a congregation for supporting its pastor during a review process? I know the Westbrook Church went further than that, but we are being asked to censure them for something that hasn't happened yet. All they've done is support their pastor who has been accused of something, but not yet found guilty."

The moderator again conferred with the officers, then turned back to the conference body. "There is nothing that says the district can or cannot censure a congregation. I will let this motion stand. The reason I allowed both of these motions to be on the agenda in the first place was because they make us deal with a very difficult issue."

The man behind Lila in line moved to the mike as she went to her seat. "I am glad you brought this issue to the agenda. We cannot allow any of our pastors or congregations to do what the Westbrook congregation did. Can't they see that marriage is only between a man and a woman? Didn't God create us male and female, to cleave to one another? How can anyone even think of something else! I know the world is going this way. I shudder at what my grandchildren see on TV. But if the church allows this immorality, then what do we have left?"

Maud Miller was next in line. She'd been on her feet and ready, making sure she could get her speech in early. "How can you call it immorality when you don't know anything about it! Kirby, our pastor, performed the union service for two lovely women, who are the mothers of three fine children. All five of them are a great asset to our congregation. These aren't people skulking around in the bushes or hidden away in spinster bedrooms, which is what we all thought homosexuality was when I was a child. These are caring, human beings. These are good women. They want the same things you and I want: friends, family, commitment, kids, a church where people love

them. Shame on you for calling them immoral when you don't know anything about them! And another thing. Stop calling this an issue! It's not the
'homosexual issue.' It's real people you are condemning!"

There were calls of "Yes, yes!" and "Amen." And there were calls for
Maud to sit down.

The moderator seemed shocked and said somewhat hesitantly, "Please.
No calling out."

The next person at the mike was Brian Hollinger. He began in a very
soft voice. "I'm on the ministerial commission and I voted for examining
Kirby Beahm's ordination…"

Several people called out that they could not hear. Louise asked him to
speak up.

"Sorry," Brian said, "I'm not used to this speaking publically; it makes
me nervous. I support these motions that Brother Fred Vogel wrote. I
don't know about what Mrs. Miller said. I don't see how two…uh…" he
paused as though the next word was distasteful, "…two lesbians can make
a family. There must be something wrong for those two women to live
that way. A person who is an alcoholic can resist taking a drink. Maybe the
need doesn't go away, but he can decide not to take a drink. Maybe there
is some homosexual need in some people. I don't know, Frankly, I don't
think so. But even if it is there, it has to be resisted. Christians can't just
give in to all their needs. We can't let Rev. Beahm's action stand. We
can't let Westbrook get away with supporting him. We have to protect
ourselves. We have to protect our children. They see enough of this stuff
on TV and even in school. We can't let them see it in the church. We have
to keep the church free of taint. The Bible calls this an abomination."

While he was speaking the eyes of many turned toward the Westbrook
group. Sam wondered how many knew that Samantha and Marianne were
sitting there listening and if they knew, would it make a difference.

"Think how it must feel if you've just been called an 'abomination'.
How would you like to be called 'tainted'?" the next speaker said, who
was from the church in the state capital. "Our congregation welcomes
LGBT people, and we are proud to say it. We cannot let these motions
pass. We know there are deep disagreements. But it seems so unfair. People on our side are willing to make a place for those of you who disagree
with us, but you on the other side won't do the same thing. You use such
harsh words. We're all people of good conscience. It's one thing to tell us
we're wrong. It's another to use words like 'abomination' and try to censure us. Where are compassion and respect?"

The speeches went back and forth. There was still a line at the microphone, when Kirby stood and joined it. Louise surprised everyone and, in keeping with her already awkward and out-of-order handling of the debate, interrupted to say, "I see that Brother Kirby Beahm has come to the line. Since he is the object of this motion—remember it's only the first motion that we are considering—I think he ought to have a chance to speak. Brother Kirby, will you move directly to the mike?"

Kirby, surprised and a bit ill at ease, moved forward. "Thank you, Sister Moderator. I would have been glad to wait my turn." He cleared his throat and looked down at the floor for a moment, then began. "This great difference is pulling us apart. But behind it is a deeper disagreement. How do we interpret the Bible? I think the Bible was inspired by the biblical writers' encounter with God, but when they wrote it down—and by the way most of the Bible was passed on by word of mouth for many years, even centuries, before it was written down—but when they wrote, their words were shaped by the world in which they lived and by their own humanity. People often say that God's Word is infallible. Well, it would be if God had given it to us directly, but God chose to work through human beings. So it's like seeing God through a lens that has smudges and bits of dirt." There were rustlings and murmurings from some of the hearers. Kirby went on, "I know some of you think what I'm saying is a terrible heresy, but it must be said. We simply don't agree on how to read the Bible. And you may also think that people who read it, as I do, don't love it as much as you do, and I say that's not true. There is no book we love more or take more seriously. Whatever you decide today about me and about the Westbrook congregation, will you give us the courtesy of affirming that we are people of faith who love God, love the Bible, love the church, and love you."

As Kirby finished his speech, John rose to join the line at the mike. Sam got to his feet too and arrived there first. The next person in line had turned his back as Kirby spoke. When he took the mike, his face was red and his hands were shaking. He was an overweight man of fifty or so wearing a pullover shirt that showed every inch of his large paunch. He had a few gray hairs that he'd combed over the top of his head in a vain attempt to cover his baldness. He looked like he would die of apoplexy. "That is just…that is just…" he sputtered, "that is just so…so…," he searched for words, "so… wicked! I am ashamed that we have to hear such things said in this…this…sacred gathering. I promise—we will all pay if we don't do what the Lord wills us to do. And we all know what that is! You know it in your heart. You know you do. There is only one answer. There is only one way. There is only one Bible. There is only one God. Brothers and sisters, think about that! Think about what you are doing!" He turned and stalked to his seat.

The woman behind him, who next came to the mike, was small and thin, almost emaciated. She had stringy gray hair and wore a shapeless dress, tennis shoes, and a short jacket that didn't match her dress. Her face was rough and weathered. She looked like she had lived a hard life. She was probably about fifty, but she looked older. She began without ceremony, and Louise had to ask her to identify herself.

"I'm Mona Mackie from the Cairo Church," she said in a rough, whiskey voice. "There's this poor boy, John. You know, he's always lived in our town, all his life. He ain't never done nothing to nobody. He ain't never hurt nobody. But all they've done is hurt that boy and hurt that boy and hurt that boy. And it ain't right and they oughta stop it. And them that hate oughta just shut their mouths. Because that poor boy John ain't a boy. That man's eighty now, but in them days when I was a kid, he was already 50 years old. He was a hairdresser, if you can think about that, in my hometown down in southern Illinois. He was...well...they said he acted like a woman, and, dear God, in that place and that time, he was gay. But, you see, to my mother, he was her best friend's brother. And when you mess with my mother's family or her friend's family, you mess with her. Ain't it a shame we don't think about people we know and love when we think about this here business?"

She went back to her seat and sat down and crossed her arms. There was silence in the room. John thought how the words of an untutored heart had authority. He was glad it was Sam who was next in line and not himself. Could anyone say anything after that?

Sam began. "Sister Mackie gives us all something to think about. She talked about hate and hurt. There is so much of that. I wonder if time might help. People in my generation grew up in a world that feared homosexuality and treated it as a perversion. It was surrounded by shame and disgust. I grew up afraid of it, and it has taken me some years to change, and if my contemporaries admitted it, we probably all still have some of that fear and discomfort left in us. On the other side, people forty or older who realized they were gay or lesbian felt this fear and rejection keenly and it was very painful. When they found the courage to come out, it was accompanied by a lot of anger. So there is fear, shame, and rejection on one side and anger and hurt on the other. But talk to the younger generation, young adults and youth. Those who are gay or lesbian are not as angry and hurt; it's been a bit easier for them. They are not treated as perverts. Those who still think homosexuality is a sin are not filled with fear and disgust. They have gone to school with kids who are gay. And those who are straight but accept homosexuality are not crusading for it. The intensity level has dropped.

"This is not a speech for or against, though you all must know where I stand. It's a speech about learning from the kids and turning down the intensity."

Fred Vogel had continued to stand at the lectern and had remained surprisingly quiet. Now he spoke. "Brother Sam, I can't accept that. Aren't we supposed to be intense about things that are wrong? Aren't we called to fight evil? How can we show respect for someone who's doing something that is just plain wrong?" There were some in the audience who nodded their heads with satisfaction.

John was next in line behind Sam, and he stepped to the mike after Fred was finished. "This is my first conference in your district. I spent my whole life until last year in another district. Though it may not seem like it, you have a greater spirit of tolerance. You are more willing to talk about things than in that district. I want to ask you something—all of you who believe that having a same-sex relationship is living in sin. I don't agree with you, but just for the sake of discussion, let's say you're right. Why is this sin different from all others? We are a peace church and we believe that Jesus calls us never to kill, yet we respect and accept people who have been in the military. Jesus was pretty clear that great wealth can be a serious spiritual problem, yet we respect and accept our wealthiest members. The Bible seems to teach against divorce and remarriage, yet we have learned to accept and respect and even put in leadership those who are divorced and remarried. Jesus thought the sin of spiritual pride was among the worst of all sins, yet we accept and live with people who are prideful and hypocritical. How are these 'sins' different from this 'sin?' To those who believe the two lesbian women who live in our congregation and for whom Kirby performed the union service are living in sin, why can't you give them the same respect and acceptance you give to these other quote/unquote sinners?"

There was only one person behind John, a middle-aged woman, but as he finished, a well-dressed man, wearing a white shirt, a tie, a sweater vest, and tan tasseled loafers came to the mike line. The woman, as well as most other people, recognized him as Robert Frantz, the respected pastor

of one of the larger downstate churches, a congregation big enough to afford a full-time pastor. The man spoke to the woman and she nodded and
gave him her place in the line.

"I'm glad for the speech you just made about sin, brother. You are asking why should we be upset by this sin. How is it different? That is a good
question. It's worth asking and answering. Let me read from Romans 1,
verses 26 and 27." He opened the small bible he carried. "I'm reading from
the New International Version." He read in a clear forceful voice. "'Because of this, God gave them over to shameful lusts. Even their women
exchanged natural sexual relations for unnatural ones. In the same way the
men also abandoned natural relations with women and were inflamed with
lust for one another. Men committed shameful acts with other men and
received in themselves the due penalty for their error.' The apostle Paul,
who wrote that, used intense language—words like 'shameful' and 'inflamed' and 'lust.' Our sexuality is a powerful part of our being, and it
needs strong guidance and strong restraint. This is why we are upset over
this, why we argue and fight so much harder over this sin than others. Our
very being is at stake. Our survival is at stake. We need natural relations
between men and women for our species to survive. Homosexuality goes
against our instincts. I agree with the last speaker, whom I have not had
the privilege to know. John, is it? It would be good if we could look at this
sin with the forbearance we have toward some of the others he named. But
we simply can't. Too much is at stake. I have a lot of sympathy for the
couple at Westbrook, as misguided as I think they are, and for those of you
who mistakenly believe that God accepts homosexual relations. You face
anger and dismay and disgust from the rest of us. But how are we to be
otherwise? We feel so deeply about this. You ask too much of us."

"We *are* angry," someone called out, and many heads nodded and
turned to see who it was. "This can't go any further," the voice continued.
It was coming from a tall man in jeans and a flannel shirt with unruly dark
hair and a full beard. His name was Gerald Dunning. "We have to put a
stop to this creeping homosexuality, and we have to do it now. No pastor
who does this should be allowed to go on. This cannot be!"

Restless murmuring could be heard throughout the gym. Several people rose to go to the mike. John saw that Sam was ready to do the same
when he saw the woman who'd raised the point of order earlier, Lila
Weaver, get to her feet and go to the microphone line, taking a place behind a man he did not recognize. He also saw a tall slender woman get in
line. Sam whispered that this was Almeda Shank and explained who she

was. Meanwhile, the moderator was asking in a pleading voice that there be no more outbursts from the floor.

The woman who had given her place to Robert Frantz moved up to the mike and made a harsh and angry speech condemning homosexuals. She said that while she appreciated what Brother Robert had said, he was not strong enough. She agreed with Gerald Dunning. She implied that homosexuals would go to hell.

Louise pleaded for people to use more moderate language.

The man who was next in line raised his voice and said it was time people woke up and got shut of their narrow-mindedness. "The people of this district are behind the times, and I'm tired of the small-town, back-woods bigotry. Anyone with any sense can read the science and see the writing on the wall. The world is changing and the district better get on board. Stop judging innocent people and look to the beam in your own eye. I'm sick of the hypocrisy and self-righteousness. There's not a thing wrong with LGBT people, and you need to open your eyes and see that! I celebrate what Kirby Beahm did and commend the Westbrook Church!"

Louise repeated her words about moderate speech, peered at the microphone, and noted that Almeda Shank was in line but with two people ahead of her. She told the conference body she was going to jump Almeda to the head of the line because she was a member of the ministerial commission and had not yet spoken. Lila Weaver and the other person, a man from the university church looked unhappy, but accepted the ruling.

Almeda stood ramrod straight and looked neither left nor right but stared directly at Louise Gingrich and Fred Vogel on the stage. She gave her name and identified herself as being from the Jonesboro church. "I support bringing these two motions to the floor of district conference, but I don't endorse angry conflict. You remind me of my fourth graders who had more energy than grace when they argued. I would not let them call each other names, and it won't do for you to call each other names. If I were your teacher, I'd give you a stern lecture and make you write 'I will speak with kindness' one hundred times." There were chuckles from the audience. "I think Brother Kirby Beahm and his congregation overstepped the bounds, but that doesn't put them beyond the pale. The two women from Westbrook may be misguided and wrong, but that doesn't put them outside either. These are brothers and sisters. When you vote, vote your conscience, but do it with kindness and respect. And, Sister Louise, put some starch in your spine. When people use bad language, give them a timeout!"

There was laughter and some of the tension drained out of the gathering. Even Louise smiled and, taking her cue from this, said, "Maybe we are ready to bring this discussion to a close and vote."

Lila Weaver, who was next in line, seized the mike and called for the question. The body confirmed that it was ready to vote. Louise reminded them that they were voting only on the first motion, regarding Kirby Beahm. She had the clerk read the motion again. She reminded the body that only delegates could vote. She said the tellers had counted 347 people in attendance. Of those there were 83 delegates from 46 congregations. She called for a paper ballot, so the tellers passed out pieces of blank paper. She gave instructions to write "yes" if you were in favor of the motion and "no" if you opposed it. People folded their ballots and passed them to the center aisle. The tellers collected them and went to a side room to count. Robert Frantz, the pastor, who was also a song leader, led the body in hymns while they waited for the outcome, which came after only a short time. The head teller gave Louise the results. She solemnly announced that the vote was 42 to 41 to censure Kirby, with no abstentions. The motion had passed. There was an audible intake of breath. There was surprise at how close the vote was. There was a growing buzz of conversation as people turned to those next to them to talk about what it all meant. John looked over at Kirby and wondered what was going through his mind. He put his hand on Kirby's shoulder.

Louise, maybe still taking inspiration from Almeda, was determined to forge ahead. She turned to Fred Vogel, who was still on the dais and asked him to present the second motion, which he did. Lila Weaver was still at the microphone, and she asked to be recognized.

"I want to point out that the motion we just passed doesn't affect Kirby's ordination. The decisions of the ministerial commission and the district board will determine if Kirby keeps his ordination. Passing this motion does nothing more than indicate the conference's displeasure with Kirby, though..." and she turned to look at Kirby "...only half of the delegates registered their disapproval, and it makes the dubious claim to restrict Kirby from holding district office. I'm not sure district conference can do this. And what's more, Kirby is not holding an office at the moment. But this second motion has teeth. It's not just censure. If we pass it, the Westbrook congregation cannot have members on the board and cannot send delegates next year to district conference. That's big! What right do we have to deprive one of our congregations of its rights? Where do you find that in our polity?"

Curiously, no line was forming at the microphone. John wondered if people were tired of the whole discussion. He knew it was mid-afternoon, the time when energy flagged, spirits sagged, attention lagged, and it was hard without a stiff cup of coffee to get up enough oomph to care about anything. He also wondered if the people had said what they wanted to say. Maybe Louise inadvertently stumbled onto a good strategy by putting the two motions back to back and wearing everyone out. She peered out at the audience, waited a moment, and said, "Do I hear a call for the question?" The man in jeans and a flannel shirt called back in a loud voice, "Question!" The body confirmed the direction, and Louise asked for the motion to be read and went through the same instructions. The tellers passed the paper ballots to the delegates and collected them. Robert Frantz led the gathering in singing. The tellers brought their result to Louise. She opened the folded paper and stared at it. Then she smiled and raised her voice, "Forty-one votes in favor of the motion, 42 votes opposed. No abstentions. The motion fails."

There were rustlings and murmurings as people moved in their seats, shuffled their feet, shook their heads, or turned to their seatmates to comment. Louise called for a 15-minute break. The Westbrook group made a huddle among the chairs where they had been sitting. John noticed Anne Kurtz on the edge of the group holding the hands of both Samantha and Marianne and speaking intently, though he could not hear the words over the noise. He saw Kirby walk over to them with a very serious expression on his face and embrace each of them. He caught the tail-end of Kirby's words, "...can't imagine how hard that must have been for you." Maud Miller took them each by the arm and herded them deeper into the circle. "Well, this is a fine kettle of fish. What does it mean? What do we do now?"

Joe Kurtz shrugged his shoulders, "We keep on with what we've been doing. We keep Kirby on salary. We support him when he goes before the district ministerial commission. It helps us that the congregation is not under censure. We continue with the standing we've always had in the district. Who would have ever thought both votes would be so close. One person must have changed his or her vote."

"It could have been that several people shifted one way or the other and it just sifted down to this," said Eve Ellerby.

John saw Fred Vogel and Brian Hollinger cross to the other aisle so they didn't have to walk by the Westbrook group and hurry to the door as though they couldn't get out of the room fast enough. Mona Mackie stood hesitantly a few feet outside the circle. He watched Sam go to her and thank her for her speech. He saw Robert Frantz and Almeda Shank talking urgently a few rows away. Gerald Dunning was off to the side, eyeing them with obvious distaste. Lila Weaver came over and joined the Westbrook circle. Many people stood in twos or threes or in small groups talking, and every so often looking in their direction.

Sam came back to the Westbrook group and said, "Look around the gym. See how people are standing. It certainly looks like it's 'us and against them'."

"Isn't that what it is!" exclaimed Maud.

"Not really," Sam replied. "Half the delegates voted in support of Kirby and our congregation. If we assume that all the attendees, the 347 Louise reported are also split, then that's one out of every two of the persons standing around looking at us. And we don't know for sure that everyone who voted against us was as angry as the ones who made the speeches. This is a key moment. We can make this division worse or we can open the way for healing. This day is not just about Kirby and Westbrook; it's also about the next time and the next time this all comes up."

"What are you saying, Sam?"

"He's saying," said Kirby, "that instead of huddling together like the persecuted, we should mix and talk and be willing to hear what people have to say, even if it's harsh and unpleasant."

"That's a novel idea," said Kurt Wampler sarcastically. "That would be loving our enemies. Seems we've read something like that somewhere."

"Just the same, that's not easy," Eve retorted. "I'd don't feel much like exposing myself. I want to stand here where I'm safe. And what about Samantha and Marianne? Do they really want to put themselves in a position to be berated by Fred Vogel or Gerald Dunning?"

"No, of course not," Sam said, turning toward them. "We owe it to you to protect you."

Marianne laughed, "That very noble, but we have heard much worse. We can take care of ourselves, though it is lovely to hear you say that."

"I'm sorry you all had to go through this because of us," said Samantha. "Maybe we never should have asked Kirby."

Kirby was shaking his head. "You did the right thing, and I think I did too. And so did the church. There are no bad guys here. Not even the Fred Vogels and Gerald Dunnings. Sometimes the only thing left for any of us to do is to act for the best and then suffer."

"I'm sure Fred and Brian and Gerald and even Bob Frantz wanted more than that. They wanted to win!" Maud paused, "And so did I!"

John, who had said nothing, put his arm around Kirby. "I think you're right. We should break up our little group and go mix. Also, if you're like me, you probably need to make a pit stop."

There were smiles around the circle, and the Westbrook folks drifted off to mingle or find the restrooms.

Chapter 32 – Heathen Friends

Sam took a chance that Oliver Larkspur would be home and knocked on his door without calling ahead. The door opened and the old man, clearly glad to see him, ushered him in, made him comfortable in the library, and went to the kitchen for some coffee.

"How's my heathen friend?" Sam asked, when they were both seated in front of the fireplace holding coffee mugs.

The old man raised his eyebrows and smiled, "That word could be an insult, but the tone makes it sound like a compliment."

"I've had my fill of church for a while," Sam said and he gave the old man a quick sketch of district conference and his ten-day trip.

The old man shook his head.

"What?" Sam asked.

"You have patience! Beyond anything I can imagine. Why would you go to all that trouble? Why not have it out with your enemies in the district, let the dust settle, and then go on?"

"Because regardless of what happens, we still have to live with each other."

"Why? They're downstate. You're up here. Just go ahead and be the kind of congregation you want to be and ignore the hardliners."

"They're not just in our church. They're everywhere. You must read the papers. Look at the Internet blogs. These deep divisions. Is there any place or group that's free of them? Maybe this is the challenge of this new century—how to build community and find ways to cooperate with and even love people whose very being you despise and reject."

"So are you saying that by going the second and third mile in order to be understanding in your little district of maybe 4,500 people, you are contributing to the healing of the global community?"

"Yes!" exclaimed Sam, sitting up and putting down his mug. "You said it! It has to start somewhere. Why not here?"

"Why would the warring madness of the world suddenly end in the 21st century?"

"Why not?"

The old man laughed, "Well, it is entirely possible that the Tea Party will embrace the president, Jews and Palestinians will be filled with affection for one another, China will give Tibet its freedom, and Southern Baptists will stage church picnics with Unitarians. That is a wonderful world image, and I am sure we are only a decade or so away from it."

"Do you do good only if you're sure it will have a positive effect?"

"Ah, nobler still! Loving your downstate enemies even if there's no hope of reconciliation."

"Your cheerful cynicism leaves me speechless."

"It does me good to know a genuine optimist."

"I'm thinking about something new," Sam said, abruptly changing the subject. "It's too new to say more. I can't talk about it yet. I don't know why, but I can't. I thought I ought to acknowledge it to you, though."

"Oh! This is interesting."

"The idea has been growing slowly and taking shape when I am writing in my prayer journal."

"So this is from God?"

"That's such a hard question. Yes, it seems to be coming from my deeper parts where I think I sense God's purposes. But you know how reluctant I am to 'baptize' every idea I have and say 'God told me to do it'."

"So it's not from God?"

"All I can say is that it seems right."

"Is it a business venture? Is there income?"

"Maybe a little income, not much probably."

"I thought your money enabled you to be free of the need for income."

"It's your money, you know. And yes, it has done that, but the money that's left does not produce enough income. Lately we've been drawing on the principal. But there's another thing. I wonder if it's good for a person of faith to have a big enough pile of money to have an assured income."

"Ah, you're saying that financial security works against faith?"

"Maybe. But I'm saying that money and resources are meant to be used, not protected. I have this growing feeling that it's not for me to sit back and enjoy the safety of this money—which is no longer a big enough pile anyway to assure financial security."

"So you're going to start a new venture and be just like everyone else who has a job or runs a business?"

"Not quite. There's nothing wrong with money. Of course, I don't have to tell you that. But when you stop following the whispers of God because you have to protect your finances, then you lose part of yourself and you lose part of your connection with God."

"Ah, so you're going to set up a business, but not worry about profit?"

"Not a business. It's hard to make your decisions as a matter of spirit. After all this time I still don't really know what I'm talking about."

"Really?"

"But I'm going to try. Before, I tried to live by listening to the thoughts and inclinations that come from this deep place, or I gave up and tried to be businesslike. I never achieved either."

"So this time, it's going to work?"

"Who knows? I am a little older, maybe a little wiser. And I don't know any more exactly what it means for 'it to work.' Does it mean I provide a good service? Does it mean that I always have the money I need? Does it mean prosperity? There are some who measure faith this way."

"Many questions."

Sam laughed, "Yes. Maybe not having the answers is the answer. I'm less worried than I can remember."

Sam's next stop that morning was Hank's home. He found Hank puttering in his workshop. Again he was offered coffee, which he declined, already feeling bladder pressure from all he'd drunk with the old man.

"You have this big idea about the rest of your life and you can't tell me what it is!" Hank exclaimed, after Sam said essentially what he'd told the old man. "Maybe it comes from God. Maybe not. Would you be doing this if the old man's money were enough to secure your retirement?"

"Well, I don't know. Do I have to know that? My circumstance is that Eve and I will need some additional income or will need to reduce our expenses. That's the presenting reality. So I ask what do I do to meet that reality. This is what comes to me. If I had all the money I needed, the presenting reality would be different."

"You don't seem worried. Hell, I'd be shitting bricks if I didn't have my pension and my wife's pension and good health insurance coverage." Hank laughed. "You already take more risks than anyone I know. Some old guy you hardly know gives you a cool half million. You have this damned epiphany in the middle of Shakespeare, for Christ's sake. You see Jesus in a vision. Now you're thinking about some goddamned spiritual adventure you can't even talk about! I want to stick around just to see what happens next!"

From Hank's, Sam drove over to John's building. He hunted through the units until he found him on the lower floor where a team of drywallers were tearing off crumbling old drywall pockmarked with holes and drying out the underlying studs with large circular fans to make way for thick moisture-resistant new drywall. The smell of damp and mold was strong in the air. Sam knew these lower units were partway below ground because the building had been built into the slope. He sneezed and asked John how he was going to be sure that moisture wouldn't come back. John said they were removing even the studs along the back wall and using a heavy sealer on the cement block before replacing the studs and putting up the new drywall.

"You didn't come here to comment on our building techniques," John remarked. "Let's go up to my apartment, and I'll pour you some coffee."

"I don't need any more coffee," Sam said.

"Well, I do. I'm ready for a break anyway."

It was an unseasonably mild November day. John carried his mug out to the balcony, offered Sam a chair, and took one himself. "So how do you feel about Saturday's district meeting now that a couple of days have passed?"

"Today I'm not talking church. I've had it for a while."

"That bad, huh?"

"No, Saturday's outcome was about the best we could hope for. I'm okay with it, maybe even glad for it. I think the discussion gave a lot of people a lot to think about. But I don't want to think about it for a while." Sam paused and remembered his manners. "But maybe you do. What did you think about it?"

"I found it refreshing. Things are better here than you think."

"Yeah, I believe that. I really do. I spent 10 days downstate talking to people because I believe that, but now I need to think about something completely different."

"So what is it?" What brings you here?"

"Discernment. I'm considering something new, starting to talk about it but not really. Sounds odd, I know. But now that I'm sitting here with you, I realize I have something else to tell you."

John nodded and sipped his coffee.

"I had a vision two weeks ago."

John leaned forward and raised his eyebrows. "A vision! Why tell me?"

"Are you saying you don't want to hear?"

"You must know I'm not a particularly spiritual guy."

"What is spiritual? You're open-minded. You ask questions. You weren't afraid to pick up and start a new life."

"Well, those are compliments, aren't they?"

"I saw Jesus," Sam said abruptly.

John shook his head. "It's not every day that I hear that before lunch."

"I was on my deck. It was just before sunset. My eyes were closed, but he was as real as you are sitting next to me." Sam gave him all the details, elaborated on the feelings, described the aftermath and the ongoing effects. John asked some questions and Sam answered eagerly.

"So you really think it was Christ?"

"What else am I to think!"

"Not just a moment of vivid imagination?"

"Well, that's a hard question to answer. Yes, my imagination was engaged. I think it always is in an epiphany like this. You and I, we're not equipped to see realities that transcend our world. Images need to be created so we have something familiar we can relate to. What better place to do this than in the imagination! But if you mean, did I make this up out of whole cloth? Was it a hallucination? No. It felt real!"

"So this was the living Christ?"

"I think so. It sure felt like it."

"Why haven't you said anything? We've had two Thursday breakfasts since it happened."

Sam shrugged. "I wasn't ready."

"Have you told Kirby?"

Sam shook his head.

"Not even your pastor!"

"Yeah, I don't know why. If anyone would understand, it would be Kirby. I've told my oldest friend, Hank. And Eve, of course. That's it so far."

"So you picked me to be the next person. That's interesting."

"I hadn't planned to tell you. It came to me to do it. Don't know why."

"So was it some word from the Lord that made you tell me? Am I supposed to get some message for myself from this?"

Sam shrugged again, "I don't know. Does it matter? It is what it is."

John leaned over and scrutinized Sam's face. "Has this changed you?"

"I don't think that's my question. The only real answer lies in what others see. I will say this. I feel less anxiety, and I have pretty good energy."

John was silent for a moment, thinking. "May I tell Angela?"

"Yeah. Sure. I'm not asking anyone I tell to keep it a secret. I'm not embarrassed by it, though I know there are some who distrust such things. I used to be one of them. I think you were, or are, too. I'm curious. Why Angela, other than the fact that she's your...uh...girlfriend—what do you call her when you're our age?"

"Girlfriend is okay. Most people don't know about her interest in spirituality. She actually teaches a class on mysticism at the community college."

"Then by all means tell her, and then tell me what she thinks."

It was just a few minutes short of lunch time when Sam left John's balcony and headed back to his office, wondering why he'd said nothing about his idea since John was the only one who'd done anything like it and why he'd poured out the whole vision story. Without realizing it, he passed Eve going south while he was going north on the main street just east of the river.

BOOK THREE

Prologue

"So your church's got itself into a pickle!" said Oliver Larkspur.

"It's not as bad as it might have been," replied Preston Krunsch.

The two old men were sitting on a bench beside the lagoon in the park on an Indian summer day in November, drinking lattes they'd picked up at the coffee kiosk out on the main street.

"I applaud you. A worthy achievement."

"What?"

"What a world it would be if nothing were as bad as it might have been! Think of the trouble averted, the pain avoided."

Preston, who seemed disheartened, made no reply.

"I am filled with admiration for your congregation," Oliver said.

"When you make a statement like that, you usually mean the opposite."

"Your congregation and your pastor showed forbearance and good spirit. How could I not admire that?"

"Obviously there is something beyond your 'admiration'."

"I do admit to dismay that you didn't fight harder."

"What do you mean 'fight harder'?"

"In your church the liberals are too nice!"

Preston shrugged his shoulders, "What should we have done?"

"Take an aggressive counter motion to the ministerial commission. Argue forcefully in your district board meetings, lean on the moderate members. Go to your district conference with a carefully orchestrated set of procedural motions. From what I can gather, the moderator was a rank amateur and didn't follow your—what do you call it—your polity very closely. Prepare half-dozen supporters from around the district with well-thought-out arguments and space them strategically throughout the debate. Have an attorney examine your polity for inconsistencies and holes. Threaten the district with legal action. Withdraw your financial support. Push the moderates in the district to speak up. It's the people in the middle who hold the key. Win their hearts and minds. Make sure every person in the district knows the Biblical counter arguments. Shall I go on?"

Preston was shaking his head. "We don't work that way? It's not in our DNA."

"Your conservatives are not above such tactics."

"How do you know all this?"

"I talk regularly with your friend Sam."

"Do you know our pastor, Kirby Beahm?"

"By reputation only."

"Then you know that's not his way."

"So if your pastor were more of a pit bull, the rest of you would go along."

Preston smiled, "No."

"Ah, well, it's lovely that you are all such nice people."

"There's something I should be saying in defense of Kirby and our alleged 'niceness,' but I'm tired. I'm drawing a blank. I concede. You're right."

"Preston, where's your spirit? Do I have to make your defense for you?"

Preston shrugged.

"Okay, here it is. You were trying to be gentle as doves and wise as serpents. You were trying to love your enemies. You were turning the other cheek, well some of you. You were following Jesus."

"That's sounds pretty good."

"It is. It's noble, saintly. And it never succeeds! It ended in crucifixion long ago. How do you think it will end now? Lovely ideas! I admire them. I wish I could believe them, but following your Jesus, really following him, puts you at risk and ends in failure."

"You're right. I have no argument for you."

"You're not going to say anything on your own behalf?"

"Only this, I guess. Crucifixion wasn't the end. If it had been, we wouldn't be having this conversation. Sometimes with God you just never know."

"Now that's an interesting argument!"

Chapter 33 – Eve

After leaving John, Sam spent the rest of the day in his office. He got some work done, though half his mind was on the conversations he'd had that morning. Eve came in mid-afternoon, went into her office, and turned on her computer, but she didn't come over to say "hi" as usual. Later he put his head into her room and she seemed preoccupied. At home she was distracted as she prepared the evening meal, and she didn't talk much as they ate. Sam, with his own preoccupations, was glad for her silence. After the dishes were cleared away and they were sitting in the living room, he asked what was on her mind. She said she'd had lunch with her friends, and it had given her some things to think about. He asked if she wanted to talk about it, and she said not yet. She assured him it was nothing to be worried about. No one was sick or in crisis. She, herself, was fine, good actually. But this reticence was not like Eve. Usually whatever she was thinking came tumbling out. Sam was curious.

The next morning, which was Saturday, she was talking with great animation on the phone to Nancy Beahm, and later that day while he was reading in the living room, he heard her in the kitchen making repeated calls. That night, they went out for dinner. Eve was in a good mood. Finally over the main course her suppressed excitement spilled out. She told Sam about the lunch conversation and her phone calls. She was starting a women's group, she said. She had no idea what it was going to be, she just knew she wanted it to be different. She wanted women to explore what women would do, how they would handle things, if they always started from women's experiences and women's sensibilities instead of trying to outdo men at their own game.

"Is that what women do—try to outdo us?" Sam said.

"No. Well, yes. Well, I don't know. But you know as well as I that when women get the power we never had, we tend to use it the way men use it. But that's not the big thing about this. You know I'm not into power. I want to be with women just being women, exploring women's identity and reality. Oh, that sounds so…so like something a man would say! Like something you would say!" Eve laughed, "I'm going to start a women's group. That's all I'm saying at this point. Let's see where it goes." She suddenly turned sober. "Nancy said something about Kirby that made me think.

We were talking about this whole district thing and how she didn't think he should have tried to resign, and she said sometimes Kirby tries so hard to do the right thing that he can't do the human thing. There! That's it! Women sometimes know how to do the human thing. That's what I want!"

Sam said nothing, but he smiled.

"Don't give me a patronizing grin," Eve said.

"I'm not patronizing you. I'm enjoying you."

Eve looked at him suspiciously. "Well, anyway, there's one thing I do know. We're not going to be like women's groups used to be."

They had their first meeting that next week, and Eve came home full of ideas. Sam sat back and listened. It was like being washed in a wave of sunlight. He'd never seen Eve so full of energy. On Thursday night of that week she came home looking very satisfied with herself, and she told Sam a long story about going to see Jack Foster.

"I've known Jack for more than 30 years, and I don't think I had ever been at his place of business. I found him in his office in the back of the building that overlooks the yard. It was neat but dusty. It actually surprised me. I thought it would be ritzier. But it is a construction business. Well, what do I know? But Jack was really nice. And we talked about the co-housing venture for a little, but then I got down to why I was there, and I asked him if our women's group could use the living room of that old Victorian house that he says is going to be the common area of the co-housing thing if it ever gets off the ground. I asked if we could use it and fix it up however we wanted. He said, 'Hell, yes! You can use the space!' You know how Jack talks when his mind is made up. I think he liked the idea. But then he said he wanted to take care of the big stuff himself, like sanding the floors, hanging doors, reglazing windows, replacing drywall, etc. I asked if he didn't trust women to do those jobs. He laughed and said he had the equipment and the men who did that work every day. 'Is that bad?' He asked. I quickly said no, that was more than I had a right to ask.

"Jack wanted to know if Jenn was involved and I said yes, whenever she's home from New York. He admitted he misses her. He said she did the right thing, and then he hesitated. I don't think of Jack as ever being unsure about anything, but he said in a quiet voice, 'Jenn always wished I'd be more like the man I'm becoming. Now when I am, she's gone.' I said, 'Maybe you're not finished with each other.' He replied, 'Nice thought. But we have to get on with our lives.'

"I thanked him and was about to leave when he paid me a compliment. He said when you and I are together, I'm usually the quiet one. I had to think about that, but I guess he's right. I don't talk as much as you. But he told me that I may not know how much everyone respects me. Is that right? Does everyone respect me?"

Sam nodded, reached across the table, and took her hand.

For the rest of November and well into December, two or three days each week Eve came home full of stories about the progress the women were making and the things they were talking about. Sam was surprised that Angela Feladucci was in the group. He laughed when Eve told him about the rather earthy ideas about prayer they'd discussed. She told him about their long talk about whether lesbian women were different from straight women and how Samantha and Marianne had joined the group and everyone had forgotten about who had what orientation, except that they all talked about their relationships.

"You talk about us?" Sam wanted to know.

"All the time, sweetie. You have no idea," Eve answered.

One night over supper, Eve was full of a long discussion they'd had about the conflict in the district. They'd decided that maybe the women should get together and begin to build bridges. They'd brainstormed all sorts of ideas. "We decided maybe women from downstate rural communities aren't really that different. They have husbands or partners, most of them. They have jobs. They have sex," she smiled, "at least we think they do. They all have mothers. They have children if they're married, and maybe even if they aren't. They get divorced, some of them. They surf the Internet. They watch cable. We laughed about doing workshops on sex, which we knew would never go over, even with us up here. Can you see any of us talking explicitly about sex!"

Sam grinned, "I thought that's what you've been doing."

Eve laughed, "Yeah, sure! We had another good laugh over doing a workshop on how to handle husbands. Or partners—we still forget to be inclusive. Someone suggested the workshop title: 'Mothers: Bane or Blessing.' Everyone's got a mother, after all. We even thought about getting women together to sing. But no one really wants to do that! Especially the younger women. The only thing we came up with that's even close to being a good idea is to do a kind of potluck/talent show/craft expo. But then we wondered why women would drive anywhere from one to four hours to a central location to get together when we're all so busy."

As Sam listened, he noticed Eve losing energy as though some of the air was going out of her balloon. For the first time in weeks she seemed discouraged.

He gave her a sympathetic look, "More power to you. I've sworn off it! No more efforts to reach across the divide. I gave it up for the holidays. Maybe in the new year. I'll see. But for now, I'm done with it all."

The next morning Eve was up early and Sam heard her humming in the kitchen. He put on his bathrobe, walked to the kitchen, and leaned against the door jamb, watching her.

"I know what to do!" she said brightly. "I had an epiphany."

"I thought there was room for only one epiphanous person in this family. Is that a word?"

"I'm going down to see Almeda Shank."

"Why?"

"She knows the women downstate. Everyone respects her. You said yourself what a great person she is. We'll see if I can sell her the pot-luck/talent show/craft expo idea. If I can get her behind it, then maybe it'll fly."

"When are you going?"

"Now! Right now. I'm leaving in 15 minutes."

"Without any preparation?"

"Oh, I've prepared. I've got my lunch and dinner in the cooler along with bottles of water. I'm making a thermos of coffee."

"Have you called her to say you're coming?"

"No. I just decided this when I woke up. If I don't do it right away, I'll lose my nerve. I'll just have to take my chances that she'll be there. If she's not, I don't know what I'll do. Maybe go find her."

****

Eve didn't get home until after midnight. Sam had stayed in contact with her by cellphone, she had told him nothing about the visit except that it was good. Reading between the lines he thought maybe Eve was a little disappointed, but he couldn't be sure. He waited up for her. She came through the door, threw her keys and purse on the table, and sat down with a big sigh.

"Is that a tired sigh or an unhappy sigh or a satisfied sigh?" Sam asked.

Instead of answering the question, Eve just started talking. "She came to the door and I said, 'You don't know who I am,' and she said, 'I certainly do!' Sam, it was just like you said. She called me 'young woman.' I thought, okay, she's blunt. I'll be blunt too. I told her I wasn't in the habit of driving 6½ hours to offer a crazy new idea to someone I'd never met. She insisted we had met, years ago at a district meeting. She has a fantastic memory. All this was while I was still standing on her step. I asked her if she was going to invite me in. That dented her self-possession a bit. She looked embarrassed and quickly ushered me into her living room.

"Sam, were you in her living room? No? Her dining room? Well, I liked that living room: small with two comfortable recliners, a wooden rocker, and a small sofa with an afghan. The end tables had lace doilies and African violets. There was one more chair, the most comfortable one. Next to it was a large end table with a stack of books, a delicate teacup and saucer, and a box of tissues. Leaning over the chair was a floor lamp with a Tiffany-like shade. In the center of the room was a large, low coffee table."

"You noticed all this?" Sam said.

"Yes, she is an interesting lady. Listen to this. On that coffee table were church periodicals. Of course, you'd expect that! Then there were the *Scientific American*, the *Smithsonian*, the *National Geographic*, and some hunting and fishing magazines. She insisted I sit in that chair with the lamp, and I did, even though I knew it was the one she always sat in. She went to the kitchen to get some refreshments. She grumbled that she'd have had something better than store-bought cookies if I'd had the good sense to call ahead like you did, but she had a glint in her eye when she said it, and I knew she was teasing me. When she left the room, I leaned forward and began to look through all those magazines and I found a copy of *People*. I was putting it back on the stack when she came into the room with two mugs of coffee and some oreos. 'You would have to find that!' she snorted. 'A guilty pleasure! I disapprove of that magazine, but I weaken when I'm in the supermarket checkout lane. I don't believe in gossip, but I'm a fallen creature.' I laughed and said, 'Well, we're all sinners.'

"She probably liked that answer," Sam remarked.

"She did!"

"Almeda likes people who come back at her."

"I must have passed the test because we had a good talk. I told her about our women's group and all the ideas for getting women together in the district. She wanted to know why I cared. 'Isn't this something we all should care about?' I said. 'Most people don't,' she replied. 'Do you?' I asked. 'Yes, I do, young woman!' she said with a lot of force. 'So let's do something about it,' I said. 'You're someone people in the district listen to.' She gave me a penetrating look, 'So you're here because you think I have influence. If you can get me, the downstate women will be more likely to cooperate in one of your schemes?'

"I stood right up to her and said, 'Yes, frankly, but it's more than that.' I said she was an interesting woman with considerable character. I told her it might be an adventure to work with her. She laughed and said, 'Young woman, I've had many things said of me, but never that I am an adventure.' I said no one has ever said that about me either. 'But,' I said, 'it's time we shook the district up a little.' She said she wasn't interested in shaking anybody up, but she would be glad for a little civility.

"I told her what you've said about the call to reconciliation being deeper than the call to it get right on sexuality. She said that was probably more than we can hope for. I asked her if she agrees that God wants us to be reconciled even when we really disagree. I was surprised at her response. She wanted to know if I really knew what God wants. I thought she'd be into the God-says-this-God-says-that mentality. We had a good talk about whether we can know what God wants and she said, 'I used to think I knew.' Sam, I really felt close to her in that moment."

Sam had been paying such close attention to what Eve was saying that he was staring at her as though looking through her. She moved her hand in front of his face and asked if he was still with her. He came to himself and nodded. "More than you know. Do you have any idea how much you are changing!" he said.

"What does that mean?" Eve said uncertainly.

"You must know what you did is a good thing. Six months ago you never would have done this."

Eve laughed. "I said something like that to her. I told her that maybe all this talk about getting people together is a whim. I said it's more like something my husband would do, not me. I said I'm not a crusader. I've never tried to do anything.

"I sat there and wondered why I was doing this. Why should I think, or why should our group of women think, we can accomplish something the district and the whole denomination have made such a mess of! I said that to her.

"She straightened up and said—you know that tone of voice—'Young woman, we don't have to know we are right. We just have to know we're not wrong. How can an effort like this be wrong?' We both sat and thought about that. Then she said, 'The question is what should we do?' She liked the potluck talent and craft show idea, but she thought it wasn't serious enough. She said the differences in the district are decades old and not just because of sexual orientation. She said there've been conservative and liberals as long as she can remember.

"Then we started talking about how people in the district used to be more connected to one another. We both wondered if the women in the district have any reasons to get together. It has to be something interesting, but nothing we talked about really turned us on.

"I'd been there two hours and it was time to leave. I got to my feet and put on my coat. I'd started the day with all this energy. Now I felt deflated and even a little embarrassed. Almeda said I shouldn't be discouraged. She said I had helped an old woman pass two pleasant hours. She said we'd started a friendship and that was worth something in her book.

"I shrugged and said, 'So is this a start then?' She nodded, 'Let's lay this before the Lord and see what comes.' I told her that's not language I usually use. She smiled and said, 'Okay then, let's see what the universe has in store.' I said I didn't use that language either but I got what she was saying."

Sam wanted to reach out and take Eve's hand, but it was one of the few times when he felt doing that might divert her. Instead he asked, "Where does this leave you?"

"Maybe the only way is one person at a time. It's slow work, isn't it! It's not just people in our little district. It's people all over the world. Jesus was probably a hopeless romantic when he said, 'Love your enemies'."

Chapter 34 – Christmas

John parked in the lot at Selby Community College, beside the building that housed the arts and humanities. He entered through the double glass doors and knew he was in the right place when he saw signs pointing to the Harvey Theatre, the college performance space, and a bulletin board with a schedule of events sponsored by the Writing Center, naming Angela, the director. He set off down the corridor in search of her room number. He'd timed himself to arrive as her last class of the morning was letting out. He made for a room at the end of the hall where he saw some students leaving and was glad to see Angela through the glass door panel putting papers into her attaché case. He opened the door and stood in the doorway until she looked up and saw him. She smiled and raised her eyebrows. He returned the smile and looked at her without saying anything, watching the play of her hands on the papers, the slight rise and fall of her breasts as she breathed, the glow of the smooth, clear skin over her cheekbones, and the fullness of her lips.

She returned his gaze, looked down and then up again still not saying anything until she cocked her head slightly and remarked, "I can match you, eye to eye."

"I know you can. It's good to see you. I like looking at you."

"You just saw me last night."

"And here I am again. Are you free for lunch? Better still are you free for the rest of the day?"

Angela laughed and asked him if he thought she was at his beck and call. He explained that what he wanted to do had only occurred to him that morning. She said she did have the afternoon and evening free, though there were things she could be doing, in particular some Christmas shopping. John said he knew this because she may not remember but she had mentioned it last night, and the activities he had in mind included some Christmas shopping.

John explained his plan over lunch. They drove to John's building and picked up David as he was walking home from school (he'd arranged this with Maggie, who had arrived back from Arizona several weeks earlier) and the three of them drove to the mall. Angela helped David pick out some presents for his mom, and then while Angela was doing her Christmas shopping, John and David went to the bookstore to find something to send to David's father in Baltimore.

Later as they walked through the mall, John was enjoying the lights and decorations and crowds of people, and David was too. John kept looking over at Angela wondering how she felt about the mall's synthetic Christmas sentimentality. She took David's hand and asked him if he wanted to visit Santa, which caused him to snort that he was too old to sit on Santa's lap. Angela laughed and rumpled his hair. She explained the literary allusions in the Dickensian scenes in the windows of the big department store. The early December darkness was falling as they made their way through the parking lot to John's car.

"How about subs for supper?" John asked.

"Great. That's just what I was thinking," David replied from the back seat.

John glanced speculatively at Angela, who said, "I grew up eating with my brothers in sandwich shops."

After the meal, John drove only a few yards across the huge parking lot in front of the strip mall to a large area cordoned off with chain-link fencing which enclosed rows and rows of Christmas trees lit up by light bulbs strung from poles lashed to the fence. In the center was a small moveable shed. Light poured from the door and a tall, friendly man in a heavy parka and a furry hat came out to help them. They went up and down the rows. John kept asking David's advice, then glancing at Angela to see what she thought. David found a short, full, round tree with long needles, and John asked if he thought his mother would like it. David was surprised and said he thought the tree was for John's apartment.

"I'll get one for myself, but this one's for you and your mom."

"We don't have a lot of decorations."

"I thought we'd pick some up on the way home. But now I have to pick one out for myself." He didn't ask Angela about her tree, because he knew she already had it up. For himself he picked a tall, slender, nicely shaped short-needle balsam fir. When he paid, he had the man throw in two wreaths and they were able to fit both the trees and the wreaths in the back of the van. The last stop was Target where they picked out lights and ornaments for both trees.

John was a bit worried about how Maggie might react. He hadn't told her he was buying her a tree. He was glad Angela was with him.

David burst into the apartment yelling, "Mom, look what we got!"

Maggie was startled as they carried in the tree, the boxes of lights and ornaments, and the bag with the gift for David's dad. John introduced Angela, and Maggie apologized for the mess in the apartment. David went to the front window and began to move the small table and the stacks of DVDs aside. "Mom, let's put the tree here." John turned to Maggie for permission. She shrugged and said, "I guess I'm outnumbered. Can I help pay for some of this? The tree and decorations—that's a lot of money." John smiled and said it was his gift, implying that he had some money left over for the month and was putting it to good use.

He set up the tree stand he'd bought, sawed a quarter inch off the tree trunk so there would be fresh wood in the water, and set the tree in place. Maggie had been going through the boxes of light and ornaments. She disappeared into the back room coming back with a tattered box from which she drew some handmade ornaments. "Those are beautiful," Angela said. Maggie flushed with pride which she tried to hide. There were some tiny, exquisitely cut paper snowflakes, several small, round pillow-like disks with Christmas scenes embroidered in the cloth, and a few origami cranes. John and David put the lights on the tree, and then John turned to Maggie and said they'd let the two of them do the rest of the decorating, knowing that Maggie needed time with her son. David gave John a disappointed look, glanced at his mom, and seemed to understand. Impulsively he hugged John, who, surprised, patted him on the back. Angela said she was glad to have met Maggie, and John and Angela went out and walked down to John's apartment, where they shed their coats and John put on some coffee.

Angela sank onto the sofa, and John was moving toward the door to bring in his own tree and begin setting it up, when Angela patted the spot beside her and asked him to sit. He was glad to get off his feet and sat gratefully. Angela took his hand and put her head on his shoulder. He wearily laid his head against hers and they sat in comfortable silence.

"I'm afraid all bets are off," she said.

"Meaning what?"

"I'm thinking of all the reasons why this relationship won't work. We've been over them before. You had a good marriage. I've had disappointing relationships. I like my independence. I don't want to be tied down. You're a lot older than I am. You're this 'good guy,' and I'm drawn to bad guys or good guys going bad. You're determined to keep this boy in your life, and I've never wanted to have children in mine. You're an active church member, and I'm a lapsed...something or other. Where's the commonality here?"

"Why are you asking these questions?"

"Because against these odds, I want to be with you."

"What do you think that means?" John asked with a smile.

"I could analyze it, but I really don't want to. I just want to know what to do."

"Why can't we do as we've been doing?"

"Seeing each other several times a week? Staying over at each other's place? Is that what you mean?"

"I'd put it differently. Enjoying each other's company. Talking about the things we care about. Going to the city together. Watching plays and movies. Sharing ordinary, daily preoccupations and events. Holding hands. Making love. Being quiet together."

"That sounds lovely. It is lovely. But…" She stopped, turned, and looked right at John. She looked away and shook her head.

"What?" John asked.

Angela laughed. "I'm disgusted with myself. I think I actually want a husband. Who would have ever thought it! I want to be married. Ordinary, everyday, garden variety marriage. The thing all my aunts and uncles and cousins wanted and, when they got it, hated. Or pretended to hate and escaped in all kinds of ways. Look what you've done to me!"

"Is it the idea of a husband I've stirred up, or does it have something to do with me?"

"You know the answer," Angela said.

"Are you proposing to me?"

"Not yet! I'm holding out. I'm hoping if I have patience, this will pass."

John laughed. "I thought I was the one who needed help. The naïve one-woman man in the presence of all this worldly experience and irresistible sexuality. But the tables are turned. You want domesticity and reliability and commitment…"

"Not the first, but the second and third."

"And you don't know what to do. What do you think God wants?"

Angela sat up abruptly. "What does that have to do with anything?"

John smiled.

Angela shook her head. "I'm rapidly reconsidering this husband bit. A woman says one word about commitment and you're suddenly turning into a religious nut!"

"You're the one who teaches a class on mysticism. I want to know what you've learned from your mystical friends about how God regards marriage."

Angela gave him a distrustful look. "This isn't some atavistic religiosity bursting out? You're not going to go all Christian on me, are you?"

"It was an honest question. I know what the Bible says. I know what the church says. But mystics seem to have a more direct line. I'd like to know what they say. Why should we get married? Marriage is for procreating, which we are not going to do. Marriage is for creating and holding together a family, which we are not going to have. Marriage stabilizes a society. But that's for the young who have children who are not yet fully adult. So why a public and legal contract made in front of the community? Why not just a private promise?"

"You're asking me when you are the one who has experienced this! Do you wish your Mary had simply made a private promise to you?"

"No, of course not. I'm simply asking if there are reasons for marriage that have nothing to do with progeny or society. I thought maybe the mystics might have had some ideas."

"Are you really interested or do you already have your own ideas and are just asking rhetorically?"

"I do have ideas, but I wonder why two older adults like us need to be married."

Angela shook her head, "It would be just my luck finally to find a man I want to commit to only to find he once believed in commitment but now believes in free love."

"No, not free love. Not promiscuity. But I am asking how sex fits into the relationships of older humans—what it means, when to have it, when not to have it. And who better to answer that question than you!"

Angela moved away from him on the sofa. "I think you just insulted me."

John took and held her hand before she could withdraw it. "I paid you a compliment."

"You'll have to explain that." She looked at her watch. "I have to go."

"I thought you might be staying over."

"Not tonight, buster!"

John smiled, "I love you, Angela."

"That's not going to work. You missed your chance."

"I wasn't saying it to get you to stay. I really do. And I am touched by your honesty."

Angela got up and reached for her coat. "Well, John Engelsinger, whatever it is you're becoming, you seem to be turning me into an honest woman. But this woman, honest or not, has to get up to teach tomorrow."

John helped her on with her coat. She kissed him on the cheek and was gone. John dug his Christmas decorations out of storage and spent the rest of the evening setting up and doing the tree. The exchange had left him happy and maybe a little pleased with himself. He knew now without a doubt that Angela loved him and wanted to be with him, and he was impressed that the tiff at the end had not made him feel bad or guilty. He went to bed missing Angela.

The phone rang early the next morning and woke him up. It was Angela.

"I know you don't have to get up as early as I do, but I had to hear your voice. I feel like a high school kid with her first crush. Believe me I'm fighting this. I'm making a fool of myself."

"I do love you. I meant that last night."

"I'm a fifty-two year old woman. I'm not supposed to feel this way. I'm ridiculous!"

"I like ridiculous."

"You're supposed to be my conquest. Not the other way around."

Chapter 35 – Disaster

Sam and Eve were sitting in the sanctuary on Christmas Eve listening to Christmas carols on the organ and waiting for the Candle Lighting Service to begin. Eve tapped Sam's arm, whispered, "Angela Feladucci is here," and pointed to a pew across the aisle where John and Angela were taking seats. "And there's David," Eve added. Sam nodded. They knew David, because he often came with John. "I wonder where his mom is?" Eve whispered. "I never see her." "Sh-h-h," Sam said. Eve watched as David sat down between John and Angela, and John put his arm around David and rested his hand on Angela's shoulder. She saw the boy smile.

At the end of the service, Pastor Kirby and Maud, who had served as worship leader, walked down the center aisle sending the candle flame down each pew until all the candles were lit and the lights were dimmed while everyone sang "Silent Night." In the last verse they all raised their candles high and the candlelight rose into the rafters and sparkled in the children's eyes and glinted in the tears of their elders.

It was snowing when Sam and Eve came out into the parking lot, and the fluffy soft flakes came down all night. The wind dropped during the night, and they awoke to white beauty glistening in the winter sun. Mid-afternoon it began to snow again. By midnight 18 inches were already on the ground. It snowed through the rest of Christmas night, and by the day after Christmas more than 30 inches had fallen and were being whipped by the wind into mountainous drifts.

Sam checked the television and the NPR station regularly to get news of the storm. Downstate the snow was wetter and heavier. Late Christmas Day the temperature began to rise, and in a broad belt across the middle of the state the snow turned to rain, which just kept coming down and coming down. By the end of the day after Christmas the total precipitation, snow and rain, was at 7 inches. The streams and rivers were rising rapidly. And the rain was still coming down.

Joe Kurtz called Sam late on December 26th to say that he had just gotten word about Tutorville, a small town near Effingham where there was a good-sized church. The creek running through town had come out of its banks. All that day the waters had been rising, and by 9 p.m. the creek had flooded all the homes along the creek. The next day Joe called with an update on Tutorville. The rain was continuing and the creek was still rising, though it was now a huge river, covering six blocks on either side of the creek bed. People were frantically putting up sandbags, straw bales, anything they could find, but to little effect. No one had ever seen a flood like this.

Sam saw a CNN report comparing it to the Great Flood of 1993, which people had called a 500-year flood. Tutorville wasn't old enough for anyone to know about more than 150 years, but this was beyond anything anyone remembered. Joe called Sam on the morning of the 28th to report that the rain had finally stopped and the creek had slowly begun to recede. More than three-fourths of the town was under water. The church had water up to the top of the backs of the pews. The parsonage was flooded to the ceiling of the first floor.

Furthermore, Joe said the Tutorville church was a community church with many members living nearby, and at least 12 church families were flooded out. All across that part of the state, the story was the same. Sam was grateful that in Selby and the larger metropolitan area in the north, the snow had never turned to rain, and the temperature had stayed cold enough that there was no rapid melting. But in the center of the state hundreds of small towns and villages were covered by flood waters, and thousands of homes were damaged.

Word went out through the district, reaching the Westbook church, that the people in Tutorville were in desperate need. An emergency meeting was called for the night of the 28th. Sam and Eve helped Joe and pastor Kirby activate the phone tree and the e-mail chain. Once a few members knew, there was a flurry of calls, e-mails and texts, and it was only a matter of an hour or two till everyone knew about the meeting. But many could not get to it because the streets were clogged by the huge drifts that still paralyzed Selby and whole metro area. It took Sam and Eve three hours to dig out.

There was no time wasted at the meeting. It was quickly decided that a delegation would leave the next day for Tutorville. Kurt Wampler had been on disaster relief projects before, and he told people to pack heavy boots; rain and snow gear; warm, but old clothes that could hold up under mud, slush, or ice; and anything that was waterproof. As Sam listened, he realized that no one knew what they would find when they got to Tutorville. People would be pouring in from all over the district. A denomination-wide disaster response was being planned. So many of the church members' homes had been flooded out as well as the two local motels that they did not know where they would sleep or prepare food. Kurt said they should bring all the sleeping bags and blankets they could muster. Joe Kurtz as board chair and Kirby as pastor were coordinating the preparations, but people really didn't need much coordination; they seemed to know what to do. Kurt Wampler and Maud Miller volunteered their mini-vans.

Jack Foster and John Engelsinger had come to the meeting together in one of Jack's four-wheel-drive pickups. As soon as the plans were clear, they left. John told Sam later that they went back to Jack's yard where he emptied one of his large construction vans, and they loaded two generators, several halogen construction lights on heavy-duty stands, shovels, buckets, brooms, two tool chests, three large propane heaters, and four portable industrial fans. The rest of the space they filled with 24-packs of water bottles and hundreds of dollars-worth of groceries. John said they cleaned out the nearby Wal-Marts and Targets of blankets, propane camping lanterns, and propane fuel cans. They picked up some old cots at the Army-Navy store and filled two 50-gallon drums with gasoline for the generators.

Sam, Eve, Jack, Joe, John, and Kurt and Cynthia Wampler were among the volunteers. Kirby reluctantly stayed behind to coordinate things from the Selby end and to be available as pastor to those who were shut in or having problems because of the storm. Eve got a call from Nancy Beahm who was annoyed and apologetic that she had to stay in town because there were structural renovations going on during the holidays at her elementary school. Maud Miller called Sam to say how badly she wanted to go, but her age and rheumatism held her back, and she was still not fully recovered from her hernia surgery. So she was going to take care of Joey, Kaylie, and Sonny so Samantha and Marianne could go. She wanted Sam to know this.

By midday on December 29, twenty people had gathered in the church parking lot. Eve saw Angela had come to see them off and was kissing John good-bye. At one o-clock a caravan of three cars, two mini-vans and Jack's construction van pulled out of the lot and headed south.

By the time they arrived in Tutorville, most of the water had subsided. The town was a sea of mud. Sam found Daryl Bender, district executive, and Fred Vogel, pastor at the nearby Effingham church, and learned that they were coordinating the volunteers from the various churches of the district. He called Joe and the other Selby volunteers over, and Daryl and Fred briefed them. Social service professionals, disaster workers, and pastors from many other churches and denominations were handling the hundreds of volunteers pouring into the area and deciding to which of the many flooded communities they would be sent. For this reason, Daryl and Fred decided to concentrate most of the district volunteers on the Tutorville church, its immediate neighborhood, and the rest of the town.

The Selby volunteers unloaded Jack's truck and carried the blankets, food, water, and lanterns to the second floor of the church's education wing, which was above flood level and which, though without heat or electricity, would keep the materials dry until they were needed. By the time they were finished, it was dark and little more could be done. Fred and his wife, Alice, were busy finding homes where the volunteers from around the district could stay. Some women from Fred's congregation had organized shuttle vans so people would have transportation to the homes where they were staying. Fred and Alice had two extra rooms, once belonging to their children who were now grown, and it happened that Sam and Eve and Samantha and Marianne were assigned to the Vogel's. Housing was at a premium, so Alice asked Samantha and Marianne if they minded sharing a room and a bed. They smiled, realizing that Alice and Fred did not know who they were, and said, with a touch of irony their hosts did not pick up, that they did not mind at all. Sam looked over at Eve and raised his eyebrows.

The next morning Eve came down early and found Alice, who was a middle school teacher, trading stories with Samantha while she fried eggs and made French toast and Samantha set the table. Marianne came into the kitchen a moment later and joined the conversation, and all through breakfast the four women continued to talk as though they were old friends. There was some awkwardness between Fred and Sam, but that ebbed away as Fred hurried through his food, all the time talking about what needed to be done and listening to Sam's suggestions.

The four from Selby with Alice joined more than a dozen others to mud out the church. The mud was heavy and stank. Sam's boots were soon clumps of oozing sludge that clung like wallpaper paste and had to be scraped off and then scraped again. Eve tried to stay on top rather than sink in, lost her balance, and sat down. For the rest of the day she carried a miry wet spot on the seat of her jeans that gradually dried, hardened, and cracked.

The pews were old and thus were made of solid wood with no veneer. They had not been in water longer than 24 hours and had survived without warping. The men loosened the retaining screws with large screwdrivers, using hand trowels to push mud away that was three inches deep. In short order they had mud on their gloves and their jeans and their faces where they rubbed themselves or brushed away sweat. The temperature stayed above freezing, but the day was darkly overcast. Dampness hung in the air. When the wind picked up, it made everything feel several degrees colder. Still the exertion produced sweat, which soaked into their already damp clothing.

When the benches were all loosened, the men carried them to one side of the church, and on the other side everyone began to shovel the mud into buckets, which had to be carried outside and dumped away from the building on the creek side of the church. When most of the mud was gone, the women with kitchen brooms and push brooms swept as much of the rest of it as they could toward the door. Then the men moved all the benches over onto the clean side and they shoveled, carried, and brushed the rest of the mud. It was discouraging work, because they could only get the worst out of the sanctuary. Dampness and muddy footprints still covered the floor. One of the members of the Tutorville church was heard to say how glad she was they had that awful tile she hated, remarking how much worse carpet or hardwood would have been.

Late in the morning while the mudding was still going on, Sam saw Jack and a man from the Effingham church carrying one of the generators to the second floor. Sam went to help. They set up a halogen light and a propane heater and some long utility tables in a large classroom; they ran an extension cord for a coffee urn. Eve recruited Samantha and Marianne and Alice, and the four women began to make sandwiches. Jack wanted to know why the women got the cushy jobs while the men were downstairs still mired in the mud, and Samantha just stuck out her tongue at him. This shocked Alice and made her laugh. Samantha seemed such a proper person. Even with speckles of mud on her pants and her down jacket, she looked neat and her hair was still in place. Marianne, on the other hand, looked like she'd rolled in the mud. Eve was enjoying the camaraderie among the four women and was watching Alice with interest. What started as lunch prep became a day-long job, as word went out that there was food, coffee, and heat at the church. Volunteers from all over the muddy town came to warm up and get something to eat.

Early on Sam saw that the church was becoming a staging area for the Tutorville volunteers as they moved out into the homes around the church. The men left the pews shoved tightly to one side. After it was swept, several women mopped the rest of the sanctuary floor, and when it was relatively clean, men moved in Jack's other generator and set up and plugged in all four fans. Even in that dank atmosphere, the floors began to dry. They moved in the rest of Jack's equipment. They put down a heavy-duty plastic tarp near the main door where people could leave their muddy tools. News soon spread, and the church quickly became headquarters for volunteers working throughout the larger area, even beyond Tutorville.

By mid-afternoon with the work at the church completed, Sam and the men and women from Westbrook went out to start on the houses nearby, joining dozens of others from all over the state who were spreading out across the town. Eve, Samantha. Marianne, and Alice continued to work nonstop, preparing food, as dozens of people made their way to the second floor emergency kitchen. Jack produced some hot plates he had had the presence of mind to throw into his truck. He even scrounged a microwave that had been on the second floor of a nearby house and thus not ruined by the flood. By mid-afternoon, he saw that the supplies of food and water he'd brought would be exhausted by the end of the day. He got into his truck and was gone for an hour and half. When he came back, the truck was full of food and supplies. By this time people were beginning to think Jack had some sort of magic, and they instinctively turned to him for logistics.

Fred and Daryl had a good grasp of all volunteers in and around Tutorville and with the help of Joe Kurtz were making plans for how best to deploy them. But people just went out and started working, and they were ignoring who came from which church or organization. Sam and John, who had been working together moving pews and mudding out the church, took charge of a house down the block from the church. A man from a church up in the south suburbs of Chicago and two women, who had driven together all the way from the southern tip of the state, joined them. The women were from Jonesboro, one of them from the Methodist church; the other turned out to be Almeda Shank. Sam smiled and said, "Well, we meet again." She squinted at him and said, "Indeed we do, young man." John looked at the two of them and laughed. The five of them set up a bucket brigade to carry out the mud. They got into a rhythm and someone began to sing old camp songs. Forever after, Sam would never hear "I've Been Working on the Railroad" without thinking about that unlikely group of older men and women, shoveling and carrying and passing buckets and ending up as dirty and dark as coal miners.

Back at the church, Eve found Jack and told him they needed something to cook with and eat on. Jack drafted two teenagers from one of the crews and asked them to carry plates and utensils up from the first-floor church kitchen, which were free of mud because they had been stored in high cupboards above the water line. The larger kettles and pots, stored lower, were coated with mud, but Jack found some dishcloths. With the help of Eve and using a couple of bottles of water, he managed to clean out two big kettles for making soup and some smaller pots. "They're a little gritty," he said, "but people will be so hungry they'll never notice. Just as long as it's hot and sticks to the ribs." He pointed out some beef he'd found on his store run and a bag of potatoes.

By late afternoon Alice, Samantha, Eve, and Marianne were dead on their feet, but there was no one to spell them. All the other women and men were exhausted too from lifting and carrying hour after hour, damp and chilled to the bone. Gradually people who'd been working all across this small town came to the end of their strength, saw the glow from the halogen lights Jack had set up, and gravitated toward the church. There were too many to serve in the small, cramped upstairs Sunday school rooms, so people carried down folding chairs and utility tables and set up an eating area in the cleared-out sanctuary space. Camping lanterns were set up on the tables. Eve and Alice carried down two huge pots of beef stew, and Marianne and Samantha brought back down the silverware and plates that had been taken up earlier. Jack quickly saw that the sanctuary made more sense as a field kitchen and made plans to move everything down before leaving for the night. Bread, butter, jam, some cheese and crackers, fruit juices, and bags of cheap cookies were laid out on the serving table next to the stew. Marianne and Samantha ladled it out as people filed by, and Alice handed out bread and cheese. There was even a small pot with a vegetarian option. Jack set up the halogen lamps around the edges and positioned the heaters so there was a cross-draft of heat. It was an oddly cheerful scene—damp, mud-smeared men and women huddled together around tables in a low, yurt-like circle of halogen light, gas lanterns, and blow-dried warmth with the dark of the peaked, cathedral-like ceiling rising above them.

After everyone was served, Eve sat down next to Sam, huddling close for warmth. He put his arm around her. They'd been cold and damp all day. It hadn't made much difference whether they were working inside or out. Everyone was cold and damp. No one really warmed up. The food, while it warmed the insides, drew energy from the extremities and everyone felt more tired and cold. People quickly helped clean up and left to find their lodging for the night. Eve got up and found Alice, Samantha, and Marianne trying to wash up. She suggested they take the pots and dishes with them back to the Vogels' where they washed everything before finally falling into bed exhausted.

That first day there was little time to talk, but during the second day the four women established a routine that left them an occasional break to sit and drink coffee. Eve commented that they knew so little about one another, yet it seemed like they knew each other. "It's the sort of knowing that comes from working so hard," she said, "and from having to think fast and figure things out together." On the morning of the third day of running the field kitchen, the four women were taking a mid-morning break, and Samantha and Marianne were talking about a cell phone call they had made the night before to their kids back in Selby. Eve was watching Alice, who was watching Marianne and Samantha. The two women had an earthy, bantering way of talking to one another that Alice liked. "You must be really close friends and do a lot together," she commented. "You talk about your kids as though they belong to both of you."

There was a moment of silence, then Marianne said, "They do."

Alice looked puzzled. "I don't understand.

"Joey is my daughter with my ex-husband," said Samantha. "Kaylie is Marianne's daughter from her first marriage. And we adopted Sonny together."

"Together?"

Marianne smiled sadly. "We thought you probably hadn't figured it out. We wondered if we should tell you or let you find out or not say anything at all. You've become a friend, Alice, and we were afraid it would change how you feel about us. You see, we are a couple."

"A couple! You're...your're..."

"Lesbians. Yes, we are lesbians."

Alice looked away. She smoothed out the lap of her apron. She looked back at Marianne. "Are you the ones your pastor performed the service for that got him in trouble?"

"Yes."

Alice began to shake her head slightly.

"You're upset," Samantha said.

"But...you're so...so...ordinary! You're like other women I know."

Samantha laughed, "We don't wear horns. We are women. We believe in commitment. We are—how shall I say it—we are monogamous just like you and Fred."

"I don't get it. I mean how does it work?" Alice's face got red and she stammered, "I mean it's none of my business. I mean it really isn't. But I just can't picture it."

"A common reaction. You wonder how it works physically," Marianne said. She looked at Samantha, "Well, I suppose if you really want to know…"

"I'd rather not," Samantha said quickly. "Marianne will talk about anything. I'm more reserved about these things. Like you actually." She reached out and touched Alice's hand.

"I didn't mean I wanted to know how you…you know…how you…"

"Do it?" said Marianne. "It's okay. It's okay to be curious about the sex. But sex isn't the only thing. Start with what makes you and Fred a couple—the things you talk about, the things you enjoy doing, the shared responsibility for your kids, the times you laugh together…"

"Fred doesn't laugh much," Alice blurted out.

"Well, he loves you. He likes being with you. He respects you. I can see that when we sit around your table. Start with that, Samantha and I have that with each other. Let the biology take care of itself. Sort that out later."

Eve watched and her heart went out to Alice as she looked at these two women who'd become friends in the crucible of mud, damp, cold, and too much work. Alice sighed. "Well, this changes things…for sure."

"It's hard for you, I know," Samantha said softly, "and for us. We'll be gone in a few days and you won't have to deal with us and this disturbing new reality anymore."

"I didn't mean that it changes how I feel about you and that I want you gone. I saw from the beginning that you are good people. This doesn't change that. But what am I supposed to think? What do I do about the Bible?" She opened her eyes wider, as something just occurred to her. "What do I say to Fred!"

There was silence. Alice began to speak again, then stopped. She shook her head as though coming to a conclusion. "I can't talk about this with Fred. Not yet. I need to think about it. We, the four of us," she looked at Eve who had been listening quietly, "are going to keep working together and being friends as though we never had this conversation. At least for right now. I have to decide what to do, what to say, how to be prepared." She looked at Marianne. "It will come out, you know. Even Fred…" she smiled, "Fred can be dense at times, but even Fred will eventually figure it out. I need some time. I can't deal with it. Can we pretend I don't know? Please? Is that asking too much of you?"

"No. We're glad you haven't turned away from us."

"Does that happen?"

"Often."

"That's terrible. That's sad." She paused, "I probably would have been one who did that." She shook herself. "Well, enough. We have a big lunch to prepare. Back to work. Okay?"

****

Sam and John and their team had taken the better part of three days to finish their first house. On the third afternoon they had moved to another down the street. By the next afternoon they had removed the worst from the first floor. Almeda Shank and her friend were in the kitchen scrubbing walls and trying to clean out and rescue the kitchen cabinets. The man from the Chicago suburbs had been needed in another house one street over. That left the basement for Sam and John. The water had been slowly seeping out, but there was still a foot and half left, too much for them to work. Glad they could put it off, they had been loading the ruined furniture and appliances onto a pickup truck, while waiting for Jack, who had found a pump, and was going from house to house when he wasn't making his food runs. It took Jack only a few minutes to pump the basement water down to a thick, three-inch muck. Sam sighed and the three men leaned against Jack's truck to rest.

"How do you do it, Jack?" Sam said. "You seem to be everywhere. You're tireless."

"I'm running on adrenaline and caffeine," Jack answered.

"Maybe," Sam said, glancing at John who smiled.

Jack saw the exchange of looks. "Don't give me your 'profound insight' bullshit, Ellerby."

"You're a good guy, better than you think you are."

"What's that supposed to mean!" Jack paused, reached down and picked up a piece of hardened mud and tossed it against a ruined refrigerator that was to be loaded onto the pickup. "I'll tell you one thing. I feel alive!"

Jack's comment was on Sam's mind as he worked. No one was nearby who could be called to make a bucket brigade, so he and John filled two buckets each, trudged up the basement stairs and out the back door, across the slippery back lawn to a low spot, where they dumped the sludge. Then they returned to repeat the process. Each bucket weighed almost 40 pounds full. They made this trek over and over. Sam's body ached until every stressed muscle began to go numb. He went into autopilot, which left his mind free but filled with a rhythm of ideas that mirrored the repetitive patterns of the work.

Why did Jack feel more alive than when he was doing his own construction work, Sam wondered. Why was he himself invigorated? He had come to know his co-workers in ways he never would have across a table or in a church meeting. Almeda was a salty delight. John—he knew John was becoming much more than a breakfast buddy. Tired as he was, he was exhilarated. Each night when he dragged himself to the church for the evening meal, he felt clean inside, purged of all anxiety, grateful to be alive, glad to feel in his body these aching muscles so very present. He'd earned the right to be at peace, to rest. The smells of muddy clothing, stale sweat, damp air, steaming soup, hot coffee, burning propane—these were human smells. He belonged here with these people. He belonged in his body. He listened with gratitude to conversations around him. It was as though he were submerged in humanity. He remembered something Eve said last night after they tumbled into bed, in the brief instant before sliding gratefully into sleep. She said she had never enjoyed anything quite as much as she was enjoying the work with Alice, Samantha, and Marianne.

Sam and Eve and the whole contingent from the Westbrook Church stayed for five days, beyond New Year's Day. At various times, as many as 100 volunteers, from other congregations in the district and from churches and synagogues across the state, made the Tutorville Church their headquarters. Working with the townspeople they managed to get the worst of the mud out of most of the houses. There was a huge stinking pile of sodden furniture, ruined carpet, waterlogged appliances, discarded clothes, soggy books—all the detritus of flood recovery—in a vacant lot not far from the church. A front-loader was slowly shoveling the debris into a flotilla of pickups and flat beds, which were carrying it to the nearest landfill five miles away. On the last day the electricity and natural gas came back on, and some of the homes had running water again, which they had to boil. The weather had held above freezing except for a short time each night, but the days were cloudy, damp, and dreary, with a small dank wind blowing most of the time, just cold enough to pierce coats and jackets especially clothing that had been sweated into—weather, Sam commented to Eve, that allowed the recovery effort to proceed, but made everyone miserable and kept everyone wet.

The people of the town were slowly moving back into their homes. Those with second floors were actually living in them already. Eve felt intense sympathy, especially for the women. With little or no edible food in their houses, they could not put meals on the table, so whole families found their way to the church building. There were nights when Eve, Alice, Samantha, and Marianne served more than 250 people in two, sometimes three, shifts. Jack made a run every day for more food supplies; sometimes he was gone for hours, but he always came back with a loaded van. He had cleaned out the gas stove in the church kitchen and was delighted that it worked when the gas came back on. He had already dried out the church fridge, and with considerable trepidation he plugged it into one of the generators to test it, expecting it to short out in a blaze of sparks. But it came on with a comforting purr. Eve was watching him and she told Sam later that she'd never seen Jack so pleased. When the gas and electric came on, Jack shifted the cooking operations from the end of the sanctuary into the kitchen.

It was January 3 and the townspeople knew most of the volunteers would be leaving the next day. Word went out and by late afternoon people began to arrive with makeshift casseroles, cookies, cakes, salads, and if they had no way to prepare food, bags of fruit, boxes of crackers, and packaged baked goods they'd found or scrounged somewhere. Every table and every moveable chair was found and brought to the space. Though the church now had electricity, Jack left the halogen lights on and even the camp lanterns because they added a warm glow to the sanctuary lights. The four women made pots of soup using all the containers they could rescue from the kitchen. A long serving buffet was set up in front of the kitchen. By 6 p.m. the church was full of more than 300 people—men, women, and children from the town mixed with volunteers, strangers who in a few short days had become friends. People stood at the tables and were packed all around the outer walls

Sam, who was standing next to Daryl Bender, leaned over and asked him to say grace. Then spontaneously a man with a strong baritone began to sing "Amazing Grace," and everyone joined in. The people from the churches in the district—the congregations were known for their good singers—dropped into four-part harmony. Tears came to Eve's eyes as the voices rose into the timbers of the peaked ceiling and out into the damp night with a loveliness that seemed to transcend the ordinariness of the people. For a moment Sam, standing in the middle of these muddy, cold, displaced townspeople and strangers, tired and far from home, was filled with a gratitude that he saw reflected in other faces...for being alive, for being with other humans in a warm place, for food, for knowing that even in bad times they were not alone. If doctrine and practice had been at issue, Sam knew, these 300 or so people would not have been comfortable with one another, but the only concerns on this night were survival, staying warm, having something to eat, and getting back home, whether to a mudded-out house down the street or to a farmhouse further downstate or to a condo in the Chicago suburbs. There was a larger reality in that room—Sam could feel it—deeper than faith and doubt, beyond the ideas about God that would have provoked argument at another time in a different place. He saw that others felt it too—this ineffable something that steals into human life at extreme moments and reminds people that it has always been there.

Eve, who was standing near the kitchen, impulsively hugged the person next to her and then began hugging everyone around her. Fred Vogel was nearby and she hugged him. He looked like he wanted to run away, but the hugging was spreading across the hall, and so he awkwardly turned to the person next to him who happened to be Marianne. Before he could move, she gave him a warm, enthusiastic embrace, and he gave back a somewhat stiff response in spite of himself. Alice on the other side of him was hugging Samantha, and she turned and gave Fred a warm embrace and kissed him, leaving him pleased and embarrassed. The room erupted in lively chatter and people began to form a line at the buffet tables.

That evening Sam and Eve, with Samantha and Marianne, went home with Fred and Alice for the last time. In the morning the six people loitered at the breakfast table. The four heading back to Selby seemed reluctant to leave. Fred wanted to talk, to make up for being so absorbed in plans and preparations on the other mornings. He asked Marianne questions about her work and commented on how much Alice had enjoyed working with the two women. Sam watched him with surprise and pleasure. Fred turned to Sam and said he knew they had their differences, but he now felt he had some friends in the Selby church even though he knew many people resented him because of his actions.

Marianne looked over at Alice, who had been looking down at her plate. She looked up and her eyes met Marianne's. She nodded slightly.

"Fred, I think we have to tell you something," Marianne said. "We have not hidden it, but it never came up. We decided to focus on the work and not be distracted. But you've extended us your hospitality. It's not honest not to tell you, to let you find out some other way. Uh...Samantha and I are a couple. We are the women our pastor performed the service of union for that you object to, that got him into trouble with you and the ministerial commission."

Fred stopped eating and put down his fork. His face went blank, unreadable.

"We're sorry. When housing assignments were made, we were astonished at the irony. We found ourselves staying with you and put in the same bedroom. Should we tell you and Alice? Would you ask us to leave if we did? Did we want to read the rejection in your eyes? Did any of this matter—your feelings or ours, your convictions or ours—when people in Tutorville were flooded out and homeless? It all happened so fast and we just let it be. But now we are friends. You deserve to know."

Fred stood up. He turned toward the door, like he wanted to bolt, as though the room suddenly held something bad for him, something unhealthy. Sam wanted to say something, but didn't know what. Marianne was visibly upset. Samantha face tightened and then sagged in sadness. Sam reached out his hand to Fred and then drew back as he saw anger in his face. Alice was alarmed and frightened. She jumped to her feet. "Fred, please don't," she said softly. "Fred, look at me."

Fred turned stiffly and said, "Did you know!"

"Only since two days ago."

"And you didn't tell me."

"I wasn't ready. I had to think."

"You had to think!"

"Fred, Marianne and Samantha are my friends. They're women, good women."

"They are doing something that is terribly wrong."

"I know, but how can such good people be all wrong?"

"If we change our minds about this, we might as well throw out the Bible."

Alice came around the table and put her hand on Fred's arm and said with surprising steel in her voice, "We can't talk about Marianne and Samantha as though they suddenly don't matter. Let's go into the other room." She firmly shepherded him into the kitchen and closed the door.

Eve sighed deeply. "I'm so sorry this happened. This has been such a good time, now it's spoiled. I watched the three of you become good friends." She looked each of the women in the eye. "Don't underestimate Alice."

They could hear raised voices in the kitchen. Alice seemed to be holding her own. They got up from the table, went to their rooms, gathered their suitcases and some muddy clothes they had stuffed into plastic garbage bags. They lined all this up in the living room and were ready for Fred to run them back to the Tutorville church where they would join with others for the drive home.

Fred came out of the kitchen. Stiffly and formally he said, "Let me help carry your stuff to the van." Alice came along and the two men and four women were silent for most of the trip. Sam asked Fred how much more time he was going to be able to take away from his own church work to do the flood relief work and received a polite but peremptory answer, and when Samantha asked if Alice was expecting to be back in school the next day, Alice only nodded. At the church Fred helped transfer the bags to one of the Selby vans. Sam held out his hand. "I am sorry it had to end this way, Fred. Thank you for all you've done." Fred shook hands briefly and looked away. He turned back and stiffly and in a monotone thanked them for their work. Alice embraced Samantha and Marianne. She couldn't help glancing at Fred as she did it. She turned to Eve who hugged her hard and whispered, "I'm glad I met you. It's going to be all right. You'll see. Call me if you need to talk." Marianne walked over to Fred, "I really do appreciate everything you've done." She made to put out her hand and thought better of it and just looked him in the eye. He returned her gaze, shook his head slightly, and turned away.

Chapter 36 – Coming Home

The first thing John saw as the Westbrook vans and cars pulled into the church lot after dark in the January cold was Angela getting out of her car. She walked to the van he was in—she could see him by the dome light someone had turned on—and knocked on the glass before he could unstrap his seatbelt and get out. He rolled down the window.

"Hello, buster. You're back from saving the world?" Angela said.

"Yes, but they wouldn't let me ride my white charger up the interstate, so I'm reduced to the back seat of a van." He put his hand out the window.

"I don't want your hand," she said and kissed him through the open window.

They heard a voice behind Angela asking for Jack. It was Jenn. John explained that Jack had gone straight to his yard. Jenn's face fell, and Eve, who had just clambered out of the other van, asked her what she was still doing in Selby, and she said she'd been with the kids for the holidays and was staying until classes started again on Monday. She said she'd drive to the yard and see if she could catch Jack. John smiled as Sam and Eve gave each other knowing looks.

It did not take long for the travelers to transfer bags and dirty clothes to the cars they'd left in the lot, and very quickly the volunteers were dispersing to their homes. As John got into Angela's car, he saw Sam and Eve saying good-bye to Samantha and Marianne. Word of what had happened had passed by cell phone among the returning vehicles. Even in the weak light of the parking lot flood lamp, John could see their sadness. He asked Angela to wait, and he walked over to where the four stood by a snow bank at the edge of the lot. "We don't want it to end," Eve said. John nodded.

Angela took John to her house. She'd picked up some things for him at his apartment, and while she made dinner he showered and changed into clean clothes. They laughed and caught up on news over the meal, spent a quiet evening talking, and John stayed the night. In the morning Angela made a lavish breakfast of fresh fruit, eggs benedict, cinnamon rolls, and coffee.

"You're very domestic today," John commented.

"I've made up my mind. I'll do anything you ask me to do," Angela said. "I missed you. Far more than I thought I would. I'm afraid. I feel like a schoolgirl. I'm probably a bad bet for a relationship. But you can have me anyway you want me."

"Is this another proposal that's not a proposal?"

"More like a giving-up. I've always held something back. Now I'm telling you that you can have it all."

John raised Angela from her chair. He kissed her lightly on her hair as she laid her head on his shoulder. Something seemed to break in her; he could feel her trembling. He held her tighter and was afraid. He sensed how tender and fragile she was behind that tough exterior.

She drew back and looked at him, smiling through tears. "Don't worry. I'm not asking anything of you," she said, toughening up. "You don't have to feel obligated to marry me. I'm a big girl. But I needed finally to let this stony heart open."

He smiled and held her.

****

Sam and Eve were quiet and thoughtful as they drove home. Neither said much until later after they'd showered, changed, eaten, and started a load of dirty laundry in the washer. Eve wrapped her robe around her and sat on the loveseat across from the recliner where Sam was stretched out.

"I'm ready for a change," she said.

Sam smiled, "What do you have in mind?"

"Traveling around, helping people."

Sam laughed, "Sounds terribly do-goodish. What exactly do you mean?"

"We have nothing tying us to this place."

"Of course we do. Our friends! The church!"

"This could still be our home base."

"What would we do?"

"Volunteer. Do short stints here and there. Or maybe some long stints."

"Where?"

"Wouldn't it be great to volunteer in Latin America? Or Europe? Or somewhere in Asia?"

"So what you really want to do is travel."

"No, I want to be itinerant. You talk about living by faith. How can you do that when you can't move about, aren't free to respond?"

"So we can't live by faith if we're settled with jobs, responsibilities, and friends?"

"Of course we can. But I'm talking about you and me, right now, not people in general. Just us and who we are—at this moment. We need to shake loose, do something completely different."

"For how long?"

"I don't know. What does it mean to live by faith, if not this? You ask each day what the next thing is and then you do it."

"What kind of world would it be if everyone lived that way?"

"You're the one who's always talking about faith. Why are you grilling me? I don't have to have an answer for everyone, only for myself and, hopefully, for you. Are you telling me after all these years, now that I'm finally talking your language, that you're not interested? That you're afraid?"

"Afraid! That's a fighting word! I never talked about faith as something that uprooted me and sent me on a mission. I talked about it as something I tried to live by in order to handle everyday life in a different way."

"Are you telling me that nothing I am saying has any resonance with you?"

Sam laughed and got up and went over and sat next to Eve on the loveseat, rumpling her hair as he sat down.

"Don't patronize me!" she snapped.

"I love you. I will go anywhere you want to go. I'll go tomorrow."

"So why the grilling, why the 20 questions?"

"I was astonished."

"You didn't think I had it in me!"

Sam shrugged and smiled, "I *have* noticed a change."

Sam stayed next to Eve on the loveseat but stretched out his legs and lay back. Eve picked up a book. Before she could start reading, Sam turned and said, "This idea comes at a good time."

"Why?"

"We won't need as much to live. We'll be given small stipends at some places, often room and board. The money we have left will go further. It wouldn't be enough if we stayed in Selby."

Eve laughed, "We are so...so feckless!"

"No. We're consistent. We didn't let the old man's money change us. If we sell this condo..."

"We just bought it!"

"I know. But if we sell it—fortunately we bought it at the bottom of the market, so we won't lose money, though we won't gain any and we'll be out the closing costs—but as I was saying, if we sell it and invest the money left after the sale along with what we still have, the income along with our social security checks will keep us going."

Eve shook her head, "Were you planning this all along?'

"No, but for once I was not worried. I knew a way would open. I just knew it."

"So this idea to travel and volunteer—you think it's coming from God?"

Sam shrugged, "My skeptical side says, 'Who knows?' Another side says the universe is more malleable and responsive than most of us allow for. But the deepest part of me says there is a God who takes careful interest in each of us—however impossible that is to imagine—and who has made a world that is far more creative and fertile than any of us imagine."

****

The next morning John was arriving back at the apartment, when Jack rolled up in his pickup. John laughed, "You never rest, do you? I was going to take the day off, but now that you're here, I guess I have to pretend to be working."

"Forget it. I came to talk," Jack said. "You got any coffee?"

Jack went to check on a heating unit that was being installed in one of the last apartments to be renovated while John got some coffee going. They sat at John's kitchen table.

"Had a close call last night!" Jack exclaimed. "Jenn found me at the yard. You know that. You told her I was there. I had the truck backed into the inside dock, and I was unloading all that equipment. I was concentrating hard, working fast, trying to get finished so I could go home and sleep. I never heard her coming. Suddenly I hear this 'Hi!' coming from the shadows. I jumped a mile and screamed like a banshee. It scared the hell out of her. There we were, face to face, shaking, our hearts racing to beat hell.

"'You could kill a man like that!' I said.

"She just shook her head. 'I had no idea,' she replied.

"'Why are you here?' I growled.

"'Are you angry at me,' she asked. I could see she felt really bad.

"'No, I'm not angry.'

"'Should I leave and let you finish?'

"'No.'

"Then she told me she missed me. What the hell am I supposed to do with that? I said, 'I never thought I'd hear you say that again.'

"'You've changed,' she said

"'So have you,' I replied.

"Then she said—and this blew me away—she said 'Would it be okay if we spent some time together when I come back to visit in the spring?'

"What could I say to that! I shot back, 'What are we saying here? We can't go back to what we used to be. We've both changed. You said it! I said it.'

"Then she asked me another question that surprised me. She asked if it was hard for me when she left. What was I supposed to say! 'Hell, yes!' Or 'No, I was fine.' So I laughed and said, 'What do you think? Does it matter? Would it make you feel better to know that I was miserable? Or would it make you feel less guilty if you knew that I was fine?'

"She said, 'You know I never tried to pretend you were okay, so I didn't need to feel bad myself.'

"But I came back to my question. 'What are we talking about here?'

"She said, 'I don't know. I just have the feeling we're not done with each other.'

Jack paused and looked hard at John. "By God, I didn't know whether to sweep her up and take her to the couch in my office or run as fast as I could in the other direction! I said that to her. And do you know what she said? She looked me right in the eye and said, 'Well, I know you don't want to do the second. I can see it in your eyes.'"

Jack just shook his head and looked at John who let out a burst of air, like he'd been holding his breath. "What did you do?" John asked.

"I still can't believe it, but I gave her a hug, I kissed her on the cheek. I said I thought that would be a mistake. I would always love her, but there was no going back. Damn it, John, I wanted her! It was probably a good thing I was so tired. But it's over. I see that so clearly. Jenn is like a shooting star on this brilliant trajectory. If she is productive into her early eighties, she has almost thirty good years ahead of her. There's no telling what she'll do. She doesn't even know how gifted she is. I've had my shot. I built my business. I slaked my ambition. Now it's her turn. She's just scared. I'd be a safe haven, but only for a while. Hell, she's going to be university literature professor by the time she's done. I'm still a damn contractor."

"You're a poet. Did you forget that?"

"Huh! Not much there. I write for myself. Geez, don't tell her! Lord knows what she'd think!"

"You think she doesn't know? You think none of the men in our group told their wives, who told Jenn?"

"What the hell! I don't care!"

John watched as Jack swirled his coffee around in his mug and looked out the window.

"You do care, Jack."

"Yeah, yeah. You're right. But I know I did the right thing."

There was a knock at the door, and John looked at Jack with surprise, shrugged, and went to see who it was. He opened the door and exclaimed, "Vi!" He stopped in stunned silence then said, "Lord! I forgot all about it. Today's the day!" He looked past her and saw a small rental van parked at the curb. "You're moving in. You got all your stuff in the van." He looked again. "In that little van! Is that all you have?"

She smiled a bit sheepishly. "Yes, that's it. All my worldly goods."

John was still dumbfounded. "We made this sudden trip downstate on disaster relief, mudding out houses. You know, the flood. We got back last night. The fact that you were moving just went completely out of my mind. I am so sorry!"

Vi laughed, "It's cold out here. Are you going to invite me in?"

"Yes, of course. I'm sorry. Come in, come in." He remembered Jack and hastily introduced them to each other. "Come in. Sit down. Have some coffee. The least I can do is offer you something hot. I can't believe I forgot."

Jack looked at Vi, peered out at the van, smiled, and said, "Looks like you're going to need help. I guess it's a good thing John and I were sitting around with nothing to do."

"Don't believe him. Jack's always working. He's the guy who owns this complex. The guy behind the co-housing thing."

Vi looked at him with interest.

John and Jack showed her the unit that would be hers, and then they did help her. It took the three of them only about an hour to unload Vi's van. John kept wanting to apologize again, but Vi was just glad to have gotten to Selby. With huge piles of dirty snow everywhere in the city, she had been afraid she'd never get her stuff out of her apartment and into the van, much less get it unloaded in Selby. When they finished, she sat down in one of the few chairs she brought, looked around, and gave a satisfied sigh.

"So you're here!" Jack said. "The least I can do is buy you some lunch to make up for my buddy's lapse. John, are you in too?"

"I can't. I have some things I have to do."

"Well, then, Viona, let me introduce you to the pleasures of life in Selby."

"How do you know my full name?"

Jack laughed, "I read it on the lease you signed."

John was carrying some trash to the construction dumpster that sat in the parking area when Jack and Vi came back from lunch, and he later came across Jack in the apartment with the new heating unit.

"Your friend's an interesting lady," Jack commented. "Not at all what I expected."

"What was that?"

"Oh, missionary-like. Do-gooder. She's got a lot of balls for a woman."

"Why do you say that?"

"Hell, the adventures she's had! The risks she's taken."

"She told you about that!"

"You sound surprised."

"She doesn't tell people, doesn't like to call attention to herself."

"Well, she talked to me! Is that a compliment? Or I'm just such a hard-ass it didn't matter what I thought. Hell, she even gave me advice!"

"Advice! About what?"

"I mentioned this hotel my company's building over in Arlington Heights. She starts telling me about all the places she stayed in all over the world: mud huts, youth hostels, small inns, mosquito-netted guest houses, a few downtown business hotels, and, on one occasion, a luxury resort. She's saying all the things that were bad and all the things that were good. She peppers me with questions about room size and elevators and laundry facilities. She wants to know the difference between the ritziest and the simplest accommodations in the new hotel. She wants to know the target clientele. She wants to know how many floors it will have and what special engineering will be needed if the building is a high-rise. Surprised the hell out of me.

"I told her she should have a second career in architecture. She said she's not interested in design as much as people. What kind of people would stay in the hotel and how would the design keep them together or keep them apart? It was a damned interesting conversation. I asked her if she wanted to continue it over dinner on Saturday."

"You asked Vi out for dinner!"

"Yeah. Is that a problem!"

"No, of course not."

"What then?"

"You're that last two people in the world I would have put together."

"Are you insulting me?"

"No. No. This is great," John couldn't help smiling.

"Come on, Englesinger! You're as bad as the other guys. Every time I do something you think is out of character, you act like the apocalypse has come."

"You're right! You're right!" John said, still laughing.

"Go to hell!" Jack said with a grin, as he walked out to his pickup.

Chapter 37 – Aftermath

Often during the weeks after returning from the disaster work, Eve thought about Alice. She wanted to call her but was afraid she didn't know her well enough. They'd shared very intense days and then the three Selby women had left. Maybe she didn't want to be reminded of what had happened. Would hearing from Eve make it harder for her? In the end after several weeks Eve decided to call. If Alice showed any signs of uneasiness, she'd politely end the call. But Alice was desperate to talk. The phone call lasted an hour and a half, and Alice poured out her whole story.

"On the night you left," Alice began, "I was setting the table and checking on the food I had simmering on the stove. I was so nervous I was constantly wiping my hands on my apron, waiting for Fred to come home from his office at the church. That's just a few steps across the lawn from the parsonage.

"Fred had gone to his office as soon as you all left that morning. He had called to tell me he had to meet one of the other ministers in town for lunch. So I'd not seen him since those terrible moments when we dropped you off. I was afraid, Eve. I was afraid Fred would become hard and rigid. I was afraid I would feel discouraged and disheartened. I was afraid there would be nothing I could say.

"But I had a lot to say. And I knew I had to say it. Not just about Samantha and Marianne being lesbians and my friends. I had to stop being afraid of Fred. I had to stop. I'd known this for a long time, like someone knows they have to stop drinking but is not ready to face the truth and the pain. I know how hard it is to stop drinking, because I have a younger brother who is an alcoholic. Why am I telling you all this, Eve? It's all pouring out."

Eve could hear the anxiety in her voice, the fear of exposure. "This is big—what you're going through, Alice. It's okay. You need to talk! You can trust me. Nothing you say will leave this conversation."

"Oh, I'm not afraid anymore of people knowing what I think. I just don't want to go to pieces on the phone."

"You're a strong woman, Alice."

"Well, there I was, listening for Fred, walking around the kitchen, straightening the canisters and appliances on the countertops, glancing out the window every few minutes, but not seeing anything in the dark. I was a mess! I was bending over to check the roast in the oven when I finally heard Fred coming up the path from the church. I stood up quickly as he came through the door. He hung up his coat, looked at me, turned and went into the living room.

"'Fred, we have to talk,' I said.

"'What is there to say?' he replied, turning back. 'You know what I think. You know what is right.'

"'That's just it. I don't know anymore,' I said.

"Then he said, 'I think you need some time to straighten out your thinking,' he turned again to go into the living room.

"'Fred, don't walk away from me,' I said sharply. I surprised myself.

"He turned back again and just looked at me. He was stern, like he wasn't going to give an inch.

"My heart sank, Eve. It's always been this way. Fred is always sure he has the moral high ground. So he didn't even bother to explain or justify himself. He just looked at me with that look—that righteous look. Like he was just so certain! He never even raised his voice. It was my job to accept his convictions and take them as mine. To see it his way! End of discussion. He began to turn again to go into the living room.

"'Those women are not wrong, Fred,' I said.

"'What did you say?'

"'I can't quote scripture, but...'

"Fred interrupted me, 'You certainly cannot. There aren't any scriptures!' he almost shouted.

"'Please let me finish. This is so important to me.' Fred didn't say anything, but this time he didn't turn away. 'Those two women are good people. They love each other. They stay with each other. They take care of their kids together.'

"'God never intended two women to be—uh—to cohabit.'

"I had to smile, Eve, in spite of myself. I'd never heard Fred use the word 'co-habit.'

"'Surely you don't think it's funny!' Fred said

"'No, of course not.'

"'It's an abomination.'

"'But Fred,' I replied, 'I really don't think it is. Even if it's wrong, it isn't that big or that bad.'

"'How can you possibly say that!' he cried. 'It goes against everything you've been taught. It goes against the Bible.'

"'But do you do everything the Bible says?'

"'I never stop trying.'

"I finally said, 'I can't argue scripture with you. I can't even argue right or wrong. I just know! I just know those two women are good people and their relationship is good. I feel it. I feel it in my bones.'

"Well, that never carries any weight with Fred. He snapped at me, 'So it just has to feel good to be right? Is adultery or fornication good because it feels good to have sex?'

"It was all I could do not to smile again. Fred kept using these words that dripped with sin. 'You have all the arguments,' I said. 'You have the Biblical education. I have nothing but my own instincts.'

"'That's not nearly enough,' Fred said. 'You must see that. How can you be a pastor's wife and say what you're saying! What will people think? What does God think?' Fred glared at me. He was bristling with judgment and disapproval.

"At that point, Eve, I felt my energy and my confidence slipping away. I was trying so hard to keep up my spirits. Then I probably said the wrong thing. I told Fred, 'I talked about relationships with Samantha and Marianne. The thing is—the stuff they deal with in living together is not so different from what we deal with in our marriage.'

"Fred's face turned red, 'You compare our marriage to their...their...I can't even speak the word. How could you!' He raised his voice. 'I cannot believe we are having this conversation! What has happened to you! You spend a few days with a couple of lesbians and your whole faith is destroyed.' He turned and finally went into the living room.

"Eve, we ate dinner in silence, and Fred went back to the living room while I stayed in the kitchen for the evening. The next morning Fred was up early and off to his office before I could get downstairs to make him breakfast. Oh, Eve, I was bursting with the need to talk. I baked some cookies and took them over to Dorothy Emmert and sat in her kitchen drinking coffee and telling her about Samantha and Marianne.

"Dot Emmert is an elderly lady, a lifelong member of our congregation. I love her to pieces, and I trust her. I told her everything, even about Fred. She listened and asked a few questions. She nodded her head and said I had given her something to think about. I couldn't tell what she was really thinking.

"While we were talking, Betsy Moeller came in and made herself at home with the coffee and cookies. She's a talker and a gossip, and she soon wormed the whole story out of me. I just can't resist Betsy. She's always dragging things out of me. When I thought about what Betsy would do with the story, I got really scared.

"But I was starting to feel a little rebellious, Eve, and now as I look back, I was maybe a little glad I wasn't going to have to carry this story alone. While I was still sitting there in Dot's kitchen, I went over in my mind what I had said. I had been careful not to say I thought it was okay for Samantha and Marianne to be together. I just reported what good people they were.

"Well, you can imagine what happened, Eve. Or maybe you can't if you've never lived in a small town. By the end of the day, nearly all the women and many of the men in the congregation knew my story.

"Of course, it wasn't Dot who was feeding the gossip mill, but she did make one call—I learned this later—to Almeda Shank who has been a friend since they both were growing up in Jonesboro. I guess she trusted Almeda's judgment and she also knew that Almeda was giving a lot of thought to this because of her work on the ministerial commission. She also knew that Almeda did not always agree with Fred. The story soon made its way around all the downstate churches, though by way of Betsy, not Almeda."

"What was that like for you?" Eve asked. "Did you feel exposed? Did you get any angry calls? Did anyone shun you?"

"Well, I learned that many women were shocked at the idea of a household with two teenaged girls and a little boy headed by two women. But some said there were all kinds of households these days. They wanted to know if Marianne and Samantha took good care of their kids. Did they provide for them? Did they keep them safe? One of my friends from the Quincy church called me and said it was maybe better to have two women rather than only one parent. She said there were too many single-parent families. But there were a lot of people who were outraged, and I did get some nasty calls. Most of the anger, and there was less than I expected, was about it's being unnatural and about kids needing a mother and a father." Alice paused, "One thing surprised me. There wasn't much quoting of scripture.

"A day or so after I talked to Dot and Betsy, Al Moeller stopped in Fred's office to tell him Betsy had been on the phone constantly and he was afraid she was stirring up trouble. Fred wanted to know what Betsy was telling people, and Al hemmed and hawed and then told him.

"Fred came straight home. 'What were you thinking!' he exploded as soon as he was inside the door. 'It's bad enough that you have these...these ideas! But you have to tell them to Betsy Moeller! Betsy Moeller, of all people! If God sends people to hell for gossip—and I surely hope he does—that woman will lead the parade!'

"I kept working at the stove and didn't look up."

"'This has got to stop! Right now! It goes no further!'

"I looked up at Fred. There were tears in my eyes. I turned off the stove. I took off my apron and quietly went upstairs. Later when Fred came up to go to bed, I was sitting in the rocking chair in my sewing room with only a reading lamp on. The door was open and Fred stood out in the dark hall looking at me. The Bible was open on my lap. I was sitting in the small pool of light thrown by the lamp; my hands were resting on the Bible. I knew Fred was there. I stirred and looked up at him. Then I closed my eyes to pray. Fred turned and went to bed. Later, when he was asleep, I went to bed too.

"Eve, we gradually began talking to each other again, but I never brought up Samantha and Marianne, and if Fred did, I quietly refused to discuss them. We talked about the things a couple needs to talk about, and I went on keeping house, making meals, washing our clothes, teaching school, and carrying out my church responsibilities. I was praying a lot. I had a new determination, and I was pretty sure Fred saw it. It was nothing I said or did, but I felt myself moving away from him. I could see he felt helpless. When he tried to speak to me, he could not hide his anger. I started to feel sorry for him. I would give him this quiet look he'd never seen before. I realized it was compassion. I was feeling compassion for Fred. I wasn't as angry or hurt as I'd been. Compassion! Can you imagine that! Toward Fred! He was indignant! But as I moved away from him, I think he started missing me. Sometimes I caught him looking at me with longing. He seemed to want to speak, but he couldn't. I'd never seen him like this. I had the oddest sense that he wanted to hold me."

Eve couldn't help herself. She laughed into her phone.

"Why do you laugh?" Alice asked.

"It's just so good, what you're doing! You know Alice, Fred loves you. But he sure doesn't know what to do with you. That's the best thing that could happen to him! And to you!"

"You think so! It doesn't feel that way most of the time. Anyway, by this time, I really needed to talk. I was tempted to drive all the way up to Selby and see Samantha and Marianne. But what would I say to them! And maybe they wouldn't want to see me. Then I thought about coming up to talk to you."

"Oh, you should have!" Eve exclaimed. "I've had you on my mind constantly. I would have welcomed you!"

"Well, I didn't know that. It was a long drive. I was nervous. I was afraid it would be awkward. I was afraid you might try to get me to agree with you."

"Oh, I wish I'd acted on my desire to call you," Eve said.

"I was asking myself where I could find someone who would listen and not tell me what to think. Dot helped some, and I went over there almost every day, but Dot doesn't have any ideas. I needed to make sense of this. Dot kept saying she wished I could talk to Almeda Shank. So one day when I knew Fred had a lunch appointment and would be gone all day, I drove the two and a half hours to Jonesboro. I called ahead and Almeda was ready with tea and four kinds of cookies laid out on the lace tablecloth on the dining room table."

Eve laughed, "I would expect no less."

"We talked for two hours and then I turned around and drove home so as to be there when Fred came in. On the drive north I kept returning to something Almeda had said to me. She said, 'The right thing isn't always the right thing.' From anyone else I would have thought that was the sort of nonsense over-educated people sometimes put out. But Almeda is known for her common sense. Everybody respects her. Dot Emmert almost idolizes her. She was a small town girl who went to college and made herself a fearsomely respected and beloved teacher. She taught generations of students for over 50 years. No one dismissed what Miss Shank said. So I asked her what she meant.

"'Sometimes there is a larger good that is more important than getting something smaller right.'

"'Are you saying that homosexuality is a small wrong?' I asked her.

"'I won't say that' she replied, 'because I don't know what to think about homosexuality. I thought I did. For years I thought it was a perversion or at least an illness.'

"'But you don't now?'

"'I said exactly what I meant. I don't know. Once I did. Now I don't.'

"Eve, I felt so relieved that someone so highly respected and intelligent could admit she didn't know! It made it easier for me. But it also made me really anxious. The ground was shifting. I just wanted to stop thinking. What else was I going to question? Fred calls it a slippery slope. I was so glad to be sitting across the lace tablecloth and fine china from Miss Shank. I looked to her for strength. But she was admitting she didn't know what was right.

"'Is there a larger good here?' I had asked Almeda hopefully.

"'You've already experienced it. You told me about it.'

"I was silent. I was puzzled. I was afraid to say something for fear it would be the wrong thing.

"'You were drawn to these women,' Almeda said with a hint of impatience. 'Your friendship with them was more important than their sexuality.'

"'Fred thinks that was just my weakness,' I said, 'my fuzzy thinking, my inability to be firm. I'm too easily swayed by emotion.'

"'Men are idiots sometimes. You saw their humanity and you were drawn to it.'

"'My heart wants to tell me you're right,' I said, 'but I don't see it. I've been taught not to trust people's humanity. That's where we get into trouble. Our sex drives are strong. If we let them go, there is nothing but trouble.' I think I blushed as I said that.

"'Almeda had looked at me and smiled, 'As an old maiden lady, I don't have much to say about that. But maybe people worry too much about sex. Both those who indulge in it and those who distrust it. I believe maybe I've done that.'

"I was astonished. I could hardly imagine Almeda Shank even thinking about sex. I wanted to ask which she was talking about—indulging in it or distrusting it—but I was too embarrassed.

"'I can see what you're thinking,' Almeda said with a smile, 'and I'm not going to go there.' She paused. 'Jesus showed compassion, and he never rejected people for their sexuality. Except for his words to the woman at the well and the woman taken in adultery (and there wasn't much judgment there) and his comments about divorce, he hardly said anything about sex. But he thoroughly disliked people who were judgmental. We are called to be like Jesus, to be reconcilers. That's the big good that I see. You can look it up. 2 Corinthians 5:18-20.'

"Eve, on the whole drive north, I kept wondering if I believed that. I wanted to believe it. And if I did believe it, what was I supposed to do? I kept returning to the last thing Almeda said to me. She said, 'You have a good heart, Alice. I think you can trust your heart on this.'"

"What a lovely thing for her to say to you!" Eve exclaimed.

"Yes, but do you know how hard that is? Look at where it's gotten me!"

In the days that followed, Eve thought often of Alice, and she came to see her as a quiet heroine, and the thought gave her strength .

Chapter 38 – Resolutions

Sam found Hank in his yard in the middle of a large building project. He was slimmer since they'd last been together. His color was better. He was in good spirits. They went to Hank's shop where he was brewing a pot of coffee. Hank unfolded some lawn chairs he kept in the corner and rested their coffee mugs on the workbench. There was sawdust on the floor and the smell of fresh-cut wood and turpentine in the air. Sam looked about with pleasure at the radial arm saw, the planer, the miter saw, the router, the table saw in the center of the room, the neat rows of tools on the wall, and the shelves with boxes of nails and cans of stain and paint. It was a workmanlike order, peaceful.

"Eve and I are going on the road," Sam said abruptly. "I wanted you to be the first to know."

"I don't know what you mean."

"We're selling our condo…"

"You just bought it!"

"Well, we're selling it. We're selling our furniture. We're giving stuff away we don't need. Throwing away what we can't give away. Throwing away all those old files and stuff we thought we should save, knew we didn't need, but couldn't part with in case someday, sometime, somebody might want to see them or God forbid the IRS might want them, even though we know, as does everyone else, that you only have to keep stuff back seven years." Sam laughed, "I'm throwing away all those old papers that I kept, thinking secretly that if I ever became famous, they might be important to my biographer. Our goal is to reduce our stuff, our material possessions down so they will fit in one 10 x 10 storage space."

"Christ!"

"Yeah, well, Christ would approve, don't you think?"

"Books! Your books alone would fill a 10 x 10 space!"

"They're going to go. Nearly all of them."

Hank shook his head and absently reached into his shirt pocket for his cigarettes, then remembering that he'd quit, rubbed his hand on his jeans, and looked around in quiet desperation.

Sam laughed.

"It's not funny. I need a smoke!"

Sam sipped his coffee and stretched out his legs, relieved to have told someone.

"And Eve is okay with this?"

"It was her idea."

"I don't believe you."

"We're leaving as soon as we can wrap things up."

"Where are you going? What the hell are you going to do?"

"Don't know. We'll probably start by volunteering to do disaster relief. We are going to get in our car, head out, and see what turns up. With the economy the way it is, there are plenty of nonprofits who need volunteers."

When Sam finished sketching out their intentions, as much as such an unlikely venture could really be planned, Hank nodded and asked, "So why, really, are you doing this?"

"I think you know why. Doesn't it follow from what I've been trying to do?"

"Yeah, it fits your pattern. I want to know how sure you are about this."

"You mean did God speak to me out of the cloud and say, 'Go forth, Sam & Eve'?"

"Something like that."

"We did not hear a voice, but both of us arrived at this, and separately. It came to Eve while we were doing that flood relief project. For me, it's a natural extension of what I've been saying. When you are on the road and you have very little stuff, it's much easier to move and change, to follow your heart, to listen to the still, small voice. You need so much less and you are so much more likely to trust that what you need will come."

"Well, you have more balls than I do!"

****

Later than afternoon, seated in the old man's house in front of the fireplace with still another cup of coffee, Sam was greeted with less surprise and even more keen interest.

"So you're taking your experiment another step?" the old man said. He smiled, "Did God tell you to do this?"

"You're poking fun at me. You know I don't hear the voice of God."

"Of course. Did this come from that deep center you're always telling me about?"

"Yes, and the amazing thing is it came to Eve, too. I'm grateful for that!"

"I should think so. Hardly possible unless both of you want to do it. What about money?"

"Your money makes it possible, you know. We could not have done this before you gave us the gift. We had debt and no source of income except what work came our way. Your money freed us to consider this. But it also pushed us. See, after paying our debts and buying our condo, we couldn't decide whether to invest the remainder or use it. We should use it, not protect it. But the prudent thing to do at our age would be to invest it and use the income to allow us to retire. Except social security plus the investment income together are not enough to live on. So we still needed to find some additional income."

"But according to your faith, if you prayed for that with purpose and an open heart, it would come."

"In a sense it did. We don't need as much when we are traveling. Some of the volunteer opportunities carry a small stipend. Room and board are covered. The international postings might include travel expenses." Sam laughed. "Our prayers won't have to produce as much as if we stayed here in Selby."

"Why are you investing the remainder of the money that came from me? Why not use it, trusting that God will provide more when needed?"

"Good question. Maybe we will. Maybe we still aren't really living by faith. On the other hand, maybe those investments are the way we are being provided for. You know, once we are on the road, we'll be learning things we can only guess at."

"You seem to have changed."

"How?"

"You're more willing that this God of yours may work through conventional things like investments."

Sam laughed. "I'm not making any theological statements. Can God work through Wall Street? God only knows. I'm taking this one day at a time."

"How will you travel?" the old man asked, changing the subject.

"We'll sell one of our cars. Use the other, the one with the most space, which fortunately has the fewest miles on it, though it's not the most economical."

The old man had been staring into the fire. He put his coffee cup on the table between them and turned in his chair so he could look squarely at Sam. "I have a proposition to make."

"Another one?"

"I want to give you something for your trip, and in exchange I ask that you write a letter or send an e-mail, oh, every two weeks or so telling me about your adventures."

"My friend, you don't have to give us something in exchange for that. We'll be delighted to write to you, pleased actually that you want to stay in touch with us."

"Nevertheless, I want to give you a gift. I want to buy you a hybrid vehicle. One with the latest technology. One with as much interior space as possible, so that if you have to sleep in your car sometime, you'll be comfortable. One with the best gas mileage."

"I couldn't possibly accept. You've done enough."

"How do you know this isn't God providing for you? It gives me perverse pleasure to do the work of a reality I don't believe in."

Sam just shook his head, "You make it too easy."

"Going on the road is not an exercise in self-abnegation. You're doing it, I think, out of joy. A spirited life is a life of adventure, not a dreary following of rules and conventionalities. Sam, that's always been why your experiment has appealed to me. It is so eccentric!"

****

Sam arrived at the Athens House as Kirby was taking his seat. The others were already there. Kurt Wampler was in full cry telling a story about almost forgetting his wife's birthday, pulling it out with a present he found ten minutes before meeting her for a dinner he nearly missed, and carrying it off with such—he actually used the word "aplomb," while every man identified with his relief and pride—that she never guessed and in fact had said it was one of the best birthdays ever.

"You didn't tell her, did you?" Sam said.

"Do I look like an idiot!"

"Why does it matter to a woman whether or not you planned it far ahead?"

"They're not men. That's why."

Sam happened to look over at Kirby, who was quietly drinking his coffee, smiling, and shaking his head.

"You look like you have something to say," Sam remarked, "and can hardly wait to say it."

"I had a most unusual phone call late yesterday. From Daryl Bender, the district executive. He called to tell me that the ministerial commission has withdrawn their effort to rescind my ordination. Apparently a member of the commission changed her vote."

There were exclamations around the table. "That's great, Kirby! That's wonderful! What a relief! For you! For all of us!"

"Fred Vogel, the chair of the commission, is very unhappy. It was Almeda Shank who changed her vote."

"I know her!" Sam exclaimed. "I drove down and talked with her before district conference. Eve talked with her too."

"That may have had something to do with her change of heart, but the story is actually stranger. Remember, Sam, when you and Eve and Samantha and Marianne stayed with Fred Vogel and his wife, Alice, when you went down to Tutorville after the flood? Eve, Alice, Samantha, and Marianne worked side by side for five days—hard 12-hour days—and they bonded. And then Alice discovered who they are."

"How could I forget that! After Alice learned about it," Sam added, "Samantha and Marianne decided they owed it to Fred to tell him too. Fred froze. He would hardly look at us as we prepared to leave."

"It seems Alice couldn't stop thinking about Samantha and Marianne. She couldn't talk to Fred, who was furious with her. So she went to see Almeda, who has the kind of influence downstate only an old school teacher can have."

"Yes, I know about this," Sam said. "Alice told Eve all about it in a marathon phone call."

"Well, Daryl was at the ministerial commission meeting where Almeda changed her mind, and he talked to her afterwards. Almeda called Alice 'a sweet and innocent girl'—Alice is actually forty-eight, but still like a girl to Almeda. She said, 'There can't be anything wrong with those two lesbian women if Alice trusted them.' Then she added, 'I don't know what's right, but those two women can't be all wrong. What's wrong here is removing a man from the ministry when he must have had the same reaction poor, sweet Alice had.'"

Sam shook his head. "It's hard to believe. People surprise you. There's more good out there than we think."

"There are still a lot of hard-edged conservatives," Kurt said. "Is this really over?"

"Maybe not," Kirby replied. "I'm still under censure by district conference, though no one seems to know what that means. But my ordination is secure. Fred Vogel is terribly upset. He can't any longer blame this all on up-state liberals and keep a righteous distance. It's in his own family now. I feel for the man. He loves his wife. He loves his principles."

"It's so odd," said John, who had not spoken. "So much anguish and trouble. All the meetings. A big discussion at district conference. And then one quiet woman brings it all to a halt."

"Almeda isn't quiet," Sam remarked.

"I wasn't thinking of Almeda," John replied. "Alice is the lynchpin. She probably never had an opinion about homosexuality. Probably never thought much about it. Probably followed her husband. Still may not have an opinion. But she had an ordinary human encounter and it changed her. If she's like Almeda, she probably still doesn't know what to think. But she changed."

"By God, you're right!" exclaimed Jack. "It's the little people that make a difference, not the big people. They just think they do."

"How would you know?" Kurt said. "You've always been one of the big people. Money, connections, position in the community."

"Yeah, well, we think we have power."

"But you do, Jack!" Sam exclaimed.

"I'm trying to use it differently, think about it differently."

"Doesn't it come down to money?" said Sam. "Jack, where would you be without your money?"

"We're changing the subject," Joe said. "The big thing this morning is that Kirby is off the hook. And it's because a quiet woman in Effingham listened to her heart, not her husband."

"Don't be surprised," Kurt said, "if someone in the district tries to come after Kirby and our congregation again."

"Daryl thinks not," said Kirby. "He's been listening as he travels around the state. He thinks people are tired. On both sides. They hear it in the media. They've heard it argued all over the denomination. They don't like where things are—neither side does—but they just want it all to stop. Except for a few like Fred Vogel. And his credibility is a bit tattered, since people know it was Alice who changed Almeda's mind."

"Well, there you are then!' said Jack. "Something to celebrate! So I'm buying this morning. Order up! Kirby, it's steak and eggs for you! Sam, we big people may have the wrong ideas about the value of wealth, but, by God, we can buy breakfast."

There was laughter and good deal of clamor and some good natured repartee with the waitress as the men placed their orders after first asking to see menus, since they were going to exploit Jack's generosity and not order the usual. When the waitress finished and called their orders in to the kitchen, Sam turned to Jack.

"You know I'm not critical of your wealth…"

"I always laugh to myself when one of you says something like that," Jack said. "You must think I'm loaded because I run a business, have a lot of employees. But by the measure of real wealth, I'm not as far beyond you guys as you might think."

Kurt reached over and patted Jack's hand, grinning, "We know you're a good guy, Jack. We love you even though you are a rich bastard."

"Be nice to him. He's buying, remember."

"Jack," Sam went on, "you're the most responsible rich guy I know…"

Jack shook his head in mock dismay, "So you're determined to put that epithet on me?"

"We love you anyway," said Kurt.

"I'm trying to say something!" Sam exclaimed. "I admire you, Jack, because you carry your wealth lightly—however big or small it is—especially since your…uh, what shall we call it…"

"You mean since he started writing poetry and meditating," Kurt laughed. "Nothing like a little poetry to put money in its place."

"It's not how much you have, but what you do with it," Sam said.

"And how you got it," said Joe. "What kind of generosity would it be if you got your money selling stuff produced in Asian sweat shops?"

"That too, but Jack isn't ripping off his clients," John said. "He's building schools, warehouses, homes, and office buildings."

"I wasn't talking about Jack," Joe replied.

"I wasn't either," Sam replied. "I was talking about myself."

"We forget that you've joined the ranks of the wealthy."

"Yes and no, but Eve and I are going in a new direction." Sam told them about their plans.

****

It took Sam and Eve weeks to go through every box and file. When they finished, they were surprised at how little they were keeping. But when Sam went through his books, he was unhappy. He owned books he'd bought when he was in college, and they were still precious even though he hadn't opened them in more than forty years. There were hundreds of paperback mysteries by authors he'd loved and still loved—books he'd reread. There were books he'd bought because he wanted to read them or thought he ought to read them, which he'd not yet read.

There was a collection of dictionaries that he no longer used because now he went to the Internet. Even thesauruses he loved, though it was so much easier now to find synonyms online. Books on word meanings, books on grammar and language, books of philosophy, theology, church history, and biblical study. Beautiful art books his mother-in-law had given him, map collections, books of photography. Novels, classics, complete collections of the works of Dickens and Austen and Shakespeare; he'd read and reread the first two, but had never spent the time he thought he ought to spend on the plays.

When he thought about giving up a particular book, he had the terrible anxiety that he would still want it. He tried to picture his feelings if his office burned. Would he miss the books? The image surprised him. He felt freed and relieved. But he hated the thought of giving books away or selling them. He was letting go of something he would never have again, and he mourned its going. He talked with Eve about increasing the storage space so he could keep more of the books.

For a day he sat in his office and felt sad. Then he ruthlessly filled four good sized boxes with the books he most loved or he felt he might need or that had sentimental value. He called his friends and told them they could have any book they wanted, but they had to come tonight. And then he called the public library and told them to come and get the rest the next morning. For the rest of their time in Selby he could hardly bring himself to enter his office. He was glad he had already cleaned out most of the desk drawers and cabinets and so did not have to go in there very often.

Eve, on the other hand, cheerfully emptied her own office, desk, and bookshelves. She went easily through their condo. The only things she kept from their dining room and kitchen were her mother's china, the silverware that had been given to them as a wedding present, some beautiful tablecloths, three gorgeous serving dishes, three vases, two table runners, and one cherished frying pan. It all fit into four large boxes. She also boxed up some silver heirlooms from her mother's family—candleholders, a tea set, and a fruit bowl. The rest went to Good Will or the Salvation Army or the auction house.

It was her clothing! She loved her wardrobe. She didn't spend much on clothes, but what she bought was always of good quality and she took care of each item. So, over time her wardrobe had grown till it was large and had many things that, though old, were in excellent condition. They were extensions of herself. To give them up was to give up part of her body. She looked at a colorful jacket she had owned for twenty years and could not imagine herself without it.

She talked with Sam about maybe increasing their storage space. He advised her to get one of those clothes-storage systems where the items of clothing are placed in plastic bags and then the air is sucked out so they are sealed and flattened almost like freeze-dried vegetables. He said maybe she could shrink almost her whole wardrobe. That made her laugh as she imagined shrink-wrapped slacks and blazers and sundresses and skirts and blouses and shoes—how would shoes be flattened!

She took her largest suitcase and filled it with her most favorite things, making sure that all seasons were covered. Then she kept out the few things she would need for the time they were still in Selby and they would need on the road and put them in a smaller suitcase. She called Nancy and said she desperately needed her help, right after school if possible.

When Nancy arrived, they carried load after load of clothing out to the van, as fast as they could and drove at breakneck speed to the thrift shop. Eve asked Nancy if she would go in and ask the clerks to come out. Several young volunteers followed Nancy from the store, and Eve turned her back and walked away while they carried everything away. When the van was empty, she hopped in with Nancy and roared out of there. When they were ten blocks away, she stopped and put her head on the wheel and began to cry. Nancy reached out and put her hand on Eve's shoulder, which began to shake. Nancy smiled suddenly, "Are you crying or laughing?" Eve looked up with tears in her eyes and a smile on her face and said, "I don't know."

Jack insisted that Sam and Eve make a room for themselves in the Victorian "common house" where Eve and the other women had created their clubhouse—a place where they could stay when they came back. Most of their friends thought they would get tired of traveling and come back again to live in Selby. This would be the place they would stay until they reestablished themselves.

Jack said this was not his reason. He said he hoped they had the courage and stamina to stay on their adventure. But he wanted them to come back from time to time so he could see them and hear about their travels and enjoy their company. He said the other friends would like that too.

So instead of selling or giving away their bedroom furniture, they moved it to an upstairs room. They donated much of the rest of their furniture to the common house as well as their kitchen appliances—mixer, food processor, toaster oven, and blender. The largest things they had and the things that in the end forced them to a larger storage space were their few antiques: a drop leaf table, an armoire, a small jelly cupboard, two rocking chairs, and an ancient clock.

One evening Kirby and Nancy and John were helping them maneuver these items into a rented truck to move them to the storage unit. Though it was a cold night in February, they were all outside discussing the space in the truck and familiarizing themselves with the hydraulic lift before trying to move the armoire. Angela pulled up and was getting out of her car to help when Nancy's cellphone rang. The discussion continued until they noticed that Nancy's face had turned grave.

"It was the retirement village in Pennsylvania," she said, putting the phone in her pocket. "My dad has weakened suddenly. They've put him in the nursing center. They think his heart is giving out. They think he's in his last days."

"I am so sorry, Nancy," Eve said.

She smiled, "It's the last thing of Dad's I'd expect to give out, his heart."

Kirby put his arm around her. "You need to go back. Right away."

She nodded.

"You go home," he said. "I'll help move this furniture and then I'll be right behind you. See if you can get a compassion fare from one of the airlines for tomorrow morning."

"You go home too, Kirby," Sam said. "We can do alright here."

"It's okay. She needs a little time alone. She's been afraid of this. Wilbur's mind is still sharp, but he has been sounding weak and tired. I'll just stay for a few more minutes and then I'll follow her."

Chapter 39 – Transitions

While they finished carrying Sam and Eve's stuff, John found himself thinking about Wilbur and realizing how much he wanted to see him one last time. By the time they had moved the furniture into the storage space, John knew he would go back to Pennsylvania. Talking it over with Angela as she drove him home, he decided he would drive, not fly. He wanted the freedom of having a car, and there were a few things he still had stored back there that he wanted to bring to Selby. Angela offered to come with him, and he was pleased and intrigued, but he realized he needed to go alone. He called Nancy and offered for her to ride with him, but she had already made air reservations. She wanted to catch an early flight and be at the retirement center by noon, instead of getting in late at night after thirteen hours on the road. But she said if John could delay until the day after tomorrow, Kirby would appreciate a ride.

And so two days later John and Kirby left before dawn to avoid the rush-hour traffic on I-294, going around Chicago. Nancy had called early in the afternoon the day before just after arriving at the retirement center to say that Wilbur was very weak, but stable. He was conscious. She had told him John was coming. She said she thought Wilbur was hanging on until he arrived. They traveled in John's van, and he drove the first shift. It felt like old times, when Kirby used to come home with John from college.

"I wanted Nancy to meet you," John said as they were starting across the Indiana Turnpike. "I felt like I owed it to her. She needed a good guy. I was the one who had introduced her to Jack Frisk. Of course, I thought he was a good guy too…"

"He was a good guy…most of the time," Kirby said.

"Not toward Nancy. But I knew you would be."

"You figured she needed a real boy scout and I was it."

"You were. You still are."

"Do you ever wonder what Nancy's life would have been like if Jack had married her? And Jacqueline's life too?"

"Aw, Kirby, do you really wonder that? Jack Frisk was—and still is—a charming flake. You are so much better for Nancy."

"Well, of course. We've been married almost 40 years. I'd say it's a moot point. But I have wondered what it would have been like if I had met

Nancy before Jack. Probably most people have the capacity for innocent romance only once. Nancy and I had to grow gradually to love each other."

"You're a pastoral counselor. You know that's the love that makes a marriage over time—even if you start with the romance."

"Certainly, but I never had the romance. When I met Nancy, she was so deeply wounded that we never really had a happy courtship."

There wasn't much John could say to that. He could reassure Kirby that Nancy loved him deeply and that they had a wonderful marriage, however it might have started. But Kirby already knew that. And saying it would not be an antidote to the unexpected longing he heard in Kirby's voice. So John said nothing, and an easy silence fell between them.

"Wilbur's been Nancy's rock—and mine too," Kirby said. "And yours, especially yours. Did you know I used to be a little jealous of your close-ness with Wilbur? I didn't give in to the feeling. I knew he was like a second dad to you. I thought it was wonderful, but I wished I had the same thing with him. I saw almost from the day I met him what an unusual man he was—the kind of man you want to like you when you're still young and unsure of yourself, as I surely was."

"Yeah, I love Wilbur. I surely do," John said. "It's hard to imagine the world without him."

They drove into the parking lot at the nursing center just after eight that evening having made very good time, stopping only for gas, restroom breaks, and sandwiches to go. It was a new facility with six 20-room units, each of which had its own kitchen, dining area, TV lounge, and nurses' station. It was supposed to have the feel of a hotel, rather than a hospital. Wilbur was in a private room with its own handicapped-designed bath, a large picture window with a deep upholstered window seat and comfortable chairs, a state-of-the-art adjustable bed, and a large flat-screen TV. Nancy was sitting on the chair next to the bed holding Wilbur's hand. His eyes were closed and his breathing was regular but shallow. His burly body looked small and shrunken under the blanket. John and Kirby said nothing as they entered, but Wilbur must have sensed their presence because he opened his eyes.

"Chon," he said softly, his eyes lighting up.

"Wilbur," John said, "It's so good to see you."

"Vell, I wonder, Chon. I don't look so goodt."

His gaze went past John to Kirby and he smiled. "Nancy said you were coming together."

"Hello, Dad," Kirby said. He had taken to calling his father-in-law "Dad" many years ago. "I'm sorry to see you so weak."

He reached out and took Kirby's hand, "You're a preacher," he said in a whisper that was surprisingly strong for being so soft. "You see people weak all the time."

"But not you. I always see you as strong."

"I guess strength ain't chust in the body." Wilbur said and turned back to John. "Vell, this is it, Chon," he said, his voice dropping so that John had to lean in to hear. "I'm going to see the Lordt." He smiled, "I have a few things I want to tell him."

John laughed, "What are you going to say?" He liked the picture of monosyllabic Wilbur talking to Jesus.

Wilbur gave John one of his knowing smiles, "I have a few observations to pass on." Wilbur coughed and stopped to catch his breath.

"Maybe we should let you rest."

"I'll have all eternity to rest," he laughed and began to cough again. "I have only a few minutes left here. So I might chust as vell use them up!"

Nancy stroked his cheek with great affection. "He's been like this all day."

Wilbur slowly and with effort pulled his other hand from under the covers and moved it toward John who gratefully took it. "I will see your Dadt, you know."

The thought staggered John, and for just a moment that tremendous longing came back, that sixteen-year-old's deep need for the dad who was gone, something he had not felt for years.

"Your Dadt and I were wery goodt friends. We usedt to talk."

John nodded.

"He toldt me one time that if anything happened to him, I shouldt look after you."

"I never knew that. Is that why you were always so good to me?"

Wilbur shook his head.

"You're saying no?"

"I likedt you."

John laughed with pleasure.

"He toldt me something else."

John waited.

"He said he vasn't sure about relichon."

"He told you that! What did you say?"

"I chust listened. I said the Lord would understand."

"Why didn't you tell me this when I was going through that awful time with the church when I was in college?"

"You needed to find your own way. And you didt."

"Why are you telling me now?"

"Your dadt was a goodt man. You are too. Chust like him. He was my friendt. Chust like you."

The rest of Wilbur's family could be heard coming down the hall—Nancy's brothers and sisters and their families. They all gathered around Wilbur's bed. Jacki was there and Nancy and Kirby's other two children, who had coordinated their arrival at the airport and driven up in a rental car. They all crammed into the room standing around the bed and gazing down at the man who'd managed in his quiet quizzical way to be something special to each one. One of them began to sing "It is Well with My Soul," and they all joined in. Wilbur smiled and closed his eyes and seemed to lean back into the bed pillows. Nancy took the hand of her brother who was standing next to her, and John took Kirby's hand and everyone took the hand of the person on each side, so they formed a complete circle with Wilbur at the top. They saw tears form in his eyes. In the silence as the song ended, he said something so softly that only Nancy could hear it. "What did he say?" one of the grandchildren asked.

Nancy began to cry, "He said he can see Mim—Mother, your grandmother."

He smiled. His breath slowed. One of the grandchildren, Nancy's brother's oldest daughter, began to sing "Blessed Assurance," in a high pure soprano. Gradually everyone joined in. Wilbur's breaths grew farther apart and just a few minutes past 10 in the evening he died.

There was a lot of laughter at the memorial service, and the church was full, and some chairs had to be set up in the fellowship hall with a TV screen for those who could not fit into the sanctuary. For a simple farmer, Wilbur had a lot of friends, but Wilbur was not simple, as Kirby said in the meditation. "Wilbur was a man of many facets and often complex thoughts who appeared uncomplicated because his curiosity and interest in the world and all his friends and family were so innocent and free of self. He had the gift of silence. He just did not need to speak. Of course, he got that glint in his eye sometimes and you knew he was enjoying the effect of his spare speech. It was that glint that gave Wilbur away; it told you, if you knew how to read it, that this seemingly simple, sometimes ungrammatical man with his heavy Pennsylvania Dutch accent was astute beyond his demeanor and was even sometimes pulling your leg. But I never felt he was playing with me," Kirby added. "I often wondered what he thought of me, his son-in-law with the advanced degrees. He had so much wisdom without formal education. Did he think people like me were windbags? But Wilbur just was not capable of that sort of reverse condescension. Wilbur was…Wilbur! A man comfortable in his own skin and glad to let you inhabit yours."

The service was long because everyone seemed to have a story to tell about Wilbur. At the end, the pallbearers carried the casket to the waiting hearse, which drove less than a quarter of a mile through the thin February sunshine to the nearby cemetery, while all who wished, followed on foot, walking across the frozen earth past small mounds of snow that lingered in the shadows of the gravestones. After the graveside service of committal, people walked back to the church for a meal provided by the women of the congregation.

After the meal, John walked back to the cemetery, taking from his van a bouquet of roses he had left on the back seat. He went to Mary's grave marker and carefully laid them at its base. He knelt down and pulled some stray strands of dead grass. Mary! The overwhelming fascination she had stirred in him when they first met. The pain, the loss of self he'd suffered during all those years when she had not seemed interested in him. Then the caution and anxiety, the skepticism and disbelief when she came circling back into his life. The wonder of discovering that she was coming to love him, now that they were both past the uncertainties of youth. The pleasure they took in each other. The disappointment that they couldn't have children. Arguing and then making up. Getting used to the little things that annoyed them with each other. The quiet easiness of their marriage. Then living with the knowledge that she would die. As the flesh began to melt from her body, seeing her spirit as he had never seen it before, seeing her grow stronger and lovelier. The deep intimacy of those final days. The aching sense of loss. Missing her so desperately. Yearning for her. Then the long sad days of numbness, the anger, then depression.

All this came to him as he knelt by her gravestone. "Where is she?" he wondered, trying to picture her somewhere in the universe. He believed in an afterlife, but he didn't have a picture. He was sure she was in a good place. He wondered why he had that assurance. It wasn't a religious faith. It was just a sense that someone as good as Mary wasn't lost to the cosmos, and if there could be goodness in one person, there must be more somewhere out there. He got to his feet with tears coursing down his cheeks and quietly, under his breath, he said good-bye.

He walked to his Mom's grave marker. It was only a few years old. He smiled. He was glad for his memories, and he was proud of the life she had led and the way she had died. She was buried next to his dad whose marker was almost fifty years old and weather-worn. Only a few memories came to him, but they were powerful, pungent. What it was like to feel his dad's male energy. He remembered how lost he'd felt when he had died.

He walked to his grandfather's grave and thought of him with such affection. He was himself almost as old as grandpa has been when he died. He wondered what that old plain-coated elder would think of him, but he knew it didn't matter. He was living in his own world, as his grandfather had lived in his. He also knew that grandpa always loved before he judged, and he remembered what it was like to be appreciated and understood by that strong, quiet, dryly humorous, wise old man.

The last grave he visited was the most ornate. It didn't really belong in this cemetery. John had been surprised when a paper was found with this old man's will asking to be interred in the church cemetery, since he had never had any interest in the church except as a cultural curiosity. Here John laughed. This old man had been an eccentric and delightful presence in his life, and he owed him a great deal.

As he walked back to his car, he passed Wilbur's grave. The dirt had been filled in, but the sod had not yet been put back. He nodded as he passed and stopped to look across the headstones to the fields and farms where his family had lived for eight generations. Surrounded by this land and this life, by all these people who had passed on—instead of grief, he felt gratitude. Something was being completed; something was coming to an end.

Kirby was staying for several more days to come home with Nancy by plane. So John drove home alone the next day after picking up several boxes and a rocking chair that had belonged to his great grandmother, which he had been storing with a friend and which he was able to fit into his van. He was leaving again, the third time, and this time he really was leaving. Selby was his home now. This place where his family had lived for eight generations, where no matter where he went or how long he stayed away always felt deep in his body to be home, no longer was. Some deep tie growing weaker had broken. He felt some sadness. He felt some relief. He felt some appreciation for his past and his ancestry. He felt some anticipation for his future. He smiled that a man in his sixties should still be having such a combination of feelings. Breaking ties was a young man's game. Settling in deeper was supposed to be for an older man like himself.

Most of all he felt like himself, maybe more than ever. He was comfortable in the place that had formed him; he was comfortable in the place where he lived; and he would be comfortable in whatever place he entered in the years still left to him. That was how Wilbur was. He wondered if his dad would have been like Wilbur and then he thought probably not. He remembered his dad as a restless man, full of energy, anxious for the next thing. But his dad was only 41 when he died, and he remembered what he himself had been like at 41 and how he'd changed, and he wondered how much more he would change till he reached Wilbur's 96 years.

He found himself thinking about Angela, anxious to get back to her. He was on a long, straight, boring section of the Ohio Turnpike when he remembered what Wilbur had said about Angela and about his own marriage.

It was still light when he came to the end of the Indiana Turnpike. He took the Chicago Skyway and worked his way over to Lakeshore Drive so he could come up along the lake and see the skyline. The sky was overcast and there was no sunset, but the clouds were high and the air underneath them was clear, and the towering buildings stood out in high relief against the gray background. Three times he'd driven this route, the first time so long ago that the Prudential building had dominated the skyline. Now it was a gathering of towers. It felt like home, but not home like the home of his roots. This was the home of his spirit, but it was not just this place and this skyline. The world was his home, and this was the part he happened to be in. He was glad for this place in the world, and he planned to stay here for a while, but the larger world did not seem strange to him. He felt he would be at home wherever there was air and sky and land and people and, yes, even in crowded cities.

He called Angela on his cellphone, and she was waiting in her driveway when he pulled up. He took her in his arms and held her. He kissed her and said, "I'm ready, if you still are. Are you?"

Angela smiled. She stood back and brushed back a lock of his hair that had fallen across his forehead. "You may regret this, you know."

"I'll take my chances," he said, and she took his hand and led him into her house where she'd prepared a late supper.

The next morning at breakfast at the Athens House he was about to tell his friends, when Sam announced that he and Eve had set a leaving date and it was next month.

"So soon!"

"Shocking news!"

"Have you really wrapped everything up?"

"We are going west to Seattle. We'll take three weeks, get off on the side roads, see if we can find soup kitchens or homeless shelters where we can volunteer a day or so. In Seattle I have an old friend who has some connections with Habitat for Humanity. I'll work for few weeks helping to build a house. My friend's wife has arranged for Eve to be a volunteer teacher's aide in a preschool program. We may stay in Seattle for a few months before we move on.

There was quiet around the table. These men had been together for a long time. Kurt stared into his coffee. "Well, you've got to do it. It's the right thing, but it is hard to imagine us without you."

Joe Kurtz nodded. "I am proud of you…I am…but I guess I wish you weren't going."

"Come on," Jack said. "Sam's doing something great, something none of the rest of us has the cajones to do. Don't pay attention to these sad sacks, Sam. Go for it!"

"They aren't telling me not to go," Sam said. "They're just saying they'll miss me." Sam looked around the circle. "You are saying that, aren't you?"

"Yeah, we admit it," Jack said.

"I'm still the new guy, here," John said, "but I wish you weren't going so soon. I'd like you to be around for my wedding."

An explosion of laughter and exclamations. "All right! John! You've done something every unattached male in Selby has fantasized about."

"Go easy now. She's going to be my wife."

"Seriously, everyone assumed Angela would never marry, ever! What did you do to change her mind?"

"In the end I was the one who wasn't sure."

"So the key was to play it cool?"

John shrugged, "I think Angela always wanted, maybe not marriage, but a mate. She just didn't want all her Italian relatives had or what she saw around her in other marriages. I don't want that either. I'm not interested in a nice little woman."

"Well, she's not that!"

John laughed, "I don't need to analyze it. I'm in my sixties. All I have to do is take it a day at a time." He paused, "I am a little nervous about it. I like living alone. I had something special with my first wife. Maybe this won't be as good. Certainly it will be different. Maybe it will be better, which will have its own challenges. I feel a bit guilty when I think of Mary. The two women are so different. But I am lucky! To have these two women in my life."

"Alright, John," Sam said. "Eve and I will hang around until after the wedding. When is it?"

"Soon actually. A small private affair. Angela doesn't want her whole extended family there, but she has to invite her brothers and sisters and their families, which is a crowd to begin with. She figures the sooner we have it the less time her mother and siblings will have to figure out how to complicate it. We'll do it in our church. Kirby will perform the service. He'll be back in a few days. I think we'll do it six weeks from next Saturday."

"That soon!"

"A quiet service in the church. Reception downstairs. Then Angela and I will disappear for a week. She's taking time off."

Chapter 40 – Endings

Early in the week of the wedding, Sam and Eve were ready to go. They had already rented their condo to a young couple on a rent-to-buy contract and were staying at the common house. They were feeling as if they were already gone, so they decided to disappear for a few days. They drove downstate to Effingham. They didn't tell Fred and Alice they were coming. They were pretty sure Fred would not want to see them, and asking Alice beforehand might put her in the awkward position of having to choose between what she wanted and what Fred would want. So they arrived in the early afternoon and had some lunch. They were in excellent spirits. It really did feel like their first day on the road. At 4:00 p.m. they showed up at the church, hoping to find Fred in his office. As luck would have it, he was there, and his secretary had stepped out for a few minutes, so that Fred himself saw them through the open door when they stepped into the secretary's office. When Sam saw Fred's face, he felt sorry for him, caught between his desire to be a good pastor and a courteous person and his feelings of discomfort and distaste at the sight of Sam and Eve.

Sam stepped forward into Fred's office and put out his hand. "We are not here to make trouble for you. We're probably the last people you want to see. We are not sure what to say. Eve and I are leaving Selby. We sold most of our stuff and packed up what's left. We're going to spend the next several years traveling and volunteering. We want to make things right with you if we can." He paused. Fred made no response. "We knew that Samantha and Marianne were a couple and we knew you didn't know. We can't change the pain that caused you—or the pain it caused them. I've asked myself many times if we should have told you. Sometimes I think it would have been the polite and considerate thing to do. On the other hand, it wasn't ours to tell, it was Samantha and Marianne's. And why should they tell you? They were two women here to work. What they were to each other should not have mattered. It was an impossible situation."

Fred motioned to the chairs in his office, and Sam and Eve sat down. "Sam's being terribly longwinded," Eve said. "I believe the things that connect us—you know what they are, our faith, our interest in the church, our love for our family—are more important than this terrible conflict.

I'm here to say that to you. You don't have to say anything back. I'm not here to change your mind. I'm also here because I like Alice very much and want to see her before we leave."

Fred sat down on the chair behind his desk. He shook his head. "You make it sound so easy. We can just get along and respect each other."

"Well, we can."

"And ignore Biblical truth and morality?"

"Even there, there is debate."

"Not for me, there isn't."

"Will you at least let us take you and Alice out for dinner, and can we make an agreement not to talk about this?"

"I can't speak for Alice. I have an early meeting here at the church to-night and I brought a sandwich and a thermos of soup to eat at my desk. What Alice does is for her to say. She's home from school and over at the house now, if she hasn't gone out to run an errand."

Fred rose to his feet and they stood up too. "I don't want to be your enemy," Eve said.

"We are on different sides. There is no getting around that, is there?"

"No, I suppose not. I wish there were."

"This isn't about hating you. The Bible is clear that we are not to hate our enemies."

"Oh, Fred, we are not your enemies."

"I don't hate you, Eve. Not at all," Fred went on as though Eve had not spoken. "But this is about right and wrong. There can be no compromise."

"Oh, Fred, this is so foolish, this separation between good people."

"That's what Alice says. She'll be glad to talk to you. I just don't agree."

"Fred, I'm sorry if this has driven a wedge between you and Alice."

A small ironic smile crossed Fred's face. "There's not much anyone can do about it, is there?"

Sam put out his hand and Fred took it. "Thanks anyway for talking with us."

They walked across the lawn and knocked on the side door and found Alice in her kitchen. Her face lit up when she saw it was Eve. It took her only a moment to finish what she was doing, shrug into her coat, and be ready to take them up on their offer. She said she hated to cook when it was only herself; she was delighted for an excuse to get out of her kitchen. The hostess had no sooner seated them than Alice was bringing Eve up to date.

Fred had been dumbfounded when Almeda changed her vote on the ministerial commission. "His plans were completely thwarted," Alice said. "He was so angry! There was nothing he could do. I felt sorry for him. Of course, he blamed me. For a while we were back to not speaking again."

"Oh, Alice. I am sorry!"

"I try to be really good to him. See, I know Fred. Underneath, he's a really nice man. He loves me and I love him. I hope he can get through this without becoming hard and bitter. I hope he doesn't make trouble in the district. He could, you know. He feels this so deeply!"

"And you, Alice. Are you holding up okay? Are you still getting calls?

"Yes. Some of the women who call want to know what lesbians are like, like they're otherworldly creatures. I think some want to be titillated. A woman homosexual! Somehow it's fascinating for them. I think for some it's kind of like reading a naughty magazine. Then I'm still getting the nasty calls, people tell me I've 'consorted with sinners.' But there are some women down here who are really thinking about this, and that really scares Fred."

Sam sighed. He'd been staying out of the conversation, listening. He shook his head. "We are a long way from bridging this divide." Eve and Alice looked at him and smiled and kept talking.

Eve began telling her about the women's group in Selby, and then she went on to tell her all about their plans. Even though these were his plans too, Sam felt like a third wheel.

They drove Alice back to her house, and Eve got out of the car and hugged her as she went up the steps of the parsonage. It was already 9 p.m. but they decided to drive back to Selby rather than stay in a local motel. They'd get back after midnight, but neither had anything the next morning. Sam was driving and Eve was talking with animated high spirits about Alice and friends and women and their road adventures. This Eve was new to Sam. She was enlivened. She seemed fearless. He watched the road and basked in the vitality that flowed from his wife.

"I want to do some women's stuff!" Eve said.

"Women's stuff?"

"I don't know. Find interesting women. Hear their stories. See what women are doing when they're just being women."

"If I said that, you'd crucify me. 'Women just being women' sounds like a putdown. You know. The stereotypes. Keeping house. Taking care of kids. Running the PTA. Juggling home and career. Talking over one another. Watching chick flicks. Gossiping. Cruise-directing the household. Ferrying the kids around."

"Any more of that and I will crucify you."

"I'm just saying that's what it sounds like when people say that."

"Suppose I said that 'men just being men' means sitting around drinking beer, watching football, cussing, smoking cigars, farting, telling tasteless jokes, and talking about sports and computers?"

"I'd say some men are like that but the men who are my friends are not like that."

"Indeed."

"So what do you mean by 'women being women'?"

"I want to learn more about what women, especially talented and interesting women, do when they are just being themselves."

"What about untalented and uninteresting women?"

"You know what I mean."

"Are you a talented and interesting woman?"

"What do you think?"

"I think I'd better say 'yes'!"

Eve was quiet for a while. It was a clear night. On the long, open stretches of I-55 between towns and exits, despite their own headlights they could see the stars. Sam settled into auto-pilot, trusting long-ingrained instincts about how fast to go, how close to get to other vehicles, and how to stay away from semis. It left him free to think and let his imagination rove. He liked to drive, especially at night with Eve beside him, just the two of them, each in their own space, yet so close and quiet in the safe, night-enclosed world.

Eve kept talking about what they would do and see. There was excitement in her voice. The anxiety that usually lay below the surface seemed to be gone. She wanted to get off the main highways and see the towns and villages. There were national parks and famous landmarks she wanted to make detours to. There were cities she wanted to see. Concerts she wanted to go to. Art museums she wanted to visit. She wanted to find stained glass windows in churches. She wondered if synagogues had stained glass. She wanted to attend a Yom Kippur service. She wanted to see the Christmas decorations in Rockefeller Center, and when Sam pointed out that they were heading west not east, she replied that they'd see New York after swinging back east through Canada after going through—she suddenly remembered that she had always wanted to see Lake Louise—the Canadian Rockies and into eastern Canada and down through Montreal and back into the US across the St. Lawrence Seaway, down the Hudson to New York City. And then she hoped to fly to England and spend time in

London before going to the continent, maybe starting in Amsterdam and definitely going to Paris.

Sam laughed with pleasure, "I thought we were going to be service workers, not tourists."

"We have our whole lives ahead of us, at least 20 more years. Who knows, maybe 30 years. I want to do both. I intend to enjoy myself!"

"How are we going to pay for all this?" Sam asked.

Eve looked over at him. "You tell me. You're the one with all this faith."

****

John watched Jack and Vi with interest. Jack was making up excuses to stop at the apartment building. One day John was leaning against Jack's pickup. It was unseasonably mild for late February. They were talking about the co-housing project. "Vi's really psyched for the idea. She's giving me all kinds of encouragement, even pushing me a little."

"Do you mind?"

"Hell, no. I like people who push. She didn't waste any time getting a job either. She's working at the Crisis Center already. I'll say this! She runs true to form! She's already on some damn committee at church, and the other day I saw her hanging out with that kid friend of yours, and his loopy mother."

John laughed.

"You laugh!"

"We both know you like her."

"Oh no! No! No! It's not like that. I'm years away from that." Jack paused and then laughed.

"Now you're laughing!" John said.

"Hell, she read one of my poems. Said she liked it. She might have been bullshitting me, but you have to be impressed by a woman who asks to read a guy's poetry."

John noticed that word about Jack and Vi was making its way through their circle of friends, though no one really ever saw them together. Nancy told John she mentioned it in an e-mail to Jenn, thinking it would be best for her to hear about it before she made her next trip back to Selby. Jenn wrote a revealing e-mail back to Nancy. It held a mixture of regret and relief. She still had feelings for Jack, she said, but they were on different paths. She was going to stay in New York and do a doctorate. She wanted to spend the summer studying in Europe. It was for the best.

"I was disappointed," Nancy told John. "I was hoping, you know…but maybe Vi is the one for Jack."

"Hold it! You're way ahead of things!" John exclaimed.

"Do you think some people need different mates for different times, different developmental stages?"

"Where is that question coming from?"

"Oh, I don't like the idea. It undermines the whole notion of a lifetime of commitment."

"Is this about you and Kirby?"

Nancy shook herself. "Certainly not. Are we right for each other at this time in our lives? I'm not even going to go there. Of course we are." She laughed, "I'll ask Kirby that question! It'll be fun to see him mull that one over!"

Partly because of Vi's encouragement, Jack ratcheted up his attention to the co-housing experiment. The rehabbing in the apartment building was almost finished. John had been supervising the last two units. All the other new units were rented, on one-year leases to keep the building free for conversion to co-housing when the time came.

Back in the fall Jack had told John he could afford to pour a bit more money into the project. So with John's support Jack had bought another house in the cul-de-sac, one where the owners were in trouble. He was able to buy it at a good price and still give them more than they'd have gotten in foreclosure.

After John came back from the disaster relief work, he began to move his attention to this house. It was rundown, a modest, two-story, square structure with a porch that ran around two sides and a second-story dormer. A tree on the front lawn shaded the porch. During the streak of mild weather in January, a crew of painters, glad for the work, had scraped, repaired, and started repainting the narrow wooden siding. The house began to look good. It was Jack and John's intention to show people how the old, rundown structures on the cul-de-sac could be retrofitted to meet the desires and tastes of the people interested in the co-housing scheme—a sort of model home. As soon as the weather was warm enough, Jack would have the front lawn landscaped and re-sodded.

Shortly after his return from Pennsylvania and Wilbur's memorial service in early February, an idea had suddenly occurred to John, so he chose the color scheme inside and out with this in mind as well as the interior design, taking out some of the downstairs walls to open the living room, dining room, and kitchen into one another. Jack's crews were in their winter downtime, and he was able to put a lot of men on the house. The back porch was glassed in so it could be used in the winter. Solar panels were installed on the roof of the back porch, which faced south. John ordered the latest appliances. He installed a master bath off the main bedroom, as well as redoing the regular bath, and putting a powder room downstairs. He wired the small third bedroom upstairs for Internet and cable as well as a small den-like room on the first floor and had one of Jack's best carpenters line one wall of each room with built-in shelves. Then before the kitchen cabinets and appliances were installed and before the walls upstairs and downstairs were painted, he brought Angela over to see the house.

She laughed as soon as they pulled into the driveway that led to a small detached one-car garage. "I see now why you never said much whenever I brought up the question of how we were going to live in one place and where that place was going to be. I began to think that you wanted us to keep our separate places for a while, until we figured this out. But you think this little house will appeal to me. You painted it outside with the same colors I used. Don't tell me. You figured out a way to get something like my sunroom. The garage is pitiful, by the way. The house is cute. You're going to landscape the front lawn, you say. What about the back lawn? Oh, I see, it opens onto the large space behind your apartment building. So you figure to get me to agree to join this co-housing thing."

John pointed out that there were two dens. She could have the one upstairs or the one downstairs. She could choose the kitchen layout, cupboards, and appliances. They could make this a place together. Jack was willing to work it either way. They could buy it from him and at the same time buy into the co-housing thing which would make them part-owner of all the common areas, which included the common house, all the grounds and lawns, the laundry and storage areas in the apartment building, etc. Or they could just buy the house and lot outright, postponing the question of joining the co-housing thing. Or they could do something completely different. Jack wasn't depending on their taking this house. Or, John made it clear, he was open to living with her in her house.

Angela laughed some more and walked through the whole house, looking at everything, asking questions, walked all around the outside and all across the large open area formed by the back of the apartment building and the back yards of the common house and Jack's house. They went to John's apartment for some lunch, and she said no more and John did not pry or probe.

****

The wedding, at 11 on a Saturday morning in mid-March, ended up being a big affair after all. All of John's friends, and all the people in the church he'd gotten to know, and Angela's large family and many of her colleagues at the community college wanted to come. No formal invitations were sent, but word went out that all were welcome and that there would be a reception in the church fellowship hall after the ceremony.

John drove himself to the church where he found Jack, whom he'd turned to for his best man when he realized Kirby couldn't do the job and be the minister. Angela arrived with one of her sisters. The wedding party was small, just a best man and a matron of honor. John was expecting to be nervous, but he calmly watched Angela coming down the aisle. He smiled and she gave him a small shaky smile in return.

Kirby kept it short and to the point. In his meditation he remembered his long friendship with John, and he said, "John has the ability to choose beautiful, interesting, and strong women. When you lose a mate that you love deeply, the love never stops, but God has given us the capacity to love again without having to deny that first love. One of the things I admire most about Angela is that she is not threatened by the fact that this man she is marrying was married before to a woman he cherished. But now it's Angela that he cherishes. It's the two of you who go together on this next part of your journey." He looked out at the congregation, "As your friends, we will enjoy seeing what you make of each other, how you journey together." He turned directly to Angela, "And Angela, you're not a stranger to love, but this is your first husband. Enjoy this new experience. Learn from it. Glory in it. This is a great blessing. Marriage is an adventure—this particular marriage beginning today!" They exchanged vows, which they had each written. They gave and received rings. And Kirby pronounced them husband and wife.

Angela's brothers complained good-naturedly that there was only a white wine punch at the reception. There was no formal cutting of the cake. Pieces were set out on plates beside nuts and mints and trays of fresh fruit. People drank the punch and greeted John and Angela who stood at one end. Gradually the din died down, people drifted to the parking lot, volunteers cleared away and washed the cups and plates. John and Angela thanked them all and left a large check on the kitchen counter for the church's hospitality fund. Twenty minutes later they walked into the upstairs space at Emma's, where about thirty of their closest friends and family were gathered. Tables were set for dinner. Janet Keller was playing the piano. There was a credenza with some gifts. The word had gone out to those attending the service: no gifts. But these friends had taken no heed of that. There was another table that had some going-away gifts for Sam and Eve, who came up the stairs just ahead of John and Angela.

John sat in the middle of this circle of people, all new friends except for Kirby and Nancy. He took Angela's hand and smiled at her. He turned his eye to the other end of the room, where some kids were gathered, sons and daughters of these friends and family. David was in the midst of them. Maggie, who had come to the service but slipped out at the end, had given John permission for David to stay for the church reception and to come along to Emma's. He happened to catch Sam's eye across the room and saw that Sam was quietly looking around too, and he remembered that Sam and Eve were leaving today.

****

Sam was thinking that these people had been friends, in some cases, for almost 40 years, in other cases, as he looked at Samantha and Marianne, a much shorter time. He was glad for his life in Selby. He wondered what he and Eve would find in the months to come. The anticipation he felt was edged with sadness and anxiety. What would life be like without these friends? Then he remembered his laptop, his iPad, and his smart phone. They could be in daily contact if they wished. He knew Eve wasn't worried or anxious or sad. She loved talking on the phone and had taken to texting and to Facebook like a duck to water. She would stay in touch. No question about it. She was ready! They were leaving directly from the reception. She could hardly wait. She had told him she felt like her life was just beginning.

Sam was talking to Kirby when he heard a spoon tapping a water glass. He thought someone was doing the wedding dinner thing to get the bride and groom to kiss, but he saw Kurt Wampler rising to his feet. Kurt's booming voice got everyone's attention. Jack called out and asked who made him the master of ceremonies. Kurt responded with an earthy witticism that made everyone laugh. Then he remarked on what a happy day it was to be gaining Angela in their circle of friends—she was considerably raising the beauty quotient—and what a sad day it was to be losing Sam and Eve to this cockamamie road adventure. He said he wanted to make two toasts.

"First to John and Angela. May your marriage be everything you're hoping for and have some surprises too," he paused, "and may it always be interesting."

"Hear, hear!" peoples said laughing.

"And to Sam and Eve. God only knows—literally—what you two will find. And maybe even God doesn't know. But God will go with you. We all know that! And know that our love goes with you too. May you have experiences that truly blow your mind!"

"Yes!" several people exclaimed. And glasses were raised.

Then Jack suddenly spoke, "One more toast. To friends!"

"Amen," several called out.

It was at this moment that it came to Sam. After all his effort, all his searching and seeking. God's ways of guiding and providing were not the greatest thing. The truth had been in front of his eyes all along. He looked at these people he loved. And he knew.

****

About an hour later, Sam and Eve stood to say good-bye. There were tears and laughter and some good-natured ribbing. Everyone was silent as they turned and went down the stairs. The car was packed. They were ready. There was nothing they needed to do. They had e-mailed Will and Rae in Seattle to remind them that they would see them in about three weeks.

Before leaving town, Sam drove to Hank's, who knew he would be coming. "I'll only be a moment," he said to Eve, getting out of the car.

"Never thought you'd really do it!" Hank said, standing on his stoop.

"You're one of my anchors, you know. You, with your off-brand faith. I'll miss you."

"Hell, you're going to be just fine."

"You and Melissa could always join us."

"In your dreams! Can you see Melissa away from her kitchen? She wouldn't know what to do if she didn't have a house to clean." They both laughed because they knew that Hank wasn't up for roaming either.

Hank looked out to the car and waved to Eve. "So go on! Get the hell out of here. Don't stand here tearing up on my doorstep."

"I'm going to hug you, you old curmudgeon."

"I'll pray for you, you bastard!" he called after Sam as he got into the car.

Their final stop was at the home of Oliver Larkspur. The old man, who was waiting, walked out to the car. Sam got out and they stood side by side leaning against the fender.

"Won't you come in for some coffee?"

"No. Eve's here with me. We're all ready to go!"

The old man bent down, looked in the car window, and greeted her.

"I want to say good-bye and thank you," Sam said.

"We both want to thank you!" Eve said leaning across the front seat.

"But," Sam continued, "maybe what I really want to say is that I love you."

The old man, surprised, said nothing.

"I have left you speechless! For the first time."

"No, with feelings beyond words."

"You're a good man! I'm privileged that you chose to make me your friend."

"Again I have no words."

Sam laughed and shook the old man's hand. "I leave you with an observation. I think you protest too much. Think about it!"

"Oh!"

"So keep the faith. No one ever said that to you, I'll wager! Eve and I will stay in touch."

Sam got into the car. Eve leaned over and kissed him. "Let's go!" she said. They waved and drove away.

****

The party wound down, and people said their good-byes and gave their final congratulations to the newlyweds. Soon only a few people were left. Nancy helped Angela put the presents in shopping bags. Jack asked for John's keys and went out to bring the van around. Vi offered to give David a ride home. Kirby carried the shopping bags down to the street. Soon they were all on the curb in front of the restaurant. As Jack drove up, David suddenly pointed and laughed, and then the rest of them heard the noise. Strings of tin cans rattled behind John's van. "Just Married" was painted across the rear window in shaving cream. Jack looked pleased with himself as he handed over the keys.

Kirby stowed the bags in the back of the van. John held the door for Angela, and then got behind the wheel. Everyone shouted and waved as they drove off in a clatter.

They had intentionally come in John's old van, assuming someone would decorate it. Now they drove to the apartment building to remove the cans and shaving cream and exchange the van for Angela's car, which was the better vehicle. The plan was to stay at Angela's for the night before starting on a road trip south into the Carolinas, hoping to catch the beginnings of spring. They had ten days, the length of Angela's spring break.

John ran up to his apartment to get his bags, and Angela came with him. She sat down at his table, and he sat across from her.

"At last we're alone!" she said.

"And free! Nothing we have to do, no place we have to be for ten days." John replied.

Angela reached across the table for his hand.

Suddenly there was a knock at the door. They both laughed.

"So much for being alone!" Angela exclaimed.

John opened the door, and it was David standing there. He smiled up at John somewhat hesitantly and peered around him into the apartment. When he saw Angela, his face lit up.

"Would you like to come in?" John asked dryly.

"My mom said I could come over only for a minute. She said you would have 'things' to do. She thinks I don't know."

"Don't know what?" John asked, laughing.

"'Things.' You know."

"Hello, David," Angela called. "You can come in."

He walked over to Angela. "I'm glad you got married to John. Now you can watch out for him and I won't need to."

"You think he needs watching out for?"

"You know he does. Are you going to live here?"

"We don't know where we're going to live, but it won't be far away," John said.

"You can come over whenever you want," Angela added.

David nodded, "Okay, that's cool." He looked around the apartment, then at Angela, and then at John. "My mom said she'd come and get me if I stayed too long. She won't, but I better go anyway." He turned and went to the door. John walked with him. Angela said goodbye. David stood by the door peering intently at John. John smiled and gathered him into his arms. John heard him sigh, and then he was out the door and gone.

Angela had moved over to the loveseat. John sat beside her. He turned sideways and took her hand. "There is no place I want to be but right here right now."

About the Author

James H. Lehman is the author of *The Old Brethren* and two children's books. He has been a freelance writer, and in the 1980s he wrote and produced audiovisuals. For more than fifteen years he did assemblies, workshops, and author residencies on writing for elementary school children, visiting more than 400 schools in 13 states. He is also a storyteller and is featured at an annual Song & Story Fest. He is married to Peg, who is a professional folksinger and teaching artist, and they have a daughter, Jessica, who is married to Steve, and a nephew Joseph who lives with them. Their son Josh died many years ago and they still think of him. Lehman is glad to return to writing fiction and has a particular fondness for the characters of this story.

www.ingramcontent.com/pod-product-compliance
Lightning Source LLC
Chambersburg PA
CBHW070352260626

47161CB00001B/111